MAGPIE'S FALL

Allison Pang

IRONHEART CHRONICLES II - MAGPIE'S FALL
Copyright © 2022 Allison Pang. All rights reserved.

Published by Outland Entertainment LLC
3119 Gillham Road
Kansas City, MO 64109

Founder/Creative Director: Jeremy D. Mohler
Editor-in-Chief: Alana Joli Abbott

Paperback ISBN: 978-1-954255-31-9
Ebook ISBN: 978-1-954255-32-6
Worldwide Rights
Created in the United States of America

Editor: Danielle Poiesz and Double Vision Editorial
Cover Illustration: germancreative
Cover Design: germancreative
Interior Layout: Mikael Brodu

Printed and bound in the United States of America.

Visit **outlandentertainment.com** to see more, or follow us on our Facebook Page **facebook.com/outlandentertainment/**

— A WORD FROM THE CRITICS —

"Pang delivers a fascinating storyline, strong character development, and plenty of plot twists which will draw readers into the first book of the IronHeart Chronicles and leave them eagerly anticipating the next tale in the series. Maggy is a plucky and loyal character that will fascinate readers but what makes this novel so enthralling is the relatable and carefully drawn characters coupled with vivid imagery throughout every scene."

—4 Stars – *RT Book Reviews*

"Allison Pang's *Magpie's Song* is exactly the sort of thing I love to read most. Beautiful prose, interesting characters that I want to know better, a carefully crafted world of that is both mysterious and almost inevitable. It's rare that a book surprises me on so many levels. Powerful stuff with enough surprises to make me smile and enough twists to keep me on my toes. I can't recommend it enough!"

—James A. Moore,
author of the *Seven Forges* series and the *Tides of War* trilogy

"Vivid, thrilling, clever, and imaginative, *Magpie's Song* is a genre-bending gem built around a kickass heroine and a compelling, beautifully-wrought SF/fantasy world you'll want to explore further. Allison Pang's talent is on every page. Fans of Pierce Brown and Wesley Chu will love *Magpie's Song*."

—Christopher Golden,
New York Times bestselling author of *Ararat*

"Pang has crafted a beautiful world with a ticking mechanical heart and a story that flies with fast-paced action. Utterly enchanting!"

—Laura Bickle, critically acclaimed author of *Nine of Stars*

"Maggy is an unlikely heroine, but Pang makes it easy to root for the foulmouthed scavenger.... [U]nique worldbuilding and impressive character work.... Readers will be eager to know what comes next."

—*Publishers Weekly*

"The world-building is a true delight, having a feel of Sanderson's old *Mistborn*, a touch of hardcore steampunk, but most of all: pure and distilled fantasy dystopia."

—Bradley, *Goodreads*

"Finally, a book that has left me speechless."

—Melissa Souza, *Goodreads*

"From the very first pages I fell in love with this story."

—A Book Shrew, *Goodreads*

"Every once in a great while I come across a story that knocks my socks off. This is one of them... This world that Allison has created is stunning. The characters are people that I want to know and go "rooftop dancing" with. Clockwork hearts, a mechanical Dragon that can sit on my shoulder, and eat pieces of coal? Yes, please. The entropic city below, and the floating, shiny city above? Yes, yes, yes. Even this plague? Again, yes! I can't wait to visit this world again. Highly recommended!"

—LIsa Noell, *Goodreads*

"Love, love, loved this book. Can't wait to get my hands on book 2."

—Seleste deLaney, *Amazon review*

— ALSO BY ALLISON PANG —

Comics, from Outland Entertainment

Fox & Willow: Came a Harper
Fox & Willow: To the Sea

The Abby Sinclair Series

A Brush of Darkness (Book One)
A Sliver of Shadow (Book Two)
A Trace of Moonlight (Book Three)
A Symphony of Starlight (Book Four)
A Duet with Darkness (a prequel short story
in the *Carniepunk* anthology)

The IronHeart Chronicles

Magpie's Song (Book One)
Magpie's Flight (Book Three, forthcoming)

Standalones

"Respawn, Reboot" (a short story in the
Out of Tune, Book 2 anthology)
"The Wind in Her Hair" (a comic in the
Womanthology: Space anthology)
"A Dream Most Ancient and Alone" (a short story in the
Tales From The Lake Vol 5: The Horror Anthology)
"A Certain TeaHouse" (a comic in the *Gothic Tales
of Haunted Futures* anthology)

When the Mother Clock sings,
The dragon takes wing…

Sing a song of sixpence, a penny for your thoughts.
Roll a ball of red thread, to untangle all the knots.
Tie me up and tie me down, the better for which to hang.
Let me dangle without regret, like no song I ever sang.

— CHAPTER ONE —

I am in the Pits.

This narrow thought fills me until I'm shaking so hard I can hardly stand upright as I stumble along the dark passage. My breath compresses with each numb step, and I hold it in even though my lungs burn. I'll shatter if I let it out.

Part of me aches with the need to turn around, to throw myself at the gates in search of clemency, but that's beyond foolish. Besides, isn't the point of this entire charade to get me down here?

I blink past the tremors, trying not to let the fear sweep me up into a sea of despair. The rest of the Tithe was forced through before me, and I can see no sign of them in the darkness ahead. Behind me, the sound of the gates locking rings through the passage with an utterance of finality that cannot be disputed. I shut it out, the crowd outside becoming a muffled rumble. I take a few more steps, and the bells strapped to my wrist jangle wildly with each movement.

One step. Two. Three.

The floor disappears with a whoosh, and I realize I've stepped off a ledge. My vision grays out in a haze, and I violently dig my fingers into the wall to keep from falling. If only that might somehow stop me from being swallowed down the gullet of the bitterest of my nightmares...

Only my years of dancing upon the rooftops of BrightStone lends me the instinctive edge to tuck and roll when I hit the ground. Pain racks my shoulders in fire, and my newly flayed skin splits beneath the impact, leaving me whimpering upon the rocky floor.

Breathe, Mags.

I lie there, mechanical heart clicking away in its usual fashion behind the panel on my chest. I take comfort in its familiarity as I take stock of myself, a mental tabulation. I wiggle my toes to ensure they still work.

The last several days are nothing but a blur in my memory: Allowing myself to be captured by Lord Balthazaar and turned over to the Inquestors. My head shaved. The Tithe procession. Whipped as *part* of the Tithe procession. The discovery that the Rot wasn't simply a punishment from the gods, but a plague deliberately spread among the people of BrightStone for reasons unknown. It's a plot I am in the process of unraveling, though to what end I couldn't say yet.

The image of Josephine and the other Moon Children saluting me from the rooftops flashes in my mind. The sharp-tongued leader of the Twisted Tumblers granted me that last bit of respect even as I allowed myself to be sacrificed in a final effort to find out what secrets lie beneath the city of BrightStone—secrets that might grant us access to Meridion and a destiny beyond what we'd become.

And then there's Ghost... Despite the rest of it, one perfect moment is etched in my mind: him fighting to get to me through the crowd, Lucian holding him back for his own good. Whether Ghost will truly come for me as he said he would or not...well, it isn't something I can rely on. There is no one to save me except myself.

For all my brave words and bold proclamations about what I hoped to accomplish down here, the reality is already far grimmer than I expected. That I volunteered for such a thing is my fault, I suppose, but knowing that at least Ghost didn't see me as merely a means to an end is comforting beyond measure. And now here I am.

Wherever *here* is...

I glance up at the spot I fell from. It's at least fifteen feet above me, maybe more. It's hard to tell. Something digs into my side. Bells, I think numbly, realizing the strap broke during my fall. I recoil from their brassy sound, shaking my wrist free as though it's coated in cobwebs.

A soft moaning echoes up the passageway, and I shift until I'm kneeling, though I've got nowhere else to go. The flickering of torchlight in the distance brushes over the edges of my vision, and I stagger toward it, the light drawing me in with a terrible need to *see*.

The passage takes a sharp turn, the sudden illumination of the torches blinding me briefly until my vision adjusts. I've found the source of the moaning in the form of the rest of the Tithe, their white robes bedraggled and torn. At least one of them is stained with blood—they undoubtedly had been caught unawares by the same fall I had been. Their masks are mostly still in place, though, the eerie serenity at odds with the miserable sounds from underneath them.

I let out a half sob. "Keep it together, Mags," I mumble. My survival depends on not losing my head.

A few of the Rotters huddle together, their terror evident in the way they shake. "Moon Child...help us... Where do we go?"

"Only one way *to* go." I struggle to get the words out as I limp past them to take a closer look down the tunnel. I have no answers. Moon Child or not, I've certainly never been here before, and no Moon Child has ever returned from the Pits to tell us what happens once the Tithe passes through the gates. I have the advantage of having studied a few old maps of the original salt mines that are now the Pits, but my brain is jumbled, the pain of my wounds making it hard to remember.

I strain to see beyond the few torches lining the walls ahead of us. I'm not sure what else I was expecting, but the only sound is the pulse of my blood pounding rabbit-quick in my ears and the panting breaths of the Rotters somehow thunderous.

And still, I see nothing but stretch after stretch of pale rock and a slanting tunnel leading deeper underground. Whatever natural light the gates let in has long since vanished, so these meager torches are all we have to guide us.

Which begs the question, who lit these torches to begin with? It's clear we are at least somewhat expected, but if so, where is this would-be proprietor of ours? And for that matter, why couldn't they have lit up that ledge we all fell down?

The very air presses down upon me, the stone closing in with an awful finality and no answers at all. As someone who has spent most of her life upon the rooftops, I can't help but whimper.

"Hello?" I try to call into the darkness, but my voice is a scratchy shadow of itself, hardly more than a whisper. My tongue sticks to the roof of my mouth, and the stink of fear hangs heavy on my skin.

I attempt to shrug out of the High Inquestor's cloak, but it's stuck. No kindness there. He'd meant to inflict as much pain upon me as possible, and the shiver of agony that rewards me when I give an experimental wriggle indicates I'll most likely black out if I keep trying to rid myself of it. I take a slow, deep breath. The fabric has the acrid stench of salt on it, but it masks the perfumed scent of the Inquestor. I'm grateful for that much, even if the dust sets me to sneezing.

Mayhap it's all a dream and you'll wake up in your bed at Molly's, a fine supper and a warm fireplace waiting.

The memory is near enough to make me weep.

"Moon Child?"

The voice startles me out of my woolgathering. On instinct, I grab the nearest torch, heedless of the way the hot oil leaks from the cloth to slicken my hand.

One of the Rotters moves beside me. "Are you all right?" She pulls her mask off to reveal a face clearly struck by the Rot—light bruising around the young woman's eyes and lips cracked with sores. She had been pretty once, I can tell, her bone structure delicate and fragile and oddly familiar.

I blink, suddenly recognizing her from the Salt Temple. She is the girl who'd been with the bird-masked Inquestor when Lucian and I went to see Archivist Chaunders. If she remembers me, I cannot tell.

She reaches out to take my arm and then seems to think better of it. "If we can find some water..."

"Why does it matter?" one of the others snaps. "We're all dead anyway."

Another moan arises from the group, someone giving voice to a coughing fit that leaves them curled upon the ground.

"That doesn't mean we should give up," the girl says. "Surely there must be a way..." She looks at me with a hopeful sort of despair. "Is it true what the fortune-teller said? Are you IronHeart?"

I shake my head, sighing inwardly. Damn Mad Brianna and her dockside prophecies. A river of grief runs through me then, remembering the way her body twitched when the Inquestors killed her, though part of me wonders if that had been the fate she'd wanted. She certainly had made no bones about her hope for Meridion's downfall.

"Do I seem like a dragon to you? Some 'Chosen One' intended to break down Meridion rule? I'm a scapegoat for a herd of sacrificial cows, eating their so-called sins," I say, shuddering against the fire licking over my shoulders when the cloak slips slightly, pulling on the wounds from the Inquestor's lashing. They've been oozing something awful, I know it.

My throat, swollen and hoarse, bobs as I struggle to swallow, and my thoughts patter like rain in my head. How do I tell them? *What* do I tell them? That the Rot has nothing more to do with sin than the wind? That the Inquestors have been purposely injecting innocent citizens with a plague so virulent that the city has been forced to quarantine the infected belowground? That the floating city of Meridion may be the source of the plague in the first place?

I've been keeping secrets for so long that I'm not sure it even matters anymore. Dead men tell no tales and all that. Besides, the truth isn't usually kind. The whole reason I am down here is to gather evidence of all those things, and I am in no shape to field questions from the others.

"Who's there?" A new voice sounds from an unseen passage before I can gather enough of my wits to give the girl a real answer. The shadows part to reveal an elderly woman, her pale hair glowing in the torchlight. I frown at her. Moon Children all have white hair—something about our half-breed lineage makes us so. Most of us are Tithed to the Pits before we reach twenty-five, but the Tithes have only been running for about twenty years. Even if one of the original Moon Children had survived down here that long, she still seems far too old for that.

A shabbily dressed man in loose-fitting trousers and a patchwork coat lingers behind her. He's younger than she is—maybe late thirties or so, though it's hard to tell. Dark hair frames a pleasant face and a scruffy chin, and his expression appears compassionate. A bonewitch, perhaps.

That doesn't mean I intend to trust either of them. In my experience, friendly faces often hide something far more sinister.

"Who are you?" I wave the torch in front of me in warning. I push the young Rotter behind me without thinking; I had protected my clanmate Sparrow for so long in such a way that it's nearly instinct now. The Rotter may not be a Moon Child like Sparrow had been, but there is something about this girl's innocence makes me want to hide her, all the same.

The two strangers squint at the harshness of the light but make no sudden moves other than to turn their heads away. The old woman smiles gently despite the glare. "Be still, child. You're safe now."

I'm lying on my stomach on a musty mattress in an actual room with real walls and a stone floor. A table laden with medical supplies stands beside the bed, topped with rolls of bandages and a tray of an odd blue liquid. The old woman kneels nearby, her head bowed.

In the distance, the moans of the Rotters have quieted some—the bonewitch had seen to them before me, but they're in another room. Not that it matters. I've got bigger things to worry about.

"Bite down on this." The bonewitch shoves a piece of rope into my mouth. I jerk away when it brushes my lips, the memories of being gagged still a little too fresh, but he sits there calmly until I relax.

I give him a nod, bracing myself for what comes next.

His movements are gentle as he dampens the wool with warm water, but it burns despite the careful treatment. He begins to remove the cloak from my back, and my shriek whistles past the rope.

"Easy now," he says. "It's stuck in the wounds. Stay still."

I have no choice but to do what he says, and I pretend not to hear the wet sounds of my skin pulling apart. I grind my teeth into the rope, my entire body shivering violently as I grip the table with trembling fingers. My guts churn, and I briefly wish he'd rip the whole thing off in one go, just to get it over with. But even I know that's foolish if I hope to make it out of this with any skin at all.

The old lady hasn't moved this entire time, and I attempt to distract myself by studying her with unabashed curiosity. I still can't tell her age, but her face is a maze of dark, craggy skin and crow's feet, and her pale hair hangs in myriad braids fastened by...seashells? They gleam in the lamplight, their spiral beauty drawing my attention.

"There now." The bonewitch lays the bloody cloak on the ground beside me. I fight the urge to spit on it. "That's an Inquestor garment," he observes, removing the rope. There's a slight tone of censure in his voice.

"Well it's obviously not my wedding gown, aye?" I mutter, unable to keep the anger from bubbling out.

"I meant no offense." He dips a series of bandages into the blue liquid before laying them upon my wounds. A soothing tingle spreads over my skin, and I exhale one long, shaky puff of air as the tension slips out of me.

My mind whirls with relief. "Well, you have to forgive me, then. I was a bit ill-used before I arrived here. My manners aren't what they ought to be." It's all I can think of to say, though I know it's not the right thing. "How long will it last? The numbing stuff, I mean." The sudden absence of pain is nearly mind-boggling in its sweetness, and I almost forget where I am.

Almost.

"Several hours, at least. Long enough to get you fed and settled." He shifts beside me. "A moment—I need to clean this up, and then I'll see about getting you something to drink."

"I did not expect the Pits to be so...hospitable," I admit wryly. Though *hospitable* might not be the right word. Regardless, it will do me no good to cross swords with my hosts, at least not until I get my bearings.

I narrow my gaze at him as he stands up and begins collecting his supplies. "Settled where?" With the pain receding, my wits have begun to return, reminding me exactly what situation I'm in. My stomach pipes up, too, growling to be noticed. Food would be a welcome distraction, but... "And where is everyone? The other Moon Children? The Rotters? Who are you people?"

The old woman lifts her head finally, a shadow crossing her proud features. "Perhaps it would be easier if we simply showed you," she says, her tone surprisingly soothing. "Whatever falsehoods you were raised to believe must be unlearned. Rest assured, everyone is properly seen to down here."

The bonewitch pats my shoulder. "Lie down awhile first... Do you have a name, lass?"

I pause, unsure which name to give him. If there are other Moon Children about, my Banshee clan name would make the most sense. I've earned more than my fair share of notoriety as "Raggy Maggy"—supposedly having been killed by Inquestors several months ago didn't help—but I'm edging toward caution over honesty now. The events of the last few weeks have left me a little gun-shy, and rightfully so. Besides, I'd been kicked out of the Banshee clan, and Moon Child clan grudges are nothing to sneer at. I'd rather not be shanked for my trouble before I even get a chance to figure out what's what. I'm not sure I want to give my real name, either, though.

"More than I care to list," I say. "Call me Magpie." I decide on the nickname only a few would know me by.

"Well, Miss Magpie, let these strips sit awhile. When the bleeding stops, you'll be able to move around some. You were lucky; most of the wounds aren't too deep. You should heal up right quick." He sits back down in his chair, wiping his hands on a damp rag. "You can call me Georges, if you like."

"Georges," I repeat. The name is familiar, but I can't place it. I turn toward the old lady to mask my frustration at my lack of memory. "And you?"

"Tanith." She gets to her feet with a gentle grace that belies her age, the seashells tinkling in her hair, and pours me a mug of water from a nearby pitcher. She sets it on the table beside the bed. "Rest. I'll get you some new clothes."

The two of them duck behind a thin curtain drawn in front of the room's entrance. I shift carefully on the mattress, relieved when the pain is minimal. Whatever that blue stuff is, it certainly works well.

The room I'm in appears to be a makeshift infirmary, judging by the additional empty cots. Bottles of concoctions line the shelves, which are built into the stone walls, and a surgical table claims the center of the space. A tray of scalpels and a bucket of plaster sit beside it. It's clean in here, too, and smells faintly of lavender, which is strange considering where we are. The bonewitch must be kept busy with the Rotters, yet somehow the odor of blood and other less pleasant things is nearly nonexistent.

Which begs the question… If only Moon Children and Meridians are immune to the Rot, how are Georges and Tanith surviving it? The salt priests always insisted that only the sinful could catch it, and while my time with Lucian and Ghost had taught me that none of that was true, I'd never dreamed that people were somehow *surviving* down here. Perhaps miracles did exist. If so, my task to discover the actual source of the Rot—whether the Meridians are spreading the plague themselves or it's being done through some other mechanism—would be that much simpler. Surely, I would find answers…

I reach for the mug of water next to me, and I sip it slowly, ignoring the bitter aftertaste. None of this is how it should be. Lucian, Ghost, and I were betrayed by our fellow conspirator, Molly Bell. My clockwork dragon disappeared. I split the skull of an Inquestor to protect Lucian and Ghost. I was whipped in front of the entire town of BrightStone for my crimes.

And Lucian just stood there at the gates and let me be taken. But what right do I have to be angry about that? After all, how many times have *I* stood by and watched one of my fellow Moon Children be subjected to the Tithe? There is nothing he could have done to stop it anyway.

It stings nonetheless. For Lucian, maybe it really is all about protecting his brother.

Oh, Ghost…

I sigh. *I* started this chain of events: finding the dragon, Sparrow's death, leading the Inquestors to the Archivist, letting Ghost get captured. And then everything had fallen by the wayside in my decidedly rash impulse to let Lord Balthazaar capture me, forcing me to be Tithed. In the end, I've no one to blame but myself.

A gleam at the foot of my bed catches my eye, and I shift so I can get a better look at the marks etched into the wooden footboard.

I run a finger over the lines, sounding out the letters. "Suck-tit." I trace the letters again and am struck by a cold certainty. Penny has been here. Of course she has. I watched my former clanmate be Tithed weeks ago, taking my place when the clan thought I'd been killed. But where is she now?

As much as I want to bolt from the room and demand answers, I soon find myself dozing off into a fitful sleep. I've been thrust into the underworld like the hero from one of those tales Mad Brianna used to tell me, Sparrow, and rest of the orphans she had taken under her wing. I will need to rest and regain my strength if I'm to have any chance of finding the other Moon Children and learning the secrets of the Pits.

In the end, you do what you do best. Hide in plain sight, and hope they do not discover you, Mags.

I have no magic sword or shining armor, but I do have a quest. And that will have to do.

—◀●▶—

The curtain flutters and Tanith reappears, holding a set of clothing similar to her own—clean trousers and a linen shirt. She eases the shirt over my head so I don't have to strain the skin on my back by stretching, and belts it at my hips. It hangs loose off my shoulders, but I get the feeling it's less about modesty and more about comfort. Without any friction, my wounds won't stick to the cloth.

She nudges my feet. "You'll have to make do with your shoes. Or go barefoot, if you prefer, but I don't recommend it."

My thoughts turn to Ghost and the toughened soles of his feet. He might not have a problem down here, but I don't need to lose a toe in some sharp-edged crevasse. I lace up my old boots, their once fine shine now quite dull.

Tanith helps me stand. "I'll take you down to meet the others. We'll be in time for supper."

"Others?" My mind races with the thought of seeing Penny and the rest of the Moon Children. Or did Tanith mean the Rotters? Or both? The casual way she speaks of mundane things such as supper makes my head hurt. But Penny was my clanmate. She's smarter than the rest of us. She can read and write, and if there was any chance of her finding a way out of this place, I don't believe she would have passed it up, supper or no.

"I'll show you. Come along." Tanith waves at me to follow her through the curtain.

She leads me down a maze of dimly lit passages lined with glowing lanterns. There's a bluish hue to them, and I resist the urge to run my fingers over the glass. Unlike the earlier tunnels made of rock above, these are clearly the well-used remnants of the salt mines from earlier days. The walls are flat and smooth and white, the turns following an obvious route. Side passages scatter into the darkness toward some distant destination.

It's all so *empty.*

"Where is everyone else?" The question seems to hang in the air, with no breeze to move it along.

"Below. Most of us don't care for the light up here. It's too bright. Gives us headaches."

I frown. "I can barely see past the shadows."

"Not yet. But you will." She pats me on the shoulder. I'm sure she means to be reassuring, but I'm more confused than ever.

"What about Georges? Where did he go?"

"He's a Rotter himself. He led the rest of the infected to a separate living facility. Everyone who isn't a Moon Child or a Meridian carries the disease, and their needs are different as a result. Not all are fully affected by it right away."

My mouth goes dry. "He's a Rotter? But I thought the Rotters…I don't know…just decayed away down here. Isn't that why Moon Children are Tithed? To help them die?"

Amusement flickers on her face. "You all think that when you first get here. But I'm a Meridian myself; the last thing I want to do is let these poor people die. Come along—let me show you."

I don't understand any of this. Everything I've ever been told is a lie—an incredibly intricate one. Apparently not even Lucian, with all his learned doctor's ways, has any idea how things are here.

I have no time to ask another question before the passage opens wide, a silvery glow illuminating what appears to be a village.

The light is gentle, whatever its source, not as glaring as the torches lining the walls up in the upper tunnels. Everything is bathed in a soft haze. If I wasn't so terribly awake I'd think I was dreaming my way into a fairy tale.

But fairy tales are peculiar. All the ones Mad Brianna used to tell me and Sparrow ended with beautiful monsters eating the children, so fair warning.

And this village is nothing if not beautiful. Excessively so. Hundreds of softly lit domes have been arranged in clusters far below with spiral pathways looping throughout. Small groups of people slowly walk along the paths as they go about their business in a seemingly casual fashion. I catch the chatter of laughter and low conversation.

Normalcy. Or whatever passes for that here. It's like a utopia built in the darkest part of the underground, somehow only serving to draw attention to how drab and awful everything else is.

I glance up, though certainly there is nothing to see except the ceiling of the cave we're in. But the village has the same ambiance as the floating city of Meridion that hovers mockingly above BrightStone, a beacon of everything I've ever wanted and would never have.

Tanith hasn't said it in so many words, but I have no doubt this village was built by Meridians. That she herself doesn't glow like they are known to do doesn't mean much. Ghost once told me the electrical current that seems to flow beneath a Meridian's skin fades away if they are away from their city for too long.

So how long has she been down here?

The trail to the village is made up of a series of steep switchbacks, the stairs carved directly into the rock, but Tanith leads us to an enormous basket attached to a roped pulley system. A small door is latched shut on its side, and she opens it with a quick pull. "Normally, we would walk down, but my old bones prefer a little less impact." Ushering me through the door, she pats my hand and then gets in after me.

The basket creaks as we are slowly lowered into the canyon. "There used to be mechanical lifts many years ago," Tanith says. "But they fell into disrepair, so we are forced to use more primitive measures these days."

Fell into disrepair? Or were destroyed?

I don't voice the words aloud, but Ghost and I had researched the Pits as much as we were able and the working theory was that the

Meridians had blown up a portion of the mines, for some reason only known to them.

And soon, perhaps to me, as well.

A man and a woman in hooded blue robes meet us at the bottom, bowing respectfully to Tanith.

"Ah, Tanith. You've arrived." The younger one, a man who appears to be in his forties, gives me a nod. He pushes his hood down, and his dark hair falls in a loose queue to his shoulders. His features are sharp and handsome, brows artfully arched and eyes half-lidded and languid as they flick over me, taking my measure the way a rat sizes up a piece of cheese.

But this man is different from the others. Like the dead architect I found who'd fallen directly from the floating city, his skin ripples as though myriad stars are trapped beneath it, beaming softly. I stumble, and his teeth flash as he grins, clearly aware of the effect he has on people. But more importantly, the fact that he still has that glow at all must mean he's been on Meridion recently. And if he's not using the gates to the Pits to get there, then there must be another way...

I file this piece of information away for later. No sense in tipping my hand too quickly.

Caught up in my thoughts, I startle as Tanith puts her arm around my shoulders. The sensation is oddly intimate, and I want to shake her away. "Prepare a dwelling for Magpie. There is an empty one in the third quad that will suit."

"As you say." He bows again and retreats swiftly, leaving the three of us beside the basket. Tanith gestures in his direction. "That's Buceph. He runs security here."

"And I'm Rinna." The woman removes her hood, revealing a mop of curly brown tresses, decorated with the same sort of seashells as those in Tanith's hair. "I see to most of the scheduling and the day-to-day tasks. Once you've recovered from your wounds, you'll get a rotation on the roster."

I blink at her. "Roster? For what? Last time I was on a roster it was to be sent down here," I say, my tone perhaps too blunt.

"Ah...yes," she says carefully. "Well, we all work to survive down here. If you have any particular trade skills, let me know your preference and I'll make sure you get that."

"Not unless you count murder," I say sourly. In truth, I've only killed one person, and Inquestor Caskers had deserved it, but still, honest work intrigues me. The concept, however, is almost beyond my comprehension. Their easy acceptance of me into their ranks seems a tad suspicious, but I'm not some innocent Moon Child anymore. And if the work allows me access to their records or a chance to snoop around without notice, I'll take it.

Rinna smiles weakly. "Don't worry, Magpie. We understand. Most of the lost ones who find their way here require a few lessons in civilization before they fit in."

I bristle, but Tanith squeezes my shoulder. "Very good, Rinna. That will be all."

"As you will, mistress." Rinna bows and heads up the path, her hair flowing behind her in soft ringlets. I cannot help but run a finger over my baldness with a twinge of envy. I've spent my entire life hiding my hair beneath a cap, and it's ironic that I might wear it so freely here when I have no hair at all.

Tanith's wrinkled hand reaches out to run over the stubble upon my scalp, something like pity in her expression. "Tsk. It will grow back, little one."

I snort, brimming with impatience. "I'm sure it will. It's only hair."

"Indeed." The two of us follow the path the others took, albeit more slowly. Tanith's pace is deliberate, with a hint of stiffness that suggests joint issues. It's noticeably pronounced on her left side in particular.

I study the others walking around us, looking for something or someone familiar. A Moon Child's hair is a peculiar shade of white—almost silver—and with all the soft light illuminating the space around us, Moon Children would stand out like beacons. But I do not see a single one.

From this distance, I can't tell exactly what the dwellings are made of—some sort of metal, perhaps—but they reflect the bluish light captured in the small glass lanterns hanging from nearby lampposts. Most of the houses are single stories with round windows. They are clearly meant for one or two people, with barely enough room for a bed and not much else, so village or not, it doesn't seem like there are any families here. No children that I've seen, at any rate.

"So, I don't understand," I say finally. "If there's a whole settlement down here, why does Georges have a surgery above? Where are the other Rotters? Where are the Moon Children?" Once it's freed, my tongue unleashes a torrent of questions with my need to understand why I've been betrayed and lied to for most of my life.

Tanith sighs. "It wasn't always this way. In the beginning, we stayed in the upper chambers simply because we were afraid to venture any farther. But when the plague didn't respond to our early attempts at a cure, we expanded our operations down here where we had more room. That said, all newcomers are checked out in the upper chambers to assess possible threats, as well as to see to injuries."

I raise a brow. "Why would you come down to the Pits at all?"

She shakes her head, and the shells jingle. "When the plague first erupted in BrightStone, a group of Meridian scientists, including myself, was tasked with finding a solution. We originally worked out of a facility in BrightStone—close to the Salt Temple, in fact." She curls her upper lip. "But before the Inquestors were able to quell the riots and fear in BrightStone, fires began to break out regularly, and we lost a number of labs that way. Frankly, we made people nervous, and it was decided it would be best to send everyone down below—both infected and our Meridian science team—to keep the other citizens safe."

The timeline Archivist Chaunders showed me and Ghost flashes into my memory. "So you've been down here for *twenty years*?"

"Nearly seventeen, actually. And we're still not much closer to a cure than when we started."

I nod. It makes sense, but I can't help wondering how easily everything is explained away. It hasn't escaped me that she didn't answer my question about the Moon Children, either.

"It's a lot to take in," she murmurs. "When you've had a chance to eat, rest, and become accustomed to how things work down here, you'll be more comfortable. Can you read, Magpie?"

Tanith asks it kindly, and I answer without thinking. "A bit here and there, but nothing too hard?"

She's clearly surprised at my answer, but maybe feigning ignorance is better. I decide to keep my thoughts to myself for a while longer. Besides, the spiral paths are diverging; one leads to a cluster of dwelling pods and one to a…

"A greenhouse?" I ask, incredulous. It's squat, with one wall made of thick glass panes, and a purplish glow emanates from within.

Tanith makes an approving sound as we approach it. "Yes. A small miracle—one of many, in fact."

"But without the sun, how do you grow anything?" Not that I'm an expert on greenhouses. But the ones I'd seen on Lord Balthazaar's estate were completely made of glass to let the light in. Down here, though…

"Would you like a quick tour? Here." She taps on the glass, and someone moves inside to open a small door on the far side. A skinny beanpole of a man emerges and stands aside as Tanith ushers me in. His wiry frame reminds me somewhat of Ghost. His hair is bound beneath a cap, and he wears a discolored apron.

"This is Joseph, one of our expert underground farmers," she says.

There's something sad about Joseph, his gaze resting upon my shaved head with a slightly furrowed brow. But then I'm inside the greenhouse proper and any thoughts about him fade away as I'm embraced by the purplish lights and the scents of dirt and growing things.

I'm half-starved for color already, even in this short amount of time. Beneath the purple light, the green leaves don't seem quite right, but there's a certain brilliance to the way they shine. Not that I can recognize one from the other, but there are pictures in front of several plants that indicate various vegetables or herbs.

"Using different shades of blue or red light allows us to determine levels of growth so we can maximize the space we use and ensure the best harvest," Tanith drones from behind me.

I leave her and walk down the rows, unable to restrain my fingers from drifting through the soil in one of the trays. In the far corner of the greenhouse is a small table covered with potted flowers. It's hard to tell exactly what color they are beneath the purple illumination, but it doesn't really matter. Flowers are hard to come by even in BrightStone. Only those who lived in the Upper Tier would have the money for something so frivolous.

Living underground for as long as they have, perhaps these Meridians are just as hungry for things other than food.

"The others find me foolish for this particular hobby," Joseph says, walking toward me.

"Sometimes foolishness is all that's left." I bend over to sniff one of the flowers, sighing at the sweetness.

"Too true." He reaches over and plucks a flower from a pot. "Here. Have a daisy." He hands it to me and then bows his head, heading for one of the other tables. I touch the flower bemusedly, my fingers slightly trembling. I'd never actually held a flower before. Not one from a hothouse.

Deathflower weeds are common enough in the BrightStone Warrens, where my clan makes its home, but they are ragged plants, tough and built for survival. The only purpose for something like this is beauty. What does one do with a such a thing? In the end, I tuck it carefully into one of the pockets of my trousers and head to where Tanith waits by the door.

Her mouth quirks in amusement as we leave the greenhouse. "Meridian technology is a wondrous thing, isn't it?"

I chew on it, sure whatever's showing on my face is not particularly pleasant. After all, such technology has been dangled in front of me for the entirety of my life. Luckily, I don't have to respond aloud, though, because the other villagers are emerging from their dwellings.

I'm greeted with open curiosity and friendly waves, and yet, I recognize none of them. Not that I have ever been particularly close to anyone but Sparrow, but shouldn't there be Moon Children here? What of Penny? She was sent here only weeks ago.

Watch your step, Mags. A society that eats its children is not interested in protecting the young.

My gut twists, uneasy. I catch a hint of pipe music nearby, but it's nearly drowned out in the excited chatter.

Tanith claps her hands, silencing the others. "Prepare the table for our guest. Tonight we shall feast and welcome our sister, Magpie. Bid her good and gentle welcome, but be careful, for she is weary and her wounds are many."

I'd nearly forgotten the lashes upon my back, but thinking about them now, I feel exhausted beyond measure and my stomach rumbles at the mere thought of food. It's stranger still to feel like I'm welcome at a banquet like a person and not some piece of street trash.

Tanith points out the various buildings as we continue walking the main path through the village. They are all squat with slight domed shapes at the tops. Some have symbols carved into the domes, noting what they are. There is a baker and a butcher, a blacksmith and a tallower, and other signs I don't recognize at all. An herbalist, perhaps, and a metalsmith.

My mind reels as doubt continues to creep into my mind. Things were starting to look too good to be true. And yet...

Where does the meat come from, Mags? What are they eating down here in the depths?

With the lack of Moon Children about, the thought chills me, squelching much of my appetite. I don't *really* think they're eating Moon Children, but I will withhold judgment until I know for sure. And perhaps I'll stick to less carnivorous fare until then.

Before long, we pass a dome larger than any other we've seen so far. "The main hall," Tanith points out. A glance through its pillared entrance shows several long tables and benches. "Wait here and rest while everything is prepared."

There is a bench outside the entrance, and I gratefully sag into it.

"Welcome home, Magpie." Tanith gives my shoulder one last squeeze before retreating into the great hall.

"Aye," I breathe, but dread sweeps over me all the same. Where are the other Moon Children?

I've silver spurs and a horse to ride,
And a golden lady to sit by my side,
With a milk-white coat and a feathered cap,
And a wooden coffin for my final nap.

— CHAPTER TWO —

S upper is a curiously quiet affair. The table is covered with plates of eggs, fresh greens, and what appears to be chicken. Next to Buceph is a bowl of mushrooms with blue caps and white stalks. They glow slightly, emitting a soft blue luminescence. Some species native to the caves, no doubt, though I'm certainly no expert on cave edibles. These particular mushrooms could be deadly poisonous, but from the way Buceph is putting them away, it doesn't seem like it.

"Care to try one?" He offers me the bowl, but I decline. I'm not picky, but I draw the line at fungus that glows in the dark.

I sip from a glass of chilled water instead and watch him eat. I'm struck again by the odd beauty of his skin. It's far more vibrant than that of the dead architect Sparrow and I found a few months ago. "How do you manage the skin effect? I thought Meridians lost that ability when they are no longer on Meridion."

I throw the words out there, knowing I might be playing my hand too soon, but some tiny piece of me wants them to see me at least as something like an equal. The way the others squirm uncomfortably makes me wonder if the skin thing isn't common knowledge.

"Ah, well, we try not to talk too much about that down here. It's considered…impolite," he says. I flush despite myself, but he holds up a mushroom. "However, in my case, it's this—bioluminescent fungus," he says. "It doesn't create quite the same effect as being on Meridion does, but I rather like it."

"Only Buceph consumes these disgusting things by choice," Rinna says, shuddering. "If you knew where they grew…"

"Not all of us can have your natural beauty," Buceph retorts, but there's no malice in it. Clearly an old argument of sorts. He turns to me. "You should try one." I decline again, and he chuckles.

A basket of steaming rolls is passed around, and I snatch two of them, slapping on a pat of creamy butter.

"Are you enjoying the food?" Tanith asks from the end of the table, sipping from her own glass with a tilt of her dainty hand.

"Aye. I cannot believe how much you are able to grow down here." I gesture at the butter. "Where do you keep your cows? Or is it goats?"

A ripple of laughter meets my questions. I frown, not getting the joke. "We don't exactly make all of it ourselves," Buceph says, passing me another roll. "We trade with Balthazaar for some of the things we need. It's turned out to be a rather nice arrangement."

The roll slips from my fingers and lands on my ceramic plate with a light thud. I struggle to swallow my last bite. Even down here I cannot escape him.

There's the rub, Mags.

As one of the most influential men of BrightStone, Lord Balthazaar has his fingers in so many pies it shouldn't surprise me to discover he is working directly with the Meridians in the Pits. After all, his wife has the Rot, though it isn't common knowledge.

So eager is he to find a cure for Lydia, Balthazaar is helping to support the very research that made the problem in the first place. I already know he assists in finding candidates to turn into Rotters, but this seems so…blatant. How is he supplying the village with such things? Not through the gates, surely. That would easily be discovered.

My heart ticks a little faster. There must be another way out of here. "How convenient," I murmur, unable to say anything else as a surge of anger rushes through me. As a former "guest" of Balthazaar's estate, I'd been subjected to days of starvation, bound and beaten and left to lie in my own filth. That I must rely on him now for food rankles.

Buceph gives me a bemused smile, perhaps hoping for a different reaction. "We've been doing it for quite a while." He gestures at our surroundings. "You have noticed we live in a cave, correct?"

Another ripple of amusement in the faces around me, but I find no humor in his words. I retrieve the roll and eat it anyway, only because it's foolish not to. Old habits die hard, even if every bite fills my mouth with bile.

"I think I've picked up on it, aye," I say dryly. My fingers itch for a smoke. I wonder if they have cigarillos down here.

Buceph nudges me with his foot, his knee lingering on mine a little longer than I like. "It's all right. Everyone who comes down here is confused at first. It's hard to accept, isn't it?"

"It makes no sense at all," I say. "This is supposed to be a punishment."

"Well, for the average Meridian, it would be," he points out. "People who live in the sky can't imagine what it's like to live below the ground. It horrifies them. As far as the Rotters go…well, having the Rot itself would be a punishment enough. Until we can find a cure, there is nothing we can do except make them comfortable." He offers me the bread basket again. "Here. And don't skimp on the butter. You're too scrawny by half."

I'm sure he means well, but the words sting anyway. I drain my glass. "You can thank your precious Balthazaar for that," I snap, getting to my feet. He reaches out to take my arm, and I slap it away. "Enough of this. Where are the others? Where are my people?" I whirl on Tanith, my hand instinctively reaching for a hammer at my hip that isn't there. "You said the Rotters went with Georges to another village. Is that where the Moon Children are, too?"

The group turns toward me, silent. Are they shocked that I've spoken out of turn? My nostrils flare. Living with Lucian and Ghost has made me complacent. I would never have allowed myself to trust these strangers so easily before.

"And all...this?" I throw my glass at the wall, relishing in the way it shatters. "Balthazaar isn't known for his kindness. I highly doubt the man would care about the Rotters or your research if he wasn't personally invested."

Tanith pales at my sudden outburst. "Oh dear. How unfortunate."

Buceph's smile becomes brittle. *A mask, then.* "Just who are you? For all the squawking you've done, the name Magpie suits you very well, but I don't doubt there's more to you than that."

My upper lip curls at him. "Little rabbits have big ears, as Mad Brianna used to say. And the High Inquestor's gotten a little sloppy with his secrets." I exhale sharply, knowing I'm talking too much, but the righteousness of my anger feels so good. All my repressed fury over the years has suddenly exploded, vomiting from my throat with reckless abandon.

But I force myself to rein it in. If they're communicating with Balthazaar on a regular basis—and surely they must be—it won't be long before he puts two and two together. The only time I spied on Balthazaar directly was in the air vents at the Brass Button Theatre the day he'd met with the High Inquestor. It was there I'd learned some of their plans, though I hadn't known what to make of it at the time. Still didn't, if I really was honest with myself. But if I'm not careful, I'm going to get my fellow conspirators caught.

I decide to do what I do best: attract attention to myself. "I'm waiting for an answer," I say, arms crossed.

Tanith clears her throat, her brows drawn together. "Perhaps it would be best to show her the rest of it now."

Buceph nods before turning toward me. "Normally we like to wait until you've had a chance to rest and recover, but seeing as you're rather insistent..." His voice trails away, and he stands, offering me his arm. "Shall we find out?"

I suppose it's meant to be a gallant gesture, but I stand there until he lowers it. This isn't a promenade. Seemingly unperturbed, he motions for me to walk beside him, and we head toward the path that leads to the trade buildings I passed earlier with Tanith.

"Our ways must seem very foreign to you." He strides beside me easily, but there's something predatory about the way he moves that sets every hair on the nape of my neck at attention.

"Of course they are. You're Meridians," I say cautiously. "Flies don't dream of anything but their dunghills. No surprise we gape at the sun when it's shining upon us."

The greenhouse looms before us, brightly lit on the inside with true white light this time. I didn't see Joseph at dinner, but there's a shadow moving behind the glass. We pass it by and continue through the village to the outskirts opposite the cliffside basket Tanith and I took before.

There's a gate here, a massive one, with thick bars embedded in the rock of the ceiling and floor. A smaller, door-shaped opening is centered within it, and Buceph swiftly unlocks it and ushers me through.

"Merely a precaution," he assures me. "The Rotter village has two of these, as well."

I swallow, unsure if they are keeping something out or something in. I don't voice the question because I'm pretty sure I won't like the answer either way.

A tunnel arcs into the darkness here, and Buceph picks up a dimly glowing lantern next to a pile of barrels. He gestures at me to follow. "Rinna mentioned something interesting about your conversation with her and Tanith this evening. Did you mean what you said? About committing murder?"

There's something pensive about the way he says it, and I don't get the sense that he's trying to mock me. There's a hint of genuine interest there, and my shoulder blades prickle in response, trying to shake off an imaginary stab in the back. I'm not sure how to answer him.

"Twice over, if you believe the High Inquestor, but I only ever killed one man. An Inquestor, in fact." The tension between us ratchets up, and my voice drops, deadly quiet. "I did it to protect my friends. And I would do it again."

"Yes. I believe you would." He smiles, but it's a snake's grin, bloodless and thin. "And an Inquestor, no less. How very... fortuitous."

He doesn't elaborate on this, and I don't want to ask.

Eventually, we make a turn and then another. The caves here feel darker than the others somehow, more constrictive. The air has a sickly sweet taste upon it, and it lingers around me like a shroud.

I hear it first—the thick, shambling moans burbling from throats gone hoarse with use. A lancet of fear ripples over my skin. "What is that?" The words deflate out of me in a wavering hiss, and my lungs struggle to breathe.

"Courage, Magpie. This first lot is beyond our help," Buceph whispers in my ear.

We round the corner, and I get my first look at the Rotters. Real ones—not like the pathetic shadows of people newly infected. Death rides these unfortunates like some sort of diseased horse. The stench rolls past, its foulness coating my skin and seeping into my nose with all the grace of a bouquet of putrid flowers. I gag, but opening my mouth only makes it that much worse so I press my palm against my nose. And then I see the Rotters up close. The smell of them is merely an introduction to a sideshow made of such horrors that it renders me motionless, every muscle in my body trembling with the need to run, yet I remain stock-still.

Flesh twists and peels from their bones, clinging to tattered clothing. Dull, vacant faces with cloudy eyes and pocked cheeks, and hair in greasy clumps. Limbs twisted or missing. Their breathing is a chorus of pendulous death rattles, wheezing from chests that had forgotten how to draw air long ago.

Buceph passes by without a word, ignoring the way the Rotters stir at our presence. Some reach out to us, as if begging for alms, but the only thing I can think of that would be worth giving them is a swift dispatch.

How long? How long does it take them to reach this stage?

I stare in unbridled fascination, my stomach churning with a horror I'll be forced to relive the next time I sleep. Lucian might know the answer, given all his hidden experiments. A twinge of unexpected sadness rolls through me, but in a heartbeat, one of them lunges at me, her hands sliding through the bars, and the feeling is gone.

Spittle froths at her lips—shriveled things that barely stretch over her rotting teeth. I recoil on instinct, her haunted moaning all the more awful when I realize she's trying to speak.

"Plllaaaz," she groans.

Buceph whisks me forward. "It's worse when they try to communicate. It's a grim reminder that they're not really dead. Not completely." There's a savage edge to his words and something mocking about it at the same time.

"I don't understand," I say. "They're conscious in there?" I spare a look behind me and instantly regret it. The woman's filmy gaze meets mine, and for that instant, it's like she sees *me*. But then Buceph tugs me away and the Rotters are swallowed up in the darkness. The urge to bolt the way we came is wretchedly strong.

"That's monstrous," I say with a shudder.

"What did you expect?" Buceph's clearly amused at my reaction, but I can't even find it in me to bristle at it. "They don't call it the Rot for nothing."

Ugly laughter erupts from me. "I didn't know. Not really."

"Don't feel bad," Buceph says, oozing sympathy. "It's a generational thing. You don't remember the days before the enforced quarantine, I expect. In those times, we had Rotters like these wandering the streets of BrightStone."

The girl Rotter who had tried to help me when we first entered the Pits flashes in my memory. Will she become this way, as well? I already know the answer, but I cannot help but ask. "And what of the people I came in with? They weren't as bad off as all that..."

"Ah, well, Georges tends to them in a village of their own until there is no longer any hope. When the disease progresses past a certain point, we bring them here. It's not ideal, but believe me, it's the most humane solution we could come up with."

"I'm not sure we define *humane* the same way." It's probably not the wisest time to bring up Lucian's theories about the Meridians and the plague at this point, though, so I bite my tongue. By now we're past the far end of the pen, which ends against a wall with a set of metal doors recessed deep into the rock. "What keeps them from trying to escape?"

Buceph points at the wire. "It's electrified, so they tend to stay away from it. The only way in is an entrance on the other side—a door that leads from inside the facility. And that is electrified, too. The back end of this particular pen is nothing more than the cave wall—far too thick for them to break through."

I study the doors of the facility, remembering the Archivist's maps. "This is it. This is what the miners were working on before the tunnels collapsed. It has to be."

Buceph frowns. "You seem to know an awful lot for someone so new to the Pits."

"I had a...a friend who worked at the museum in BrightStone. Her father was a miner, and she said there was an explosion many years ago, when the Pits were first built."

"Indeed." My response seems to satisfy him, and he fusses with a keypad on the right side of the doors, his fingers moving too fast for me to follow.

Something buzzes on the other side of the metal, followed by a flashing red light above the door. A moment later, one door swings in to grant us entrance. He takes the lead, brushing by me and waiting until I follow before shutting it again, leaving me face-to-face with a disgruntled young woman dressed in a white coat. She's of medium height—a little shorter than me—with light-brown hair and eyes that somehow seem even less alive than those of the Rotters outside. She might be considered pretty, but I cannot help but wonder if her scowl has been carved permanently into her skin. On the other hand, there's nothing particularly cheerful about living or working down here as far as I can tell.

She turns to Buceph in exasperation. "This is not proper protocol."

He shrugs. "Seventeen years of following procedure, Sora, and where has it gotten us?"

"She's contaminated," the woman snaps. "We can't let her inside."

Now it's my turn to snort. "Moon Child, aye? I can't get the Rot."

"But you carry it," Buceph admits, sighing heavily. "She's right. Rot or not, there are several experiments inside that could be affected by the introduction of other sorts of microscopic organisms." He waves his hand. "You'd think as head researcher here I'd have the power to override, but..."

"Rules are rules," Sora states flatly, unconvinced.

"Then we'll decontaminate her. Simple as that." He gestures toward another door. "The showers are in there, if you wouldn't mind. I'll see to it you're brought a set of scrubs."

"Scrubs?" Their words are confusing, like Lucian's sometimes are—Meridian terminology and technology I don't understand.

Sora sniggers, but the sound cuts off when Buceph glares at her. "Special clothes," she says finally. "Meant for places with potentially high contamination levels. If you want in, you must wash. There is no other choice. Leave your clothes in the basket beside the door."

"Fine, then." I trudge off in the direction she points and find myself in a simple room coated with metal tiles. Pipes emerge from the walls with copper knobs, reminding me of Lucian's laboratory. It takes a minute of fussing with them before I manage to turn them on.

Water hisses from the faucet above, and I yelp at the chill. The sound echoes harshly, but the water heats up fast as I strip and toss my clothes in the basket. I scrub down with a bar of chemical-scented soap, avoiding the cuts on my back as best I can. I crane my head at the wounds, but it stretches the skin in a way that makes me grunt. A burning prickle throbs through me, leaving me inhaling slowly. The numbing gel Georges applied is definitely wearing off. With any luck, Buceph will have some here, as well.

True to her word, Sora has left me a set of...*scrubs* outside the door. They certainly don't seem like anything fancy. How such a thin set of trousers and shirt make a particularly good barrier to the Rot or anything else, I couldn't say. Mayhap they stop those invisible phage things Lucian had told me about when he was showing me his laboratory.

As I emerge from the shower room, Sora regards me with cautious suspicion before handing me little cloth shoes that slip easily onto my feet. "So you don't track anything inside."

I shrug at her, unsurprised when she turns away without responding.

"It's good enough." Buceph strides toward me from an opposite door. He's dressed the same as I am now, all the way to the cloth shoes.

"I still think this is a bad idea," Sora says, "but it's your call."

"Yes, it is. And I think Magpie has earned it." He gives me another one of his reptilian smiles, like he's trying to pin me to the spot. I don't remotely like the sound of his voice, but I refuse to look away.

Something tells me that if I retreat even the slightest amount, he'll somehow take advantage of it. I'm not going to give any more ground than I have to.

Buceph nods curtly at Sora, and she clicks something on her desk. Another set of doors opens up behind her, these made of a thick, frosted glass.

There's nothing intricate about them, but I know a cage when I see it. I exhale sharply when I pass through it to a dark, metal corridor. I can't see the blood, but I can smell it, damp and coppery, a sluggish reminder of how alive the people outside once were. In here it feels almost obscene, a viscous odor that can't ever be washed away.

"So who are you really?" I ignore the shiver of panic in my spine, the animal part of my brain insisting I *flee, flee, flee.* "Tanith said she was part of a group of Meridian scientists in search for a cure for the Rot."

"Well, that's one way of putting it, I suppose." Buceph sighs, his tone as matter-of-fact as mine. "More like we're the ones responsible for creating the Rot to begin with."

I struggle not to recoil, my terror at his admission turning me cold. "And you decided to what? To slaughter BrightStone citizens in some game? Some disgusting power play?"

"Well, it wasn't intentional," he says mildly. "Not the part where it got out. It wasn't created for the people of BrightStone at all. It was meant for us."

"Oh aye. Lady Lydia was rather clear on that." I shake my head in sudden fury. "Immortality, was it?"

He stops. "Well, aren't you an interesting puzzle? And not far off. How old would you say I am?"

"Forty?" I guess it at random, and he chuckles.

"Would you believe I was only thirty-eight when I was sent down here? And that was nearly twenty years ago." A sideways smirk crooks his mouth. "I've barely aged a day. Alas, in Meridians, the serum only slows down the aging process, but in the case of the BrightStone populace, it appears to stop aging altogether. Unfortunately, the very cells making up the body no longer replicate or refresh, eventually breaking down even while the person still lives."

I bare my teeth at him in a snarl, and he laughs. "Lady Lydia was a rather happy accident as far as the Rot goes—at least for us. Meridion gave up on funding our little project some time ago. We knew we needed more support, so how better to get it than to ensure the richest man in BrightStone was beholden to us? Not that we had do much, mind. A few rumors about the possibilities of immortality and she was all too eager to get her hands on it."

I just blink at him, stunned. "And when she got the Rot, Balthazaar offered you his services in hopes of finding a cure for her..." I put the pieces together, remembering the way Lady Lydia's chest struggled to rise and fall, clinging to the last shreds of her humanity.

"Yes. As long as she remains ill, we have his undivided attention." He stops beside a door. It's out of place down here, the burnished wood gleaming like a portal to another world. "And we don't actually have a cure yet, but we give her enough transfusions of our own blood to keep her alive." He pauses to fiddle with another keypad above the lock and grunts when the door opens. "More or less."

I point back the way we came in, my hand trembling with rage. "Those Rotters out there...they're *people*."

"Well, not so much anymore." He waves me forward. "Come in."

The room inside is elegant and cozy in a bookish way, but it makes the rest of this place seem all the more horrible for its starkness. Stacks of cigarillos and bottles of brandy, inks and papers and soft pillows—all kinds of luxuries are piled up in almost obscene quantities and nestled beside the finely carved furniture.

"I spend a fair amount of time in here." Buceph takes a seat behind the ornately carved desk. The top of the desk is slightly curved with a softly glowing lamp to illuminate the papers scattered on its surface. "It's only right for me to enjoy what I have, being down here as long as I have been."

"If you say so." All I can imagine is setting this whole place on fire and him with it. "So why exactly am I here? I thought you were going to show me something."

He fixes his eyes on me hungrily. "When you killed the Inquestor, how did you do it? I'm curious."

"I shoved a fireplace poker through his skull," I deadpan, confused by this line of questioning. "He deserved it. Why do you care?"

He eases away from the desk with an air of satisfaction. "Excellent. No shy violets here, eh? I've a proposition for you, Magpie. One that will benefit us both."

His smug, wheedling tone echoes the triumph of his words. He clearly thinks whatever deal he has in mind will be accepted without question. But I've been on the raw side of several deals now, and I want no part of whatever this is. But I don't tell him that. Not yet.

"Go on," I say, my gaze sliding slowly around the room. Looking for escape. A weapon. I'll settle for either, but I'll be happier with both.

He snaps his fingers at me like he's trying to catch the attention of the dog. "I want you to kill the High Inquestor."

"You want me to *what*?" I shake my head, unsure I'd actually heard him correctly. "From *here*? Besides, you're all Meridians. I thought you were working together."

"I suppose that depends on who you talk to." He lets out a humorless chuckle. "I can't begin to tell you how happy I am with your answer. You barely flinched at my request."

"I didn't say I'd do it, either," I retort, my mind whirling. "I've no love for the man, and his death won't exactly make me cry, but why should I help you?"

"Well for one thing, it will get you out of this hellhole. Surely showing you the way out is worth something, isn't it?" He waves me off. "Make no mistake—all of us want to go home. Very much so. The team down here is as trapped as you are. As trapped as the Rotters."

My ears prickle at the idea of a way out, but I school my expression into something indifferent. It won't do for me to be too eager about it. I pull a cigarillo from the pile on his desk without asking, studying him sourly. "Oh aye. I can see how taxing it must be walking around in an actual body that isn't falling apart. The horror." There isn't an open flame on which to light my cigarillo, and I tuck it behind my ear for later. Too bad my clockwork dragon isn't here with me. The little beastie was always good for a quick spark.

Inside, I'm laughing at how much trouble I'd gone through to get down here only to find the tables turned to allow me to escape. I cock my head. "So, what? You're saying the High Inquestor is keeping you down here?"

"Yes," he says softly. "You weren't wrong about the immortality bit, and the High Inquestor is a rather ambitious man. To be quite honest, most Inquestors aren't in BrightStone by choice. Meridion does exile our more...unsavory citizens from time to time. What else would they do but become the man's bullyboys? And to ensure their loyalty, he has each Inquestor injected with the immortality serum, to at least make their time more bearable."

I frown, trying to puzzle it all out. "And?"

"He will not allow us to leave the Pits until the serum is perfected. Not until it can slow down aging to a complete halt." His mouth purses. "Tanith had the idea of testing the serum on the Rotters—under the guise of a cure. If we could refine the process on them, well, we'd make everyone happy, right? Hence the Tithes. It's a necessary deception so that we can have all the test subjects we need without worrying the general populace of BrightStone."

My nostrils flare at his matter-of-fact tone. "I'm sure that's a great comfort to the ones out there in the pen," I grind out.

Patience, Mags. Think of the information. The evidence. Remember why you came here. Find the other Moon Children.

I turn away from him to peruse the bookshelves, trying to think of another way to keep him talking in the hopes of finding something I might use as a weapon. Most of the shelves are full of esoteric leather-bound books I can do nothing with. Then I stumble upon a photo on the nearest shelf.

It's of a group of men and women, young and eager. I recognize some of them. Buceph. Tanith. Joseph. Some of the others I'd just seen at dinner in the village. They're dressed in white coats like the one Lucian wears in his laboratory, and they have hopeful expressions on their faces. Yet, there's a certain smugness there, too. They've found their answers, tugging on the strings of the fabric of reality to weave it to *their* will.

One woman in the picture stands alone, looking pensive.

"Ah, the old days. How quaint." Buceph nearly sighs in my ear, and I startle away from him. I've been so absorbed in the picture I didn't realize he'd come up behind me. He taps the frame, pointing at the solitary woman. "Madeline d'Arc was part of this little project, too, you know."

Madeline d'Arc. I should have guessed. Who else could it be but the legendary architect of Meridion with those cool eyes filled to the brim with the knowledge of her creations and a bit of sorrow that perhaps she had gone too far.

All I know of her is that she invented a number of the Meridian wonders, including whatever made the city fly. I rub the panel on my chest out of habit, feeling the comforting *tick-thump* of my heart. The fact that my mechanical heart bears her mark is a mystery I've yet to solve, but nothing about this conversation with Buceph makes me want to bring it up.

I glance over at him. "And what happened to her? To d'Arc?"

He shrugs. "She didn't join us, if that's what you're asking. She may have disabled Meridion's engines in her infinite 'wisdom,' but she disappeared long before we were sent down here. I suspect the High Inquestor had something to do with that, too, but at this rate, we'll probably never find out what happened to her."

He raises a brow at me as the conversation swings back to the High Inquestor, and my stomach twists. I switch topics. "You still haven't answered my question from earlier tonight. Where are the other Moon Children?"

He grasps my arm, his fingers curling into my flesh like the talons of a hawk. The endgame of this conversation is at hand. "Let's find out, shall we?"

He escorts me from the room, the door shutting behind us with an echo of finality, as though his offer involving the High Inquestor is also closing. But the Moon Children come first, murder for hire or no.

We head to the right, passing by a number of hallways. Mentally, I'm tracking which direction we go and how many doors we pass. I catch a glimpse of Sora at the other end of the hall, but she pays us no mind as she heads into another room, her arms loaded with books.

A large window illuminates us from the left, its light harsh. I squint, unable to make heads or tails of what I see. Tubes and tables, whirring machines and steaming copper pipes. Vials of bubbling liquid and viscous fluids, and devices with sharp edges gleaming like malevolent insects.

"We mix serums in here," Buceph says. "Attempts at blending different blood types between Meridians and BrightStonians. We still haven't figured out why the serum mutated to a virus within those from BrightStone." The smug dismissal in his tone makes it clear he doesn't expect me to understand.

He's not wrong. Lucian and I had had a conversation about such things once—not that I understood the concept then, either. But Lucian was a Meridian-born bonewitch, a real doctor trained in things I could only dream of.

"Phages," I mutter in a halfhearted attempt to pretend some semblance of knowledge of the subject. Lucian's laboratory had several sketches of such things in it, though I'd never quite grasped the concept. His drawing looked like spiders to me, but he'd said they were too small to see in reality.

Buceph slams me sideways against the wall. "Who are you really, Magpie? Who are you working with?"

"I hear things is all." I push him away, wincing at the way the wounds from the High Inquestor's lashes burn from the sudden movement. "Leave off."

I *am* working with the BrightStone rebellion, at least via Lucian and Ghost, but the light gleaming in his eyes echoes a madness born of too many years living down here in the Pits, surrounded by the sick and the dying. I've only been here for a day, and already I want to claw my way out.

All semblance of friendliness is gone now, and he shakes his head. "I think not. You know far too much for some half-breed gutter rat." He taps the top of my head, and peers at my Moon Child clan brand on my neck. "If you're even a Moon Child at all.

Hard to tell without any hair. Well, we'll find out soon enough." He takes me by the arm and half drags me down the hall to another window. "I think you'll find this room much more interesting."

I look through the window, my stomach churning as I take in the empty chairs and worn straps, the tables meant to restrain. "So you resort to threats now? Will you bind me there and take my blood to prove what I am?" My lip curls. I've no intention of allowing him to do this to me. At least not without a struggle.

"If we have to," he snarls.

My fingers twitch as we approach another window. It's an expansion of the previous room, though there is a curtain drawn between the windows so you can't see from one side to the other. But instead of chairs and tables, the walls are lined with narrow glass tubes—large ones. And they aren't empty.

It takes me the span of two breaths for my brain to comprehend what's inside them: Moon Children. At least twenty. Maybe more. Nearly all are mutilated in some fashion, with scars and missing limbs and vacant expressions.

I choke against a wave of vomit, staggering to my knees. "What have you done?" I whisper hoarsely.

He stares through the window with an air of almost parental satisfaction. "Moon Child blood has interesting properties, you know. There's no immortality or agelessness present, but the immunity to the Rot makes it particularly tempting to work with. We've been trying to determine if it's from the Meridian side or if some mutation has allowed you to build up a natural antibody." He snorts. "There are always complications during our experiments, though, as you can imagine."

He's still not looking at me, but I gather myself to my feet, blinking away tears of fury that this is what it comes down to. That the road my people walk ends here, in a place of utter darkness, not even granted the mercy of death.

"Let them go." Inside, I'm screaming, but the air lodges in my lungs like wet feathers.

"Go? Whatever for? Even if I did, none of them are cognizant of anything. They won't follow you. They certainly won't thank you. At this point, they're not much more than Rotters themselves." A soft chuckle escapes him. "I bet you're wishing you'd taken me up on my offer to kill the High Inquestor. Think of all the unpleasantness we could have avoided."

"I'll kill myself before I help you," I snap, my body poised to run. My mind is still half-numb with grief, but I've lived my entire life on the streets; even though I know my odds of getting away are slim, the urge is still there.

"As you will." He snatches at my shoulder, and I turn to bite him, but he slaps me hard across the back. A shriek erupts from me, my cuts burning, and I wonder if they've split open fresh. I slump, and my consciousness begins to drift as he jerks me up and shoves me through the door to the holding room. Something pricks me in the side of my neck, and everything fades to darkness.

What hits me first is the smell—blood is something I'm all too familiar with. But it's the salty flavor of old fear that wakes me. It permeates this room, staining everything. The walls. The curtains. The chair I'm in reeks of terror and piss and damp shit, the stench of it so thick I can barely breathe.

Blink.

Blink.

A soft halo of light blurs my vision. My eyelids feel heavy and swollen. A shadow slithers beside me, but I can't seem to focus on it long enough to see what it is. I squirm, wriggling my fingers and toes. My hands are bound to the chair, but my feet are not. Some lucid part of my brain files that away, though for now, I can only focus on trying to move.

"Ah, I suppose it's wearing off. Tsk." Buceph is scolding me, but it takes me a minute to understand the words.

My head rolls to the side as the light is moved slightly. I try to make sense of the metal table beside me, the tools gleaming upon it with a wretched sense of menace, each honed to a specific purpose. I've been to enough bonewitches to recognize most of them—scalpels, syringes, and the like. But there is one I have no name for. It has a long narrow shaft embedded into a handle, grooved with measurement ticks and ending in a sharp point.

I mumble something at it, but whatever I've been drugged with has made me sluggish.

"Now, now, none of that." Buceph tips my head back, holding my right eyelid open critically, and makes a little huff. "If you haven't guessed by now, Moon Children aren't exactly cooperative subjects. Giving a little blood here and there, sure, but they tend to fight against limb or organ extraction. We find removing a little piece of their brain fixes that problem rather quickly. Nice and simple, right through the inside corner of the eye."

He smiles fondly at me, but I don't think he's so much seeing me as remembering the ghost of every Moon Child who's ever sat in this chair. I'm reliving the echo of their presence, each cry for help, each sobbing whimper, until I want to clap my ears against it. The walls ooze with it—this utter devastation that removes the humanity of a person, reducing them to nothing more than a shell.

Buceph pats my cheek. "No fuss at all, afterward. So much easier to collect the samples we need—organs, bone marrow, you name it. You can never have too many samples, you know. For controls, replication, that sort of thing. Our testing is very thorough."

"I'll show...show you 'thorough.'" I cough as I struggle to catch my breath.

"A vial or two of your blood first," Buceph says, taking an empty syringe from the table. "Now, make this easy, Magpie. Keep me interested and maybe I'll even let you live a little longer."

The needle pricks my arm, and the pain is an exquisite welcome, jerking me into action with all the rage I can muster. I head-butt Buceph, and his nose crunches in a spray of blood. A gasping breath of a scream whooshes from his lips, the needle still stuck in my arm, obscene and sharp. His fingers clutch at my clothing as he pulls away, and he tears the collar of the scrubs to reveal the panel on my chest, my clockwork heart whirring with panic.

Tears blur my vision from the impact with his skull, and he bares his teeth at me. I cringe as he raises his hand, ready for the blow, but he stiffens when he sees the heart-shaped panel. His hungry fingers trace the edges of the metal as though he intends to pluck it from my body.

"I'd recognize that style anywhere. Rather strange to find it on a Moon Child, but d'Arc never did anything without a reason." His voice grows hungry, calculating. "Guess I won't be killing you quite yet. D'Arc was notorious for her little games and hidden devices. Let's get a closer look at this one, shall we?"

I spit at him, but he's already prying up the edges of the panel from my flesh with a scalpel. The blade scrapes over the metal, and the vibration rolls me to my bones. White-hot pain arcs across my chest, the *hitch-click* of my heartbeat becoming a high-pitched whine until…

Clunk. Clink.

Fire fills my lungs; I have no breath left to scream. Reduced to panting, I pull against my restraints, but he snatches me by the throat and presses me down. Everything is bloody, a red haze coating my vision, and I realize I'm about to black out again.

But my legs…my legs are still free.

My foot snaps up, catching him in the balls as hard as I can manage. He staggers, the tray of medical devices half-upended into my lap as he snags the curtain and tears it, exposing the Moon Children on the other side of the room.

Something grinds inside my heart, stuttering, only to be released a moment later. I erupt into a coughing fit and scrabble for a scalpel, my fingers brushing the handle of one balancing on the armrest.

Buceph groans as he struggles to get to his feet, the curtain twisted around his legs. I arch my wrist until I line up the blade with my strap as best I can. I wince when I nick myself as I slice through the binding. There! The rope snaps. I undo my other arm and lurch out of the chair, the scalpel tight in my fist.

One of the Moon Children moans something at me, halting my flight. She's missing both her legs and one of her arms, and there are wires shoved into her sides. In my mind, all I can see is Sparrow and the way her life was ripped away from her. This girl is no different, except she cannot even end it herself. None of them can.

There's a panel on the side of the tube with a series of buttons on it, and I press the largest, watching in horror as the top of the enormous cylinder slides away, exposing her to the air.

"No!" Buceph pushes past me in a fury and slams on the panel so it starts to close again. "They will die immediately if they're removed improperly! Stupid girl!"

"I'm sorry," I sob at her. "I'll come for you. I promise."

Somewhere an alarm is blaring, but I barely hear it. Sora rushes into the room, brandishing one of those electrical pig-stickers the Inquestors are so fond of. She jabs it in my direction, trying to force me toward Buceph, but her movements are stiff and unskilled. She's no trained Inquestor, and subdued Moon Children are undoubtedly easy subjects to control.

I slide beneath her arm and through her legs, snagging her ankle to yank her down before bolting for the outer hallway and toward the exit. The heavy steel doors are shut tight, but there must be a way to get them open. Copper-plated buttons and switches line the wall, and I push them frantically until I'm rewarded by a rumble in front of me.

The doors start to slide open with a loud creak.

"Magpie!" Buceph limps up the hallway, clutching his face. I launch over the desk, slip through the narrow opening between the doors, and hurry out of the facility.

Stumbling on the rocky cave floor, I limp across the cavern. Another tunnel, different from the one Buceph took to bring me here, looms in front of me. Clutching my chest, I tear into the darkness and I don't look back.

The sun and moon swing round and round,
Dancing with the stars in space.
Night and day are swallowed down
By a snake with a grin on his face.

— CHAPTER THREE —

I've probably made worse decisions than running through tunnels in the dark while injured, but not many. Not that I have much of a choice. I can't return to the Meridian village. Undoubtedly, they all knew what was supposed to happen, and any appearance by me now would only result in my capture.

The path is sharp beneath my cloth shoes, and my back burns from where Buceph slapped it, the entire area flushing with heat. My throat is swollen, my wrists bleeding. But all of that pales to the roughshod way my heart clicks and whirs, the way the metal panel feels loose. I swallow hard into the darkness, but aside from some dimly glowing slime on the cave walls, there is nothing here, and I force myself to continue, taking turn after turn and choosing forks at random.

Inside, I'm screaming in panic—at my heart, at what I've learned, at being alone. But my bones feel as though I might walk them into dust, their aching fragility a painful reminder of how precarious my situation is. I'll mourn my brothers and sisters later, but right now I can only focus on my immediate needs: food, water, and a place to rest. I slow, my free hand skimming the tunnel wall. It's slick with dampness. My body hurts too much to think about anything other than when I will be able to sit down, so when I come to a small hollow I don't stop to ponder the wisdom of hiding inside.

It's not quite a cave—more of a shallow impression carved into the side of the tunnel. But there's an overhang offering a bit of shelter, and I crawl as far into it as I can. A shudder erupts over my spine, making my limbs tremble with exhaustion. The damp chill of the rock penetrates through my scrubs, but my consciousness is already fading away, my last thoughts of Ghost and a warm fireplace before the blackness swallows me whole.

"Told you this one escaped!" The low voice hisses nearby, jerking me awake hard enough that I smack my head on the rock. Terror rockets through me. I've been found.

Every muscle in my body is screaming bloody murder, stiff and cold, but I attempt to shift anyway. Any chance of escaping this time is laughable, but what else can I do?

"Show yourself," I snap, fisting a loose rock. As roughed up as I am, I won't be taken without at least injuring one of them. Whoever they are.

"Easy, there." A man's voice comes closer, and I catch a bluish glow glittering in the darkness. I blink as additional points of illumination appear, and I realize I'm seeing eyes. I kick at the barest silhouette of a shadow, grunting when I make contact with something soft. A high-pitched whimper stops me from a second assault.

"Enough," another voice says, a girl's this time. A rustling of cloth and then four heads poke up from lowered hoods, pale hair shining like moonlight.

Moon Children?

The girl moves closer, and I gasp. "Penny!" I half sob her name, nearly delirious with relief.

She grimaces and crouches beside me. Her cheeks are smeared and dirty, and a long narrow scar slices across her nose. She's missing at least two of her teeth, and her hair falls in greasy snarls down her shoulders. But it's her.

I wave my hand in front of her when she doesn't react. "Penny? Penny, it's me. It's Raggy Maggy." Her face flickers in recognition at my name, but there's confusion there, too. I tap my prickly stubble. "They took my hair, Penny. The Inquestors. But it's okay. It's still me."

One pale brow cocks high. "How did you get here? Rory said the Inquestors killed you and Sparrow."

"Not exactly." I hesitate, unsure of how much to tell her.

"Well that's reassuring," she says dryly. "Considering I had to take the fall for it, color me excited to find out you've been alive all along."

"I'm sorry for that," I say, meaning it. "But they killed Sparrow. They did. I survived, but Rory didn't know. And I was badly injured. Besides...Rory kicked the two of us out of the clan." I sag, tired of explaining myself. Tired of all of this. "If you want to kill me for it, then do it. I'm in no shape to fight you, and I'm not sure I care anymore."

"Penny?" One of the Moon Children steps closer. I don't recognize him, but he's older than me, though maybe not quite as tall. It's hard to tell in the glowing light of his hair, but there's a jaded weariness in his voice that makes me think he's been through a lot. "We should get going. She's in rough shape."

"Aye, Bran." She holds out her hand to me—the one missing several fingers from some previous accident before she was Tithed—and I gently take it. I wriggle out of my hiding place, hissing when my shirt pulls on the reopened welts on my back. I cough, my metal chest panel rattling, and limp to my feet.

"Come on," Penny says. "Let's get out of here before the suck-tits show up."

The others scatter into the darkness, hair bobbing away until I can no longer see it, leaving me with Penny to follow. Admittedly, it is easier to stumble along with the glow of her hair leading the way, and I focus on that until the tunnel narrows down to almost nothing.

She moves past me. "I'll take you to our shelter. It's tight quarters, I warn you."

"It's not a dead end?"

Her teeth flash, the space gaping wide between them. "That's what we want you to think. Last thing we need are Rotters or those arse-lickers finding their way here. Not that any of them could fit."

Before I can ask her what she means, she shifts a chunk of rock to reveal a small hole.

"You weren't jesting." I'm frightfully glad I'm not much taller than she is. It will be rough if the tunnel goes on for any length, though.

"Don't worry. It opens up in a bit." She wiggles her fingers at me. "There's a hard bend a few yards in, and then it widens so you can stand."

I exhale sharply and duck into the tunnel. It's a damn good thing I don't mind narrow spaces, but even so, I can't imagine traveling like this for long. I'm slithering on my belly, grit sticking into my hands as I wriggle forward. Every movement I make feels like something is tearing along my spine, and I bite down on my lip to keep from whimpering.

Penny squeezes in behind me. A grinding sound indicates she's pulled the rock back over the hole. A grunt escapes her when she attempts to twist her body forward. "Move it, Mags."

"*Mmmph.*" I push on, twisting my hips to squeeze around the bend, gasping. The tunnel is now snug, and the weight of it compresses tightly enough to suck the breath from me. Sweat drips into my eyes, but I've got no way to wipe it off. I blink away the salty burn and peer into the darkness to find my way.

"Not too much farther," Penny says. "There's a drop-off at the end there, so take it slow."

All I can do is grunt in acknowledgment. My scrubs catch on an outcropping of the wall, and it gives suddenly. I pitch forward, my hands slipping into nothingness. I jerk my head up to keep from going over the edge.

Pain floods the left side of my temple as I smack my skull sharply on the rock above. "Fuck me."

"I *told* you to go slow." Penny grasps my ankles to keep me steady. "There's a ledge about three feet down. I'll keep you from falling."

"At least there's no chance of the Meridians chasing us in here," I mutter. "So there's that."

"Can you imagine Buceph worming his way through this? Those shoulders of his would never let him past the bend." She pauses, her voice becoming small. "It's not like they said it would be, is it?"

"No," I agree, easing my way down. "It's worse."

"The glow comes from the mushrooms," Penny tells me as I hunch before the tiny fire pit in the Moon Children's cave, my hands shaking against the chill. "They only grow in a few places down here, usually in piles of bat shit, but you eat them and after a while, your hair shines like a lightstick and you can see in the dark."

"Buceph didn't mention that particular perk when he tried to get me to eat them," I say. "Night vision would come in mighty handy, aye?"

Penny flutters her lashes and tosses her head. "Oh, but he is *so* proud of that flashy face of his, isn't he? Arse."

"That's not the word I would use." I inch a little closer to the fire, noticing how Penny flinches away from it. "What's wrong?"

"Whatever the mushrooms do allows us to see in complete darkness, but it makes us far more sensitive to natural light." She squints at me. "It hurts."

An angry chuckle escapes me. "And what happens when you reach the surface, I wonder? Are you blind under the brunt of the sun?"

"We may never see the surface again. Why risk death down here for what may never be?" She shrugs. "In a few months, you'll come to realize there is no hope of escape. And then you'll get tired of bumping your head on the rocks and eat the damn things."

I wince as my hand brushes my scalp where I'd banged it on the tunnel. "Point taken. That's all of you, then?" The ragtag band of Moon Children stands before me—six of them, including Penny. Three boys, three girls. All surviving by the barest skin of their teeth.

But they're cheerful enough for all that, even given their sunken cheeks and bony limbs. Like living scarecrows.

Penny smirks. "What's left of us. You'll remember Dafyyd and Rosa, I'm guessing?"

"Aye." The two of them had been Banshees with me and Penny, though I hadn't been particularly close to either of them. Rosa in particular seems frailer since I'd last seen her. She's built small like Sparrow had been, all large eyes and copper skin. Dafyyd is stocky, with a square jaw and thick brows, his hair cut short against his ears. I can't remember how old they are, but they're younger than me. Maybe fifteen.

The two of them nod at me as Penny points to another girl. "Gloriana is a Twisted Tumbler, and the boy there is Conal from the Spriggans. He doesn't talk much, though, so don't worry about it if he ignores you."

I give them each a once-over. Gloriana is a pale beauty with a thick braid and an even thicker scar roping its way around her neck. She's cool and quiet as I study the brutal markings. Conal doesn't even bother looking up from where he's sitting against the edge of the cave wall, his hands crossed over his knees. From here, I can only see the curve of his jaw and that he has a patch over his right eye.

"And then there's Bran." Penny's voice fills with satisfaction as the last Moon Child steps forward. No mere boy, Bran is the oldest Moon Child I've ever met, though since most of us are Tithed before we're twenty-five, that's probably not saying much. His hair falls halfway to his waist in ragged fashion, greasy and matted. Its glow is diminished beneath the grime, but it's still there, like the others.

"Spriggan," he says, watching me warily. "A former leader, in fact." He seems somewhat unassuming, but I recognize the air of leadership when I see it. He's used to keeping Moon Children in line.

The cave the tunnel led into is narrow and cramped, but it stretches up a good thirty feet. In the center of the cave is the fire pit where embers continue to smolder with a soft burnished glow. A thin trail of smoke wisps upward and disappears through some minute opening I cannot see, and a rivulet of water streams down one wall and drips into a bucket. And in true rooftop dancer fashion, they have fashioned hammocks for themselves, high above the ground.

"Clever," I say.

"We learned quick," Penny agrees, pointing toward the high arched ceiling. "The only other way out is up there—by way of a wyrmhole."

"A what?" I follow her finger, trying to figure out what she's talking about.

"There's a series of small tunnels that crisscross through the caves up there. Not sure where they came from and they're not particularly easy to maneuver, but one of us always keeps a watch, even so." Gloriana smirks. "We'd hear anyone coming long before they arrived."

Bran lets out an ugly laugh. "I've got some large rocks I'd like to drop on them if they try."

"How long have you been down here?" I ask him, not sure if I really want to know the answer.

Bran shrugs. "You lose track in the dark. Days, nights. It doesn't matter much. I've been here the longest. Maybe three years? Four?" He goes silent then, and we drift off in our own thoughts.

Three years of rough living down here... How do they bear it?

Penny dips a rag into the bucket now and uses it to wipe away the blood from my forehead. "So how'd you get away?"

I cough, pressing my hand over the panel in my chest to keep it from falling off. "Head-butted Buceph and broke his nose." Now that I've finally found a place of relative safety, every sore place on my body has woken up, my nerves screaming.

Bran leans against the far wall, smoking a cigarillo he had produced from a spare pocket earlier. He chews on the end of it, exhaling deeply. "Should have killed him."

"I was preoccupied with not dying at the time," I retort, then pause for a beat. "Have you been there? Have you seen...the others? Are we really the only ones left?"

"Yes, I've been there," Bran says shortly, giving me a pointed look. "And we are it. At least as far as I know. Not all in our little group actually made it to the facility. Some, like Penny, escaped before that."

"I knew something was off the minute I ran into that Tanith bitch," Penny snarls. "No one is that nice. Not to sin-eaters. I don't care who you are." She spits, her tongue roving over her broken teeth.

I can only grunt at her. Trusting Tanith was my mistake, and it is not one I plan on making again.

Bran moves away and climbs the wall to one of the hammocks. He retrieves a haversack and tosses it at my feet. I open it to reveal a pair of trousers and a shirt. The others don't meet his eyes when he climbs down, and he nods at me. "Go on."

I'm not sure what's going on here, but I don't need to be told twice. The scrubs are torn and filthy, and aren't doing anything to help with keeping me warm. Careful to keep my balance, I let the scrubs fall to the floor, tearing the top the rest of the way through.

Penny lets out an audible gasp, and I know she's looking at my back.

"Is it bad?" My voice is ragged, tired. "It was healing, but I think it started bleeding again during the struggle with Buceph."

Bran frowns. "Who whipped you?"

"The High Inquestor," I grunt, trying to slide into the shirt without irritating my skin. "Murder. Treason. Conspiracy. I'm all sorts of trouble, apparently. Maybe I should have taken Buceph up on his deal and killed the man."

Bran curls his upper lip, flicking the ash from his cigarillo. "He offered that to me, too. Guess you and I are 'special.'" He turns away without elaborating, taking a seat on the far side of the fire.

I'm not sure I want to press just yet, so I let it be for now and change the subject. "I'm less worried about that than I am about this." I gesture to the panel on my chest, peeking through the low collar of the shirt. "Buceph tried to pry it off me. I think it's broken. Loose, anyway."

"What the fuck is that?" Penny reaches out to touch it.

"My heart." I sag down beside the fire. "Do you have somewhat to eat?"

"Not much," Penny admits. "Every couple of weeks there's a supply crate or two delivered to the Meridians. We usually steal from them. Other times we sneak fish from the Rotter village."

Rosa brings me a bowl of a pasty, doughlike substance. Not quite bread, but it seems it's trying to be. I shovel it down without chewing, sipping water from a ladle in a water bucket. My actions are met with silence, but even through that, I can sense their weariness. Our bones ache with the condemnation of our birthright.

But so much of my life has been built on distrust—between BrightStonians and Meridians, between the Moon Children and everyone else, even between the Moon Child clans. I'm not so naive as to think everyone can be trusted, but if we had communicated better somehow, maybe we would have seen the pattern sooner.

Secrets got me into this mess. Maybe it's time to share them.

And so I do.

The explanations pour forth in the darkness, wrapping us in a hidden cloak of soothing cadence. It's unnerving in a way, to have them listen so raptly, and if there's a measure of skepticism present, I can hardly blame them—it sounds like a fairy tale. Clockwork dragons and iron hearts, floating cities and conspiracy theories, plagues and immortality serums, and all of it swirled up in the desperate need to understand who we really are and where we come from. And then there's Ghost and Lucian, and Molly Bell's betrayal.

When it comes out that I killed Inquestor Caskers, even Bran stares at me, but his expression merely turns thoughtful. He waits until I finish before taking a long drag from the last of his cigarillo and cocking his head at me. "That's a hell of a story."

"Aye. But it's true. For whatever it's worth."

"Not much," he says with a shrug. "Not down here." He turns away and taps Conal's shoulder. "Anything on the watch earlier?"

"Nothing of any note."

Bran grunts, gesturing to me as he points above us. "There's an empty hammock near the top. It's yours if you want it. Dafyyd, take the next watch."

Dafyyd begins to climb, disappearing into the darkness above. The others scrabble up the rock walls and into their respective beds. I'm offered no help, but I don't really expect any, even as injured as I am. No self-respecting rooftop dancer would. I flex my fingers, running them over the wall with an experimental touch. Small nooks make it easy to find footing, and I scale it without issue, albeit stiffly.

When I find the hammock Bran pointed out, I settle into it as he settles into his. I don't miss the glimmer of sadness in his eyes, but I don't ask whose bed this is. Or whose it was, really.

I shift in the sturdy netting. Scavenged from one of the villages, I have no doubt. It creaks slightly, swaying beneath my weight. I turn onto my side as best I can, my reopened wounds still burning. The embers of the fire below fade, and eventually go out, leaving us in the dark. The others fall asleep quickly, and I'm surrounded by a soft chorus of exhalations and snores. If only I might be that lucky.

Bran sighs in the darkness, and I know the clothes I'm wearing and the hammock I'm sleeping in belonged to another Moon Child who meant something to him. A lover. A sister. A friend. It doesn't matter much.

I hesitate, listening to him breathe. He doesn't sound like he's asleep yet, and the weight of living underground is pressing down against me. The image of the haunted Moon Children in their glass tubes crackles against the backs of my eyelids, making me restless and sad. I struggle to calm but finally give up.

"The others..." I whisper to Bran. "The Moon Children in the facility..."

"It's all of them," he says before I finish my question. "Everyone that's ever come down here and hasn't either escaped or died... That's what's left of them. I've tried to break into that hellhole so many times I've lost count. All it's done is force Buceph to increase his security."

"I'm sorry," I murmur. "If I'd known what was happening, I would never have let—"

"How would you know? How would any of us?" He shifts in his hammock, the ropes creaking as he turns away from me.

"We'll set them free," I say, though I have no idea how. "Somehow. I swear it."

"Yes," he agrees. "We will."

Tiptoe, tiptoe, sneak and hide,
Run from my master and run from his bride.
A burning fire and a heating pot,
A destiny for which I'd rather not.

— CHAPTER FOUR —

I wipe my hands on my trousers and move out of the way as Rosa and Conal pass me. "Are we almost to the waterfall?" I ask.

Bran points down the tunnel. "Along this way and two turns to the left. It's another tight squeeze since the shaft has partially collapsed, but there's enough space for all of us to make it through."

I have to hand it to him—his sense of direction is brilliant. Maybe it's the amount of time he's been here. He's a bit like Ghost in that respect, gifted in some strange way when it comes to moving about. Though any envy I might have for such a skill pales at the idea of having to live here so long it becomes a necessity.

The thought of Ghost sobers me. What are he and the others doing up there on the surface? Have they been captured? Are they getting by? I had taken my freedom for granted far too easily.

Aye, and what wouldn't you give to be racing across the rooftops with him right now beneath the moon and the fog and the rest of it instead of crawling through these holes like some kind of insect?

It's been several days since I was found by Penny and the others. My wounds aren't exactly healed, but they've scabbed over enough that I'm no longer afraid of openly bleeding. The panel is another matter, though the humming rattle inside dulls whenever I press the panel flat against my skin. I don't know if the damage is mostly cosmetic, but I surely don't have the skill to remove it and check. For now, all I can do is ignore the vibrations and hope that the thing continues to work. Still, it's uncomfortable to leave it loose, so the best I've managed is binding my chest tightly with ragged strips of the leftover scrubs. It's not perfect, but it will do.

The tunnel turns and turns again. Our pace is fast and light. I have to keep my fingers upon the wall to make sure I'm not left behind, but the others have no such problem, their eyes glowing a silvery blue.

"So what's so great about a waterfall?" I ask.

"You'll see," says Bran.

We've come to what appears to be a dead end, but he doesn't pause, shifting his body to climb up. The cave walls here are easy to scale, too, though I cannot see how far up we go. Thankfully, a fast rushing sound echoes past us, making the path easy to find.

I line up what I know of the cave maps in my mind, trying to remember if there's an underground river and where it goes, but before long, we find ourselves before a roaring waterfall. The frothing waters rocket past us and disappear below. The spray flecks over my face, bone-chillingly cold.

I look up at it. "Where does it go?"

"The sea, I suspect," says Bran. "Eventually. None of us have ever dared to find out."

"Not voluntarily," Penny says, rolling her eyes.

I should be curious, but I'm not. Inside, my brain beats with the possibility of escape and the despair of not being able to swim.

"The Rotters come here," Penny notes. "No reason we can figure. They watch the water and then move on."

Gloriana snickers. "Assuming they don't 'accidentally' fall over the edge."

"Rotters? You mean the ones from the facility? Aren't they penned up?" I rub my forehead, confused.

"There's a village full of Rotters that is run by Georges. They aren't allowed to leave voluntarily." Bran scratches his nose. "When the disease progresses to a certain point, they're transferred to the facility holding pens, but some are allowed to...free range, I guess. I'm not sure what the criteria are."

A silence overtakes us then, the crystalline water shunting into the darkness. How easy it would be to drop into that current and let myself be swept away. I shake my head against such thoughts. "Tanith said somewhat about that bonewitch Georges. That he was a Rotter, too."

Bran stares off into the distance, his expression twisting into something savage. "In some ways, he's as much a victim as any of us, as tainted as he is. Not that it'll save him. Or any of them. Come on."

He stalks off, leaving me to follow in his wake. The others remain where they are, and I hurry to keep up, focused on the dim glow of his hair. When he slows down, I nearly stumble into him, catching myself on a craggy outcropping.

"Hush." He points up. "We'll do better to take the wyrm passages from here. It's cramped, but this close to the Meridian village, it's a safer approach."

He maneuvers up the wall, and I struggle along after him, finding footholds in the dark until I've caught up to where he is crouching. The tunnel is low hanging, and I have to crawl on hands and knees until it widens enough that we can sit side by side.

"Where are we going?" I ask.

"To see the Rotter village. We don't go there often, but you should be aware of it."

"Will we let them see us?"

"Of course not. We wouldn't be any more welcome there than we are anywhere else." His face grows tight. "It would be a mercy to kill them all, to be honest."

He says it so gently, and I frown. "So, what? You're proposing mass execution to a group of people who've contracted an illness through no fault of their own? I mean, I hate the BrightStonians as much as any Moon Child, but that seems...excessive."

He shrugs. "They're already dead. They just don't know it yet."

We move on after that, crawling out of the wyrm tunnels to a wider passageway. Soon we're in another large cave, similar to the one the Meridians settled in. This one has an immense pool of water, and great stalactites hang from the cavern's ceiling, dripping in an off-kilter harmony to make the surface ripple.

"No one knows how deep it is," Bran says when he notices me staring. "There are hot springs in various tunnel offshoots, but this particular lake must empty into the sea somewhere. Every once in a while, some great beast is rumored to be seen within, but I doubt it. The only useful thing about it is the fish."

I shudder, remembering the massive skull hanging in the great hall of the museum in BrightStone, and decide to give this particular body of water an extremely large berth.

On the shore of the lake is a village, its docks jutting into the inky blackness like little wooden fingers. Several coracles are tied there, rocking gently on the soft ripples. I can only guess what sorts of horrors the fishermen would find in their nets here.

"If you haven't guessed already," Bran says, "the population in the Rotter village tends to fluctuate for obvious reasons."

I nod and study the dwellings. They look like they are crudely made of mud and rocks. Most don't seem to have roofs, but instead a section of beams from which ragged pieces of cloth and twisted bits of string mixed with dried fish hang. There's a narrow pathway leading from the village to the gate, lined with torches so bright they make me squint.

Bran winces away from them. "The Rot takes their sight. They make up for it with all the extra light, but that's one of the reasons we don't come by this way much. They don't have anything worth stealing, anyway. Except fish," he amends a moment later.

We pause beneath an arch that looks like the threshold to the Hells. It's gated and locked. I run my finger over the rusted bars. "For their 'protection,' I suppose."

Shadows move around the lake—the Rotters going about their daily business. It's quiet, their spirits long since burned away. Several women are huddled by the water washing clothes.

In BrightStone, the washerwomen squawk like half-mad chickens as they run their linens over their tin washboards. Not that they have much by way of soap—no one does—but the process is a social necessity. Gossip spent like wages, a currency of words and rumors cackled in a crowd of tired mothers and old crones while half-naked children and mangy dogs roll beneath the sour waters of the public fountain.

There is a certain contentment in knowing your neighbors are as miserable as you are, and thus, there's some level of camaraderie there.

Not so with these women. Their hands might move in the same ways, their elbows bent as they scrub, but all I can hear is the *scrape, scrape, scrape* of cloth being dragged to and fro. The air of despair here is thicker by far.

A sudden shriek echoes through the cavern. "No! No! No, you can't...I won't!"

The women pause in their work but bow their heads an instant later. Bran gestures at me to come quickly, and the two of us scramble up the arch until we're perched above the gate.

A flare of torchlight comes down the path on the other side of the gate, bright enough that Bran turns away. I peer below as the bonewitch who treated me the other day—Georges—steps into the passage. He's still wearing the patchwork robe. His eyes are more bloodshot than I remember, but my vision is unfettered by pain now and I can see the details of his appearance more clearly.

Although dreadfully pale, he seems no different from most of the regular BrightStonians above us, except for the prominent veins spiderwebbing at his hairline, but it's far different from what I remember of Lady Lydia's appearance. Balthazaar's wife looks like nothing more than a hollow shell of a person, lingering in a body that has already died. Perhaps Georges receives more of the Meridians' blood than Lydia does. It would make sense, given how much of Georges's work is directly tied to this village.

A hollow-faced young woman crouches in the dirt at his heels, her fingers scraping at the stone with jagged nails. Clumps of hair have started to fall out, leaving patches of gray-stubbled skin. It's one of the Rotters I led into the Pits—the girl who stopped to ask how I was. But the disease has ravaged her almost beyond recognition. The telltale purple lesions of the Rot blister her cheeks and neck. She begins to rock back and forth, a nervous grunting falling from her lips.

"Anna?" The bonewitch kneels beside her. "It's nearly time now."

Anna jerks away from him, drooling. "No," she moans. "No no no no no no." Blindly she reaches out and grabs the hem of his trousers.

The bonewitch tsks at her. "Anna, we have no choice. These are the rules. You have to leave the encampment now. There's no longer a chance at a cure for you. We cannot waste food on those who are too far gone." There's true sadness in his voice but no actual mercy. He will do what he needs to, even if he's lying through his teeth to do it.

A thick sob escapes her, and it's all the more horrid for the way it burbles from her throat, her lungs filling with fluid.

The death rattle.

My nostrils flare wide as I realize she's going to become like those Rotters in the pens. I start to move, though I have no idea what I'm going to do.

Bran snatches at my hand, his fingers digging into my wrist. "Stop. There's nothing you can do for her. If you go down there, you're on your own. I'm not risking myself or anyone else."

Anna lets out another sob. "Please. I'll do anything. I don't want to die."

"I'm sorry." Georges is handing her a lightstick, and something inside me crumbles. "I'll help escort you to the Meridian facility where you can pass peacefully."

I yank my hand away from Bran, outrage flooding me.

"Oh aye," I snap, clambering down from my perch as Georges gives Anna a little shove forward past the gate entrance. Bran hisses something at me, but fury fills my ears with a roar. "Help her like you help all of them, is that it?" I shove the bonewitch, unable to watch such deceit play out again. "How many have you lied to?"

"Magpie," he says with a cough. He rubs his head where it hit a rock. "How...good to see you again. It appears your wounds are healing nicely."

"What do you care if you were going to turn me over to those butchers anyway?" I spit at his feet. "You're disgusting."

Anna's head snaps up at the sound of my voice. "IronHeart?"

Georges glances at me. "What is this, now?"

Anna struggles to her feet. Her breath reminds me of a half-eaten kitten Sparrow once found in the slag heaps. Inwardly, I recoil, but I do my best to stay steadfast as Anna's skeletal fingers dig into my arm. After all, she'd been the only one to try to help me when we'd first entered the Pits. Surely, she deserves the same compassion now.

Her skin is leathery and cold, and flakes off when she lets go. "The witch...the witch of the docks said she was IronHeart...that she would bring down Meridion..."

"Is that so?" Georges asks softly, raising his hands toward me. "Don't worry. I have no wish to harm you, though I'm afraid Buceph's rather vexed with you."

"Like I care." I lower my voice. "Next time our paths cross, I'm going to kill him."

Alarm flashes over Georges's face, but our little commotion has attracted the attention of the village Rotters. Some of them are already making their way down the path toward the gate.

"Another time, perhaps," he murmurs, closing the gate behind him and locking it, leaving Anna and me out in the tunnel.

I look around and find Bran is gone. "Useless," I murmur. "Step out of line one time and he abandons me. Delightful."

Maybe he knows something I don't. Maybe he's just an asshole. I'm not sure it really matters at this point, because now I'm stuck here, not knowing how to get back to the Moon Child cave. I can't yet see in the dark, either. Which makes me a fool twice over, I suppose.

But then, haven't I always been?

Georges spreads his arms as he makes his way to the group of Rotters. His voice is a slow, soothing tone as he speaks to them. Whatever he says, it doesn't take long for them to turn around and head back the way they came.

"Don't leave me alone." Anna's jaundiced eyes fill with tears. "Please."

I shiver, only able to see Sparrow's empty face staring at me.

You couldn't save Sparrow. You can't save Anna.

But I can be with her when she dies.

"All right, Anna. Let's go."

The flickering of the torches disappears as we feel our way forward. Anna's fingers crab-claw the lightstick, the skeletal knuckles like the segmented joints of some pale spider. It seems to steady her some, but she still sniffles off and on. The lightstick illuminates the small space about us in a pale golden gleam. The tunnel is similar to the others, the air stale and humid and clinging to my skin.

"Thank you," she says.

"You're welcome, I guess. Not sure how much help I'm going to be. I'm not even armed."

She stumbles on the rocky ground, nearly losing hold of the stick. "Careful," I warn. "It's the only one we have."

Something shuffles in the tunnel ahead of us. We freeze. I flatten against the wall as she gapes, fear paralyzing her to the spot.

"Get down," I hiss at her, my voice startling her into movement. We crouch.

"What is it?" Anna squeaks.

"Not sure," I say, though I can smell the acrid miasma of necrotic flesh announcing the presence of at least one Rotter. I remember what Penny said about the free-ranging Rotters and pause. "We might be in trouble."

"Here." She presses something into my hand.

My thumb slides over the hilt of a dagger. "Where did you get this?"

"I stole it. Georges left it on the table when he took me into the village infirmary. I don't know what I thought I was going to do with it. Stab him, maybe. Survive out here longer." Her voice grows smaller. "End it sooner."

The Rotter comes into view, and if there's anything still intelligent trapped in that body, I can see no sign of it. A shiver of horror prickles over my spine, and I grip the dagger that much tighter.

It was tall once. Male. Beyond that, I can't tell. It's stooped now, limping on the tattered remains of its legs, flesh peeling from its bones. Its mouth looks like someone's fed him a torch at some point. It lets out a low groan of longing when it sees me. And then it lunges, its charred mouth open wide.

I don't hesitate. I drive the dagger beneath its chin to lodge it into the brain. The Rotter squirms like a beetle pinned to a piece of parchment but continues to reach for me, bony fingers snatching at my cloak. I wince as its teeth graze my forearm. I may be immune to the Rot, but a bite will still hurt something fierce.

I pull on the knife to dislodge it, but it's stuck. I kick the Rotter's knee out from under it, and the entire joint bends backwards, causing the Rotter to lose its balance, and the momentum allows me to retrieve my dagger.

Foul black blood coats the blade, and the stink nearly sets me to retching, putrescent brain matter spattering over my hand. The Rotter rolls on the ground trying to get to its feet for another attack, but Anna runs over to it with grim determination, her booted heel stomping on its head with enough force to shatter its skull.

What's left of its nose crumples. It tries to grab her, but I finish the blow with my dagger, slicing through its decomposing neck tendons with ease.

Anna lets out a hysterical little laugh. But she can't seem to stop, her body shaking violently. "That's going to be me," she hiccups with a distant sort of terror. "That's what I'm going to become."

"I'm sorry. I really am." The words are hollow and patronizing, but they're all I have to give her. I wipe the dagger on what's left of the Rotter's pants, grimacing at the smell. Anna still watches the body. I tug on her arm as she clutches the lightstick like a talisman.

I don't know where we're going, but we'll have to rest at some point, and I surely don't want to do it here. If we're lucky, maybe we'll find a cavern with a high ledge to make camp.

"How long?" I ask her after a long silence.

"I don't know." Her voice is soft and sad. "Some of the villagers have been there for quite a while… But I guess some of us react faster than others. Or are more sinful."

A bark of laugher escapes me. "Sin has nothing to do with it. *At all*. Whatever story the Tithers told you when they rounded you up..."

She shakes her head. "No. I got sick on my own. The salt priests diagnosed me in their temple. They said I must have done something terrible, but no matter how much I confessed, nothing seemed to satisfy them." Her mouth trembles, spittle coating her lips. "I didn't mean to be bad."

Her words strike me cold, but I'm unsure of what to say. Anna's mental state seems to be growing more fragile by the minute, and I'm not sure I have the right to strip whatever beliefs she has from her. And yet...

"The sin is on those who did this to you. To all of us," I amend.

She sniffs and wipes at her face. "The Hells can take them, then."

"We can only hope," I deadpan. "Come on. Let's keep moving. Lingering here will only attract more of them." One at a time we could deal with, but if we run into a group? We step gingerly around the fallen Rotter.

"When I first arrived in the village with the others, we were rounded up in a holding pen," she tells me. "Georges separated us into groups depending on how far gone we were. The ones that seem to fight the Rot best or have skills worth saving are brought into the main village. The rest of us exist on borrowed time," she growls. "I was a rag-picker in BrightStone. Sometimes a lantern lighter on the docks, but that's not a skill needed down here."

"Expendable, aye?" I give her a wry smile. "We're in the same boat, you and I."

A soft sigh escapes her. "Yes. I suppose we are."

My feet are burning by the time we stop walking. I have no idea how much time has passed or how deep into the Pits we've gone, but my legs ache with weariness. At least we haven't seen any more Rotters. There's been no sign of shelter or any of the other Moon Children, either.

I sink to my knees with a groan, my stomach clawing in on itself. "Wish we had some food."

Anna slouches against the wall on the other side. "In another day or so it won't be necessary for me." She doesn't elaborate, but the unspoken words hang there between us.

My fingers twitch. "I don't know about you, but I could do with a shot of whisky right about now."

"Georges has wine, but he kept it for himself." She shivers, wrapping her arms about her legs.

"Georges seems to have a lot of things he doesn't want to share," I observe.

"Some of the Rotters get better treatment than others. Injections of medicine, I think? Definitely better housing." Anna shakes her head. "Georges gave us a place to sleep and some basic necessities, but there wasn't much time to discuss what was going to happen." She reaches up to stroke her cheeks, flinching at whatever she feels. "Guess I was too far gone to bother with."

"I saw you once, you know. Before we were Tithed. You were in the Salt Temple." I hesitate, unsure of what to say exactly but needing to fill in the silence with something other than the rough burble of her breathing.

"Yes," she says softly, holding out her arm. "I was getting a Tithe mark." She traces the outline of the tattoo on her forearm—a series of concentric circles nested inside one another, the one in the middle drawn in solid red.

All the Tithed Rotters were given them before the procession. Moon Children had their clan names branded in the back of their necks, so I suppose the Inquestors didn't need to waste any more ink on us.

Wait...

I squint, bringing the fading lightstick closer to Anna. Her skin is a gray color in the yellow light, but the second tattoo is there, unmistakable and primitive. All the bonewitches in BrightStone are required to mark their patients for things that require cutting or injections. It's part of how the Inquestors keep track of medical procedures. Patients become a living calling card, showing their scars to the world and inadvertently advertising the work of those who practiced on them.

And the tattoo on Anna's upper arm is a wavy line and a dot I know incredibly well, bearing several of the same marks myself. "Sally NimbleFingers," I mutter. "I know her. She's patched me up a few times."

Anna nods. "I wasn't injured. I was getting an injection. Last winter, when the Chancellor declared we might get some of those fancy vitamin shots? I'd been real ill two winters before that—caught a case of the grippe and nearly starved since I couldn't work. Figured I'd pay up front this time. For all the good it did." Her voice is even smaller than it was before, the hesitant cooing of a mourning dove, quiet and pensive.

Blood fills my mouth when I bite down hard on my lower lip. "Any chance you know of anyone else in the Rotter village who saw her, too?"

"Maybe. At least two I recognized?" She frowns. "What are you going on about?"

"I don't think those were vitamins," I admit. "I think you were injected with the Rot. The Meridians down here, they have a lab they use for experiments. It was full of Moon Children, but Buceph indicated the Rot was distributed on purpose." Her nostrils flare wide, and there's nothing but sour bile on my tongue. "They needed subjects, and the Rotters are nothing more than stock. And the only way I can think of that they'd be able to infect people unnoticed would be through the bonewitches."

Tears slide down her cheeks. "Then it's not true about sins? What the salt priests tell us? None of it?" She turns away from me, and I can only imagine the horror and heartbreak roiling behind that haunted gaze.

"I'm sorry." Guilt flushes through me, and I wish I hadn't brought it up.

She swallows softly before I can say anything else. "I'll take first watch, if you want."

I waver. I need the rest, but it wars with my usual distrust of the unknown. Anna seems nice enough, but she's desperate. And desperate people tend to do drastic things, some of which there's no undoing.

She lets out a laugh at whatever she sees in my expression, but there's no humor in it. "Go on. You might as well take advantage of the time while you can."

She's right enough on that account, and in the end, my body makes up my mind for me. I pull my hood up, bunching it into makeshift pillow, and with a sigh, I slip into a fitful sleep.

Jack and Jill went up the hill,
But the well is old and dry.
No way to fish or make a wish
And naught to say but good-bye.

— CHAPTER FIVE —

Iron Heart?" Anna's voice is a hoarse whisper that pulls me
from sleep. Bleary, I blink up at her, but she presses her fingers
to my lips. They're chilled and clammy and shaking. "Listen."
I hear it then. The low, shambling footsteps of Rotters. A lot
of them. They're coming up behind us. Wordlessly, I gather my
things and take Anna by the hand to lead her as fast as I dare.
"Hells. Where are they all coming from?"

And maybe more importantly, where are they all going?

Anna's breathing labors at our speed, and before long, she's not
trying to hide it, her fluid-filled lungs wheezing with each gasp. I
slow, my ears pricked for any pursuit, but we've managed a bit of
distance. At least the Rotters aren't particularly quick.

"We need to keep moving," I tell her, holding the lightstick up to
her face. She doesn't react to the light, though; her eyes are nearly
completely clouded over. I wave my fingers in front of her, but she
doesn't stir and I bite my lip. *Oh. The poor thing.* "Are you blind,
Anna?"

"Yes," she whispers, her voice shaking. "Everything went
completely dark about an hour ago." She swallows hard. "It won't
be long now, I don't think. I'm so cold. It's like I don't belong in this
body anymore."

I squeeze her hand. "Come on. Let's see if we can't find a place to rest."

"Tell me if there's something in the way." Her words are brave, but it doesn't hide the way her chin trembles.

"Aye." We set off again, slower this time. The tunnels are becoming narrower, and she skims her hand lightly over the sides to keep her balance. The passage splits and then splits again until we find ourselves at a crossroads with tunnel offshoots in four directions.

Anna's footsteps slow and grow heavy, her worn boots grinding into the stone as if they are made of iron. "Need to…rest," she mumbles, sinking to her knees. "I cannot go on any longer. Leave me here."

I waver, my instinct for survival warring with sorrow. I should do as she says. Everything indicates I should cut my losses and go. Instead, I squat down beside her. She's begun to rock in an aimless fashion. I babble questions at her, as though it might stop whatever is happening. "Do you still know your name? Who were you before?"

"I almost can't remember. Isn't that strange? It's a dream somehow, but the sleeper is a stranger." There's an almost singsong quality to her words that reminds me of Mad Brianna, though my foster mother had barely been lucid at the best of times. Anna goes silent, and I kick at a loose stone, listening to it bounce down the tunnel. She lets out a low cry as something emerges from the shadows beside us.

Rotters. The tunnel is abruptly filled with the ripe stink of them.

I pull us into one of the side tunnels, her dagger in my hand, but the odds are well out of my favor. Even if I can fight a few of them off, I won't be able to stop them before they overwhelm us completely. But instead of attacking, they shuffle past us down a different shaft.

Anna turns blindly around and around in confusion. "What's happening?"

"Rotters." Three more pass by, slack-jawed and empty, the last one missing both arms and most of its jaw, its desiccated tongue lolling.

Anna straightens. "We should follow. I can keep up."

"If you think I'm going to follow them to some undead lair, you're half-mad."

"Probably." She limps forward in the direction they went. "You can stay here if you like. I've nothing left to lose."

I grind my teeth, my gut rippling with ill-contained fear, but I follow her. We keep a good distance behind the line of Rotters. No sense tempting fate.

Anna is a woman on fire, her determination clear in the thrust of her jaw. Whatever her purpose is, she's found a vehicle toward it. Almost like finding her own people, I suppose. Something I know entirely too well. I glare into the darkness. Damn Bran for abandoning me, anyway.

We don't have far to go before the Rotters slow down, and when I glance up, I am surprised at the flood of light before us. The mine shaft opens up to reveal a glittering cavern, the walls coated with those glowing mushrooms. I study them, remembering Penny's comment about bat shit. Bats mean a way out.

But where is it?

Anna doesn't pause when I do, instead following the Rotters with some otherworldly sense. They skirt along a shallow lake and congregate on the far shore. There appears to be a stony outcropping there, but it's narrow, twisted like a tree made of granite and streaked with thick veins of silver. But most importantly, far above us is a stream of brilliant light bursting through an opening at the very top of the cavern.

A hole.

And beyond that...

"The moon," I breathe, nearly hysterical with relief. I've lost all sense of time the last few days, so just the knowledge that it is night grounds me, even if the sudden illumination hurts my eyes.

I flex my fingers. And if I can scale the Mother Clock in Prospero's Park, I can climb a cave wall. But a question niggles in my mind. Why are the Rotters even here?

I slink away from the opening of the tunnel. More might be coming through, and the last thing I want is to be caught unawares. A low overhang nearly covers a small crevice on the near side of the cavern wall. It's easy to slip inside, my body flattening to wedge itself within, but something sharp digs into my spine, and I shift my hips to ease the pressure. I've been in worse places, just not many so tight. I've got a good view of the lake and the granite slab, at least—enough to see what the Rotters are doing.

Anna has begun to pace among them. She's humming beneath her breath, a foolish snippet of song about a courting blacksmith and a wedding. I suspect she's going mad, the Rot finally eating the last of her wits. The other Rotters shift, almost uneasily, but there's an air of expectation coming from them, too.

A scuff from the hole at the top has them jerking their heads skyward, moving like a single entity. The moonlight is shadowed by a moving figure.

"Meal time, you blighty buggers!" a familiar voice calls.

Lord Balthazaar?

More shadows move in front of the hole, blocking the moon entirely now. The Rotters stir, making eager sounds as something scrapes along the ground above, as if being dragged. Whatever it is appears at the lip of the hole. I can't make it out, but a moment later a high-pitched shriek sounds out—a woman.

She wails as she's shoved into the opening and hurled into the cavern below. Her cry cuts off when she hits the ground with a crunching thud, and I choke back the urge to vomit. It's a mercy in its own way because the Rotters converge upon her unmoving form. They tear into her without ceremony, rending flesh from her limbs in bloody splendor. Bones crack and her insides spill over the rocks in a crimson wave. I sink deeper into my hiding spot in horror; if I press my spine against the rock hard enough it will swallow me whole.

The Rotters have hardly finished their meal when another body is dropped through the hole. This one an old man. And then a young man... He doesn't die from the fall like the other two, and his screams echo around the cavern until I can bear it no longer and clap my hands over my ears.

Some foolhardy part of me imagines drawing the Rotters away from him, but that's pure suicide. And even if I succeeded, I'm no bonewitch, and the wounds he's suffered from the fall will be septic within hours.

But still... Long after he's gone I can still hear him begging for mercy.

Coward. Coward. Coward. My clockwork heart ticks its mocking cadence.

When they're finished with their meal, the Rotters begin to stagger through the tunnels, their chins stained scarlet. Anna is the only one who stays behind, and she sinks to her knees. I emerge from my hiding place. There is nothing left of the three victims, save a few scraps of tattered cloth and bits of flesh. Their bones have been picked clean.

I place my hand upon Anna's shoulder and give it a squeeze.

"IronHeart?"

"Aye. Are you all right?" It's a ridiculous question, but it's all I can think of to say.

"What have I become?" She shakes her head, then another coughing fit overtakes her, stealing her speech for several long minutes. "No. No, I can't. I won't. You'll take care of it, won't you?"

My mouth goes dry at the thought. "The hells, Anna. I mean, you're asking me to...kill you. Are you sure?"

"Would you settle for this?" she snaps.

I shake my head at the thought, not even having to think on the monstrosity of it all. Imagining day upon day as my body decayed all around me, my mind slowly putrefying into insanity?

"No," I say.

"Then do me the courtesy of releasing me. I will not suffer to become a monster." Her nostrils flare. A prickle of terror seizes me, shoving away whatever moral arguments I might make. Is this who I am? Someone capable of such a mercy in cold blood? The fact that I'm even considering it terrifies me more than the idea of the act itself.

And yet, is it fair to let her continue existing in this shadowed life in which she finds herself, with no escape and no end to it? My finger runs over the hilt of the dagger, but I cannot look away from her face, those unseeing eyes piercing straight through me with a plea of such utter despair.

I cannot save her. But I can free her.

"I'm sorry," I croak, unsheathing it, the metal clammy against my skin and burning me to the bone. And still I hesitate, my clockwork heart whirring rapidly. *Coward, coward, coward.*

For all my fine words to Buceph about killing, it's one thing to kill someone in the heat of passion or in self-defense. But Anna is still technically alive. And maybe she's not exactly a friend, but this tastes more like murder than I care for.

"Please," she begs. "I cannot bear it any longer."

I exhale sharply and hold the blade to her neck.

Her blind eyes somehow roll up to capture mine, boring into me with agonizing clarity. "Now."

I steel myself against my own revulsion. I make it quick, slicing over her jugular the way I remember seeing a member of Mad Brianna's gang put down a dog for butchering. Her skin has a disturbing velvety texture to it, almost seeming to disintegrate beneath the blade's pressure like an insect escaping its old carapace.

She slumps immediately, the wound at her throat spraying thick black blood, her body's corruption even more evident than before. She makes no sound when she dies, the remaining spark of life fleeing the shell of her humanity like a bird.

I drop the knife and it falls at my feet. I squat beside her, a soft sob escaping me. Ignoring the acrid stink, I swallow huge gulps of air trying to comprehend what I've just done. I close her eyes, but it's a foolish gesture. She died when she contracted the Rot. The end result just came later than it should have.

"This lot should be nearly ready now." The voice echoes from the passage across the cavern. "And none too soon."

My head jerks toward the sound, and I leave what's left of Anna's body where it is, retreating to my hole as Georges enters the chamber holding a blue-light lantern...with Buceph. I bite off a swear when the two of them walk around the stone outcropping. Buceph pauses here and there to collect some of the glowing mushrooms from the far wall, tucking them neatly into a sack at his waist. I note his limping walk with satisfaction.

"It would appear we've missed the dinner bell," he observes, nudging a skull out of his way. "They're learning much quicker than the last batch did."

Georges clambers up the rock platform and cups his hands over his mouth. "Hallo, topside!"

Buceph winces at the echo. "Shut up. You'll attract the the Rotters' attention, and I don't want to be forced to kill any to protect your sad waste of skin."

Georges ignores him and shines an electric torch up the hole, flashing it twice. "Finally," he mutters after an answering shout is returned. There's more shadowy movement above to block out the moon, but this time a crate is lowered into the cavern. Buceph immediately opens it with a crowbar, murmuring in approval at whatever's inside.

"We'll have to return with the others. The replacement lab equipment is going to be too heavy for the two of us alone. Ah good. New syringes. And how nice—they've sent us a Festivus ham."

The offhandedness of this last comment fills me with a weary anger, but these last few days I've been run roughshod and I have no energy to deal with this particular outrage. But still. To casually discuss their supplies as though they merely met at a dinner party, ignoring the skeletal remains nearby and the obvious carnage, makes it even clearer that the Rotters are not the monsters down here.

Buceph loads up as much of the supplies as he can into his large shoulder bag. "Tanith will be pleased. She's needed more paper for ages."

"Remember to leave some for me. Half, as per our agreement." Georges presses his lips together, watching Buceph with a weary expression.

"How could I possibly forget with you always here to remind me?" Buceph asks.

A grinding rattle sounds from above. The cave grows darker, and I realize the moon is gone. Whoever was topside has closed up the hole. Damn.

I panic at the sudden lack of light, though Georges still has his lantern and Buceph glitters like heat lightning crackling over a dusky sky. They climb down the rock and take another look at the bone pile.

I'm more than ready for them to leave. My limbs are cramping, but as soon as I'm alone, I'm all for looting what's left of the crate. I shift, easing my tight muscles, and then freeze when I realize the two men have stopped.

They've found Anna's body.

Buceph squats down next to it. "How very interesting. You did say one of yours left with our Magpie, didn't you? Or maybe it's IronHeart, after all. She's a survivor, that one. Best not to underestimate her."

"Like you did?" Georges snaps. "You're talking about a fairy tale when she's just another Moon Child you couldn't manage to keep a hold of. Your precious d'Arc is as much a myth as whatever hides inside your floating city. And none of us will see either."

"Indeed." Buceph scans the cavern, sweeping right past my hiding place.

Don't breathe, Mags.

"Well, whatever she is or isn't, I'll expect you in the village tomorrow with the rest of the supplies." Georges grimaces in pain as he flexes his fingers. "And tell Tanith I'll be needing another infusion soon."

"Of course," Buceph agrees. He watches Georges disappear into the shadows before glancing at Anna's body again. He chuckles, picking something up from the ground. "You might want to keep track of your dagger better next time, Magpie. Never know when you'll need it."

Fuck.

The blade flashes in Buceph's hand, dull with Anna's blood, but he makes no move to return it. Instead, he wipes it clean upon her cloak and tucks it into his belt. "I like a challenge, Magpie. I'll be interested to see what you do."

And with that, he leaves in the opposite direction Georges did, disappearing into the darkness and leaving me with nothing more than the *drip, drip, drip* of water as it falls into the lake.

I wait awhile before approaching the crate. Exhaustion has set in, as well as newfound caution. Buceph is a crafty bastard, as is the plague-ridden bonewitch, and I wouldn't put it past them to set a trap for me. But eventually I have to creep out of my hole.

My limbs are stiff, my hands still crusted with Anna's blood. I rinse them off in the pool, avoiding the shriveled skin of her body and keeping my mind as blank as possible. If I look at her too closely, I'll probably break down and I can't afford that right now.

It feels good to stretch my legs, my fingers flexing into the crags of the rock. Without the light of the moon, I'm left in the faint blue glow of the mushrooms again as I move to the crate. It is mostly full of things I cannot use—great devices of metal and glass. The old me twitches at the sight. I'd had to make my living collecting scrap from the junkyards for so long that my first thoughts are always about how much jingle I can get. How much are these worth?

But no. If I can't eat it or use it as a weapon, it's useless to me now. Several loaves of bread sit in a separate compartment, along with some dried meat and a wedge of cheese. I don't think twice before taking nearly all of it.

Georges can ask for another crate if he chooses.

I tear through the first loaf of bread, my stomach rumbling as I fill it. I polish off the cheese, as well, and then stuff everything else into a small bag I found beneath a pile of paper. I fill it until the seams are nearly bursting.

A last search of the crate leaves me with several lightsticks, an extra cloak, and a flask of ale. No weapons, but there *is* a ball peen hammer. I test the heft of it, humming in approval at the balance. "Like an old friend."

Somehow its presence makes me feel more like myself, all the confusion of these past weeks melting away until all that's left is me.

IronHeart.

Raggy Maggy.

Magpie.

Mags.

Four names for my life so far. Hopefully I'll get the chance to collect a few more. I don the cloak and tuck the hammer into my waistband, its weight comforting at my hip. Washing down a last bite of bread with a few sips of ale, I scramble off the rock slab.

"See you've found the Arse."

I nearly slip into the lake as my ears register who is speaking— Penny. Along with Bran and the others, judging by the sudden flare of pale illumination.

"The Arse?" I ask.

"What else would you call a great opening in the cave that rains shit down upon us?" A gasp of hysterical laughter escapes me at the words, but only because it's so terribly fitting. Penny sucks on her lower lip so it smacks faintly. "You find any food? I saw you nosing about the crate."

I touch the pouch at my waist. It's squished from my earlier gymnastics, but the insides are intact. "I've some rolls. Think there's a sausage or two in here, too." Almost as one, they turn toward the sack. I barely get it open before hands are grabbing at it, knuckles curled into desperate claws. "Hey, leave off. You'll make me drop it."

Bran snaps his fingers, and I'm left with a few inches of breathing space. Somehow I don't think it matters if the food hits the ground, but I appreciate the attempt at manners. I dole out everything as equally as I can.

It's gone in seconds, and their expressions remain just as hungry.

"All I have." I tuck away the now-empty sack at my waist. "Buceph and Georges took the rest."

Bran rummages through the crate to pull out a cigarillo, and he lights it with a lucifer. "They usually leave us a bit here and there. It's a game to them. We can pretend it's charity, but they're rubbing it in our faces that they know we're here."

"You could have told me all that before leaving me behind over at the Rotter village." I narrow my eyes at him. "I don't exactly appreciate wandering around in the dark with no way to defend myself."

"You were the one who took off despite my warning, *Magpie*. There's a balance down here, and you're disrupting it," Bran snarls.

"Well, maybe it *needs* to be disrupted," I shoot back. "It was still a shit thing to do. We need to be better than that. Fight, find a way out of this hellhole, and free the other Moon Children from the facility," I say, glancing at all of them. Bran winces at my words, but I pretend not to notice. "Clearly whatever you're doing now isn't working. Haven't any of you ever attempted to escape through the…Arse?"

Bran glares at me, exhaling a puff of smoke. "It's the first thing I tried. But it's electrified. Get too close to the edge and you're fried like one of those elegant Meridian pig-stickers. And I don't fancy falling to my death, do you?" He quirks an eyebrow. "Most of our days are spent trying to find enough food that we don't starve to death and avoiding the Rotters. There's no point to anything else. There's not much by way of bandages or bonewitches to fix you up, if you haven't noticed."

I recognize the defeat in his voice, and the energy drains out of me. "We need to form an actual clan. One that won't leave its members to wander around in the dark because it's the easier thing to do."

"Whatever for?" Rosa juts her pointed chin at me, her cheeks stark and gaunt. "We get along okay now, aye?"

"It's not *us* as much as what we represent. With a name, we become a single unit, not merely a ragtag band of survivors. I know I haven't been down here long, but even I can see that there's too much…discord among us."

Penny grows thoughtful and rewards me with a little grin. "Just think of all the creative graffiti we could come with."

"Aye. Warnings. Directions. Something to alert other Moon Children that we're out here. Waiting for them." I point to the supplies in the crate. "They've already started trying to repair the damage to the facility. None of us should be subjected to that ever again."

Bran extinguishes the last of his cigarillo. "All right. Then let's start with this." He digs into the crate again and finds a cluster of glass instruments. He chucks them against the wall, and they shatter. The other Moon Children follow suit, destroying whatever they find, voices raised in cries of anger and frustration.

Penny digs through a pouch at her waist and thrusts a fistful of blue mushrooms into my hand. Our eyes meet, and she gives a little nod.

Without hesitation, I begin to eat.

A silver moon and a golden sun
Shining ice and fiery burn
A celestial dance too late begun
With delicate steps I cannot learn.

— CHAPTER SIX —

I already told you—there's nothing we can do for them," Bran says, stretching lazily and cracking his knuckles. We're lingering in the outskirts of a narrow tunnel that leads to Buceph's facility. Even from here, the stench of the Rotters in the pen wafts over us in a thick miasma that nearly sets me to choking.

I haven't been down here long enough for the mushrooms to affect my vision much yet, and I don't want to risk wandering around down here alone until I have a better idea of where everything is.

Our makeshift clan name is now the NightSingers, though there was a brief altercation between Penny and Gloriana about it. Penny wanted us to be the Meridian Suck-Tits. Gloriana insisted such a thing should be beneath us. Bran overrode the final vote and named us the NightSingers, though he's not particularly partial to that, either.

For whatever it's worth, it's who we are. The name doesn't really matter as much as what it stands for. Moon Children are not bred for independence, and there is something soothing about being in a clan again, even if it's purely for survival. It's taken time for us to sort things out, even as small a clan as we are, but I've convinced Bran that there are too many issues at hand to have a single leader in total control. To that end, we've split the decisions among the three of us. Bran is technically in charge, but Penny and I have worked together as part of our old clan for years; it only makes sense for the two of us to continue, especially when it comes to vandalism.

I peer around the edge of the tunnel into the cavern, studying the way the facility door is built into the rock itself. There are no external windows, except for a narrow horizontal slit in the door itself, and that is so small even if I smashed it, it wouldn't help us break in.

"Where does it draw power from? That would be the obvious thing to disrupt, aye?" I frown, not spotting any generators like the ones in the Meridian village.

Penny shrugs. "Somewhere inside. The generator that electrifies the Rotter pen has a box fixed to the cave wall on the other side of the fence. There's no real way to get to it, short of climbing the walls, but why would we want to shut that one off? The Rotters in the pen are barely cognizant of their surroundings anyway. I'm not sure they'd even notice."

"And the last thing we want to deal with is an even larger horde wandering the tunnels." Bran lights up a cigarillo and takes a draw before passing it to me and Penny. "Like I said, I've gone through or tried nearly every scenario I could think of the past three years, and they all turn to shit."

"So what?" I snap. "The only way we're going to have any chance of getting out of here is if we make ourselves such a pain in the ass they have to stop operations. The petty thefts can be ignored, as you've said, but stealing their test subjects? Wholesale vandalism? How fast do you think they'd notice if we destroyed that precious greenhouse of theirs?"

"Maybe if we had a guaranteed way out." Penny leans her head on Bran's shoulder. "Otherwise it might end up biting us in the ass all the sooner."

Bran takes the cigarillo from Penny and flicks the ash away, grunting something noncommittal. "There are some days I might actually welcome that." Without another word, he shifts, extricating himself from Penny with an oddly gentle nudge, and disappears into the tunnel, the glow of his hair fading away.

Penny watches him leave. "It's easy to forget he's been down here so long. I think he's given up on any of us ever getting out. Sometimes I think it's cruel to even bring it up to him anymore."

"All the more reason to share the burden of leadership."

"I suppose. He's spent so much time trying to survive—to help *us* survive—I'm not sure there's much room for anything else." She looks over at me. "It was his sister, you know. The one who's clothes you're wearing? She was taken by the Tithers against his will. He offered to go in her place, but they ended up taking both of them."

"I didn't know. I don't remember that. But to be honest unless it was one of our clan, I didn't much pay attention."

"And that's why you and Sparrow were so reckless," she says sharply. "Because you didn't pay attention. Maybe if you had..." Her words trail away and I bite down a retort at the insinuation.

Because in the end, she's right. If Sparrow and I had been more careful that night, she might still be alive. Or maybe she'd be down here in my place. Or I might have been Tithed anyway. And then I may not have met Ghost or Lucian.

That's the shit of it. We can never know what might have happened. I probably wouldn't be in this mess of intrigues, though.

Sometimes ignorance truly is a blessing.

"As you say. But I can't undo the past. All I can do is try to change the future." I rub the top of my fuzzy head, still not used to the way it feels beneath my fingers. "Where are the others?"

"Setting snares. There aren't many rats down here, but every once in a while, we get lucky." Penny's upper lip curls. "You'd think the little shitbags would be down here eating the Rotters. With that flesh falling off them and all."

"Even rodents are smart enough to stay the hells away." I snort. "Doesn't say much about us, I suppose. All right. I think I've seen enough for now."

"To the den, then?" Penny inclines her head in the right direction as she turns to go.

"You go on ahead. I've got some thinking to do, aye? I'll whistle if I get lost." I let out a little trill. We haven't quite decided what clan signals to use—every clan has its own collection for communication—but some of the basics are the same no matter which clan we belong to.

"Try not to do anything too stupid." She runs her tongue over her broken teeth with a grimace before disappearing down the tunnel.

"When have I ever?" I call after her, chuckling. In truth, I want some time to think. I head away from the facility, as well, one hand on the wall to keep me balanced in the dark. Though there are pockets of total blackness, there is a faint bioluminescence coating some of the walls that at least grants me some sense of direction. Not that I have a particular direction I'm going in.

I allow my mind to wander, retracing the steps of the previous days, my thoughts returning to Ghost and Lucian. How are they getting on? Are they any further along in their attempts to unlock the gates of the Pits to get me out? For that matter, everything happened so fast before I was sent to the Pits that there had been no time to discuss when such a rescue might occur, let alone how to communicate about it.

I glance behind me, wondering if I might be able to find my way to the gates on my own. Somehow, I don't think Bran or the others would be too keen on it, however.

I head back toward the facility hugging the opposing cave walls to slip past it and hurrying past the Rotter pen as quickly as I can.

Thankfully, I see nothing but a few shadowy figures, their moans chasing me up the next tunnel.

I slow down as I approach the Meridian village, pulling my cloak more tightly around my head. It takes me awhile to gauge how many people are about, but most of them seem to be in the great hall for their evening meal. My mouth waters as I catch the scent of meat cooking, but I don't have time for that now.

Sneaking into their village isn't possible, not with the gate closed, and the mechanism isn't a standard lock by any stretch. Nothing I could readily pick at any rate, even if I was so inclined.

Someone grabs my shoulder. "Don't be stupid," a voice hisses in my ear. I struggle to reach for my hammer at my waist, and then I realize it's Bran. "What in the hells are you doing?" Anger radiates off him, but he reminds me somewhat of a cat that's had a bucket of water dumped over it. I can nearly see a tail bristling behind him.

"I wanted to…I don't know. Go to the gates at the front of the Pits." I keep my voice pitched low.

"Ah yes. Your so-called rescuers. Fine. I'll take you there, but there's a better way than making yourself an obvious target the way you are. Come on." He jerks away, tugging my arm behind him so I'm forced to stumble in his wake. He leads me down a series of passages I didn't know about, eventually taking us to a wyrmhole that drops us beside a shallow pool.

Before I realize it, we've reached the end of the tunnel. We've actually managed to circumvent the Meridian village entirely, finding ourselves where the path switchbacks up to the salt mines.

"Ah," I say. "I didn't know about this route…"

"You could have asked. And this is a bad idea, by the way, but might as well get it out of your system." He brushes past me, and together, we carefully head up the switchbacks. Bran's tucked his hair deep into the hood of his cloak, but I still catch the barest hint of it shining from around the edges of the cloth and that's enough for me.

We pause when we reach the top. It's the first time I've returned this way since I was forced down here with the others, and I gaze down at the glowing village. I'm struck again at the peaceful beauty of it, but now it gleams with all the sweetness of poisoned candy. I don't linger on it, heading farther toward the surface, retracing my steps to the infirmary where I'd been treated.

It grows warmer as we ascend. Bran lets me take the lead, keeping a slower pace behind me. The caves below tend to maintain a constant temperature, but without much of a breeze, even chilly often feels stifling. But from here, it's intolerable since I know I'm heading toward the only possible escape route—and it will be closed off.

Biting hard on my lower lip, I spend the time getting a better look at the salt mines proper, the pale walls gleaming in the darkness as Bran's hair lights the way. I try to overlay what I know of the layout, struggling to remember the maps I studied with Ghost.

The ceilings are low and the passages are narrow, my footsteps echoing throughout like sad sighs. It's almost like walking through a tomb, and I suppose it's not a bad comparison given how many people die down here.

The main passage widens as the floor slants upward. Here and there are doorways to various rooms. Most are long emptied of anything that might be useful, leaving only bare white chambers with no windows and one exit.

I begin to run, choking back a wave of vomit. The walls seem to press around me and my breath is coming in shallow bursts, but I can't seem to stop. I'd taken my days living upon the rooftops of BrightStone for granted. Here, I've become nothing more than a mouse in a maze, no different from the ones Lucian kept in the secret room off his bedroom so he could study the effects of the Rot on their tiny bodies.

"Oy, Magpie!" Bran trots behind me. "Don't forget the drop-off."

I'm running faster now, ducking past torches that are no longer lit. I suppose there's no reason to keep them aflame except on Tithe days anyway. The drop-off looms in front of me, and I skitter to a halt, almost slamming into the wall.

Bran catches up to me a moment later, tsking as he grabs me by the shoulder and spins me around. He studies my face with a critical eye. "Not seeing it."

"Seeing what? I didn't hurt myself." I pull away to press my fingers against the wall, trying to judge if I can climb it or not.

"I figured you must have a crack in that thick skull of yours," he says dryly. "I can't think of any other reason someone would tear into the darkness like that. But there's no damage, like you said, so guess you're as stupid as you look."

A hot flush rolls over my cheeks. "Why do you care anyway? If you hate me so much…"

"I don't care. Not really. But I care about *her*." He skims his own hands over the wall.

I blink at him. "Her? You mean Penny?"

"Who else?" His voice grows softer. "She might not show it, but the fact that you're alive has made her very happy. Happiness is hard to come by down here, if you haven't noticed, and I'd like to keep that going." A frown wrinkles his forehead. "This is how she broke her teeth you know, falling from here when she was Tithed."

"She never said anything to me about that."

"You probably never asked," he mutters, finally finding handholds and launching himself upward. "Come on."

The heat of my cheeks grows sharper at his rebuke, but I follow suit, my feet digging into the rock. I struggle the last bit of it, my fingers slipping. Bran doesn't help me at all, watching impassively as I finally wriggle my way over the edge.

Panting, I stagger to my feet. "No wonder they're not afraid of the Rotters climbing out of here."

Bran shrugs, tugging me along. "There used to be a ladder, but it broke. Guess it wasn't a priority to have it fixed. Besides, the real reason they're not afraid of us escaping is just ahead." The gates are in front of us now. A rush of fresh air rolls past me, the metal gleaming with the brittle strength of starlight.

I fight the urge to throw myself at the bars, something within me breaking as I peer into the darkness of the edges of the Warrens, the tumbledown ruins that were my home for so long. I sink to my knees, a bitter despair washing over me. It was foolish to think it would be so simple, but so maddening to have freedom dangle in front of me. But for all that I'm a few inches away from it, I could have been atop Meridion.

From this angle, I catch only the merest glimpse of the floating city drifting through the clouds. At one point, it might have seemed a comfort, but it's nothing now but a hollow void. Knowing about the creation of the Rot and the Moon Children, I don't think I can see the city as anything other than an enemy, even if their citizens are as ignorant as Lucian likes to claim.

And where is Ghost? I don't know if I was somehow expecting he'd be here, magically waiting on the other side like the hero from a fairy tale. But how did those really go, anyway? Not that it matters. I'm no princess and this is no tower, and the only dragon I know is the little clockwork one I'd found, and I have no idea where it has run off to.

Leaning against the bars, I press my forehead against the metal. The chill burns into my skin, and out of habit, I let out a soft warning whistle, the notes discordant.

Death lies here…

"I wouldn't touch that for too long." Bran pushes me back and squats, tapping the bars. "Such peculiar metal. Normal steel would have rusted away ages ago with all the salt down here."

Glancing up at Meridion, I sigh. "If this is what Meridion is made of, too, it will probably last up there forever."

"I don't care what it does as long as it leaves us alone." Bran pulls a snared rat off his belt. "I was going to save this for later, but…" He lays the unfortunate rodent down so that it's touching two of the bars at the same time. "One. Two. Three."

The rat vibrates, its little body bursting into flames as an explosion of sparks crackle. The scent of burning hair and sizzling flesh sets my stomach churning. "They're *electrified*? And you let me touch them?"

"You'd only have done it the once." Bran smirks, scooping up what's left of the rat. He picks away the charred bits and then sighs. "Probably not worth eating." He chucks it between the bars. "And as far as the electrics go, aye. That's why you don't see any Inquestors patrolling around here much. Anything touches these bars for longer than a few seconds and *poof*."

"And that's the same as what's around the Arse?" My heart sinks as he nods. "I didn't realize…"

"Well, I wasn't lying when I said I've tried nearly everything since I've been down here." He sucks in a deep breath. "I figured you'd find your way to the gates eventually. Everyone does, at least once. Better to get it over with early and realize there really isn't anything we can do."

"I can't live like that," I tell him. "There has to be another way."

"Who said anything about living?" he retorts. "This is *survival*, Magpie. No more, no less. Living is a luxury we don't have time for. If you need to pretend it's something else for now, then so be it, but the sooner you realize it, the better you'll manage. There's no point to hope at all. It will only drive you to madness that much faster."

"I have to believe Ghost and Lucian will come through," I maintain. "I at least need to let them know I'm still alive. Maybe if I came up here on a regular basis…"

"Don't be stupid," he snaps. "You're trapped here. You've seen the passageways. Between those and this electric gate, do you really think you'd stand a chance if Buceph happened to wander this direction?" He taps the hammer hanging from my hip. "The man's a sadist, and that little thing won't be enough to stop him if he's really coming for you."

I press my hand to the loosened panel of my heart and swallow. "I know full well what he's capable of."

"No. You don't." Bran's mouth curls up in a snarl. A sudden burst of rage clouds over his eyes, and it's clear whatever he's seeing hasn't faded from his memories at all over the years. "I got to watch that bastard tear my sister apart one piece at a time for weeks while he had us locked up in that hellish operating room of his. And once he discovered we were related, he took a special sort of pleasure in not harming me at all."

Ice spreads out from my belly, his words leaving me chilled. The timbre of his voice trembles slightly, but there's a sharpness lurking below, a promise of pain beyond imagination.

Perhaps he's right. I *don't* know. Not really. The height of my misery has been mere weeks. Bran has been down here for years watching his fellow Moon Children be butchered, surrounded by death on all sides. It's a wonder he hasn't gone mad himself.

Uncertain, I reach out to touch his shoulder and give it a soft squeeze. "I don't know what's going to happen, but I promise you, I'll do everything I can to find us a way out."

"Don't make promises you can't keep, little girl. You don't know anything." He lurches to his feet and disappears down the passageway. "Don't stay here too long," he calls back.

And with that, he's gone.

I let out one last set of whistles into the Warrens but am rewarded with nothing more than the lonely echo bouncing through the crumbling alleys.

And then, in the far distance, is an answer. *Here... What news?*

My heart beats so loud in my ears it feels as if they might burst, but whistle signals aren't complex enough to convey everything that needs to be said. I need to talk to Ghost, but the two of us didn't agree to any code words. We didn't have enough time to develop the same repertoire I'd had with Sparrow or my other clanmates. Ghost doesn't even know what most of the basic call signs are, let alone how to communicate with them. Besides, why would he trust what a random Moon Child tells him anyway? He has no way of knowing it's me. There is only one phrase he really knew and that was…

A half smile crosses my face, and I let out a series of short whistles. There's a long pause and then a questioning repeat. I whistle an affirmative and then repeat it again myself: *Magpie fancies a shag with Ghost, three days hence.*

It is the only thing he'll probably recognize, and while most Moon Children know Ghost as clanless, a message like this will surely stir up enough curiosity that some of them might pass it on.

The Mother Clock strikes the hour, and her song is so familiar I want to weep, but the time slips away as easily as rainwater through a sieve. Despite my hopes of meeting Ghost tonight, when the dawn starts pinking the sky, I'm left with nothing but retreat.

A half chuckle escapes me, but it's a sad, lonely thing swallowed up by the darkness as I make my way back down into the Pits.

Ding-dong bell,
Up she goes and down she fell.
Who pulls her out will find her dead
Asleep upon her watery bed.

— CHAPTER SEVEN —

Move over." Rosa nudges me slightly to peer into the crate. We're in the Arse, post-Rotter feeding but before Buceph has made his appearance. It's the third such looting I've participated in since I've been down here. The overall schedule feels random, and we don't always get there before the Meridians, but today we were lucky enough that Dafyyd saw the supplies first.

We're like vultures picking a carcass clean. Bran snaps up a carton of cigarillos and a bottle of brandy, even as the rest of us scramble over food and other assorted goods. Penny takes several pieces of parchment and some charcoal sticks. Anything that looks useful and is portable enough to take is squirreled away and divided among us. The rest we destroy.

And then we're gone, ducking our way through the tunnels and to the den as silently as we can. We run in pairs, usually in different directions, doubling back or climbing to a wyrmhole if we need to.

This time I'm running with Conal. He's a short lad, younger than me, with a wide cowlick on his forehead. He doesn't talk much, but his one good eye never seems to stop darting about, as though he's constantly on the alert for an attack. Perhaps he is. Most of the others haven't been particularly forthcoming with their own stories about how they escaped Buceph, and there's enough misery down here without me forcing them to dredge up old memories.

We don't head to the den right away. We've started caching what we can spare in various hiding places, if only to spread things out in case any of us gets separated for a time.

The feral Rotters are growing bolder, and as a clan, we've decided that while taking out a few here or there is manageable, the risk is far too great to confront more than that.

We pause in a wyrmhole to take stock of what we have. Conal watches me as I dig through the food I've taken—bread, jerky, a wedge of cheese, and two small jugs of ale. He has a jar of pickled eggs and a packet of sardines.

"That's new," I note. "Slightly higher class than the bread, aye?" My stomach grumbles. I eye the sardines, but Conal's face is far too eager. "Take them."

That quiet gaze stares at me, his whole body seeming to shrink in on itself. "Are you sure?" His voice is tremulous and fearful. Whatever happened to him may have occurred before he was Tithed to the Pits, though his innate distrust of me could mean anything. Or nothing. Maybe he just isn't fond of clan leadership.

I thrust my jaw at him. "Aye."

He doesn't wait to be told twice and tears into the fish quickly, swallowing them down without chewing. I store the bread and cheese with some of the water flasks we've already put up here.

"So what now?" Conal asks, running his fingers through his cowlick so it spikes.

My stomach rumbles again. "I wonder if there's any use in trying to get something fresher..." My voice trails off as I think of my lessons with Lucian and his insistence on me eating vegetables. Something about scurvy, but he hadn't enlightened me on it. There were hardly any fruits or vegetables among the storage crates, though. At least not since I'd been down here. But the greenhouse in the Meridian village had some.

I'm not so foolhardy as to simply waltz in there, but these last few weeks have made it clear that Bran is correct. We spend so much of our energy finding food that there is little room for much else. I've revisited the gates to the Pits only once, but there was still no word or sign of Ghost.

"We need more food. If we could get that done more efficiently, we'd be able to spend more time searching for a way out." A twinge of guilt runs over me. I've certainly achieved my original goal for being down here—searching out evidence of a conspiracy—though it will do me little good if I starve to death before I can relay the information. Not to mention the word of a Moon Child won't be taken too seriously in BrightStone. I need concrete evidence of what is happening and how.

"Don't suppose you've ever thought of breaking into the greenhouse, aye?" I wonder aloud.

Conal shakes his head. "It's right smack in the middle of the village. Maybe Bran might do it, but all that glass..."

"Too easy to be spotted," I agree with a sigh. But desperate measures might lead me to try it anyway.

Conal brightens. "There is a...a garbage pile, I guess? It's in one of the tunnels next to the village. On the far side, so they don't have to deal with the smell."

I haven't rummaged through the trash since I started living at Molly Bell's.

And look at you now, Mags. Putting on airs, are we?

I can almost hear Sparrow's deriding chuckle, and I laugh bitterly. "I suppose I'm not too good to go garbage picking. Where is it?"

The garbage heap is exactly as Conal described. There's a small pit in the far corner of one the tunnels and a huge pile of...not trash exactly. It smells like a privy, but somehow it's a more comforting scent than that of the decaying bodies of the Rotters. More honest, maybe.

It doesn't make me want to get too close to it all the same, and I hover around the edges. Rotting vegetables, or maybe plant cuttings, are stacked in various piles, but pride or not, I'd have to be pretty damned desperate to go rooting through actual shit.

Beside me, Conal whirls around as a brush of blue light creeps into the tunnel. I follow suit, one hand on my hammer, only to be confronted by the greenhouse keeper's bemused visage. Joseph has a satchel slung over his shoulder and a floppy hat on his head, though it's so threadbare he's probably only wearing it out of habit. It's not like there's any sun to protect against down here anyway.

"Ahem. I didn't realize Moon Children had such a need for my compost. Planning a garden, are we?" He's not mocking us exactly, but he doesn't seem overly upset by the concept, either. He gestures at Conal. "You're too thin, lad. Both of you."

Conal launches himself past Joseph with a violent swipe, pushing the older man down and rushing into the darkness. I go to call him back and then stop. I'll never catch up to him anyway. I let out two sharp trills and then a short tweet: *Report to the clan.*

Joseph sobers as he gets to his feet, his brow furrowing. "That one...he had a rough go of it when he first got here. I don't think he ever quite got over the shock."

"And which shock would that be?" I hiss. "The one where he first realized his entire life was a lie? Or the one where he was nearly butchered by your people simply so you can all extend your perfectly miserable lives?"

He exhales slowly, picking up his lantern from where it fell. "I let him go, Magpie. Before Buceph could take him. The same way I did some of the other few I could manage to save."

I heft the hammer in my hand. "Of course you did," I retort. "That's why he's so terrified of you. Victims always fear their rescuers."

"It's not something to make light of." He sighs and turns away. "Come with me."

"Where? The facility? A trap? I think not." I edge toward the wall, ready to take off at the nearest sign of another Meridian. And not that I trust the man at all, but...

"My greenhouse," he says. "Pull the hood up on your cloak and walk beside me. Most everyone else is doing their own work; no one will give you a second glance if you're with me. Just try not to attract attention."

"Oh aye. Because I'm so good at that." He chuckles at this but waves at me to follow.

I hesitate. Though I've wanted to do some basic reconnaissance of the village since the NightSinger clan was formed, walking directly into the lion's den feels bold, even for me. Still, the greenhouse tempts me with its secrets, and my clan needs food—more than we can reasonably manage on our own.

I do as he instructed and walk a pace or two behind him, keeping my head mostly down as we enter the village. There are a few Meridians walking a lazy patrol, but they don't seem concerned by me, or anything else for that matter. Joseph tips his hat at them as we pass, and that is apparently good enough.

And yet, this all feels terribly familiar. Like I've done this before. And I have—with Lucian. The morning we'd gone to visit the dying Archivist at the Salt Temple, we'd walked in almost the same fashion, only he'd been hiding me from Inquestors.

But Joseph is not Lucian, and I'll be the better for remembering that.

The heady glow of the little homes that seemed so magically welcoming when I'd first arrived now turns my stomach, and I cannot help but keep a wary eye out for Buceph. The others may not recognize me, but he will. There's a sharpness in my bones that sings of death when I think of him, and I know one of us will destroy the other upon our next confrontation.

"He's not here," Joseph murmurs, glancing over at me when I move closer to him. "So calm yourself. At least until we're inside." We approach the greenhouse, and he ushers me in, cocking a brow when I keep a tight hold on my hammer. "It's glass," he reminds me. "Should you wish to leave, you have only to break it."

I cross my arms when he closes the door behind us. The scent of growth slams into me, and for a few heartbeats, I simply *smell*. It's not the salty tang of the caves, dark and musty with despair, and that's a vast improvement.

"Why are you helping me?" I ask.

"Because I'm sick of this." He sighs. "All of it. I want to go home. I want to be done with whatever it is Tanith thinks we're doing. And I'm tired of watching people die."

"Then why don't you do something about it? You're one of them." I spit on the ground, my nostrils flaring wide. "Words mean less than nothing down here. How many years have you been here doing nothing but watching, hiding in your plants and your fancy lights? Have you even seen what Buceph is doing in that facility? He's dissecting us! Making our blood into a…a *product*."

"You're right. And I have no excuses. Not anymore." He grimaces. "My biggest regret is not stopping it when I had the chance."

"How would you?" I ask. "Buceph said the High Inquestor was keeping you here until you found a *solution*. So if what he said is true…" *Solution* isn't really the word I want to use, but as polite euphemisms go, it will do.

I slowly edge my way around the greenhouse, silently taking stock of everything there. Food versus flowers. How much can I carry? Is it ripe? Would it be easy to transport?

"It is. The High Inquestor was not sent to BrightStone because he was a good person. The Pits weren't his idea, but he saw the advantage of having us down here. Should we actually be successful in perfecting the serum, I imagine he'll use it as a bargaining chip to return to Meridion." His lips curl into a mocking expression. "And should we be so bold as to kill Buceph and stop him from doing more dreadful things, Lord Balthazaar will stop providing us with supplies."

"Now *that* I don't believe." I shake my head. "I've seen Balthazaar's wife. He wants her cured of the Rot. I doubt he cares who he deals with to make that happen. So you're just using that as an excuse."

He flinches. "Your opinion notwithstanding, it is very true that the only way to communicate with the outside world lies within that facility. How else would we order the supplies we need? Or know when the Tithes will occur?"

"And here I thought you tied little messages to the tails of trained rats," I retort. "So how does it work?'

"It's a simple mechanism—a wire enclosed in a tube that runs from the facility to, well, I'm not sure exactly, but the High Inquestor does. They use a special device to tap a code up the wire where it's recorded on wax tablets." He raises a brow at me. "When they built this place, they wanted something that would always work and wouldn't be easily discovered. A more complex technology would be bound to break down somewhere along the way."

"And naturally, only Buceph has access to it, aye?" I rub my temples.

"Well, to be fair, we didn't expect to be down here this long. But yes. It complicates things a bit," he agrees.

"If you say so." I nose around a large tree with broad, flat leaves, grunting in satisfaction when I see a small basket of plantains beneath it. I scoop one up and peel it, the sweetness exploding on my tongue. I wolf the rest of it down and pocket two more.

"You shouldn't take those, you know." There's a bitter ache in his voice, but somehow it feels like he's not really directing the words at me as much as someone else. A memory, perhaps.

I thrust my chin at him. "Don't be greedy. You owe me—*us*—this much."

He continues to regard me with a weary resignation. "Yes. I simply meant that the plantains won't keep very long. If you want staples, you might consider the carrots or the potatoes. Perhaps an onion."

"No strings attached?" I clamp down on the flutter of elation that I might be able provide my clan with more food this easily. Surely there's a catch somewhere. "How about an entire bag of potatoes?" I counter, testing the waters further. "And some carrots."

"Fair enough." Joseph ducks behind one of the aisles and pulls out a burlap sack and begins filling it. "We had a decent enough crop recently. I think we can manage. I'm sorry that I can't do much else for you right now, but I'll provide you with whatever food I can spare without the others being suspicious."

"Why here? Why now?" My eyes flick to the door behind him. "It would be so easy for you to simply turn me in."

"Nothing is ever that easy. And as I said, I am simply tired. I never thought much of Tanith's ideals."

A snort escapes me. "None of you are innocent, least of all the ones who pretend it isn't happening."

"No. She meant well, in the beginning. We all did, I think. But she prefers to leave the distasteful parts to Buceph." He looks away. "And it is all distasteful now. There is no use pretending what we're doing here is remotely anything other than sadistic or self-serving."

"And how do the other Meridians feel?" I cock my head at him, curious.

"Much like me, for the most part. With the exception of Sora, none of us do our work at Buceph's facility. It's mostly theoretical in nature, anyway. None of us really have the stomach for that sort of experimentation." He pales. "You have to believe me—we're no happier than you are."

"You certainly manage to live longer, though." I bite down on the inside of my cheek. Evidence of the Meridian creation and propagation of the Rot was one thing, but to possibly hear it from the lips of one of the floating city's scientific citizens? Someone who has been here since the beginning?

"And if we got you out of here somehow? Would you be willing to make such statements in public? Before the Chancellor of BrightStone? Tell her of your part in this and which Meridians were involved in the planning of the Rot release? Explain what you've been doing to all these innocent people ever since?"

He hesitates and then finally nods. Whatever arguments he's having in his head remain unspoken, and I can't even begin to know if he's telling me the truth. But I'm pretty sure I don't really have a choice but to believe him.

His people have betrayed mine often enough. He might as well betray his own, too. It's a start in either case.

"If you truly have a way out of here..." His voice trails away as though the idea is more than he can hope for.

"I'm working on it," I admit, unsure of how much to tell him. In the end, prudence wins out and I shrug. "Let's say I've got a few tricks up my sleeve and leave it at that." I grin despite my doubts. "But I'll hold you to your promise," I tell him softly. "Show me that some Meridians have at least that much honor, aye?"

"I'll do my best." He holds out his hand to me. It's rough and dirty, and that, at least, is honest enough. I take it, sealing the bargain, for whatever it's worth. He tips his hat at me, and I smile.

The potatoes are heavy, bumping awkwardly into my hip, but I'm already imagining roasting them in our fire pit. It won't be enough for more than a meal or two, but we're so strung out as a group, every bit helps.

"Getting cozy with the enemy, are we?" Bran croons from one of the side tunnels. He nudges the sack. "If there's food in there, I'll forgive you."

"Aye. Potatoes." I shift the sack to ease the weight on my shoulders. "And I think we have an ally. Joseph, the man who runs the greenhouse, is willing to talk to the Chancellor when we get out of here. That would be enough to break everything wide-open, wouldn't it?"

A bark of laughter escapes him. "Oh, I'm sure. At least you're enthusiastic about our chances," he grumbles, taking the potatoes from me as we scramble up to the wyrmhole that leads to the den. "Just make sure you know the cost of his help. Nothing comes without a price."

"He wants out of here, same as us. Said he would assist in providing us with food, and that might make things easier on us, so we can spend more time searching for a way out. And a way into the facility…" The words sound stupid in my own ears, and I can tell by the way Bran looks at me, he thinks I'm stupid, too. Stupid for trusting a Meridian. Stupid for even thinking we'll ever get out of here.

And maybe he's right. But I can't sit here like a lady in a tower, waiting for a rescue that may never come. I won't apologize for that.

Before I can say any of this out loud, Penny pops her head out of the wyrmhole, her face pale. "Oh, thank the Hells you're back! Hurry up!"

"What's going on?" Bran shouts, her panic bleeding into him.

Penny's lips tremble. "It's Conal and Gloriana. They've been poisoned."

Humpty Dumpty sat on a wall
Convinced that he could fly.
Down he fell and broke his shell
Leaving him as hollow as I.

— CHAPTER EIGHT —

Bran and I scramble into the den, Penny behind us, and
Bran drops the potatoes next to the fire with a heavy thud.
Gloriana is lying on the floor moaning, her head in Rosa's
lap, her pale skin taking on an almost waxen appearance. Her
breath is slow and labored. Rosa's eyes shimmer with tears.

Next to them is Conal. Dafyyd wipes some sweat away from the
boy's forehead, and spittle foams at the corners of Conal's lips. He
gapes at me like a fish gasping for air.

I narrowly avoid a puddle of vomit as I dash over to him. "What
happened? He was fine a little while ago…" Penny's glowing hair
reflects off a glass jar lying on its side, the contents spilled onto the
ground. "Pickled eggs?" My head whips toward Conal. "Did you
eat those? Did Gloriana?"

Dafyyd kicks a half-eaten egg by his foot. "They were eating
them when I came in. I think Conal had more, though."

My mind races with the implication. Had it simply been food
gone bad, or had it been intentionally poisoned? I need to know,
but there's no time to figure it out now.

"What do we do? What do we do?" Rosa asks between quiet
sobs.

My upper lip curls as I look at Bran, who's staring at us all with empty horror, as if he's caught in a personal nightmare from which he'll never wake up. I snap my fingers to get his attention, and he startles.

"I don't know," he says finally. "I don't know."

I tap my nose, not coming up with anything satisfactory. There's only one real option, and I have no idea if it will even work. But I have to try.

"Come on." I get to my feet and point at Penny. "We need to move them."

"Move them? Where?" She runs her tongue over the edges of her broken teeth.

I'm already climbing up the den walls to the wyrmhole. "Meet me by the gates of the Rotter village. I'm off to bag myself a bonewitch."

I stumble along the tunnels, my hand skimming lightly over the cave walls for balance. Although I'm starting to see better in the dark, I'm nowhere near as capable as the others yet. I still tend to get mixed up, but in this case, I know where I'm going. Or at least I know the right direction.

Moving my two clanmates will be hard, but there's no way we can get Georges into the den, so this will have to do. Assuming he will help us at all.

I shove that thought away and pick up another burst of speed, narrowly avoiding a feral Rotter who comes shambling out of the tunnels in front of me, his toothless maw gaping wide. My hammer's already in my hand as I slow down. Normally, I'd avoid him and keep going, but if the others will be following my path, I can't leave the Rotter here to attack them. I let out a yowl of frustration.

I ignore the sad groan he makes and take a stance a few feet away from him. He grunts eagerly, but this one's been around for a while.

"I don't have time for this," I mutter, launching at him. It takes two blows with the hammer to knock him to the ground, and his knees explode when I slam the hammer into his legs. He makes a confused burble, and I bring the hammer down one more time. His skull collapses beneath the impact. The bone seems to simply fold in on itself, the structure of his face bearing only a hollow resemblance to what he must have looked like alive.

"I'm sorry," I mumble, wiping my hammer off on the side of the cave wall.

No matter how necessary it is, the wrongness of it burrows deep in my bones. These aren't Inquestors who have beaten a populace into submission with their electric batons. Not Buceph who has hurt so many in his quest for knowledge. Not Balthazaar who imprisoned me. It's Anna and even Lady Lydia, their bodies dying all around them, exposed to a plague they didn't deserve to catch.

But none of that matters now. I can do nothing for them. But I can focus on saving my clanmates, so I shove all the rest of it away and hurry down the tunnel.

This way, that turn, here, here…

I let my mind patter on, taking me where I need to go. When the flickering of torches finally glimmers into view, I breathe a sigh of relief. At least I managed to make it this far without getting lost. The gates to the village are locked, but I pull out my hammer and slam on it as hard as I can.

"Oy! Let me in!" I bang on it several more times, calling out across the lake with a series of high-pitched whistles. If my clan hears them, they'll know I'm here, but my only goal right now is to draw attention to myself.

The lake water ripples, and in the distance, the shadows of the villagers move wildly until a small group of Rotters heads for the gate, a low murmur rumbling from them. They stare at me, the despair clinging to them like a cloak. The group parts suddenly, and Georges approaches me through the center with a deliberate gait. His face is haggard, but he has a calming presence about him somehow, almost an aura of peace that seems to roll over the Rotters like lapping waves on a quiet shore. Compared to the miasma of death that hangs over the facility and much of the caves, it's mesmerizing.

"Brilliantly done," he says, his mien softening as he looks upon the frightened Rotters. "All right, you lot. Let's take a minute to forget this intrusion and then return to our supper, shall we?" The Rotters slowly quiet, and I blink at him, amazed at the gentle command in his voice.

When the Rotters have trailed away he crosses his arms. "What do you think you're doing?"

"I need your help. Two of the other Moon Children...they've been poisoned!" A sudden rush of agitation rolls over me, and I jiggle the gate door in emphasis.

Georges frowns. "Poisoned? By what?"

"We stole some pickled eggs out of the supply crate you got from Balthazaar. Both of them ate some."

"Well, that's very unfortunate," Georges states. "But I fail to see what that has to do with me."

"You're a bonewitch, aren't you?" I demand. "Aren't you supposed to help the sick?"

"And I have my hands quite full." He gestures behind him. "We're all sick here, as you can see. I certainly don't have antidotes for poison."

"You owe us," I hiss at him, slamming the hammer on the gate again for good measure. "You healed me when I first got here. The least you can do is try to help the others." My eyes flush hot with tears, remembering how Sparrow had died. "Please. There are so few of us left..."

The bonewitch pinches the bridge of his nose, that aura of peace wavering slightly. "All right, then. Bring them here, and I'll see what I can do. But I make no claims as to whether I can actually help them or not. And if not, I trust there will be no trouble between us?" The question is polite, but the warning threads through the words all the same.

"Aye." I tap my hammer on the gate as I turn to go. "I'll be back with the others as soon as I can. And thank you!" I pelt away up the tunnel, whistling shrilly to my clan.

Conal's breath is rapid and shallow as he lies upon the mattress, his body racked with fever. Gloriana is on the bed next to his, lying on her side and vomiting noisily into a bucket. At this point, I'm not sure there's much left in her, but she dry heaves until she's shaking.

Georges has injected them both with something that is supposed to calm their stomachs, but it doesn't appear to be working. Rosa was smart enough to bring the remainder of the pickled eggs with her, and the bonewitch is studying one as the other Moon Children try to help as best they can.

Bran paces by the door, tension radiating off him in waves. He's not looking at anyone, and I can tell all that biting rage is all inwardly directed. Any moment he's going to burst, and whatever the end result is, I doubt it will be anything good.

I nudge Penny from where she sits beside Conal and gesture at Bran. "Get him out of here. He's making the rest of us nervous."

She blinks up at me and then nods, taking Bran by the arm and leading him outside the infirmary. Not that we couldn't use more help in here, but watching a clan leader implode isn't something the others need to see right now.

Georges sighs. "I'm afraid I can't determine exactly what was used to poison them. There are any number of things that it could be, and I don't have the tools necessary to research it further. The best we're going to be able to do is to keep them hydrated." His brow furrows when he sees Conal, and he shakes his head. He hasn't said anything, but I recognize that clinical, detached mien. Lucian had it when we saw the dying Archivist in the Salt Temple. I suppose it's a defense mechanism. After all, patients die all the time.

Dafyyd continues to sit vigil beside Conal's bed, stroking the boy's hand with grim determination. I turn away, unable to bear it anymore. Georges taps my shoulder and quietly gestures for me to follow him into the little room beside the infirmary. It's a shoddy place, but clean enough —the desk and the shelves rudimentary but serviceable. Certainly nothing like the piles of hoarded goods in Buceph's office.

Georges's bloodshot gaze flicks toward the infirmary. "I think you already know what I'm going to tell you," he says, his tone formal. "But you must know things are not going well for that boy. The girl…" He shrugs. "I think she'll manage if she can survive the next few hours."

"What can we do to save them?" I cross my arms.

"There is no saving them, Magpie. There is nothing else we can do for them now, and there is no way to make things better. Not down here. Not for these people." He raises a brow at me. "Not for Rotters or Moon Children. Not even for myself. All I can really offer is sympathy."

"Oh aye. Because kicking out diseased townsfolk into the caves or escorting them to a pen to die is the epitome of compassion, right?" He says nothing, taking a seat in the chair behind his desk and flipping through whatever records he has. He's far gaunter that I remember, his yellowed eyes seeming to bulge slightly. I can nearly make out a hint of cloudiness that seems to be settling over the pupils. Anna had appeared much the same, but she had been in a far later stage of the disease.

"What do you want me to say?" he asks. "That I'm sorry you're stuck down here? That I regret what's happened to these poor unfortunates in my care? That I can't make a cure?"

"Apologies are wasted on anyone living down here." I slip into the seat across from him, placing my feet on the paperwork on his desk. Obnoxious, I know, but this way he can't use busywork as an excuse not to talk to me. "No. I want to know why you do it at all."

His mouth thins, lips like bloodless worms twisting in the mealy pockmarks of his face. "Do you think I have a choice? I stop doing this, and Buceph stops giving me my serum. And then I die. I know you and your little 'clan' out there think you're rebellious crusaders, but all you're doing is interfering with our work in finding a cure. I do what I must for those who have skills to help us survive. The rest have to manage as best they can."

"Sounds like an excuse."

"Of course it's an excuse," he snaps, glaring at me. "How easy it is for you to pass judgment, you who have no fear of rotting to death in your own body."

I lunge across the desk at him, my fist held up high and shaking with fury. To his credit, he doesn't even attempt to avoid the blow and I pull it short at the last minute, smashing it into the shelf behind him so it tumbles to the ground with a crack. "How. Dare. You." My throat is so tight with anger I can barely manage the words.

"I'm dying anyway," he chuckles, coughing slightly. "Go on. Relieve me of my misery."

I shake away the sting from my knuckles. "Too easy."

"Yes, it would be. But I don't know what else I can give you. I'm as trapped as anyone else down here. Buceph certainly doesn't enlighten me on the specifics of his...work. I'm not from Meridion. The most I can hope for is that he actually finds a solution. That's it. That's the only reason I do any of this."

Lady Lydia had begged me for death from her bed, cocooned in her sallow face and patchy skin, the room filled with the acrid smell of flesh gone rancid. Georges has all these symptoms, albeit to a lesser degree. Whatever Buceph is giving him, it's probably not much better than what he's giving to Balthazaar to apply to his wife, and undoubtedly, the end will be same no matter what.

I suppose I can have sympathy enough for that, though it doesn't balance out the rest of it. "You tried it, didn't you?" I ask softly. "You didn't accidentally get injected by some random occurrence. Someone tempted you with the idea of immortality, and in the end, they got what they wanted—a bonewitch they could trust beneath their thumb. And well, I suppose you got a form of immortality, if what Buceph says is true." I shrug, pretending not to notice how he looks away.

"It's not as simple as all that," he protests. "You know as well as anyone how they work down here. How they work up there." He points toward the ceiling. "Why I did what I did isn't important anymore. This is where I am and who I am. And for all that, I've never stopped being a doctor. But I'm forced to make decisions doctors should never have to make—life, death…" He lets out a sharp bark of laughter. "We all die. The only thing I can do is attempt to ease their suffering."

"You're a coward, Georges," I say, and he glances away. "And that's the truth of it, using their deaths to prolong yours. Because whatever this is—" I gesture about the room "—is a far cry from living, and we both know it."

"What is it you want from me? My resources are somewhat limited, as you can see."

I eye him shrewdly, leaning across the desk. "Tell me something, bonewitch. Just what is Buceph planning with all these Rotters wandering about the caves? He explained what he was doing with the Moon Children—I saw it for myself in that facility—but I'm rather confused as to the purpose of the Rotters. You all know the serum doesn't work on BrightStone citizens, so why this constant farce of the Tithes?"

"I don't know," he admits. "I do my job here, I take my serum, and I die a little more each day. As for the Rot...imagine it weaponized. Imagine holding the potential cure. Imagine unleashing it upon an unsuspecting populace and then swooping in as medical saviors...all for a price." He snorts. "Perhaps they only attempt to refine it in BrightStone with the hopes of moving along to conquer the rest of the continent. Who knows?"

Bile stings my tongue at the thought. "It always comes back to money," I spit. "Meridian currency might as well be corpses for all they seem to make so many of them."

"Indeed. Haven't you learned anything? Those in power always make payments in lives." He rubs at his eyes. "Listen, if you have anything else to say, do it now. I need to return to my other patients."

"Do you actually care for them? Or is it more like keeping cows alive long enough for slaughter?" The words fall from my mouth before I can stop them, my bitterness making me cruel.

He stands up from his desk, but before he can say anything, Dafyyd tears into the room. "Please...he's getting worse."

Georges pushes past him, and I follow Dafyyd as the other Moon Child skitters after the bonewitch. Conal is gasping on the bed, his hands struggling as he reaches out to touch something. His good eye is nearly swollen shut, but it tracks Dafyyd intently.

"Do something!" I snap at Georges, as Bran and Penny clatter in from outside and Rosa wails in despair.

"There is nothing else!" Georges roars, shoving me so that I nearly stumble into Gloriana's bed. She's somehow sleeping through all of this, the edges of her lips swollen, but at least she's still breathing.

"There *is* nothing," Georges repeats, running his fingers though his thinning hair. "It's respiratory failure, and I don't have any anything here to stop it. All I can do is end it painlessly."

Bran shoves past me, agony blazing from him as he kneels beside Conal's bed, his hands on the boy's forehead. Conal wheezes something, a guttural plea trapped in his throat like a dying bird.

"Do it," Bran commands Georges. "Now."

Dafyyd lets out a cry, and Bran holds him back as Georges prepares a syringe, tapping the glass vial. "It will be quick," Georges murmurs, taking Conal's arm and injecting him in expert fashion.

Dafyyd struggles in Bran's arms, and the clan leader finally lets him go, watching as he throws himself over Conal, his fingers curling into the other boy's hair, a litany of soft sobs echoing through the room.

I shatter at the sight and turn away, lunging out the door and into the village. The Rotters pause as I dash past them, but if they say anything to me, I cannot hear it and I don't stop. The gate to the tunnels is still unlocked, and I slip through it, tearing into the darkness as though I might somehow outrun the rattle of my own heart.

The gates to the Pits loom in front of me, a scattering of stars straining to be seen through the fog of BrightStone. Despair washes over me as I whistle shrilly into the night, calling for Ghost, or Josephine, or anyone. Anyone at all.

But no one comes.

Among the leaves and frosted grass
A breath of ash, frozen blue.
A body mourned, encased in glass
One moment thus to capture you.

— CHAPTER NINE —

Dafyyd says nothing as we wrap Conal's body in rags. The glow from his hair has faded with his death; whatever biological process drove it to light up fled when he left his body.

The hissing roar of the waterfall overwhelms my thoughts. I know Dafyyd blames me for what happened. Not that he's said as much, but he's wrapped his grief around him so tightly I can hardly breathe when I stand beside him. He's drowning in it.

When the last rag is tied, Dafyyd and Bran pick up Conal's body and gently roll him over the falls. He tumbles into the foaming water and disappears into the darkness below. Penny cracks a lightstick and hands it to Dafyyd. It flares in his hands, and he kisses it once and then drops it, watching as it streaks away like a shooting star into the void.

"In case he needs it where he's going," Rosa explains to me, tear-streaked and weary.

I nod at her. I'd never really thought much of the idea of an afterlife. Hells, I'd never thought much beyond avoiding the Pits. Even when Sparrow died, I'd been too injured to see to her body.

Ghost said he'd had her burned and her ashes scattered upon the bay. My hands creep up my neck, clutching at nothing. Sparrow's necklace was the only thing I'd had left of her, but the High Inquestor had broken it when he sent me into the Pits. It's bitterly hollow knowing I've lost my last connection to her.

And while I hadn't been very close to Conal, he had been a clanmate and a companion. To lose him so easily hurts more than I expect, and a wave of despair rushes over me. I clamp down on the emotion, fighting against the helpless feeling with all the strength I can muster. The frustration and anger flutters deep in my gut, and it presses down on my spine, coiling around my anguish.

Someday, it will escape and expose me and all my vulnerabilities. I know this. But not today, I tell it silently. Not today.

Bran is slumped against the cave wall, watching the water rush past. The rest of us simply wait there, saying nothing. There isn't anything *to* say. Gloriana is the only one who isn't here. Although she survived the night, she's still far too weak to be moved. For now, we've left her in Georges's care, though one of us usually stays with her on principle.

Dafyyd stares at the waterfall and sighs. Rosa takes his hand and leads him away, letting him rest his head upon her shoulder.

Penny watches them and shakes her head. "At least he didn't jump."

"I didn't know they were so attached," I murmur.

"That's because you're too wrapped up in trying to get out of here," Bran observes. "Which is understandable, but..." He pulls out a cigarillo and sucks on the tip before lighting it with one of the myriad lucifers he apparently stashed upon his person. "I know you're new to the whole clan-leader thing, Magpie, but part of the gig actually involves knowing what's going on with your clan. All those little relationships—" he swirls the cigarillo around for emphasis "—they're all interconnected. Like a web."

"Well, at this rate, we're not going to have a clan for me to know anything about," I retort sharply, stung. Perhaps he's right, but that doesn't make it any easier to swallow. "More important is the whole poison issue, aye?" I waggle my fingers at him. "Not dying seems like a slightly higher priority than romantic entanglements."

Penny licks the edge of her broken teeth. "Well we aren't going to be able to trust anything from those crates, that's for sure. Why would Balthazaar even do that? If we hadn't taken it, the Meridians would have, and I doubt they're immune to poison."

"Joseph gave me some potatoes the other day," I remind them.

Bran frowns at me. "Oy, and you're planning on trusting him? We aren't touching anything those shits give us until we have at least a rat or two to taste them first. And that goes for anything we pull out of those crates." He points at me with the cigarillo. "You're in charge of catching a rat, by the way. We can put it in one of those buckets, maybe."

Penny takes the cigarillo from Bran and puffs a smoke ring. "It's too bad we don't have a way to grow our own food down here. Some of those lights from the greenhouse and some seeds, and maybe we'd manage a bit better."

"And maybe if we had wings we could fly out the Arse." Bran winces when she cuffs him lightly, but there's a hint of amusement on his face.

"Wings," I say. "I wonder if Josephine ever got those wings of hers to work. She already had a prototype built when I was Tithed." The leader of the Twisted Tumbler clan is nothing if not resourceful. If anyone could turn Meridian technology into something we could really use, it would be her.

"Believe that when I see it," Bran scoffs. "Is Josephine really still running her dog and pony show beneath the Brass Button Theatre?"

"Aye. She skims off the theatre's power so she can operate her forge." I snap my fingers, suddenly struck by a thought. "What if we did the same?"

Penny lets out a grunt. "What, tap into the theatre?"

"Not that. I'm talking about your idea with the greenhouse lights. We don't have the resources, true, but Georges does." I shrug. "I mean, his infirmary obviously runs off some sort of power, and I think they're completely dependent on the Meridians for their food, except for fish."

"So you're saying we somehow get them lights, and they, what? Share what they grow?" Bran cocks a brow at me. "For someone who has repeatedly insisted we're going to get out of here so quickly, you certainly seem to be planning long-term."

His words make me pause. Am I? Perhaps so.

"It's called being practical," I mutter.

"Call it whatever you like. It still doesn't answer the question of how we'd get lights like that over to the Rotter village." His smile turns sour. "We don't have the numbers to break directly into the greenhouse and get away, and I doubt Joseph will be too keen on the idea of simply handing them over."

"I don't know," I admit, overwhelmed. With everything that's happened over the last few days, my mind is a blur. Questions thicker than flies around a dung heap buzz around my brain, and there are no answers anywhere.

I glance up and realize the two of them aren't really paying attention to me anymore. From the way Penny's leaning on Bran, it's clear enough that I don't need to be here, so I slip away.

I can't blame them, really. If I had a choice between catching rats or a quick shag, I know which one I'd pick. And grief is a funny thing. I suspect if we had any real amount of alcohol, the entire clan would probably be drinking ourselves into a stupor. Failing that, whatever makes you forget is probably good enough. But somehow it merely serves to highlight how terribly lonely we all are down here. Clan or no, our bonds are fragile at best. There is no one here to be my Sparrow. No one here like Ghost.

The thought of the two of them washes over me in a miserable wave, but I shake it off. Wallowing down here is an indulgence, and there is no time for that.

"But I miss them, aye," I whisper fiercely into the darkness as I head toward the den, the words somehow lingering like a fever dream. "I miss them."

The thing about catching rats is that it's relatively easy when you don't care if they're alive or dead. In my case, I've got nothing but bleeding fingers for my troubles, the skin on the top of my right hand a mess of gouges from the rat bites. The fact that I've been trying for almost two days stings a bit, too, but at this point, it's a matter of pride. Rosa already took pity on me and caught two rats the day before. They've been set up in the den in a makeshift cage made of some old wire we found outside that Meridian compost pile. Leavings of the greenhouse, maybe.

So far, neither rodent has died from anything we've fed them— not that anyone's had much of an appetite to take advantage of it. I set the bucket down and blow on the cuts on my hand, though it does little to ease the pain.

"Still at it? I thought you'd have given up by now," Penny says, tapping on the wall to announce her presence. I've set up my traps beside a small pool of water that the rats are known to frequent, but it's a tight squeeze.

"Aye, well." I plunge my hand into the pool, letting the water wash away the blood.

"Come on. Let's go do something more interesting." She holds up a small satchel and a rudimentary paintbrush that I think she actually fashioned out of her own hair and a broken piece of wood from the supply crates.

"Do tell," I drawl, drying my hand on my pants.

"Oh, just a distraction." She smirks, leading me down a series of tunnels until we reach the hidden path to the Meridian settlement and up the switchbacks to where the cave meets the more finished part of the mines. "Don't worry, we're not going any farther. I wanted a nice flat surface, aye?"

I cock a brow at her as we enter the main passage. Its walls are smooth and pale, and Penny opens the satchel and dips her brush into it, pulling out a glittery, goopy mess that she then smears on one side of the passage. "These crushed mushrooms don't last too long, but it's fun to play with."

A snort escapes me, but I already know what she's going to write. *"Meridians are suck-tit bastards,"* I read aloud when she finishes.

She blinks at me in surprise. "When did you learn how to read?"

I tip an imaginary hat at her in a jaunty fashion. "I'll have you know, good madam, that I was taught by the finest bonewitch BrightStone has to offer. In Molly Bell's brothel, no less. Not that I'm particularly fast, mind."

"Heh. All right, then." She shoves the brush at me. "Your turn."

Bemusedly, I dip the brush into the satchel and give it a test smear, watching as the illumination flares up, then settles into its usual blue glow. I chew on my lower lip. My writing skills are fairly poor even at the best of times. In the past I'd always resorted to rude symbols, but today...

Carefully, I trace out nine letters: *I-R-O-N-H-E-A-R-T.*

Penny whistles. "Now that's probably gonna piss some of them off. Good." She takes the brush from me and then stills. "Someone's coming," she hisses.

Farther up the tunnel, I catch the glow of torches heading toward us. We duck into one of the abandoned side rooms, flattening ourselves against the wall behind the doorway.

"It's a Tithe," Penny whispers in my ear. "It must be."

I exhale softly. There hasn't been a Tithe since I arrived, and my heart whirs nervously. The Rotters are one thing—at least they can go to Georges—but there will be another Moon Child. Someone new for the Meridians to harvest.

I reach down and grip my hammer tightly. If it was only Georges and Tanith as it was for my Tithe, we'd have a chance. But if there are guards or Buceph...

I can hear it then, the quiet sobs of the Tithe echoing off the walls like a litany of prayers offered up by the damned. It was eerie when I entered the Pits, and it's as haunting to hear this Tithe now. It's all the worse since I know what actually awaits them.

"They should be here by now." It's Georges, striding past our doorway toward the exit. "I wonder if they're waiting below." Bemusement fills his voice. "What the hell is this? 'Suck-tits'?"

He's seen our graffiti.

"How...distasteful," Tanith murmurs. "What is this IronHeart nonsense all about, really?"

Georges grunts but doesn't elaborate. "Paint's still wet, too. We must have just missed them." He sounds tired, as though even speaking is something laborious. I think of Gloriana, still recovering at the Rotter village. Will he betray us?

"At any rate, make sure the Tithe doesn't see it," Tanith says. "Last thing we need is for them to get all riled up about fairy tales."

I start to move toward the door, a cold rage sliding over me. My skin ices over as my vision narrows. Penny's fingers dig into my arm, and she shakes her head at me. I let her pull me away, and we press our heads against the wall.

Georges grumbles something noncommittal, but whatever else he might have said is drowned out by a sudden wail of despair. The multitude of footsteps along the corridor is thunderous, punctuated by each panting, terrified breath. And above it all is the discordant jangling of the Tithe bells.

The sound makes me want to curl in on myself, but I grip my hammer harder, mind racing for a plan. I'm not about to let another Moon Child enter this nest of vipers.

Penny's face is pensive, but there's a hardness to her expression. She gives me a slight nod. I'm not sure how we're going to do stop this exactly, but our best bet is to wait until everyone is out of the passage and on the switchback ledge.

"Are we all set? I think this fellow here is in need of a bed." Buceph's smooth voice slithers into my ears, all honeyed words and confident lies. My clockwork heart whirs as I rapidly exhale, terror and fury compressing my lungs as I forget everything but the fact that our tormentor is *here*.

I peek around the doorway of this little room, catching a quick glimpse of the Rotters being led outside by Georges, with the bowed, pale head of a Moon Child bringing up the rear.

Tanith lingers in front of the graffiti, and Buceph chuckles. "I see our Magpie has become even bolder."

Tanith frowns. "What makes you so sure it's her?"

"Did you see any of this type of thing before she arrived?" Buceph shakes his head. "No, I'm quite certain she's involved somehow. She keeps it interesting for me, at least." His voice drops into something far crueler. "Hopefully I'll do the same for her."

My brain stops, and this time, when I launch myself from our hiding place, Penny doesn't stop me. My hammer swings wide, the arc aiming for his head, but some noise escapes me. A sigh? A grunt? Whatever it is, the trapped bit of whatever is left of my humanity roars in a rush to set itself loose, to bury my need to hurt the one responsible for so much pain.

Regardless of whether it's a mistake or some ephemeral battle cry of the soul, it's enough to catch his attention. When he ducks, my hammer misses him by mere inches. The wall behind him isn't as lucky, and spiderweb cracks emerge from the center of a fairly impressive dent.

Tanith lets out a cry of panic, darting out of the way as Buceph whirls to face me. "Ah, Miss Magpie. We were just talking about you. Ah, ah," he murmurs as I lift the hammer to take another swing. "None of that now. We wouldn't want anything bad to happen to your fellow Moon Child, hmm?"

I hear the humming crackle of the electric Tithe wand before I see it, practically tasting the burning prickle in the air. The wand slams into me, fiery pain leaving me sprawled on the ground. It is as if I've thrown myself into a wasps' nest, leaving my skin coated in sharp thorns.

My muscles spasm, and my limbs lock into place. For all the stiffness of my body, my brain seems fluid, all thoughts melting away until there is nothing left. But I've been stung by such monstrosities before, and the instant he lets up on the power button, I attempt to roll away, making it about two steps before he's pressed the Tithe wand into my neck.

"That's quite enough of that," he murmurs. "Be a good girl and drop that hammer, won't you?"

When I don't comply quickly enough, he zaps me again, but only for a few seconds. Enough time to get the point across. The hammer drops with a thud. Penny still hasn't made an appearance, but I don't dare look behind me.

Buceph prods me forward, and I step over the hammer and out of the tunnel. Tanith glares at me, irritation flickering over her face, but I ignore her. Georges is already leading the Rotter Tithe away to the tunnel that will take them to his village. If he has any idea what's happening with me and Buceph, he gives no sign.

I almost call out to him but catch myself. Gloriana is still recovering there. If Tanith and the others realize that, they'll take her for sure.

But the Moon Child boy crouched on the ground, holding his head in his hands, is all I really want. He's young. Maybe barely twelve, he's a child who can only recently have discovered what he is. That a clan leader would choose such for a Tithe is beyond revulsion.

"Oy. What clan?" I snap my fingers at him to get his attention, but he doesn't react, even when I whistle a danger trill at him.

Buceph grabs the back of my neck, pressing the Tithe wand into the soft spot at my throat. "Do that again and I'll set this off on your jugular. Your windpipe will seize up, and you'll suffocate right here." He lets out a soft chuff. "He's been drugged anyway—perhaps too much for his size. I doubt he'll know which way is up for at least the next few hours."

I turn so I'm staring at Buceph directly, ignoring the wand as best I can. "What are you going to do with him?"

"Tanith is going to be a dear and lead the poor lad down the switchbacks to our village," he says pleasantly. "And you're my hostage to ensure good behavior on the part of whoever else happens to be lurking about." He lowers his mouth to my ear in an almost seductive croon. "I've heard your group has decreased in size by a member or two. My condolences. I do hope they weren't in too much pain."

My head jerks up at him, and he chuckles. A thousand things unsaid flee from my tongue, words as useless as wet cotton. "And what exactly do you want from me?" I ask finally, honing my voice into something barbed.

He taps my chest and shoves me toward the basket that will take us directly to the cave floor. "I think you know. Come along now. We're taking the easy way down."

Tanith glares at me as Buceph and I approach the basket. If Penny's lurking in the tunnel, I cannot see her past the lantern light. Internally, I'm running through what my options are, but if Penny can manage to get the Moon Child away from Tanith while I distract Buceph, that will be a good enough start.

Sometimes distraction is all I'm good at, so for now I'll play along.

The basket creaks on its rope when we board, and Buceph flips the switch that will allow for our descent. He hasn't eased up on the Tithe wand at all, but I don't really have any intention of going with him to the facility. Surely he must know that.

I let out a bitter laugh as I turn to watch the blue glow of the village. "I'm going to feed you to your own Rotters, you know."

"I can't wait to hear that saucy tongue of yours begging for me to end you once I've got you on the operating table." He nudges my neck again, the hum of the wand vibrating against my skin. "I'm not going to kill you, though. Not for a good, long while."

"You're a right fortune-teller," Penny calls down to us from the top of the ledge. Tanith reaches for her, but Penny shoves the old woman to the ground, vibrating with fury. "Don't move, hag."

"What are you going to do, Moon Child?" Buceph asks mockingly. "You'll never make it down here in time." He presses the wand higher on my neck. "Don't strain your mind too hard. I can outwit anything you half-breeds come up with."

Penny grunts something and pulls my hammer out from behind her. "Aye, but can you fly, you pompous fuck?"

Buceph lets out a startled grunt as she sweeps forward with the hammer, smashing the pulley that holds the basket. It lets out a screaming wail as it bends, partially uprooting from the rock it's fastened to. One of the wires snaps and the basket pitches forward, leaving me free-falling into the darkness.

I scrabble at the cave wall, letting loose a high-pitched cry as my fingers snap against the rock. My feet are marginally more successful, and I come to rest a few lengths below the basket. "The hells, Penny?"

Buceph drops the Tithe wand as he clings to the basket, and it hurtles down, shattering against the cave floor as it strikes. I give him a vicious grin. "What's that about my saucy tongue?"

His expression grows murderous as I find a better foothold and begin my ascent. I give the basket a wide berth until I'm above it. "Oy! Penny! Do you think I can break this thing the rest of the way if I hop up and down a few times?"

"Hurry up," she says. "We'll do it from here. Less chance of you getting bisected by the wire when it snaps, aye?"

"Good point," I concede. Even as dark as it is here, between the mushrooms and growing accustomed to life in the Pits, I find it relatively easy to pick my pathway. Years of rooftop dancing has at least prepared me for this much, and I clamber up the rest of the way without issue.

I shake out my cramping fingers when I reach the top, staring out at the Meridian village. A cluster of people are headed toward us, undoubtedly alarmed by the sudden breaking of the basket. Tanith is already limping down the switchbacks, wailing a torrent of epithets both impossible and improbable.

"You let her go?" I ask Penny, craning my head to see if Buceph is still hanging on to the basket.

"She snuck off when I was watching you climb." Penny grunts, handing me my hammer. "Let's finish this, aye?"

I don't need to be told twice, and I bang the hammer down on what's left of the pulley. Once. Twice…

"Please, Magpie. Don't." Buceph's skin is flashing in something akin to panic, the electrical pulses fluttering like a half-mad moth beating itself against a lantern light. "I'll make sure you get out of here if you let me go. I promise."

"Aye, promises," I mutter, bringing down the hammer again so that an explosion of tiny rocks scatters down the cliff face. "Your promises and the howls of a feral dog—both hurt my ears and are about as useful."

Crack!

With a final blow from my hammer, the pulley snaps.

I watch him fall, committing to memory the way the basket tumbles down the cliff wall with all the grace of a bag stuffed with millstones. The mewling shriek that warbles sweeter than any bird I'd ever heard. The particularly nasty snapping sound of what can only be bones breaking through the flesh that holds them inside a body.

I smirk when he reaches the bottom, only to sigh when I realize he's somehow not quite dead, his legs jutting out at a horrific angle. Short of chucking my hammer down after him, I don't have anything else to finish the job with from up here.

And the hammer is far too valuable.

Penny nudges me sharply, thrusting her chin at the newly Tithed Moon Child. "We've got to move. He needs to rest." Her gaze grows dark as she looks at the growing crowd of Meridian villagers at the base of the cliff, and she pulls her cloak up and over her glowing hair. "And we're targets up here."

I grunt in assent. The Moon Child doesn't react when I wave my hand in front of him. No help for it but to carry him. Somehow the two of us get him on my back, his arms draped over my shoulders. His fingers curl tight around my collarbone, so at least he's cognizant of that much.

"All right, then," I say to Penny. "Let's go."

Raggy Maggy has grown so fine,
She sits at table and pretends to dine,
But throws her fork and bends the tine,
Tips her cup and spills the wine.

— CHAPTER TEN —

A nd you're sure no one followed you here?" Georges eyes me shrewdly from the other side of his gated tunnel. Behind us are only the scattered torches used to show the Rotter Tithe the way to their new home.

"Hells if I know," I snap, shifting the boy so he rests higher on my hips. "But that risk goes up the longer you leave us out here, aye?"

He unlocks the gate to let us in. "You should have let the Meridians take the Moon Child," Georges says. "The Rotters are my domain anyway, so you coming to the village won't change anything. But Buceph won't look too kindly at the additional loss of that one."

"Caring about what Buceph thinks isn't exactly our top priority, if you haven't noticed," Penny retorts as we slip through. "Besides, he's probably dead by now. Or wishing he was." She flaps her hands like wings. "For all they're raised in the sky, Meridians can't fly for shit."

"I...see," Georges says weakly. "Enough. Come or go, but I've things to do." He turns away, gesturing at the Tithe to follow him into the village proper. The other villagers there ignore the wailing newcomers.

Once they're all standing by the infirmary, he gestures at them to remove their masks. Hesitantly, they do so, and he studies each of them in turn, assessing what stage of the Rot they're at. Sometimes he touches a cheek, or peers into an eye, asking each of them their name and what part of BrightStone they are from—all the things a bonewitch ought to do when introduced to new patients.

After determining none of them has any outright injuries, save their exposure to the Rot, he has them escorted to the little dwellings where they could find beds and something to eat. "They'll have questions," he says as the forlorn group slinks off. "They always do." He gives the Moon Child boy a gentle poke. "I see the Inquestors are as thorough as ever when it comes to their sedation. You can leave him in a bed in the infirmary for now. He'll need to sleep some of that off before he'll manage anything."

Penny nods at me. "Watch him for a while. I'm going to go find Bran and let him know what's happened. The others should be aware in case the Meridians decide to retaliate."

"Tit for tat," I agree, wincing under the weight of the boy. I head off to the infirmary when she leaves, wondering what Bran's reaction will be.

Gloriana is actually sweeping Georges's office when we enter, and she brightens when she sees me. With as terribly ill as she was only a few days ago, the fact that she's up and about is a good thing. She almost seems normal, except for the tremors in her hands. That part Georges isn't sure how to heal, so all we can do is wait and see.

"Hired help now, aye?" I drawl at her, unable to keep from teasing.

"It's something to pass the time," she says, flushing. She holds out one hand, watching impassively as it trembles, and then makes a fist, picking up the broom again. "Busywork keeps me from thinking about it."

"I would think so." I lay the Moon Child boy in the closest bed and get him settled. His cheeks are filthy and tearstained, so I snag a clean bandage off the shelf and wet it to gently wipe his face.

Gloriana comes closer. "He's so...young. Poor thing." Her smooth brow wrinkles. "Was he...Tithed?" The sonorous vibrato of her voice grows husky, and the sharp intake of her breath speaks volumes of her fear.

"Yes. Penny and I rescued him from the Meridians. We threw Buceph over the cliff. I don't know if he survived or not, but there's probably going to be trouble later, aye?"

"I see." She lets out a half sob. "Good. I hope he dies. I hope they all die."

"Yeah. Me too." I turn the boy's head slightly to find his clan brand on his neck. "Banshees," I say flatly. "Rory needs a stern talking-to. With a hammer." Rory was the clan leader of the Banshees and the person who had abandoned me and Sparrow to our fates instead of standing up for us as our clan leader should have. He had never been what you might call *protective*. In truth, most of his actions were entirely self-serving. Or perhaps, *self-preserving* might be the better term for it. But I still wouldn't have thought he had it in him to Tithe a child.

Gloriana shakes her head. "I'll watch over him while I'm here. Georges says I should be cleared in another day or so." She wiggles her fingers ruefully. "As much as I can be."

"I hope the lad has some news from topside," I say softly. "My friends... They're still going to get us out of here."

Gloriana's smile becomes a little sad. "I wish I still had hope like you do. Hold on to that, Mags."

"I'll try." I sag onto the bed next to the boy and rest my head in my hands, trying to sort it all out.

I'm interrupted a few minutes later when Georges arrives. He examines the boy briefly and then squares on me. "I feel like I'm running a hostel for wayward Moon Children."

I open my mouth and then close it, shrugging. "It's a fair cop."

"*Mmmph.*" He turns to Gloriana. "Would you mind gathering ten of those folders off the top shelf? Make sure there's a sheet of parchment or two in each one, please."

Gloriana disappears into his office. The sound of shuffling papers rustles past us, and there's something cozy about it. For a moment I'm transported into my old room at Molly Bell's, where Ghost, Lucian, and I would sift through documents as they tried to teach me how to read.

"What an odd creature you are," Georges says wryly. "To be honest, if what you say about Buceph is true, I can't imagine what the fallout will be. For all their outrage and false civility, the Meridians are also terribly stuck in their ways and will do anything to keep whatever comforts they have. With Buceph possibly out of the way, they might not challenge you at all. It's hard to say."

"Somehow, I doubt that. But I'm not letting them have another Moon Child. Ever."

Georges sighs. "Well, then what will you offer me?" He gestures at the boy sleeping on the bed. "You're using resources that belong to my patients. And medicines. Food." His eyes flick to where Gloriana fusses with the folders in his office, and they become gentle.

I frown at him. "So what is it you want? You know we have almost nothing."

"I know." He turns to me. "I require three things. One, if Gloriana will allow it, I'd like her to stay here. I've need of an apprentice, or simply someone who can help. In return, I'll teach her some bonewitchery." He squeezes his hands together. "My time is growing short; my sight is rapidly failing, and I do not want to leave my patients completely helpless."

"You don't think the Meridians would help?" I don't even know why I ask it, and from the way he snorts at me, he doesn't either.

"Look around you, Moon Child. If this is all the assistance they can provide me, what makes you think they'll be any different once I'm gone? The Rot will take the Tithers, whether I'm here or not. I only hope to ease their burdens, which is what I want from *you* when I am gone." He gestures for me to follow him into the office and points to the folders Gloriana set on the desk. "I record everything in these."

My ears perk up. "Record?"

"Like this." He browses one of the shelves and pulls out a folder to hand it to me. "This was Anna's."

I flip it open, unsure of what he's getting at until I see the notes. All her bonewitch marks, the dates when she got them, his treatment plan for her, her family information…and one small section that is labeled Last Wishes. In roughly written script, there are only three words: *To get well.*

The words pierce me, and I sag into the chair. Such a simple thing to want and yet seemingly so impossible. There is no cure for the Rot.

"I know you think me a monster," Georges says, his voice quiet. "And I am, in my own way. But every last person I've had to escort to those pens, I've sat and listened to. Written down whatever it was they wanted me to know. In the off chance that someone reads these records, or finally frees us from this particular hell, at least they will know a bit about the people who were trapped here. In that way, I suppose, they'll live on."

Gloriana cocks her head at them. "What…what do you want us to do with them?"

"Well, for one, keep it up, when I finally succumb to the Rot and can no longer do so myself. But should you get out of here, as I suspect you might, I think it might be a nice gesture to provide the families up in BrightStone with some last memories of their loved ones. It's not much, but… Even if the gates were to be opened, the fact is that all of us in this village are infected. Without regular infusions of Meridian blood, there is no hope for us at all." He shakes his head.

I nod. "All right. We'll make it work. Somehow."

"Very good. As to the other thing..." His voice trails away, and he taps the hammer on my hip. "What you did for Anna... As awful as it may sound, granting some of these people a choice is the last thing I can do for them."

My head snaps up, ice pooling in my belly. "You want me to... kill them?"

"You've already shown you can do it. I know it was a mercy for Anna. It would be a mercy for all of them, to be frank, but even I cannot ask you to do that. And not all of them would take the offer. For some, there is always hope, even until the end." He hesitates. "As to why I do not do it myself...I am a coward, as you so keenly accused me of being, and it hurts too much to destroy what I cannot save."

A bitter laugh escapes me. "So you use a Moon Child to do your dirty work, the same as everyone else. Aye, it's monstrous enough. Sin-eaters are what they call us, aye? Why not this, too?" I hand the folder to him, not sure how I'm supposed to feel.

"It would be a mercy." And then I understand what he's really asking, the question beneath the question. After all, he's been trapped in that dying body far longer than any Rotter should have to be, walking an unsustainable road between the living and the dead.

There's a sad sort of acceptance in his eyes, the distant look that appears when you know your fate. "I've been down here too long and done things I can never undo," he says quietly. "And whether they stemmed from the selfish reasoning of a sick man or the altruistic intentions of a bonewitch, it no longer matters. I...want some peace."

I exchange a look with Gloriana, who is growing paler by the second. "Go lie down," I tell her, my words sounding harsher than

I mean them to. Making these sorts of decisions is not something I want to do.

"When the time comes," Georges rasps, "please..."

I pinch the bridge of my nose, suddenly wanting to get the hells out of here. "Aye, I'll think about it. But I need to clear my head. It's been a long day."

I retreat into the infirmary where Gloriana sits on the Moon Child's bed. The boy is still fast asleep, and I can only hope he has information about Ghost, Josephine, or the world topside. Something hungry kindles to life inside me, a burning, aching need to *know*. I stare at him as though I might pull him from his drug-laden sleep with the sheer force of my will but am rewarded only with a soft snore and a sigh and a small tinge of disappointment.

"I'll let you know when he wakes up," she says, clearly sensing my need to get out of this place.

"All right." I wave her away and make a hasty retreat into the Rotter village proper. I'm more than ready to take refuge in the den and sort through everything that's happened. Penny and Bran are there, neither one of them seeming particularly happy, but I'm in no mood to have a clan meeting or discuss what Georges told me, so it's fine by me.

Bran steps forward, and I can't tell if he's pissed or merely thoughtful. It probably doesn't say much that I can't read his expression very well—or that he's getting better at hiding it from me.

Before he can say anything, one of the Rotters passes by. The plague isn't far along in her, but perhaps there's a hint of it about the tightness of her mouth. Her bearing is proud, her shoulders thrown back in that haughty thrust that screams Upper Tier.

The woman's head cocks to one side when she sees Penny. "Don't I know you?"

A smirk flickers over Penny's face. "Aye. And I know you. Marie, was it?" She glances at me. "An old schoolmate of mine from my earlier days." Her voice becomes sour. "Much earlier."

Marie coughs awkwardly. "Well, this is a rather unfortunate way to meet again. I'd always wondered what happened to you, Penny...when you and your mother... Well, you know how fond I was of you."

"I'm sure you were. Now can it," Penny snaps, turning away and throwing her hands up in dismissal.

Marie stares after, her mouth open. "You have no right...no right to be so rude to me when I'm like this. You have no idea what it's like to have everything taken from you because of the way you look." She goes silent as Penny whirls on her, her expression so ugly and full of self-loathing it takes my breath away.

"Don't I?" Penny's voice is unwavering and cold and brittle as ice on a pond. The Rotter blanches, her pallor gray, but she says nothing. Penny stalks off, her face a thundercloud.

"Brilliantly done," says Bran with a sigh. "And probably our cue to leave."

The two of us follow Penny trotting up the path to the far side of the lake and the gate there. Penny picks it with a hairpin and then locks the gate behind her when we leave.

"Useless thing." She kicks the gate halfheartedly.

"So...an old friend?" I nudge her shoulder, and she snarls at me.

"Nothing so nice. My mother..." She shakes her head and starts again, a stricken expression on her face. "I was Upper Tier, you know. Born there among the gentry of BrightStone. I was trained and educated in all the ways that mattered. My parents were even frequent guests at Lord Balthazaar's estate."

I take this in, realizing how much sense it makes. Penny's intelligence has always seemed so far beyond the reach of normal Moon Children, but it never occurred to me to think of where she'd actually come from.

Bran lets out a snort. "So, what? Your mother dallied with an Inquestor?"

She kicks him in the shin. "My mother swore she was never anything but faithful to my father. She swore it on every oath she could possibly make. Hells, she even went to the Salt Temple for purification to prove her innocence, and the salt priests verified it." Her brow furrows with old hurt.

"But...?" Bran prods.

"Aye, well, maybe she lied. I don't know. Didn't stop my father from leaving us once my change happened. His parents couldn't deal with the scandal of having one of our sort as part of the family. By that point, it wasn't like they could really hide me away."

"How'd you end up with the Banshees?" I asked. "I'd think you'd be closer to Spriggan territory near the Upper Tier." The three Moon Child clans have three distinct territories about the BrightStone quarters, and you usually end up in whichever one is closest to you out of sheer necessity.

Beside me, Bran shifts uncomfortably, but he says nothing. "I should have been," she says finally. "My mother was forced to leave the family home, but her own family wouldn't take her back because of me, either. So she ended up living in the Cheaps—down by the docks."

"Ah," I say, nodding. "And Mad Brianna obviously advised her of what to do with you." My foster mother had an entire army of orphans at her disposal—myself and Sparrow included at one point. And when our hair whitened overnight, declaring our Meridian half-breed heritage, she immediately sold us off to the Banshee clan.

"Aye. I was nothing but a hindrance to her at that point anyway. No one wants to do business with the parent of a Moon Child. I needed a clan." She lets out a humorless chuckle. "I'm not like your friend Ghost, able to slip in and out of territories without fear. So to the Banshees I went. My mother died of consumption a few years later. Her constitution wasn't the best, aye..." Penny sighs.

"Anyway," she says, her voice stiff and awkward. "I'm sorry, you know. That bit with Marie— I just couldn't. The woman was nothing more than a complete bitch to me and my mother when we were forced out of the Upper Tier. I'm sorry she contracted the Rot, I am. But I don't care what happens to her," she says brusquely.

Bran's upper lips curls at Penny. "Fair enough." He pauses, cocking his head toward her. "If it were me, I would have gone to my father's house and given him a piece of my mind. Make him at least acknowledge my existence."

Penny draws herself up in red-hot fury. "Shut the fuck up, you half-wit. That's what I was doing when you—" She tears off into the darkness, the pale outline of her hair bobbing away as she slips farther into one of the side caverns.

"Now I've done it." Bran winces, getting to his feet. "It's my fault anyway." And with that cryptic comment, he slowly follows her until I'm left to wander by myself, my thoughts trailing behind me like leaves in the wind.

The problem with being alone in a cave for too long is that eventually your thoughts stop altogether. I take refuge in one of the wyrmholes and help myself to a cigarillo and a sausage link wrapped in burlap. Since Conal's death, we've all been hesitant as far as eating goes, and that's undoubtedly what Buceph wanted.

It's too easy now to half starve ourselves in the hope that we don't die all the faster. But everything that remains has been at least tested by the rats, and so far, nothing else appears tainted. And so I eat because I must, my thoughts turning over and over.

What if we had killed Buceph? What if we hadn't? Am I wasting time on survival when I should be searching for escape? Or am I starting to somehow accept my fate, content to become another lost Moon Child?

I light the cigarillo and take a long drag, tipping my head to rest against the smooth tunnel wall. And what of Georges's offer? To become an executioner? Acts of mercy I can understand, but how many Rotters would I have to kill? And it would have to be me who did it. Or maybe Bran. But I cannot see subjecting anyone else to such a task. Certainly not Dafyyd, who jumps at shadows now and barely speaks. Or Gloriana. Or Rosa.

I flick the ash of the cigarillo. Perhaps this is the burden of leadership, but I'd give anything to be unfettered upon the rooftops again, with no more to worry about than where my next meal was coming from.

My thoughts drift further away, arcing into visions of Sparrow's and Conal's deaths, the way Anna slipped away as her blood pooled upon the ground—and by my hand. They had been butterflies in a perfect storm, and they had been crushed by it.

So what does that make me?

A magpie, collector of shiny trinkets and clever tricks? A ragamuffin street rat with a clockwork heart and a penchant for finding trouble at the worst possible time? A dragon, perhaps, slumbering within a form of my own making, simply waiting for the right moment to take flight and rain vengeance upon my enemies?

My bitter chuckle grates on my ears. Even Ghost insisted the prophecy of IronHeart was nothing more than a myth. He would know, having been born in Meridion himself, I suppose.

I, however, am no one at all.

Exhaling sharply, I stub out the last of the cigarillo and slide through the tunnel, my hammer banging into my hip. I barely know which direction I'm going, tracking my way in the dark by the bioluminescent slime and my own slowly growing night vision.

Dread slices through me as I approach the Meridian village. Dread of what I will or won't see. Of if I will even be able to find out what happened to Buceph. Of if what Joseph had said about only Buceph knowing how to communicate with the outside world is true. What would that mean? Would we finally be able to gain access to the facility and release my fellow Moon Children?

It's all almost too much, and before I know it, I'm in the hidden passage that leads to the Meridian village. I peek about the entrance to the cavern carefully, but there's no sign of the chaos of earlier today.

The village itself seems terribly subdued. There is little movement coming from the buildings—only a few shadows slipping about here and there. The main hall is lit up, though, an angry conversation humming from it like a discontented beehive.

"Probably discussing how to kill us all," I mumble to myself.

I walk as calmly as I can, keeping my cloak drawn tight about my head and my face pointed down until I reach the greenhouse. The one guard I do pass gives me a quick once-over before he hurries away toward the main hall, clearly distracted.

My breath escapes me with a rush, and while I'm relieved at somehow managing to have slipped through their watch, I don't have much time. Despite my luck, I've been tempting fate a few times too many recently. Sooner or later, it will run out.

The greenhouse isn't locked, so I let myself in. It's empty. That's just as well; I'm not sure Joseph really wants to see me right now anyway. Besides, it's harder to steal things when you have witnesses.

That said, I already know I can't reach the greenhouse's ceiling lights—not without creating too much of a fuss, that is. But I spot a light that's a little closer to the ground, which might do, and then my gaze settles on a midsize one above a shelf of small pots. And not that I know much about plant lights or how they're put together, but I've spent half my life lurking around junkyards collecting scrap, so I sure as hells know how to take something apart.

Doing so without breaking it outright and silently is another matter altogether. There's a garden trowel on the workbench, and I use its blade to undo the screws holding the light in place. Then I grab some nearby shears and snip through the wires that secure it to a beam in the ceiling.

And then I do the same to the wire that powers it, which I wrap carefully around the fixture. It's about four feet long and will undoubtedly be an awful pain to transport, but if I can get it to that hidden passage by the pool, I'll be able to stash it long enough to get help moving it the rest of the way.

I gingerly pick up the fixture and tuck it beneath my arm. Ideally, I'd wrap it in something, but it's too risky to take my cloak off here and I want to be on my way as fast as I can.

"What are you doing?" It's Joseph. Of course.

But is he still a friend? Or has he become an enemy?

"Borrowing somewhat," I say bluntly, readying to drop the fixture or throw it at him if I need to bolt. The older man's eyes brim with disappointment, and a thread of anger needles through me. What right does he have to judge me?

"I see. Go on, then." His breath comes out in a hiss, and it's such an angry sound, vibrating so hard it feels as though the very glass might shatter.

I shrug it off and go to move past him when there's a sudden knock on the door. Turning away from the entrance, I bow my head, my free hand resting on my hammer.

Behind me, I hear Joseph open the door. "Good afternoon, Rinna. What can I do for you?"

I stiffen. Rinna is the guard who originally escorted me and Tanith to the village when I first arrived in the Pits. Will she recognize me?

"Is everything all right?" she asks.

"Yes," Joseph says tiredly. "I was getting some assistance with the removal of one of the lights. It needs repair, and my back isn't what it used to be."

"Ah, I see. We missed you in the second half of the meeting." There's a slight tone of censure in her voice.

"Yes, well. Given the current circumstances, I thought it might be prudent to take stock in what we have and what we'll need." He pauses, an underlying tremor in his voice. "How is he doing?"

She gives Joseph a sympathetic look. "About as good as expected. He'll pull through, but I don't know if he'll ever walk again. It's hard to say. He's been escorted to the holding facility, so he has our best medical resources at hand. Sora will be caring for him in the meantime."

I sneak a peek her. Her expression is blank, but it seems fake, a facade of disinterest to hide the panic. I cannot help a little roll of satisfaction at the thought.

Good.

Let them be afraid, then.

They say their good-byes, and once she's gone, Joseph crosses his arms. I turn to go. "What will you do with it?" he asks.

"It's not for me." I refuse to look away. "It's for Georges."

He blinks, surprised. "Georges?"

"Aye. Seeing as Buceph *poisoned* us, we can't trust the food that comes from you, either. Even if I were inclined to, my clan is not. So I take this to Georges, and maybe he grows somewhat for us." I'd hoped to keep Joseph an ally for a while, but somehow knocking one of his cohorts off a cliff probably didn't fall within range of acceptable. "I'd stay away from the pickled eggs, incidentally."

He pales. "I'm sorry. I didn't realize... Are you sure it was done on purpose?"

"It's what he told me before we knocked him down the cliff. Not that I expect you to believe me," I admit, letting out a regretful chuckle. Meridian or not, I actually liked the man. "But I won't trouble you any further in either case." I gesture to the light fixture. "Let me go with this, and we'll call it even."

"Even," he repeats weakly. "Well, I suppose that changes things. For what it's worth, I'll try to encourage them against hunting you all down."

I give him a tight-lipped smile as he opens the door for me. "You can do what you like, aye? However…what we did today? That was to rescue a Moon Child from the Tithe. From here on out, we'll do the same for every Tithe that comes through." I tap the hammer at my side. "And if we need to go to war with this village to do it, we will."

"You couldn't possibly defeat all of us," he points out, though there's no malice in his tone.

"I don't need to," I retort. "All I have to do is destroy all the lights in here and then we'll see how far you get, aye?"

"That's uncalled for," he mutters, raising a finger at me. "Hold up." He rummages through a few bins beneath the tables, finally retrieving a small black pouch. "Here. Lights won't get you very far if you don't have seeds."

A hot flush rolls over my cheeks, and I can see him biting his lip. "I'm an idiot," I say finally, taking the bag from him.

"Yes," he agrees. "But I think you're trying your best. That has to be worth something, doesn't it?" He gives me a gentle nudge out the door. "Good luck, Magpie."

"My thanks." I doff an imaginary cap at him as I leave.

There are a few more people around now, but apparently, looking like I'm headed somewhere specific is camouflage enough. So I work my way through the village and to the edge of the secret passage, breathing a sigh of relief when I gently place the light fixture in the wyrmhole and myself after it. I don't know how much good one lone light will do, but it's the best I have for now.

"He says his name is Haru," Gloriana says quietly as I study the boy in the bed, his chest rising and falling in a deep sleep. "He wasn't awake very long, but enough to get a name and some basic information. And you were right: he's a Banshee. Though only for about a month." Her face grows grim. "He only found out about his Moon Child heritage a short while ago... And to already be thrown in here?"

"Aye, well, at least he's safe enough now. I'm going to go check on that light. Georges says he'll have it set up in the shed outside the infirmary." It had taken me several hours to get here with the light fixture, gingerly dragging it through the wyrmhole. It arrived a bit more battered than I would have liked, but a quick test showed that it's still at least somewhat functional.

I find the bonewitch setting up a few shelves in the shed. The light is hanging from the ceiling, but instead of the fine wires of the greenhouse, it appears he's made do with twine and some netting. The lights are actually connected to the power now, too, the illumination bathing us in violet.

I pull the pouch Joseph gave me from my pocket and hand it to him. "Lights aren't much good without seeds. Joseph allowed me to take some of these."

Georges brightens. "Did he, now? How unexpected... Perhaps I might persuade him to provide me a few seed potatoes later."

I glance down at the buckets Georges has lined up on the shelves. "Not that you really have dirt, so I'm not sure how this is going to work."

"We don't need dirt. We'll do this hydroponically. We have plenty of water, as you can see." He gestures toward the lake. "Fish live in it, small as they are, so at least it's good for something."

"Hydro-what?" I ask. "Never mind, explain it to me when it's set up and then maybe I'll understand it. All right, then. What next?" I cross my arms, trying to finish the rest of this negotiation as best I can. "We'll expect at least some percentage of whatever you grow. In return for services rendered."

"Indeed. We'll start the hydroponics with these lights and see where that takes us. With any luck, we'll have something to show for it in a few months, though I do believe some of these beans might be ready to harvest earlier than that."

"I suppose that's worth something down here." I rub my neck, my limbs heavy with exhaustion, and I debate the wisdom of asking for a bed in the infirmary. In the end, I decide against it.

Georges fiddles with the placement of one of the buckets. "Have you given any more thought to what I asked before? About...you know."

I take a deep breath. "Can you promise me that it's something they want? Something they asked for?" I swallow, some small part of me screaming that I'm even considering this. But there are no good answers here—only small mercies.

He nods, solemn and serious. "You have my word."

"All right, then," I say softly. "I'll do it."

The elves in brown have gone to town
To buy a pig and an iron bell.
One to eat and one to wear
Around my neck to make me drown.

— CHAPTER ELEVEN —

*S*critch. *Scritch. Scratch.*

I carve another line into the rock wall of the den, mentally trying to count them up. How many days have I been here?

"I don't know why you bother." Penny swings in her hammock. "It's depressing as hells."

"Passes the time. And it helps me plan things." I shrug. "I think I missed a birthday, aye? Might be twenty now."

She's right, though. In the beginning, every day that I scratched a new line was one more day that I dared to hope Ghost and the others would make good on their promise to save me.

I add up the days and sigh. *Eight months, three weeks, and two days.*

I cannot help the wave of despair from washing over me. Still, I etch in the lines, like some sort of affirmation that I exist. It's too easy to let time slip away until all we're doing is surviving.

There have been three other Tithes in that time, and our clan has managed to rescue each Moon Child that's come through the gates, expanding our number to nearly ten. Though to be fair, without Buceph to prod the Meridians into action, they haven't expressed any more interest in us. Tanith didn't even show up to the last Tithe, leaving the whole thing to Georges, who brought the Moon Child along with the Tithers to the Rotter village.

Perhaps that is Joseph's doing.

We know nothing about Buceph these days, save what Georges has told us—that he somehow survived his fall but that his injuries were severe and disfiguring. He never leaves the facility now, not even for the supply crates.

I finish my carving, shove the nail into my pocket, and loop an empty haversack over my shoulder. I tuck a dagger into my rope belt alongside my hammer, my thumb stroking the hilt as I try to ignore the sudden whirring of my heart.

Penny glances up at me, staring at the dagger at my waist, and then looks away. "Another one? How many has it been now?"

"Two today." I climb up the wall to the wyrmhole that will lead me from the den. "And as for how many in total..." I pause, trying to make the sums in my head. "I don't know. Forty-six? Fifty? Georges keeps all the records, but I don't really like trying to remember."

She shudders. "Maybe I'll meet you, then. Just past the waterfall. We can check the traps after. You know I can't stand these... things."

"I know. I'll be waiting," I say, slipping into the darkness. And I do know. The fact that I have taken Georges up on his offer to be his mercy executioner leaves a bad taste in everyone's mouth, but none of the rest of the clan can deny the bargain isn't somewhat advantageous, at least in the form of food we could trust.

As to my end of it... Well, I prefer not to think on it much at all. In some ways, my heart has truly become iron, beating bloodless and cold as the metal inside me, even as I shut away whatever bits of emotion that remain shrieking within, horrified at what I've become, the necessity of what I've had to do. If I dwell on it for too long, I'll go mad.

But instead of wallowing in it, I've turned my attention to survival...and escape.

I've explored as many of the tunnels as I can already. Over the last several months I've crawled over each one I've found, using a piece of charcoal and a spare piece of parchment to map out where I've gone. Not that I don't trust Bran and his exploration abilities, but a record is helpful. Besides, it's easy enough to miss things after living in the same place for so long. Or so I tell myself. It's really the restlessness that drives me to it, the same restlessness that pushes me to climb the walls of the Arse to test and retest its electric edges.

Bran is right about them, of course. Everything I threw at the edges had been blackened, burned beyond recognition, in seconds. Bran and I debated trying to somehow throw water on it, but that would require timing. After all, shorting it out will do nothing for us if the opening itself is covered. I have no doubt it's sealed in some fashion from topside, but even if it isn't, we have no leverage to open it from here. As far as I know, none of us has mutated into being able to walk on ceilings.

Bran smirks at me whenever I return from my wanderings, but there is always a gleam of disappointment there, too. It's as if, somewhere inside him, there is a part that isn't broken, that hopes beyond hope that I will find us a way out.

But I never do.

The water rumbles over the edge of the falls, disappearing into the darkness so far below that even my enhanced vision can't see where it goes. I turn away from it, now facing the two Rotters who are crouched at my feet, and take a seat beside them.

It's Marie this time, as well as an elderly man named Tobias. He hasn't been down here long, but the Rot has run through his body at a surely painful speed. He says he remembers seeing me at the docks with Sparrow long ago, but I have no recollection of him at all.

It doesn't matter anyway.

It's just as well Penny declined to be here. Whether she and Marie were enemies in the past or not, there's still something troubling about watching a piece of your memories literally decay before you.

The two of them sit there, eyes growing milky and blind.

"Are you in pain? Is there anything else you want me to relay to Georges for your families?" I ask. I always confirm, though the answer is nearly always the same.

Marie shakes her head, a chunk of her matted hair sliding into her lap. "No more than usual. In fact, in some ways, it's easing. Maybe the nerves are dying off finally. My fingers always seem so chilled, but it feels distant now. Like I'm seeing myself from far away." She presses her fingers to the curve of her cheeks, and I catch the glitter of tears. "As far as my family goes... I don't know. Tell them I died well, I suppose. They aren't to mourn me for too long; my husband must find another mother for his children." Her face tightens. "Assuming he hasn't already."

I reach out and squeeze her hand. It's cold, bloodless. "All right, then. What about you, Tobias?"

The old man shrugs. "Never hurt no one. No family to speak of. I just...don't want it to be painful," he admits. "I don't expect it will be anything other than a release from whatever horror this is. I don't know what I did to deserve it, but I wouldn't wish this upon anyone."

He sounds stoic enough, here in the darkness, but I can't tell whether it's an act or he really doesn't care at this point. From the reactions of the others we've escorted to the falls, it seems to be a mixed bag. Though by the time we're here, they're usually ready.

Perhaps Georges had pushed Anna out too soon; she'd been terrified. But he had been much less open with the other Rotters about what was really happening to them. It had been more important to preserve whatever illusions they had about finding a cure. At least now they could leave without regrets, knowing they wouldn't be forced to wander the caves as nothing more than shells of their former selves or be put in pens like animals.

They sit quietly after that, their breathing starting to slow into the guttural death rattle that signifies the end of their consciousness. Some of the other Rotters have held hands as they die, but neither of these two even make the attempt. Marie is far too proud for such a thing, I suspect.

Tobias lets out a soft sigh as I remove the small dagger. "I'm sorry," I murmur, but before I can move toward him, he rolls over the edge into the waterfall and disappears into the darkness. It's a momentary relief, if I'm honest, not having to do it myself, and inwardly I thank the old man for this small kindness, even if it wasn't intended.

Marie trembles, turning her milky gaze toward me.

"Tell Penny I'm sorry," she says, lifting her chin. "Now."

An unfortunate truth to carrying out this particular task is that I've gotten rather good at it. The fact that it's an act of mercy doesn't make it any easier, but we give the Rotters the choice, for whatever it's worth.

I make it as quick as I can, the blade slicing clean across her neck. I force myself to watch her die. It's the least I can do, really, to try to remember they were all alive once, with families and hopes and dreams far beyond the reality of what they'd become.

Her blood is thick and sluggish and black, like that of all the Rotters before her, and she slips away with a soft gurgle. When she's gone, I roll her over the falls. There's no place to really bury the dead down here, and fire is out of the question. The smell would be intolerable, and there's not enough fuel to do it anyway.

I clean the blade in the rushing water of the falls, wiping it dry on my trousers before tucking it into my belt. As Georges's executioner, I never know when I'll be called to perform this particular ritual, and I don't want to be caught empty-handed.

Penny is waiting for me in a tunnel just outside the falls. Her face is pensive when she sees me, as though she's weighing some dark question within herself, but in the end, she merely sighs. "Time to check the snares?"

I nod. "Aye. Maybe we'll actually have a rat or two to show for it."

Together, we crawl through the tunnels, adjusting to the total darkness with ease. My eyes now glow the same silver shade as the others' do. The mushrooms are a steady part of my diet, and the shadows no longer hold any secrets for me.

The upper tunnels twist and turn in strange patterns, unlike the ones hewn by the miners. The remains of some ancient river perhaps. Bran still insists they were created by great wyrms many years ago. I think he's full of shit, but what do I know? The museum never had anything about giant creepers in it, and I am more inclined to believe the museum.

Then again, Archivist Chaunders had never been to the Pits herself, so maybe Bran *is* right. If so, I'm grateful the creatures are long gone. The last thing we need is to be swallowed into the guts of some mutant night serpent.

Penny and I emerge into one of the main tunnels, climbing down the wall with quick fingers and quicker feet. The first two traps are empty. The third has caught a rat large enough to eat. The fourth has snared a feral Rotter. The elderly woman has a rope tied tightly around her ankle, her sagging flesh wrinkled and sad.

I hoist the hammer from my belt, hefting its familiar weight, but I don't move forward.

"What are you waiting for?" Penny asks, annoyance thick at the edges of her voice. She wants to get back to the others. Or to Bran, really. Whatever his past, it's clear they've worked out an arrangement—for comfort, if nothing else.

Annoyance heats my cheeks. "Nothing. Just trying to determine if we're making a dent in their numbers at all. If it's even worth trying anymore."

The Rotter in question lunges at me, but she falls to her knees when the rope brings her up short. At one point, I'd tried to look the Rotters over for bonewitch marks like the ones I'd memorized from one of Lucian's books, but most of the time, their skin was so badly damaged it was impossible to tell. Plus, they stink like the hells.

"You want to let them roam free?" Penny retorts.

"No...I don't know. Maybe Bran and I need to try to short out the Arse again." I swing my hammer and the Rotter's head caves in, her body slumping to the ground in a heap. "I would prefer to stop doing...whatever this is..."

"You and me both." Penny watches as I wipe off the blood from my hammer on the Rotter's clothes, her nose wrinkling. "Suppose we ought to see if Georges has anything to trade for this." She hoists up the rat with an air of distain.

Not that we have much to trade these days but at least this way, we could pretend it was even when we swapped for the measly vegetables the Rotters managed to start growing.

The two of us make our way to the Rotter village, silent. I've run out of things to say over the last few months. Nothing changes, and there's no point in discussing the obvious, not even to simply hear myself talk.

Beside me, Penny is humming, and I snort. "Nursery rhyme, is it?"

"One of Sparrow's creations, I think. How did it go?" Penny asks. *"The Pits, the Pits, give you the shits..."*

"Run and hide, you've already died," I finish with a bittersweet chuckle. "Aye, that was the one." The sting of her absence has dulled with time, but I still feel a constant twinge of sadness that she is no longer with me.

There's a subdued feeling in the air when we reach the Rotter village—more so than usual. I don't think on it long, letting Penny go to the makeshift trading post to see what she can get for the rat while I head toward Georges's office.

I walk into the infirmary to find Gloriana wiping down a bed. The astringent odor stings my nose. "He's in his office," she says quietly. "But don't take too long. It's not one of his better days, aye?"

The bonewitch has slowed down considerably over the last few weeks. Our meetings have grown shorter, and we both know his time is running out. Whatever effect the serum had on him seems to be gone. Either whatever the Meridians are providing him with is not the real thing or it's stopped working.

Georges is curled up on the chair behind his desk, but even before he moves to greet me, I can smell it—the sweet scent of decay grown thick like flowers in a dung heap. He shifts his head toward me when he sees me, his breath wheezy, and I freeze.

The death rattle.

"Are you all right?" I force out. It always chills me, this sound. I knew his time was approaching, but I'd been ignoring that fact for quite a while. Georges and I had come to an understanding over the last several months, but to realize he would be leaving us, as well...

"Not dead yet," he grumbles. "Soon enough, for all that." He breaks off into a hacking cough. "Need to do my rounds anyway."

I eye him dubiously. "I don't know if that's such a good idea."

He laughs. "Are you suggesting I stay in bed and rest in the hopes I'll get better? No, don't answer that." A long sigh escapes him. "And you're right. It's nearly time. I hope Gloriana will be able to manage. There's still so much I haven't taught her..."

"Does she know?" Surely, she must. Gloriana isn't blind, and she has the beginnings of actual medical training now.

"Yes. We've discussed it. I don't know how the Meridians will react when I'm...gone. They may not choose to provide her with any additional serums, so that's one of the things we need to sort out. I wonder..."

I pause, then keep my next words quiet. "Did you want an... escort?"

"Yes. I think that might be appropriate. But not to the falls. There's something I want to do first." He struggles to his feet, waving off my proffered arm. His hair sticks out in all directions across the top, but a pile of it suddenly falls out and lands on the desk, leaving his scalp a scaly mess, the skin an angry purple.

"Ah," he says, his voice trembling now. "Perhaps it would be good to skip rounds today," he admits. "I'm not one for good-byes anyway." This time he does take my arm when I hold it out to him.

I try not to recoil from the fog of his breath when it hits me in the face. His teeth are worn down to nubs, the gums swollen when he smiles.

"Let's go see Tanith," he says. "I want to show her something. And I want everyone to come with me."

The journey through the caves to the Meridian village has been without incident so far. Penny is beside me and most of the Rotter village is trailing behind us, with Gloriana bringing up the rear.

"It's like a parade of the damned, aye?" I listen to Georges's labored breathing in front of us. I'm not entirely sure why he's bringing everyone with him, but as a last request it seems reasonable enough. I doubt the Meridians will be happy to see any of us, but I don't care.

Penny taps me on the shoulder as we take the last turn. "Listen."

Shouts echo up at us from farther down the tunnel, and we head toward them. The tunnels snake forward and to the side, and I walk down the one closest to the sound, half expecting to see a herd of Rotters attacking someone, but it's a Moon Child.

Ghost?

My ridiculous heart stutters beneath the binding, and I stifle a cough at the way it vibrates, pressing my hand against my chest. No. Not Ghost. It's Tin Tin, one of the boys from Josephine's clan, the Twisted Tumblers.

Bittersweet disappointment flares deep in my gut, but that's unfair. Tin Tin had been instrumental in helping me spy on Lord Balthazaar and the High Inquestor, and he would undoubtedly have news from BrightStone. But where had he come from? I don't see any Tithers with him.

Then I realize he's partially surrounded by a handful of Meridians: Tanith, Joseph, Rinna, and a few others I don't know.

Penny makes a questioning hum behind me. "Go get the rest of the clan," I hiss at her, pulling my hammer from my belt.

She grunts in affirmation and disappears, leaving me, Georges, and Gloriana to handle the situation for now. Tin Tin has been roughed up, his clothes ripped and tattered. Still, he thrusts out his chest, proud and courageous.

"Where is she?" He's shouting, turning round and round, his pale braids swinging. "Where is Magpie?" My heart aches at his confusion, but it's overridden by the anxious need for information. Questions patter around in my head: Where is Ghost? How do we escape? Are the others at the gates waiting for us?

But my tongue lies rooted in my mouth.

Tin Tin shoves Rinna's arm when she attempts to snag him, easily rolling away from the guard's grasp. "You don't understand. We don't have time for this. If you only knew what was happening topside—"

"What does it matter?" Rinna waves him off with a flick of her hand. "We're beyond those petty squabbles down here, and perfectly happy to be so."

"It has nothing to do with squabbles. BrightStone is in the process of a revolution. They're closing the Pits."

"Don't be ridiculous," Tanith snaps. "Balthazaar has said nothing of the sort. Why would he keep supplying us with food if our project is to be shut down? We're working on a cure for his wife."

Tin Tin frowns. "Lady Lydia died weeks ago."

The stillness that follows Tin Tin's statement is that hollow disbelief that only fills up the full space of the tunnel because it's true.

Georges straightens himself, letting go of my arm, and limps toward the group of Meridians. "Was there a Tithe today I wasn't aware of?" His voice is a raspy shadow of itself, and even Tanith recoils from him.

Tin Tin shrinks back, then darts past the Meridians toward me. "Magpie!" Tin Tin cries, his face a map of fear and relief. "Your eyes...they're glowing."

"Long story. Are you all right?" There's a lump in my throat I can't seem to make go away, a hint of ill-timed laughter threatening to bubble out of me, but I swallow it down. I can't afford to lose my senses.

Before I can say anything else, he thrusts something into my hand. "From Josephine," he whispers.

I know without even looking at it that it's one of the Inquestors' miniature Tithe wands that Ghost stole for Josephine. How Tin Tin had managed to sneak it in here isn't something I want to investigate too closely right now, and I quickly tuck it up my sleeve as discreetly as I can.

I look back at the Meridians. Georges is standing directly in front of Tanith now. "You haven't answered my question," the bonewitch presses. "Where are the Rotters that were Tithed with this Moon Child?"

Joseph coughs apologetically. "The others decided that, given your obvious decline, it might be...easier on you if we took them directly to Buceph's facility. If you haven't noticed, we've been decreasing the overall number of Rotters that we send to you over the last few Tithes. We wanted to lessen your burden... And we've had several come through without Moon Children at all." He glances at me with a little nod, and I can't tell if he's doing it out of solidarity or if it's a secret handshake or what.

"Lessen my burden, eh? I see." Georges bows his head, his shoulders shaking. I can't tell if he's laughing or crying. Maybe both. "Tell me, Tanith...was all this deception by design?" He gestures behind us to where the village Rotters have collected, staring straight ahead with faces carved of ice. "Your entire audience is waiting for your answer. Why not be honest for once? With yourself, if not with us."

His breath shudders out of him, and he stumbles. It won't be long now. "Wait here," I murmur to Tin Tin, gesturing for Gloriana to stand with him. "And don't watch."

I'm burning with the desire to ask questions, but this needs to be done first. And if it's in front of Meridians and the rest of the Rotters, then so be it. There's only one road for them to take. May as well truly let them see what lies at the end of it.

Georges sinks to his knees, legs buckling. Joseph actually leans forward, seemingly to help him, but he is pushed away by one of Tanith's bodyguards. "In denial until the end, then," Georges says. "Were you even trying to cure me at all these last few months? Or did you simply decide to ease my burden by ignoring me, as well?" His regret filters through his words, and when Tanith doesn't respond, he gestures at me. "Magpie. It's time."

I brush past the Meridians with single-minded purpose, the dagger at my hip unsheathed.

Tanith frowns at me. "What are you doing?"

"Undoing, aye? I'm undoing." My hand rests on the top of Georges's shoulder, and I can feel the vibration of every breath that racks him. He reaches up, his fingers resting on mine, and he gives them a squeeze.

He gasps. "Please…"

I close my eyes for a brief moment, trying to gather the courage to do what needs to be done, and then I tip his chin up. His gaze is empty, the cloudiness gleaming an eerie blue, reflecting from the Meridians' blue lantern lights. A whimper escapes him, desperate and small, at odds with his size. It diminishes him, even more than the Rot itself. From the soft sound emerges the knowledge that he is still a person. Not merely the shell of man but simply a mortal wrapped in the cloak of a disease that he'd refused to allow to define him.

And perhaps that's what he hoped to show the other Rotters. Despite all that he'd done and all that had been done to him, by allowing me to kill him here, in front of them, he reveals that he is still more man than monster—and so are they.

His mouth trembles. "It hurts. IronHeart…"

"I'm sorry," I whisper. His suffering drags me from my thoughts, and I swallow down all the grief, all the hopeless fury, tucking it away for later. I try not to think as I swiftly draw the dagger across his throat, his black blood spilling out hot and thick. It's almost half-clotted as it falls, as though his heart stopped pumping long ago.

Maybe it had.

Tanith lets out a soft cry, but I don't spare her another thought as Georges's body slips to the cave floor. She's been spending all this time avoiding the realities of the situation down here; she can avoid this, too.

Despite my warning, Tin Tin has clearly watched me release the bonewitch from the hells he's been trapped within. I'm not sure what it says about what he's seen so far in his short life that he barely seems to register the act, but if he's hiding his emotions he's doing a damned good job of it.

"What news?" I ask him finally, my need for answers overwhelming.

He looks away. "The Tithes... They're stopping the Tithes. I'm, uh...the last one." His voice shakes. "Josephine sent me to tell you...you and Ghost."

The floor drops out from beneath me. I'm wavering on the edge of a cliff, but there's no step forward or back, simply darkness all around. "Me and Ghost? What do you mean?" I suck in a heavy breath. "Ghost isn't here. I've been... We've been waiting all this time—for him, for you, for Josephine to open the gates..."

Hysteria bubbles up from some awful location deep inside my chest as he looks at me, horrified. "But... Ghost was Tithed months ago."

"But how?" I croak. "We've been watching all the recent Tithes come through. We've managed to snag all the Moon Children before this one..." My voice trails away, something like a husky sob making it hard to breathe.

Ghost doesn't even have a clan brand; he isn't supposed to be Tithed. It's possible he could have convinced Josephine to make him a member of the Twisted Tumblers, at least in name, but Lucian would never have agreed to it. And something like that would have been too obvious anyway. Brands take time to heal, let alone getting him on the Tithe roster.

Something breaks inside me. "He came here as a Rotter, didn't he?"

Tin Tin shrugs. "I don't know. But Josephine said... She said we was running out of time, that whatever he was doing down here, he better hurry up and give the signal."

"What signal?" I explode, launching to my feet. "Gods damn them all keeping me in the dark like this. Both ways," I add savagely, whirling around to glare at Joseph. "You said you were taking Rotters to the facility, aye? For how long? How many?"

"Several groups." Joseph holds his hands up to me, trying to calm me down. "But it wasn't done out of malice. We really did think it would be better in the long run…"

"For who?" I snap. How long? How long would Ghost have been with that butcher? My stomach rolls, and I struggle not to vomit. Every instinct I have is screaming at me to find Ghost, even as terror floods my limbs.

What if I'm too late?

A stricken Tanith gestures at me, breaking the tension. "Enough. Magpie. It's time to stop all this foolishness." She cranes her head to get a better look at the Rotters and sighs. "Bring them all with you to our facility, and we'll take care of them."

Her words break me out of my frozen stance, my brain snapping to life. I gesture rudely at her. "Oh aye. I'm going to willingly lead them to the slaughter, only to be dissected in your laboratory to soothe your conscience that Moon Children are nothing but animals?" I point at Tin Tin. "Did you not hear what he said? You think Balthazaar is going to keep giving you supplies if he has no reason to anymore?" I shake my head, then point at the Rotters behind me. "You think they're going to line up and lower their heads onto the chopping block for you, simply because they're ill?"

The Rotters from the village begin to murmur, their anger reverberating off the cave walls in a cacophony of distress. My nostrils flare wide, but Gloriana pulls Tin Tin aside as the Meridians close ranks around Tanith, a hiss of Tithe wands lighting up as they start to retreat.

I let out a shrill whistle. *Gone to shit.*

"Mags!" Bran shouts at me from the wyrmhole at the far end of the cavern.

I grab Tin Tin's hand so he doesn't stumble. "Come on. It's going to be a fight. And an ugly one, at that." One that has been a long time coming, and not one I need to be involved in at this point. The Meridians are on their own.

Besides, there's someone else I need to find.

My clockwork heart vibrates with fierce longing, though I know I need to see Tin Tin to safety first.

I help Tin Tin clamber up the cave wall to the wyrmhole; Gloriana follows after, wiping away the sharp glitter of tears. Bran and Penny are there, along with the others, watching in fascination as the Rotters move toward the Meridians, desperation driving them forward with furious voices and raised fists. They outnumber the Meridians by quite a bit, and even without weapons, they are a force.

It won't be enough in the end. Bodies that are already falling apart and weak from illness have little chance in the long run, but I don't begrudge them their anger and I have no more options. No more plans.

Save one…

"Here. Make sure he gets along okay," I give Tin Tin a gentle shove toward the others as I turn away.

Penny stumbles after me, catching me by the wrist. "Mags, where are you going?"

I pause long enough to extricate myself from her grip, shaking her away as if she's a fly. "The facility," I growl. "It's the only place Ghost could be. If Tin Tin says he came down here as part of a Tithe and we haven't seen him…"

"Or maybe you're jumping to conclusions," Bran points out. "For all we know, he hit his head stumbling around in the dark and was eaten by Rotters."

"I don't give two shits what you think," I tell him bluntly. "I am going to that gods-be-damned facility, and I *will* find him if he's there. You can choose to come or not." My fingers touch the little electric Tithe wand that Tin Tin gave me. My upper lip curls. "And this time, if Buceph's there, I'm going to take him out once and for all."

My words linger between us, and I finally see a spark of that great and terrible fury Bran's been carrying all this time. Maybe it's tempered by Penny's presence, but I know it won't take much to push it into a full-on inferno.

It's not right and I shouldn't do it, as tempting as it is. What I need is Bran with his head on straight. I cannot help but give a mocking chuckle at the thought, knowing that I am nearly about to break apart over the fact that Ghost is here—*has* been here for who knows how long.

The idea that he's possibly been in that facility for months makes me beyond ill. If Buceph has figured out he's a Moon Child—and by now, he surely has—there's no telling what state I'll find my friend in.

Bran sighs. "All right. Go on ahead. We'll meet you there."

I don't think twice on his words, and I launch my way out of the wyrmhole, scraping my knees as I go. The sounds of fighting rend the air around me, rage spun on by years of lies and deception, but I turn on my heel, breathing hard through my nose, just thinking, *Ghost, Ghost, Ghost, Ghost...*

His name beats a cadence in my chest, and it's all I can do to try to think calmly. Panic won't help him, and it certainly won't help me. But still, I have to try.

All around the hangman's tree
I chase you and you chase me.
The noose is loose and away I run,
And yet I trip and come undone.

— CHAPTER TWELVE —

The cavern that houses the facility is like a monstrous gaping maw, its stony teeth jutting from the floor and ceiling. I can hear the grunting wails of the feral Rotters in their pens, and I do my best to shut them out. There is nothing I can do for them at this point, and there are too many to try to kill individually.

Steeling myself, I wrap a shaking hand around my hammer and start my descent to the cave floor, stopping short when I see a few of the free-range Rotters wandering about. They pass by me aimlessly, going up to the main door and staring into the window. It reminds me of the mice in Lucian's experiments, getting rewarded with a pellet if they hit the right button.

In the end, they stagger away, heading farther into the caves. Normally, I would follow them and give them a quick, merciful death, but I have other business to take care of right now. At some other point, I might have approached the facility with more caution, but anger ripples through me, and my fear and desperation lends me more confidence than usual. And so I stride straight to the door and knock.

Which does nothing.

I knock harder, finally pulling out the hammer and smashing it against the little yellow window until it shatters with a satisfying crunch. "Let." *BANG!* "Me." *BANG!* "In!" *BANG!*

"I think that's quite enough, Magpie." Buceph's voice crackles over the speakers. "Did you want something?" His voice is deceptively mild, but there's something mocking in it, too, an easy smugness at the fact that he's inside the building and I am not.

"I'm pretty sure you know the answer to that," I retort, slamming the hammer against the door for good measure. A groan behind me takes me by surprise, but I pivot quickly to see the two feral Rotters from before ambling up the passage toward me.

I attack them without hesitation, swinging my hammer left and right until I make impact. It caves in the skull of one and blows out the knees of the other so that he falls forward, impaling himself on a stalagmite.

"I'm sorry," I murmur as he frantically wiggles his fingers at me. There's something that looks grateful flashing on his face as it collapses. Surely, I'm mistaken, and yet I'm still not quite sure I can comprehend such an emotion.

But then, that's why we offer the Rotters a choice, isn't it?

I shake my head. I've got more important things to worry about. More important *people*, I correct myself, staring at the thick metal door. *Ghost.* He's waiting for me.

My nostrils flare wide as the door creaks open, revealing Buceph, the electric lightning flashing beneath his skin like a storm. He's deeply scarred on the right side, deep ruts in his cheeks that pull his lips into a ragged sneer. A hard knot of tissue ribbons across a discolored eye socket, though beneath the crooked lid, that brilliant blue eye flashes nothing but pure malice.

His head twitches to one side, but it appears involuntary. "I must say, your penchant for killing my subjects is becoming rather vexing, Magpie."

"A pity I couldn't have finished the job with you," I snarl.

"Indeed," he says, the corners of his mouth tugging into a horrifying rictus. "That's what I find so fascinating about you, you know. Coming down here, a helpless Moon Child, and now you've become a monster, so quick to judge that which you don't understand."

"I'm not interested in exchanging philosophies," I say coldly, hefting my hammer in my hand. "Though if you'd like to step closer, I'd be happy to at least you introduce you to the basics of mine."

He snorts. "No doubt. So tell me, Magpie. Just why are you here?"

"You have something that belongs to me." My heart is thumping rapidly, and I'm unsure if he'll call my bluff but not sure I want to give him all the details up front. I have no doubt he'll take advantage of any weakness shown.

"I see." His face flattens. "And what is it you think I have? You know as well as I do that your little group steals from us without shame. I hardly think I owe you anything at this point." He cocks his head. "Ah. Unless you mean *someone*? In that case, yes, I do have a subject or two in the labs, but that isn't really any of your concern, is it?"

I pause, doubt fluttering with every beat of my pulse. "That's for me to decide, isn't it?"

"And what difference does it make, Magpie? What will you give me for a chance to study that heart of yours?" He taps on the door with his fingers, bored. "Will you allow me to start taking what's rightfully mine from the Tithes? Will you stop this ridiculous notion of humanitarianism you've started with Georges, freeing Rotters from their misery, or whatever it is you're doing now, and turning Meridians against their own in a misguided effort to help our pitiable offspring?"

Of course. Of *course* he would have figured out about the lights and the plants and Joseph. The community is too small to hide anything for long. But he doesn't know about Georges's death yet. Nor about the Rotter uprising currently taking place. Did Balthazaar even tell him Lady Lydia had died? For now, I'll keep these things to myself. Anything he doesn't know can be made into a weapon later, and I need every advantage I can get.

I stand up straighter. "And what if I am? Would you prefer it if I simply roll over and let you butcher me like a cow? No. For all your fancy airs, you like it when I challenge you, don't you?"

"It's certainly more interesting with you here, I'll grant you that. As to what I want... I think you know." He gestures at my chest.

"Show me what you have first," I counter. I don't really have any intention of granting him access to my heart, but we both know that if I go in there, the chances of me coming out alive are nearly nonexistent.

But Ghost is in there.

I hope.

Buceph gives a little half bow. "Very well. Though I don't think you're going to like what you find."

A shiver rolls down my spine, and I grip my hammer that much harder.

He shakes his head at me. "Sorry, m'dear, but what the hells makes you think I'll allow you to enter with *that*?"

At least I still have the Tithe wand. And in some ways, that will better my chance of escaping. Because it's going to come down to a fight, no matter what else happens. I steel myself and leave the hammer outside the door. I figure if Bran or the others see it, they'll know I'm inside. I damn near sleep with the hammer as it is. Any time it's not on me is a dead giveaway that something's up.

Buceph watches me with his usual smug amusement, but I stifle the urge to pat my sleeve where the Tithe wand sits, concentrating on the comforting way it brushes against my skin. Instead, I simply follow Buceph's little gesture, emerging into a waiting room directly inside the facility. The fall from the basket clearly had not been kind to him, though I hadn't realized how much so, as reclusive as he'd been. His handsome features and proud bearing of earlier days are long gone. There's a stooped curve to his spine, and his right leg is twisted severely, braced with a series of metal brackets around his knee and upper thigh.

He taps it wryly when he sees me looking. "Admiring your handiwork? The others didn't think I'd ever walk again, you know." He snorts to himself. "That's why I finally kicked Sora out of here. Couldn't stand the pity."

"Pity is the last thing on my mind," I retort, unsurprised by the familiar electric hum of the Tithe wand he pulls out. He doesn't attempt to do anything, just uses it to gesture at me to walk in front of him.

"Fancy that. Same for me. I won't bother with the formalities of decontamination," he says. "I think we both know that it doesn't mean anything anymore."

"Not like I would have done it anyway," I say bluntly. "Let's hurry this along, aye? Some of us have things to do." The words are all empty bravado, but they make me feel better. I simply let Buceph push me along as he limps past the table with the little picture boxes and then down the dark hallway to the laboratories.

It takes everything I have not to run screaming from here, the flickering of the lights and the sickly blood smell hitting my nose like a slap to the face. It's fresh. Not like the stink of Rotters but of something alive.

We pass by the first room with the all the tubes, glass vials, and devices. It doesn't appear much different from when I last passed through these doors. It's perhaps more worn down in places; whoever has been working here hasn't been cleaning up much.

The energy drains out of me when I see at the metallic table in the center of the room. The body on it was human once, but whatever lies there now is nothing more than a poor shadow of it. I'm not entirely sure if it was male or female from this angle. The hair is light brown, but the skin has been flayed so all that's left is the ruinous tangle of muscle and tendons, red and white and brutally mocking.

"Who...?" I cannot bring myself to finish the question, knowing the answer will probably destroy any semblance of sanity I have left.

He shrugs. "Some Rotter boy who came through the Tithe a few months ago. We've been testing new strains of the Rot recently; I needed to check on certain biological markers."

My knees sway slightly, and I reach toward the wall for support, trying to keep myself up as I struggle not to vomit. I take a deep breath. It could be someone else. It's not necessarily Ghost.

"How disappointing. You know, Magpie, for someone so prone to violence, you're remarkably tenderhearted when it comes to your methodology." He leans in close, amused. "Would it help you to know this one was already dead by the time I removed his skin? I mean, he didn't start out that way. I needed something fresher than what the Rotters normally provide, but at least he didn't feel any pain. Well, not *much* pain," he amends with a shrug.

All my fine words to Bran about stopping Buceph topple in an instant, and despair rolls over me in a wave. I must have made a whimpering sound, an ugly sobbing mumble that should have been Ghost's name but instead came out as an agonizing croak.

"So the Magpie has a weakness after all," Buceph murmurs. "Magpie, Magpie...Maggot Pie? I must admit I've been calling you that in my head for quite a while now. Amusing, isn't it? I really rather prefer it."

"You're mad. Completely nutters." I force the words to form. I have to keep the gibbering anguish from taking over. Ghost might be in there, lying on that table. I still couldn't believe he'd been part of a Tithe months ago and I hadn't known. Hadn't been able to do anything. Hadn't done anything at all nearly the entire time I was here.

For a moment, I'm lost in my own self-loathing. I can't hear anything but the roaring of the blood in my ears, and my vision is swept away into a narrow focus. Everything around me is gray and misty, and there is only the banging of my heart as it pounds in my chest, my body shaking with it.

When Sparrow died, I became empty, and here it seems such again, my emotions draining from my feet to trickle away into the hallway and the shadows.

When I stand, it's with the calm acceptance that I'm going to kill Buceph. Tithe Wand or no, there's nothing left for me except to end it here. I'm not even thinking of escape or what might be going on topside. Everything I've hoped and worked for is crumbling before me.

Something inside me protests, knowing it's not as simple as that, that such things never are, but I ignore it, sliding my way toward Buceph like some predatory cat that's suddenly found a wounded mouse.

Something unreadable flashes over his face, and his smile fades away. He nearly backs up a step but catches himself. "What do you think you're doing?"

"Removing you from the equation," I say softly. The Tithe wand hums in my palm as I pull it from my sleeve, flicking the button with my thumb. It crackles, and I shift my grip.

"Where in blazes did you get that?" A note of genuine panic escapes him, but it merely strengthens my need, even as he lifts his own wand.

"You're not the only one with secrets," I snap, launching myself at him. Time seems to slow, as it always does when I'm fighting for my life. It's different from last time when I was so scared and uncertain, wounded and confused and half beside myself. Now, though, I have no such restraint.

He sidesteps me, but that's all right. My feinting jab causes him to turn his head, and I knock the wand out of his hand, striking with my own, the electricity sparking from my palm. He dodges it neatly, kicking my knee so I stagger forward.

He's on me before I can regain my balance, driving me to the floor, a dagger aimed at my chest. I struggle against his greater weight, and the ticking of my heart grows louder. The blade scrapes over my collarbone, pain flooding my senses. No mere nick, but a bone-gouging strike that slides off the panel in my chest, loosening it even further.

I flail, snatching up the Tithe wand from where I dropped it, and twist my legs to kick him the chest. His eyes widen in surprise, but by then, the wand is pressed into neck and I hit the button. He drops to the floor, frozen in shock.

I've been on the receiving end of one of these little brutes. I know the burning sensation of joints locking into place, the white-hot pain that arcs across your skin. And I don't give two shits.

I hit him twice more for good measure, using the momentum to drive my elbow into his throat. He gags, and I straddle him, my fists slamming into his face in an uncontrolled fury.

Somewhere in the recesses of my mind, I'm gibbering, but all I can see is the way the blood blossoms under my knuckles, the way the electric pulses of his skin dance beneath each blow. My hands sting, but I can't seem to stop, even when his nose crunches crookedly.

I'm screaming at him, the words making no sense, and though I know he can't hear me at all, I cannot seem to stop until the fight sags straight out of me, leaving me spent and trembling. He moans, but it's a feeble thing. I hit him again with the Tithe wand and that knocks him unconscious.

Something like laughter escapes me, but it's all wrong, high-pitched and cackling. The echo of Mad Brianna rumbles its way through, and somehow, I'm on the docks of the Cheaps, listening to my foster mother braying her prophecies over the crowds.

My savagery stuns even myself. Though I've killed before, somehow the use of my fist feels far more primal than I'm ready for. But the thought of Ghost lying on the table in the other room hardens any regrets I might have had. And really, what else is there? Do I simply break his neck or slit his throat? Do I bind him up and let Bran have him...Bran, who has suffered so much more at the hands of this monster?

I swallow as something hot runs down my cheek. I brush the tears away and set about finding rope to bind his hands. The medical lab has bandages and tape, and I gag him before knotting his arms behind him, and then doing the same to his ankles for good measure. Even if he retains consciousness, I don't want to hear anything he has to say.

With him safely bound, I steel myself for another look at Ghost's body on the table but find myself turning away.

Not yet, not yet.

If I acknowledge it—that he's truly gone—I'll shatter into a thousand pieces. "I can't," I breathe, though I don't know if I'm saying it to him or myself. I don't want to do it here, surrounded by the stink of death, in the presence of the Meridian butcher who'd done this to us.

I swallow away my cowardice because there's something else I need to do first. I vowed to free the Moon Children trapped in the laboratory from their misery, and I am here now and intend to see it through.

The curtain dividing the room comes down easily enough, crumpling with a soft sigh. I leave it where it falls, freezing when I see the tubes, still mounted on the walls like the glass coffins of the damned. It was horrific seeing them before, but last time I'd been here, I'd been wounded and trying to escape, not to mention make sense of what was to become my new reality.

Now I am surrounded by the ghosts of my people, floating upon a sea of bones. There are small boxes beside each tube, beeping at various intervals, numbers and gauges and who knows what.

I count only ten tubes with anyone in them. Were there more before? I don't remember. Or maybe it's that I don't want to remember. Most of them have their eyes shut, but the girl I'd tried to free before is staring straight out at me. Nothing particularly intelligent flickers behind that stark gaze, but it pierces me down to my toes all the same.

If there is anything I can tell her to ease her suffering, the words will not form. I'm numb, drifting through the room like a spirit made of grief, but there's an emptiness inside me, a hollow wind scraping through me. I shiver and push the button on her tube so that the top slides away, exposing her to the air. She doesn't twitch, but a soft moan burbles out of her mouth, her tongue poking between parched lips. I don't know how long she'll live for; Buceph only said exposure would kill them.

The box beside her tube starts chirping in a panicked fashion, so I turn it off, pressing the buttons one by one until the beeping stops, and then she sighs and goes still.

Something drips onto my hand, and I realize I'm crying, my tears somehow taking form despite my best efforts. I open the rest of the tubes and turn off their breathing apparatuses, too. Do I know any of them? I think I must—old clanmates Tithed long before me—but it hardly bears thinking about, so I focus on the task at hand until I'm done.

And then all is silent. The quiet closes around me, compressing my lungs until I can barely breathe. I glance around at those pale, broken bodies as I exhale a final apology for everything I couldn't do, for everything they had endured.

I flee, but it is only to further enter the nightmare this place has become.

I'm shaking as I approach the room where Ghost's body is sprawled on the table. The smell hits me instantly, fresh and sweet with the scent of decay on the edges, and I gag, trying not to vomit as I force myself to take another breath. It's shallow and rapid and trembling as memories of the last time I saw him wash over me: seeing him struggle in his brother's arms as he tried to get to me in front of the gates of the Pits. My eyes blur against it, because he'd come here to find me like he promised...and I failed him.

I stare at the ruins of his face, trying to picture it as it had been, with the sharp jawline and the strong nose, the pierced ears, the gentle curve of his mouth when he smiled...

The brilliant blue of his eyes pierces me with an anguish I cannot begin to describe. "I'm sorry," I mumble, the words cutting off into thick sobs. "I'm so, so sorry."

I need to do something with his body, but I'm so numb inside I hardly know where to begin. I reach for a towel to cover him, to give him at least that dignity.

And stop.

Blue eyes?

Ghost doesn't have blue eyes. His are dark, like mine are. Or like mine used to be, anyway, before the mushrooms silvered them up. I swallow hard. If this isn't Ghost on the table, then who is it? And where is Ghost?

An ugly cry of relief escapes me as my stomach sinks. What if he's already gone? I place the towel on the dead man's face, for all it's worth. Which I know isn't much. Setting things to rights, I keep the Tithe wand fisted in my hand and take off down the hall and into Buceph's office. It's the same as it's always been, although a little messier, but there are no other signs of anyone else. My upper lip curls, and I grab Buceph by the hair and lift his head.

"Where is he?" I demand, knowing it's useless. He's unconscious, after all. And I doubt he's going to give me any answers at this point even if he weren't. But if I can't get him to talk, I'm sure Bran will.

There's a certain satisfaction in dragging Buceph by his feet down the hall, but it's short-lived. He's large and heavy, and the flood of terror and anger that had given me such furious strength before has subsided, leaving me all the more drained and bewildered. My knuckles ache something fierce, and my clockwork heart is hitching in a terrible fashion, my shirt sticking to the open wound on my collarbone, making it burn.

When I exit the facility, I'm confronted by Bran and the rest of our clan, standing in a semicircle around the front door. A mishmash of homemade weapons hangs at their sides, but Bran waves them away as I emerge, his eyes widening when he sees Buceph.

"You've trussed him like a turkey," he says with a hint of admiration.

Penny cranes her neck behind me. "Where's Ghost?"

"Not there. There's a body...but it's not him. I'd already knocked Buceph out before I could get any more information out of him." I exhale sharply. "And the trapped Moon Children are...free now. As best as they can be, at least."

Bran turns to head for the door, but I catch his arm and shake my head, hoping to spare him that. "Don't," I whisper. "You don't need to see it."

Penny crosses her arms, glancing over at me. "This is getting out of hand. Most of the Rotters from the village didn't make it. The entire cave looks like a charnel house."

Bran kicks away a loose stone. "All that effort you put in, and for what? I told you it was a waste. They all died anyway."

The emptiness inside me gives way beneath his words. I'm so tired of trying and failing.

I drop Buceph's legs and grab my hammer from where I left it beside the door. "Well, we can drag this sorry sack of shit to Tanith and demand she tell us where Ghost is. Trade Buceph for him if we have to."

Bran shakes his head. "Oh no. If you think I'm going to simply hand over the one who murdered my sister and our clanmates for a fairy tale, you're sorely mistaken, Magpie."

"Until I know where Ghost is, we need him. *I* need him. It's the only bargaining chip we have. If they're stopping the Tithes, we're going to be trapped down here forever."

Beside us, the Rotters in the pen next to the facility are growing restless. Can they understand us? Bran and I have talked about how to put them all out of their misery, but we have never had any weapons large enough to do so.

Buceph groans and blinks his one good eye at us, jerking away as he realizes where he is and who we are. A huffing protest grunts past the towel I gagged him with, but I'm not in any hurry to remove it.

"So now what?" Bran's face is unreadable, flat and emotionless. Finally confronted with vengeance, he doesn't seem sure where to start. "I mean, we could toss him in the pen over there, aye? Poetic justice and all to be torn apart by the very creatures he's created?"

Bran says nothing, but Buceph starts choking, a wheezy sound that shakes his entire body. And then I realize he's laughing.

Bran removes the gag. "What's so funny?"

"You are. All of you." Buceph shifts his jaw, ignoring the bloody spit pooling in the corners of his mouth. "You have a remarkably strong fist considering how scrawny you are, Magpie. I think you've loosened a few teeth."

"Good," I say. "What did you do with the Rotters from the last few Tithes? We know they were sent to you directly."

"Well I certainly wasn't interested in feeding them. Like I told you, we've been trying some new serum strains." He manages to roll himself over so he's kneeling. "But most of them I dumped straight into that pen. Might as well be with their own kind."

My head jerks toward the pen, my stomach falling out of me. "What?"

"I kept a few around—like the one you saw inside." He lets out a wheezy laugh. "And one turned out to not be a Rotter at all. I'm assuming he's the one you want. Do you know who he is? Who he *really* is?"

"Where is he?" I snap. "I didn't find him inside."

Buceph continues to chuckle to himself. "Have you tried listening?"

"What are you talking about?" Everyone pauses then, silence punctuated by soft breathing and the rustling moans of the Rotters shifting about in the pen. Seconds tick by, my heart rattling in my chest...and then I hear it. A panicked moan, half pleading, coming from the Rotter pen. The hair on the back of my neck rises as I whirl toward the pen.

"It's electrified, idiot!" Bran shouts, but I'm already turning for the side of the cave, my fingers digging into the rock. The pen wires are anchored directly into the wall, spanning the length from the facility corner to the far end of the cave. The wires must be at least twenty feet high.

My feet slip out from under me slightly, but I force myself to stay calm. Wherever he is in here, he's safe enough to make noise. It does none of us any good if I fall into the staggering clusters of Rotters, too.

When I'm high enough that I can finally see into the pen, I note that only one side is fenced in; the rest of it is surrounded by the cave walls. So there's that much. But getting in is only part of it; I suspect getting out is going to be tougher.

"How do we turn the fence off?" I shout at Bran. "I'm going to need you all to create a distraction."

Whatever Bran says is lost in the shuffle. I see him kick Buceph in the balls, but I don't even remotely care because there, in the center of the pen, is a platform, just high enough to be out of the Rotters' reach. There are no bars surrounding it, but a single chain hangs from the ceiling. And attached to it, is Ghost.

An ugly sound escapes me, reverberating through the pen loudly enough that even the Rotters pause their incessant groaning. Ghost kneels on the platform, blindfolded and gagged with his hands bound behind him, the chain keeping his arms up at what must be a terribly painful angle.

There's blood on his face and on the tattered shreds of his clothes. I lock eyes with Bran, thrusting my chin at Buceph's prone form. "Kill him." My voice shakes with fury.

Bran lets out a cry of triumph, even as Buceph shouts at him. There's a scuffle, and then I can't tell what's going on as a cluster of Moon Children surround him.

I have more important things to worry about anyway. "Ghost! I'm coming! Don't move!" I eye the platform and realize I can't make the jump to it, but I can reach the chain. It's attached at an angle so that the part connected to the ceiling is closer to where I'm hanging.

"This might hurt, aye? I'm sorry," I call out to him, unsure if he's heard me until he jerks his head in an obvious nod.

"Don't fall," I mutter to myself, sucking in a deep breath, my body tensing.

I make the leap, my trembling legs bunching beneath me as I arc through the air, barely snagging the chain. I slip, catching myself as Ghost lets out a grunt, his arms jerking up against my sudden weight.

"Almost there." I carefully lower myself down the chain onto the narrow platform. It's barely large enough to fit Ghost as it is, and I'm forced to straddle him so we both can fit.

I rip off his blindfold, and for that one instant, an electric pulse shoots through me, an eternity of things to be said and shared and hidden and lost. And then his gaze becomes confused as he takes in my glowing hair and the eyes that light up the darkness.

"It's a long story," I mumble. "Hold on." I carefully slice through the gag with my dagger. He lets out a long, coughing gasp as he sucks in one breath after another.

"Mags?" His voice is husky and raw from screaming. Unbidden, my hand finds the top of his head, and I draw my fingers through the ragged cut of his hair, my heart breaking as he winces away from my touch.

"Wait until I get you out," I say gently. "We have to free your hands first." The bindings around his wrists are merely rope, hooked around the chain. My dagger makes short work of the rope, and the chain swings away from the platform. He hisses softly when he lowers his arms, wiggling his fingers to try to get the blood flowing again.

I crane my neck to see above the crowding Rotters. They are split between watching us and paying attention to the goings on beyond the fence. I whistle a question at the other Moon Children, but except for an exasperated shriek from Penny, I can't get an answer out of them.

I eye the chain, now hanging a fair distance away from the platform, wondering if I might not somehow swing across the space, but that does nothing to help Ghost, and judging by the way his arms are shaking, he's in no position to follow me. And I will not leave him here.

But my clan needs my help, too.

"Fuck. I don't suppose you know how to turn this fence off?" I ask Ghost offhandedly.

He shakes his head but then sags. "Box," he mumbles. "Far wall. I think it's wired from there. Inside the facility is the switch, but if you can break the box…"

"Got it. You stay here."

He lets out a humorless chuckle. "No choice, there."

I suck in a deep breath, not entirely sure what the hells I'm doing. Releasing the Rotters into the caves is probably the worst thing I can imagine. Shutting the fence off will be pandemonium.

I pull the hammer from my belt and whistle a warning to my clan: 'Ware the Rotters.

Then I launch myself into the writhing mass of bodies, my hammer swinging to and fro as I duck past gaping mouths and reaching fingers. It's only a matter of seconds before all the Rotters turn their attention to me, and I twist away, crying out as one of them manages to bite a chunk of skin from my arm, its mouth leaving a wet smear over my bicep. It's not deep, though the pain nearly makes me falter.

In a desperate move, I slide to the ground, shoving my way through the decaying legs. At least there are no teeth down this way, and I emerge from the tide of bodies on the far side of the cave, the metal box blinking like a beacon in a hazy green light.

Without hesitation, I slam the hammer down on it, ignoring the sparks that shoot from the top. The humming of the fence fades away and then goes dead, and I scrabble up the cave wall to pull myself to safety.

"Fence is off," I shout to the other Moon Children. "Break it down!"

Abruptly, the Rotters turn from me, pressing against the fence, and I realize they truly must be able to understand me. The wires groan beneath the sudden strain, an almost musical sound echoing as they break, whip sharp. The Rotters explode forward like a wave, and I hear the wet sounds of destruction as my clan circles up, weapons swinging as they cut a swath toward the platform.

I clamber down the wall to join them, ignoring the splatter of gore as it hits me in the face, the putrid stink of it awful. But the

Rotters aren't really paying much attention to us, just moving forward to surge into the tunnels.

I cannot see Buceph at all. Though if he's dead by Bran's hand or the Rotters', it makes no difference. In the end, we're left standing in a stinking pile of bodily fluids and corpses.

"Well, that's done it," Bran says tiredly. "I'm not sure how you always manage to take things from bad to shitty, Mags, but here we are."

I snort. "One does one's best."

Ghost is still on the platform, his expression feral. He stumbles as he attempts to climb down, and Bran helps pull him to his feet. The fact that he's here feels like a fever dream, and I'm not quite ready let myself believe it's real.

Tin Tin has no such compunction and barrels past me into Ghost's arms. "Oy! You're alive!"

"Am I?" Ghost lets out a shaky breath.

"For the moment, it seems we all are," Penny says, staring off into the distance. "Perhaps we ought to move to the den. I'd rather not be caught if the Rotters come back this way."

"Tin Tin said somewhat about Josephine and a signal?" I ask Ghost hurriedly, trying to somehow rationalize my thoughts into something approximating coherent.

Ghost blinks at me as though he's seeing me for the first time. I reach up to touch my hair. The magpie streak dyed in my hair is long gone, and what's left of my shorn tresses has grown out just past my ears. Without a proper mirror, I've no idea what I really look like, but surely, I must be the same as I used to be, shagginess and all.

Or mayhap it's the fact that I glow in the dark. Or the brittle thinness of my form. I feel transparent, the very blood beating through my veins exposed.

"Mags?" he breathes.

My eyes wander over him, seeking purchase in his very existence. His own hair is longer, and there's something about him that makes him seem older than his twenty-two years, a hollowness that wasn't there before. A jagged scar runs down the side of his neck, Lucian's bonewitch mark beside it, but the rest of him seems unchanged. A sudden, aching despair overwhelms me.

"You're bleeding," he says suddenly, and the sting of my wounds ripples over my skin. I press my hand over the loose plate on my chest and realize I need to rebind it, the slice on my collarbone raw and burning, the bite on my arm clotting.

"My...L-Lucian," Ghost stutters. "If we can find our way to the front gates, he'll get it open. He and Josephine," he adds. "I don't know how much time we have."

Hope beats fiercely in my breast, tempered with caution. "They've figured out how to do it?"

"Yes, but it will be a very small window of opportunity." He turns to Tin Tin. "I'm assuming Josephine sent you?"

Tin Tin nods, but Bran brusquely cuts him off, his clan leader instincts apparently kicking into high gear. I should be annoyed by it, but one look at the others' exhausted and blood-spattered faces and I know he's right.

"Discussions later. Let's head upward." Bran surveys all of us and sighs. "There should be additional supplies left in the Rotter village. Once we're patched up and fed, we can determine the next course of action." He cocks a brow at Ghost. "This signal of yours, perhaps. I don't know about you, but I'd like to get the hells out of here, aye?"

Relief flickers over Ghost's face. "Aye."

Lucy Locket had a pocket
Filled with needles and thread.
Sharp and fine and silvery twine
To capture all within her bed.

— CHAPTER THIRTEEN —

Bran and Penny take point climbing to the tunnels, and the rest follow. I wave the others on, slowing my pace for Ghost. "Go on," I say to Bran. "We'll catch up. I need to rest for a few. I'll take him to one of the wyrmholes—the one near the Arse. Penny, can you bring us a few of the extra lightsticks and somewhat to eat?"

Bran grunts at the plan. "Understood. Each of us will take what supplies we can and meet you at the Arse." He spares a look for Ghost. "Let's hope our friend here can help us out."

The others disappear into the shadows, leaving Ghost and me alone.

"Can you see anything at all?" I already know what the answer is, but I have to fill in the awkward silence somehow. My tone is casual, professional, the words a shield I thrust between us and hide my emotions behind.

And yet, my heart whirs, vibrating in frightening fashion because Ghost is *here.*

He's here, I crow inwardly. I still hold myself back, so afraid I'll blink and none of this would have happened at all.

"Not really," he admits. "Your eyes are glowing. And your hair. Everything else is black."

"Well, follow my hair, then." I glance at him, and all I see is sorrow and regret. There's nothing I can say to fix it.

He hesitates and then follows along behind me. To his credit, he makes no noise other than the occasional grunt when he bumps his head. I move as slowly as I dare, but he's still surprisingly nimble and has little trouble moving up the cave wall.

My own curiosity burns quietly, but I've learned patience since being in the Pits and I want to get to a safe place before explanations are made.

We reach the tunnel and hunch to get through the narrow entrance. "Watch your head. There's not much room."

"You don't say," he mutters. "Quite the leader you've become, I see."

"More like co-leader. Bran handles the logistics; I do the spy bits. And Penny points out everything we might do wrong. Not that there's many of us to lead if you haven't noticed. The NightSinger Moon Child clan is woefully tiny these days." I smile sadly, remembering his late-night lamentations upon the rooftops so long ago. "And you're welcome to consider yourself a member, if you like."

"After all this time of being clanless, it finally takes falling into a cave full of Rotters to gain acceptance." He sighs, but that wry humor of his twists into an answering ache in my chest.

"How did you manage to get down here?" Guilt makes me ask it, if only to clear my conscience. If only I'd known sooner... But what's the point in worrying about that now? He's here. And alive.

That seems the most unbelievable thing of all.

He pulls up his sleeve to show off a new tattoo. Curled and winding down his wrist is a Tithe mark, meant to keep track of the newly diseased. "Snuck in with the infected as part of the Tithe. Then I made the mistake of telling Buceph I was from Meridion. And once he discovered I was looking for you, well, he decided I made better bait than test subject. That's what he was getting ready to do, incidentally. It was only dumb luck that you showed up before he could finalize his trap."

I wince. "He wants my heart. He...recognized it was d'Arc's work. He probably planned on trading you for a chance to open it. I don't know. We would have tried to free you if we'd known you were..." My voice trails away, the words stuck in my throat. "I'm sorry."

"Don't be. You weren't expecting me to be here." He exhales sharply.

We travel in silence after that.

I tap his shoulder when we reach the wyrmhole. It's not much more than a depression on the left side, but we can both manage to sit in it, albeit in cramped fashion. And there we crouch, staring at each other, the quiet and the dark pressing in around us.

"You left me here," I whisper, finally, unable to control the way my voice cracks into something husky.

It's not fair to accuse him. I know this. But it all comes rushing out in a whimper of despair at the bitter realization that I am so close to losing who I am, who I was. The fear of being trapped in these dark warrens as the air is slowly sucked from my lungs doesn't help, either. Fear of being buried beneath tons of rock, dust coating my throat until all is fire. Of being forced to kill innocent people again and again and again, until I'm so wrapped in shadows I don't think I'll ever see the light again.

"You said you'd come for me," I croak. "You said you'd get me out."

"I'm...I'm sorry, Mags." Regret dances over his face. "I tried. You have no idea how hard I tried to find a way to free you. We all did. Lucian. Josephine. Even Molly attempted it while she still had the power to do so. I'm not sure why. Maybe she felt guilty."

"Oy, that's rich, seeing as she sold me out to Balthazaar. And you, too."

He shrugs. "Lucian got rip-roaring drunk one night and went over to the Conundrum and had it out with her. I'm not sure she knows how to be loyal to anyone but herself, to be honest."

"Words mean nothing here," I remind him, snorting in wry disbelief. "I can't eat them or wear them or use them to protect myself. None of us can. Intentions mean even less."

"I'm sorry. That's not even remotely enough, but it's all I've got to say." He wipes at his wet, gleaming eyes. "I never meant for this to happen." His voice is a ragged tremor, reminding me that he's had his own trials to deal with. I just never figured his worry for me might be one of them.

His hand slips into mine. I cannot seem to stop trembling, and there's a part of me that hates that I can't. But the rest of me hovers on the edge of breaking down entirely because I haven't been abandoned after all.

When his head tips forward to rest against mine, I don't retreat. "You didn't forget me," I whisper, fresh tears burning down my cheeks.

"I didn't, Mags. I couldn't." He presses a kiss upon my cheek, pulling me tightly against him. "I was going mad knowing you were down here. That we'd sent you here…" He swallows, clearing his throat. "So much has changed up there. Lucian has gone underground with Josephine. They've managed to double the weaponry output of the Twisted Tumblers, and the Chancellor has rallied the citizens to her side. This is the last Tithe the Inquestors plan on allowing. After this…they're going to round up anyone infected and kill them."

"But that doesn't make any sense. The Rot… Ghost, your brother was right. The Inquestors have been spreading the Rot. The Pits, the Tithes—all of it. It's all a lie. That facility was housing the remains of so many Moon Children. They were using us to find the key to immortality." A chill runs through me. "Unless they've somehow found it? Buceph could communicate with the High

Inquestor through the facility, so there's no way of knowing what the true story is."

I grunt. "Perhaps we were a bit quick to kill him. Though I don't think we could trust anything he said. Considering he actually wanted me to kill the High Inquestor, I can't figure out what sort of game he was playing."

"I don't know. Something happened after Lady Lydia died. Maybe a falling out with Balthazaar and the High Inquestor. Whatever came of it, it's a right mess, Mags. And I can see no way out of it." He pulls away. "That's why we need to get out of here—you and the other Moon Children. I've seen the Rotters here and the Meridians, but I haven't lived it. Not like your clan has. If we can bring everything to light..."

"You make it sound like I had a choice," I say bitterly. "Don't you think if I'd found a way out of here I'd have left by now? And here I thought you'd come to find me simply because you promised to."

He rewards me with a humorless laugh. "After almost nine months, Lucian insisted you would be dead by now. Coming down here to find you was a suicide mission, but I had to try." He cups my chin so I'm forced to look at him. "I did, didn't I?"

I choke out an affirmative, unable to deny the truth of his words.

And then his mouth is on mine, but all I can taste is blood and dust and ashes. His fingers quiver as we cling together, his hand sliding over my neck. I can't seem to stop shivering, but he pulls me closer, both of us shaking with the sad knowledge that we are somehow still alive in this place.

"I can't believe Lucian actually let you come down here," I say. "After ensuring your safety at every turn, why would he allow it now?"

Ghost coughs. "Ah, well, technically he doesn't know I'm here. I mean, he probably does *now*, but I did this on my own."

I pull away from him. "But you said that you snuck in as part of a Tithe."

"And I did. Actually, I snuck into the Salt Temple and stole a robe and a mask, and then I left Lucian and Josephine a note."

I pinch the bridge of my nose. "Gods, you are so stupid. If you knew half of what it's been like down here, the things I've had to do..."

"Fighting like an old married couple already. Shall I leave you two to it, then?" Penny snorts, tossing a handful of lightsticks at our feet. "I told Bran you were sweet on someone else, even if there was no hope for it."

To his credit, Ghost says nothing, but he picks up one of the lightsticks, cracking it so it flares to life. Penny and I both wince at the brightness of it. He cups his hand over the edge in apology, blocking the golden gleam.

I slump against the rock. "You've only said a few words since you've been here, and I'm already starting to believe there's a chance we'll get out of here alive. How do you do it?"

"It's hard to think it, but you can trust me, Mags. And Lucian. Trust may be a bag of cats, but I—"

An ominous rumble cuts off his words, sets the tunnel to shaking. We scramble to our feet and crouch to keep our balance. The floor shakes again, faint explosions rocking the tunnels in the distance. I can feel the weight of the caves pressing down upon us. We've had small cave-ins here and there before, but nothing like this. And the thought of a slow death via starvation or suffocation makes my throat close. "What is it?" I manage.

Ghost's nostrils flare wide. "We have to go. Right now." He grabs my hand. "Come on!"

"But the others!" Penny shouts, moving through the tunnel toward the Moon Child den. "Bran! We have to warn them."

I'm already partway down the cave wall when the reverberation begins again. It starts as a soft tremor, a thin vibration beneath my fingers. It arches into my wrists and through my bones. The very rock has come alive, threatening to buck me off like a wild horse.

I curl my toes into a deep crevice as I cling to the rock face for a moment. If I fall from this height, I won't have to worry about anything ever again.

"Mags!" Ghost is right behind me, the lightstick dangling from his belt. I quickly turn from it, continuing my descent.

"Damn these missing fingers," Penny swears, bringing up the rear. "I can barely climb a wall that *isn't* moving, let alone whatever bullshit this is."

And then we're in the main tunnel on the ground. I reach to take Ghost's hand. Whatever happens, I don't want to be alone again.

Does that make me a coward?

Haven't you always been?

The floor shifts again, and a low cry escapes me. An explosive shockwave erupts behind us, followed by a surge of stale air. I peer into the dark tunnel only to realize it has collapsed almost entirely.

"Move," Ghost barks, breaking me out of my stupor.

I run. I'm being pelted by bits of rock and rubble. But there's no slowing down. We pass by the Moon Child den but it's empty. No one answers my whistles, and in the end, we can only continue on. We meet one Rotter along the way, but my hammer makes quick work of her. I leave her twitching on the tunnel floor, the remains of her brains oozing.

Is the air growing thin? Sweat burns my face and I force myself to calm. Panic will get me killed quicker than anything else.

"Mags! Penny! What's going on?" Bran's voice cuts through my thoughts.

Relief floods me when I see him and the other Moon Children above us in another one of the wyrm tunnels. "Don't know yet."

Ghost nudges me. "We need to go."

"Come on. We can take the shortcut to the Meridian village and see what's happening." Bran waves us up, and Ghost and I follow behind Penny as quickly as we dare. It's tight going with all of us up there, but we've developed a system for moving through smaller spaces. Stealth has always been of utmost importance, even up here, so we signal with quiet taps on the rock or a gentle stroke of the ankle in front of us.

We pause when the tunnel stops, leaving us at a drop-off of nearly thirty feet. A rumble sounds from below, the tromping of feet and slide of rotting flesh scraping against itself.

Rotters. A great herd of them shambling together with a mindless focus.

"Hells above and below," Ghost breathes from just behind me. "Where are they going?"

I scan the nightmarish parade, but the ground heaves again, a wailing moan exploding as the ceiling falls. I lose Penny in the rain of rocks as Ghost snatches me from the entrance of the tunnel. A chunk of debris cracks me in the temple, pain blinding me for a few precious seconds.

Ghost thrusts something over my face. A piece of his shirt? "Don't breathe in the air." He coughs and tucks his chin into his collar in an attempt to cover his nose.

Penny's high-pitched shriek shatters the silence, and I struggle toward the sound, tipping precariously at the edge of the tunnel.

She's fallen.

I let out a guttural cry. How can she, who has taught me so much, be brought down so easily? Ghost wraps his arms around me, holding me against him.

"No! Let me go!" But Ghost doesn't loosen his grip, even when I bite him on the arm, my body racked with this final indignity. My vision blurs through my tears, leaving everything in a hazy cloud of ash and burning salt.

Her body is ravaged by the ever-hungry Rotters, her bones picked clean in minutes.

"I'll kill you, you bastard. I'll kill you!" I don't even know who I'm saying it to. The Rotters. Buceph. Georges. Any of them. All of them.

"Mags, stay with me." Ghost's voice is a hushed litany of calm. Practical. His usual sardonic wit is subdued, but there's a faint hint of irony, even so.

I shove my grief away like I always do. It's a wonder my body hasn't exploded into a pile of bloody anger, my skin popping open to reveal that I'm nothing more than a core of hatred and bones.

Bran lets out a sobbing moan, but it's too late; there are too many of them for us to fight. "Oh, gods dammit all, Penny."

When the last of the Rotters have fled into the darkness, Bran gives me a stricken look of such utter heartbreak that I can barely catch my breath. His face flattens, and I know he's pushing it down, compressing his grief into whatever space he has left for such things.

Behind him I suspect the other Moon Children are doing the same. Except for a few low wails, there is no other sign, save a single mournful trill whistling through the caverns.

It's not enough, but there is no time.

I reach over to squeeze Bran's shoulder. "Let's go."

Without another word, he slides down the side of the shaft. I scan the tunnel below us, my brain deliberately blind to the pile of white hair on the ground. When no more Rotters appear, we follow suit, running in the opposite direction.

We don't speak, but the silence this time is hollow. Somewhere along the way, Ghost's hand slips into mine, and I cling to it.

"What in the hells..." Gloriana stares at the mangled, twisted metal that once was the entrance to the Meridian village.

"It's like they broke right on through." Ghost drags one of the large pieces aside so we can move around it. "Where are they going?"

Bran's mouth is turned down so sharply you could cut yourself on it, and he's got my electric pig-sticker clutched in his hand, but

I'm not sure he's even aware of it. "Only one way to find out," he says abruptly, striding past the tattered gate.

The rest of us trail behind as he leads the way. There's a faint moaning sound from the bend up ahead, and I immediately grab my hammer and take a place next to Bran, pushing Ghost behind me. The other Moon Children fan out a little wider. I'm not sure how armed they are, if at all, but we've been doing this particular formation for several months now and it's become a habit.

As we enter the cavern of the Meridian village, we're hit with the scent of burning flesh and the distinctly acrid odor of an explosive. A collective gasp echoes through the tunnel.

"It's like an abattoir," Ghost breathes, his hand on my shoulder.

"A what now?" I roll the unfamiliar word on my tongue. Inwardly, I'm still trying to process what I'm seeing—which is the complete and utter destruction of the entire village.

"Slaughterhouse," Bran says curtly, pressing forward.

And I suppose that makes sense. Most of the domed houses have caved in on themselves, and the dining hall appears to have imploded from the inside, the roof collapsed, the beams of wood splintered like the broken rib cage of a whale. The greenhouse is nothing more than broken glass and twisted metal. But worst of all are the blackish stains misting the ground and the fallen walls of the buildings. Blood, I realize, spattering everything as far as I can see.

"What happened?" I peer into the wreckage as though I might divine the answers if I stare at it long enough. "I mean, there's clearly been an explosion, but—"

Bran thrusts his chin toward the far end of the ruined village. The feral Rotters we released from the pen have surrounded the one building that still stands, and atop the roof is a cluster of Meridians.

I can't make out who they are from this distance, but there are too many Rotters to risk getting any closer.

"Can we make for the main gates?" Ghost frowns, squinting. "If Lucian's there, he'll get us out."

"If we can manage to sneak around them," Gloriana murmurs. "Perhaps if they stay distracted..."

The fact that we'll be using the Meridians for such a thing is not lost on me, but I'm not particularly brokenhearted about it. The loss of Joseph sets my plans askew as far as the rebellion topside goes, but given the current situation, it's a loss I'm willing to overlook.

Bran only shakes his head, and the group of us sprint toward the switchbacks, sticking as close to the shadows as we can. My breath comes in short gasps, each footfall a mocking cadence as it echoes past me.

We're nearly to the switchbacks when I hear it—the awful screeching of metal grinding above us...

"That's it!" Ghost shouts, heedless of the way the feral Rotters turn their heads toward us. "That's Josephine and the others! They're forcing the gates open!"

"Oy, now you've done it," Bran snaps as the Rotters lurch toward us.

Ghost scoops the shorter Tin Tin onto his back. "Go, go!"

Our clan hurries along behind me, and I look over my shoulder to see Bran taking the rear with his Tithe wand. When we reach the top of the cliff, I pause to catch my breath, biting off a shriek when I see the sheer number of Rotters stampeding behind us, their ragged bodies and puppet limbs somehow moving in rhythm like an undead murmuration. It might even be considered beautiful were it not for the fact that the entirety of the Rotter horde is tearing up the switchbacks with a speed I've never seen before.

"Move it," Bran snaps, herding us forward.

My heart rattles, the panel vibrating, and I punch it once, trying to get it into place as we round the last turn and head into the mines. Another shrieking wail rockets past us and what sounds like—

"Gunfire," Ghost shouts.

It's too far away to be a threat, but if we're not careful we're going to be sandwiched in between whoever is firing and a wall of flesh-eating Rotters. We're not going to make it. I'd forgotten about the drop-off coming up. I'd barely managed to climb up it by myself, and with Haru, Tin Tin, and even Gloriana, who never quite regained her strength, we aren't going to be able to get all of us up and over it before the Rotters catch up.

"Dammit." I turn into one of the side rooms, motioning at the others to follow me.

"What the hell are you doing, Mags?" Bran snarls at me as we flatten against the wall.

"We'd never make it past the drop-off. Not with them behind us," I murmur. "And I don't want to be trapped there."

He grunts. "No one make a move, aye?"

A minute later the first of the Rotters shambles by us. None of them seem to notice, so hell-bent are they to move in their chosen direction. They crash through the mines like a wave of fetid flesh upon a sea of bones.

"Gods," Ghost chokes, earning him a sharp nudge from Bran.

It's unbearable, this many of them crowded into such a small space. They leave more than a stench behind, making the tunnels slick with their corpse juices. But they continue ignoring us, their attention rapt on whatever is going on at the gates.

I'm paralyzed between despair and disgust, every bit of survival instinct screaming at me to flee. They could turn on us any second and rip us to pieces. And there are no upper tunnels here. No warrens to retreat to.

But the song of freedom hums so much louder.

So we hold our place, waiting for them to pass. Maybe they'll hit the wall and return the way they came. I tremble at the thought of what will become of me topside. I'll be blind.

"Blind but free, Mags. Surely that's worth the price of your vision." I cannot help but whisper it as regret at possibly never seeing the sun again fills me.

But in the end, it doesn't matter. I crane my head over the others, straining to hear past the shambling mutters of the damned. Voices. Shouts. The crack of bullets skitters through the halls as the Rotters surge forward. How are they getting over the wall? Unless they're climbing over each other?

Then the floor lurches beneath us, the walls seeming to shimmy beneath my palm.

"Another explosion? It feels different than the last one." I frown, taking a firmer grip on my hammer as the floor shakes again, followed by a sudden rush of heat from the gates washing through the corridors like a wave of fire.

"We have to go!" Ghost shouts, tugging on me. "They're collapsing the tunnels!"

Bran and I look at each other, and he makes a little gesture with his head toward the hall. The steady stream of Rotters has died down a little—enough to give us a chance if we take it now. Not that we have any choice.

The next explosion sets the cave ceiling to rattling, and the collapsing brickwork smacks me in the head. I suck in a deep breath and squeeze Ghost's hand. "Give us a few seconds head start and then follow, aye?"

Before Ghost can even reply, Bran launches himself into the hallway with me right behind him. It becomes almost rote, the two of us falling into a rhythm—Bran with his Tithe wand shocking the Rotters into falling to the ground and me finishing the job with my hammer.

With such a narrow field, there is no time for mistakes and no space in which to correct any. By the end of it, I'm sliding through a river of gore, my feet coated with black blood, the very air nearly misting with the stench of putrescent guts and diseased flesh.

I gag on my own bile and then vomit twice. Somehow Bran manages to keep his stomach, but his skin has taken on a greenish cast by the time we emerge from the mines.

The last of the Rotters are either still in the tunnel heading toward the entrance or dead inside it. The rest of my clan clatters behind us. I pause long enough to take a quick head count, and then we gallop down the switchbacks as another explosion rocks the mine. Salt dust explodes over us like burning snow, the entirety of the mine passage collapsing.

Rosa lets out a scream as she stumbles, and Dafyyd snatches her up before she falls down the cliffside. Panic floods my limbs, as I realize we're about to be buried alive. Whatever I'd thought before, I'd always known that at least the gates to the Pits were there. Mentally, it was a chance for escape, a window to the outside world; there was still some sense of normalcy left.

But now?

A high-pitched cackle pierces my ears, and then I realize I'm the one making the noise. Only it's not really laughter as much as sobs with the final crushing knowledge that we are going to die.

Tin Tin lets out a little whimper, and I swallow my despair. Going half-insane now isn't going to help my clan. I wipe at my eyes, ignoring the crusting black blood on my sleeves. I'm sure my hair is coated, too, but for right now, I push it all down, down, down, and away.

My heart seems to be whirring out of rhythm, and I poke it again, trying to make it stop and failing utterly.

"What now?" Gloriana asks hoarsely, her face covered with salt dust.

Bran shakes his head, glaring at Ghost. "I don't know. Take stock of our supplies maybe? If there's even a point. What the hells was all that about? I thought you said they were opening the gates. That they were going to let us out!"

Ghost flinches. "They must have met with some resistance. The Inquestors were... Well, I suppose it doesn't matter now, does it?" He smiles wryly, but it's an ugly, self-mocking thing. "Maybe it's better to focus on us for now."

We limp our way toward what's left of the Meridian village. If nothing else, we might scavenge something that will help us survive a little longer. Not to mention the three Meridians still sitting atop the last standing building.

One of them waves his arms at us as we approach, and I squint. It's Joseph, blood-streaked and weary. I stagger in their direction, watching as the older man partially slides off the roof and snags a rope that's been fastened to the top somehow. He carefully lowers himself down.

His eyes seem to have lost focus as they roam over our little clan but narrow when he sees Ghost. I glance up at the rooftop, at the other two Meridians left: Tanith and Rinna. The guard is shimmying down the rope, Tanith clinging to her shoulders until they reach the ground. Rinna is stoic, as always, but Tanith gapes at the carnage around her.

For a moment, it seems as if none of us can move, and we stand there together, bleeding and filthy and despairing. My breath is somehow the loudest thing I've ever heard, thunderous in each ragged exhalation.

Finally, Bran digs through his pocket and pulls out a cigarillo, lighting it in the smoldering flames of one of the nearby buildings. He puffs on it for a minute. "So what the hells just happened?"

His voice is calm, but I've lived with him long enough now to know he's about to break. I can see his almost feral wildness combined with an unwavering hatred as he studies at the three surviving Meridians.

Tanith lets out a soft sob, sinking to her knees. "There was an... an accident."

"Oh no," I snarl, pointing at the warped gate at the far end of the village. "That's not an accident. None of *this* is an accident." I gesture all around us.

Joseph limps forward. "The...Rotters. The ones that came with Georges. We...we stopped most of them, but a few got away. Next thing we knew there was an entire army of them on the other side of the north entrance. We were going to try to drive them off, but a few of Georges's group let them in." His voice starts to tremble at the end of the sentence.

"Can't say I blame them for that." Rosa clutches Dafyyd's hand as though she's never going to let it go.

Ghost points at the remnants of the village. "But surely the Rotters didn't have explosives?"

Joseph shakes his head. "Those were leftovers from when this place was built." His gaze darts to Rinna, loathing dripping from his words. "Someone decided it was the only way to stop the Rotters, never mind that after nearly twenty years the blasting caps were perhaps unstable."

Tanith lets out a bitter laugh. "I don't think *unstable* begins to cover it." A huge cut on her cheek has started bleeding, and she wipes her shirt across it.

Beside me, Gloriana shifts, her fingers flexing as if she wants to examine the wound, but Bran shakes his head at her, following it with a short whistle. *Not now...*

"So what do we do?" I run my fingers through my hair and push it off my forehead. I immediately regret it as my hand comes back coated in a congealed black sludge.

"Well, clearly, we can't exit through the mines." Tanith straightens up. "We should go to the facility. Surely Buceph can help us communicate with Balthazaar and let him know we need a rescue."

Bran sneers at her. "He's dead."

Rinna's head snaps toward him. "You're lying. He can't be..."

Bran says nothing, simply staring at her dully until she turns away.

"Maybe we should go there anyway," Dafyyd says. He swallows hard. "I mean, there's bound to be some supplies there, right?"

"Fair enough." Bran gestures for the rest of the clan to follow him. "We'll start there. Maybe that communication device still works." He starts off, and I let him lead, deciding to bring up the rear.

I heft my hammer in my hand and turn to the three Meridians, weary of talking to them. "Follow if you want. Or don't. It's up to you."

With that, I follow my clan through the village, giving Ghost a gentle nudge from behind as I catch up to him. He takes my hand, and I squeeze his hard, both of us pretending not to notice how much we're both shaking. Together, we head back the way we came, leaving the Meridians to trail in our wake.

Splish. Splish. Splash.

By the time we reach the facility, it's become terribly clear that something isn't quite right, namely because we are now in ankle-deep in water that's more like a cold sludge. It stinks of putrefaction.

Up ahead, Bran cranes his head toward the facility. "Damn. The explosions must have knocked the river off course. Be a bit like drowning in your own coffin, aye?"

"Then we're doomed. I cannot swim, and if the tunnels fill…" I suck in a gulp of air. My heart is a bird taking flight in my throat. A clean death was all I'd ever been able to hope for. But to suffocate, my lungs filling with putrid death water… It was unbearable.

"Courage, Mags." Ghost lowers his mouth to my ear. "I'll not let you drown."

I cannot allow myself to hope it will work, but I nod at him anyway.

Joseph sloshes up behind us and tries the facility door, tugging on it several times. It doesn't budge, even when he tries the keypad on the side. "Maybe if the water shorts out the electricity?" he suggests doubtfully.

"Not sure I want to stick around that long," I mutter. "Besides, if the electricity dies, how will we send a message topside?"

"We need to get to the Arse," Gloriana says. "Maybe it will be open."

"It's got more room, at least," Bran says, laughing sharply. "But that's about all it has going for it. Still, it's probably our best chance."

The thought of escape spurs us on. Tanith trails us like a confused quail, Rinna resting one arm around her shoulder with Joseph at their heels, his head hanging low, as though he's making peace with whatever's coming.

I wonder dimly if Rotters can swim. I imagine the cavern of the Arse with us floating atop it, the bodies of the dead teeming below, forcing their way through the current with a sluggish grace. But there's no time to worry about that now.

By the time we reach the Arse, we're wading through a chest-high flood. I find myself walking on tiptoe in an effort to keep the panel to my heart dry. Loose as it is, I have no idea how it will react to being submerged, and I have no desire to find out.

Tanith has slowed down considerably, and when we reach the cavern, Bran and I immediately begin to scale the walls. Floating or not, it can't hurt to get as high as possible in the meantime. He points above us. "If we can get to the wyrmholes that should buy us a little time."

I'm about to suggest the same to Ghost, but a sudden flare of light at the entrance of the Arse captures our attention as the ceiling cover slides away.

"'Ware below!" a smooth voice booms down at us, a rich baritone I'd recognize anywhere.

Balthazaar.

"Help us," Tanith cries, staring up at the hole. "Please, they've caved in the tunnels."

"Yes, I know all about it. Prospero's Park is currently being overrun by the plague-ridden masses. However, I have closed my gates to them, so I fail to see why I need to do anything."

"Then why come here at all?" I counter, trying to keep the panic out of my words. "Why not collapse the hole and be done with it?"

"You're not helping, Mags," Ghost snaps.

"Oh my word." The spotlight is shone down upon us. I have to turn away, my mouth twisting into a grimace. "Is that you, Magpie? To think that all this time you've been lingering down there. Pity. I was rather hoping you died."

I snarl, but I don't need Ghost's warning hand on my arm to tell me to shut my pie hole. He's our only ticket out of here, so I have to play nice. And I *can* play nice. I think.

Some distant part of me awakens, reminds me to bow my head and simper, but I find I cannot do it. I want to glare at him, but the light makes it impossible.

He takes my wincing for something else and chuckles, obviously pleased. "So again, I ask you. What have any of you to offer me?"

I hesitate, the water nearly lapping at my panel now, but Tanith steps forward. Somehow she keeps her eyes open despite the light, though I can see how much it pains her. "A cure."

"You've had far too long to produce such a thing and with no success," Balthazaar retorts coldly. "My wife lies buried beneath the ground, no thanks to you." He cocks his head. "Where's that charlatan Buceph?"

"Gone. There are only a few of us left. Surely you can see your way to mercy? We can work for you directly, start over." She pauses, something sly rippling over her face. "You know the High

Inquestor has kept us down here against our will. Should you free us, we will do everything in our power to ensure that a cure is found—one that would be solely in your possession."

I glare at her. The wheedling of her words grates on my ears. Balthazaar pauses for a great length of time. I cannot imagine what he needs to decide, but we need to start climbing the walls.

"All right," he says finally. "But only you."

She shakes her head. "No. All of us or none of us. Think about how much that information is worth to you and then decide if you can be without it. Besides, blood from myself and my Meridian cohorts carries the original serum, which I will need if I'm going to replicate it. A cure without knowledge of using it is worthless." Her gaze sweeps past me. "And I'll require these Moon Children as additional subjects, of course. My work will be faster if we don't have to hunt down new ones. They're the key to it all."

"Tanith!" Joseph rebukes her sharply, even as an exhausted anger settles in the pit of my stomach. But I'm almost too tired to care.

Almost.

"I can't wait to bash your head in," I tell her pleasantly, ignoring the way Rinna thrusts herself between us.

"This is all fascinating," Ghost says dryly, ensnaring my wrist with his fingers and giving me a warning squeeze, "but maybe we could discuss it someplace higher? Where we're less likely to drown, perhaps?"

"Very well," Balthazaar says. "But you will tell me everything about this process." A rope slithers down the opening, the woven temptation dangling in the center of our group.

"You first." He points to Tanith, but she shakes her head.

"Not until the others are taken up. Go on, boy." She gestures to Bran.

Bran's nostrils flare wide the instant his fingers brush the rope. He sucks in a breath and begins to climb.

Envy and exultation burn in my breast. And fear. Always fear. To have freedom so close and offered by so fickle a master is a dangerous game. Bran's arms, toughened from scaling the cave walls, lend themselves to the task with an easy grace.

I shift closer to the rope to hold it steady and start to flail in panic, even as Ghost takes my shoulder. "Easy, Mags. You're next."

"What about you?" Panic lances through me. I've just found him again; I don't want to be separated already.

"I can swim. I'll be right behind you." He gives the elderly Tanith a tight nod. "I'll make sure you're tied into it."

A vicious protest sits on my tongue, but the call to freedom refuses to loosen it. Always the practical one, Ghost knows we need Tanith as part of our evidence for the rebellion, and it's his nature to go about it in altruistic fashion.

Bran is at the top. He's snatched by several pairs of hands, Balthazaar impatiently gesturing at us to move along.

Ghost steadies the rope. "I'll be right here if you should fall." He kisses me, and though there's something terribly desperate in it, it's enough to steady me.

I tug on my hammer out of habit, reassured by its weight on my hip. The rope is slick beneath my fingers, but I loop it over one foot and start my ascent. I have to shut my eyes against the glare of the lights above. But if I look down, I'll never move. So I climb in darkness, my pulse beating a cadence I find hard to match. It's too fast and too shrill, hitching quickly. And still there's a part of me that refuses to believe I might actually escape this place after so long.

When I finally reach the top, Balthazaar's men reach for me, yanking me out of the Arse and onto the grass. I let out a whoop of hysterical laughter. "Like being born, aye? From the wet womb of the Earth."

Bran doesn't do more than grunt. Sparrow would have understood what I meant.

My breath rasps in my lungs, cool and crisp. The taste of a late-summer night, even through the filter of my own stink, is sweet beyond measure. Not even the fact that I can't see dims this joy.

One by one, the rest of the Moon Children climb up. All except for Ghost, that is. Tin Tin hugs me with relief when he finally makes it. Rinna and Joseph follow after that, and finally, Tanith.

"Not so hard, you clumsy idiots." I cover my face when I hear Tanith's grumbling, catching the barest shadow of her silhouette. The ropes creak beneath her weight. "Turn those lights out."

Balthazaar snorts. "We'll do nothing of the sort, my good lady. Remember, this little rescue is an inconvenience to me." He pauses. "If you prefer the darkness, you're welcome to stay down there. Speaking of which, I think that's quite enough Moon Children for one day."

"No! You cannot leave Ghost behind! You promised!" I lurch up, my vision blurred in all the light.

"He's been a guest of my establishment before. I find myself rather loath to invite him in a second time. Bad business, you understand." A foot nudges me until I'm nearly rolling into the Arse. "But then I feel the same way about you."

"Mags!" Ghost shouts from below.

Something slithers past me. The rope.

"No!" I clutch at it, my hands coming up empty.

Pain burrows into my side, my bones crying out in protest. Balthazaar has kicked me, but I bite down on the anger, swallowing the sob that threatens to emerge. When I give him no satisfaction, he lets out a grunt. "Take the old one to my estate and set her up in one of the…guest rooms."

"Yes, sir." One of his men steps forward, and I dig my fingers into the lip of the Arse, bracing myself for an assault of one sort or another. "And the others?"

"Tie them up and put them in the wine cellar. I'll figure out what to do with them later." His bitter laugh echoes past me. "And close up this fucking thing. If any of this mess is traced to me, we'll have more than Rotters to deal with."

I twist to my side, panic suffusing my limbs past the blindness. I can't leave Ghost behind. Not again. Not like this.

"Ghost, they're shutting you in! They're shutting you—" This time the kick takes me across the chin, my jaw clacking shut hard enough to nearly take off my tongue. Blood floods my mouth, and I can do little more than purse my lips and whistle a pathetic mockery of the old signs.

Danger. Betrayal.

Beside me, Bran makes an answering noise I can barely hear, and my breath hitches into a sob as I gather myself to my knees. My ears ring with the impact, a dizzy whirling that leaves me completely disoriented. I draw in thick breaths of air, ragged and burning, into lungs that have known little but the warm damp of the underground for so very long.

A grinding of mental nearby indicates the shutting of the hole, but I roll toward it even so.

"Stop her!" One of Balthazaar's men tries to snatch me back from the edge, but it's already too late. I fall through the swiftly shutting Arse into the darkness below.

Falada speaks and truth follows,
But far sweeter are the lies.
Easy to taste and easy to swallow
And just as filling as the flies.

— CHAPTER FOURTEEN —

Water flushes through my lungs and fills my nose, coating my insides with a putrid chill of filth and soot and shit.

Inside my chest something sputters, stops, sputters again. A deep ache clamps down hard against my heart.

"Mags! Mags! Stop fighting me…"

Ghost's muffled voice cuts through my waterlogged ears, and somehow I manage to stop flailing. I cough up the damp foulness, finally cognizant of how he's got one arm around my waist and another gripping the cave wall.

"My panel!" I gasp. "It's loose. Have to keep it above water…" I twist, pressing my hand over the panel as hard as I can.

He adjusts his grip to ensure I'm floating faceup. "Stupid, stupid woman. Why did you do that?" Terror and anger make for a heady mix, but it's tempered by how tightly he squeezes me.

"Why did you come down here to find me?" I counter, avoiding any of the other reasons pattering through my thoughts. *Because I'm blind topside. Because you're blind down here once your lightstick fades. Because you'll die if I'm not here. Because you came back for me.*

Because I don't want to be alone anymore.

A shuddering breath escapes me as I swallow down another wave of terror at the feel of the slick water surrounding me. Above us, the sliding of the metal grate echoes harshly as the opening to the Arse closes, and we're left entombed in darkness once more.

But my hair illuminates us somewhat, brushing over Ghost with a gentle light, his face filled with quiet fear. I scan the darkness of the swiftly filling cavern. There's no sound but our breath and that hitching heartbeat in my ears, the flush of water slapping the walls of the cave.

"We have to get higher. Into one of the wyrmholes." I exhale sharply, swallowing down a ragged sob. "The only one nearby is across the way."

"We'll have to swim for it." His grip around me tightens, panic already making me twitch. "A few strokes at a time. I won't let you go. I promise. Just kick when I tell you, okay?"

My throat is dry when I swallow, and I can only nod at him, my hands clenching into fists to keep from clutching his shoulders.

He kicks away from the cave wall, moving in some sinuous motion I can only mimic. He stops me. "Don't. You'll slow me down. Stretch out and relax. Or hold your breath some, if that helps you float." He turns so he's partially beneath me, one arm still about my waist and the other cutting through the water in front of us. "Kick, Mags. With me. One. Two. Three…"

The calming cadence of his voice slides through the clouded haze of my thoughts, forcing me to move in time with him. Before too long, I realize we've reached the other side. "How in the hells did you learn to swim? Surely not Bloody Bay—you'd have been sliced to pieces on the rocks."

"We have pools in Meridion," he says. "And Molly's bathhouse suited when I was younger. Lucian insisted."

"Small favors." I shiver and cling to the cliff with a ripple of relief to be perched on solid ground. "Come on. If we're lucky, some of the other tunnels haven't flooded."

I've nearly made it to the wyrmhole when Ghost lets out a cry. A Rotter is hanging on to his ankle. "I can't shake it," he says, struggling to retain his grip on the wall. The lightstick falls from his belt, illuminating the water beneath us with an eerie yellow glow as it sinks to the bottom.

I scramble down the wall, reaching for my hammer to take out the Rotter, but Ghost beats me to it. He lashes out with his heel, crushing what's left of the Rotter's decaying nose. It isn't a killing blow, but Ghost still manages to wiggle free.

"Come on." I reach down to help him up. "Let's get out of here before any other stragglers find their way."

"Lead on, Mags," Ghost murmurs, gently pushing me forward.

I squeeze my hammer and imagine the sound of Balthazaar's skull splitting beneath it. The anger beneath my fear gives way into something that allows me to move and before long we're in the wyrmhole. We take a few minutes to catch our breath. Inwardly, I'm taking stock of our situation. Depending on the state of the other tunnels, we could very well be without food, drinkable water, or air, never mind any chance at escape. It's tempting to sit here forever. My weary body is aching to lie down, to wake up from this horrid nightmare of an existence.

Ghost brushes my hand. "We should move on," he says quietly.

"Aye." But which way? Bran and the others had scouted these tunnels for years without ever finding an exit. Where could I possibly go now with even these limited routes cut off?

But still, I take the lead. I wind us back to where we'd been before the tunnel collapsed. The other lightsticks are still there, and Ghost gathers them up, along with the small satchel of food Penny left behind.

It's something. We keep moving until the end of the wyrmhole. I peer over the edge. The water is only about ankle deep from what I can see and doesn't appear to be rising as quickly as it was in the

Arse. There's no sight or sound of Rotters below, and the "all clear" whistle echoes from my lips out of habit.

"We can walk from here," I say.

I descend before him, reaching the bottom first to watch as he holds a lightstick between his teeth. The shadows play over his face, illuminating the scar on his neck.

So armed, he scrambles down to where I am. "I'll follow you."

"Like old times, aye?" Our eyes meet with a grim humor. "Just let me take care of any Rotters we run into. I've had…practice."

"I've noticed," he says dryly. His mouth twitches, and I can't tell if he's going to laugh or cry about it, but what else is there to say? I only did what needed to be done.

We walk in silence for what seems like hours, my ears constantly pricked for the sounds of Rotters or anything else. Several of the tunnels are blocked, and we're forced to turn around or squeeze through nearly impossible spaces again and again.

Ghost treks along beside me, eschewing the lightsticks until he truly needs them, which suits me more than fine. After a time, we rest, nibbling on the now rather soggy stores of what Penny had given me earlier.

"There's no end to it, is there?" Ghost slumps against an outcropping.

"No." I search for another wyrmhole in the upper reaches of the tunnel, craning my neck for the telltale signs of a recessed space. "The Rotter village is over that way, I think. We might find some additional supplies there. And if we can scrape out a place to rest that would be good."

He nods, and we climb up the wall and into another tunnel. This one is so narrow we have to wriggle through most of the way, but by the end of it, we're rewarded by the sight of the Rotter village nearly entirely submerged, the sunken remains of their huts jutting from the water like bones. Odds and ends float in clumps here and there, offering us little in the way of comfort or aid.

"Either the lake overflowed or the river flooded it." I exhale raggedly, swallowing against another throbbing pain in my chest. "I don't have any other suggestions. And there's something wrong with my heart. I think some water got in there. It keeps slowing down and lurching back up."

His brow furrows. "Is there anything out there we could make a raft from? At least give us something to float on?"

I thrust my chin toward one of the larger piles of debris. "Aye. Looks like a door or somewhat over there. Might suit, but it's hung up on some rocks. I should be able to free it if you make sure I don't fall in."

We creep down the cave wall to the edge of the door. Something pale clings to the corner… A hand? Closer inspection reveals part of a bloated arm. Its owner is long gone.

Ghost crouches beside me, taking my elbow so I can lean out over the inky water, one foot reaching to hook the door with my ankle. My clockwork heart hitches again, and I pause, willing myself to calm.

The door floats toward us, and Ghost helps snag it so it steadies. "I'll test it first." It wobbles under his weight but remains upright. He gestures to me, saying nothing when the makeshift raft nearly capsizes from my frantic leap onto it.

I white-knuckle the edges, ignoring the splinter that slices into my thumb. "Now what?"

"Now we find something to use as a paddle and see if we can't navigate our way easier." He's so matter-of-fact about it, but I catch the faint tremor in his voice, as if hiding his own panic will soothe mine.

I slide to the center of the door, my grip loosening when he leans over to use his hands to push us through the water.

"There." I point to a shaft of wood leaning against another outcropping of rock. It's a broomstick, an oily film glistening off the soaked bristles. He aims for the rock, and I snatch it from its resting place and hand it to him.

He pushes us away toward the center of the cave. The stillness is suffocating, nothing more than the gentle slap of water against the door and the splash of the broomstick as Ghost rows. After a time, I realize he's humming a dirty little ditty under his breath.

"Your clock's wound up tight while mine sits on the shelf... If your old clock needs winding, I'll wind it myself..."

I join him on the last chorus, our voices echoing in a harmonious cacophony.

"Too-ra-lam-a-lam-a, too-ra-lam-a-lam-a too-ra-li-ay. Too-ra-li oo-ra-li oo-ra-li-ay," we sing together.

"Didn't think you'd know that one," I say wryly, though I shouldn't be surprised. He lived in a brothel, after all.

"I know all sorts of things," he says with an exaggerated eyebrow waggle. It's ridiculous, but it makes me laugh all the same. It's a tremulous thing, such laughter, but I hold on to it as if it's the last good sound I'll ever make.

Ghost rewards me with a wink and returns to his paddling, leaving me to point us in what seems like a good direction. Most of the time there is no choice at all, only channels of varying degrees of narrowness. We get stuck here and there, forced to twist the door sideways to slide past an outcropping or a fallen bit of rock. But the water always flows, so that's the path we take.

At some point I doze off, the rhythmic slap of the water on the door hypnotic. With anyone else I would remain alert—or try to, at least. But Ghost... Ah, well, he is someone different, isn't he?

And so my head tips forward onto my chest despite everything. Minutes, hours, I don't know how long I'm out, only that reality has faded away.

"Mags? Wake up." Ghost's voice is a whispered mumble, breaking me out of my stupor.

I jerk forward, nearly tipping off the door as I suddenly realize where I am and what's happened. "Have we stopped?" I rub my eyes with my palm, blinking rapidly as my jaw drops. "What...?"

We're in a cavern. And not one I'm familiar with. Perhaps the earlier explosions had opened a passage into it. But it's not the cavern itself that's so surprising but the way it glitters a brilliant bluish silver, illuminating the entirety of the cave in myriad tiny lights. The very walls and ceiling are covered with...something.

"What is it?" I squint at the walls. It's different from the bioluminescent mushrooms but nothing I recognize.

"Some sort of insect. Glowworms, I think. If you watch them long enough, you can see them moving." Ghost nudges me. "I thought you might want to see it."

"Oh. Yes." I struggle to find my voice. The cave is beautiful, and it's been such a long time since I've seen something that could be called beautiful. Delicate. Untouched. "I've never seen anything like it down here," I admit.

I lean against him, my head tipped up to take it all in, and for a moment, I can imagine I'm outside and I'm looking at the stars. If I sit here long enough, the rest of this will disappear and I'll awaken on a rooftop somewhere, the busy streets of BrightStone below me and Meridion shining above, as always.

I ache for it, a deep yearning that lingers within me for some past memory etched upon my mind. The shadows of regret dance through such thoughts—of what was, what could have been, what will never be again. Perhaps it's only my melancholy that colors my interpretation of my past. After all, as bad as I thought I'd had it at times, it was nothing compared to where I am now.

Yet, I am not alone. Ghost's warmth seeps through my skin, a gentle reminder that at least I have him. But we're already drifting farther into the cavern, the glowworms fading away as we slip past them and into a narrow passage. Before long, it becomes evident that Ghost doesn't have to paddle quite so hard.

I trail my fingers in the water. "There's a current."

He grunts, pulling the broomstick from the water. And indeed, we're moving along by ourselves now. My stomach twists as I realize we're heading for the falls.

"Hush," I tell him, listening. Normally, I'd never lead us this way, but with the tunnels collapsed and flooded, I've lost my sense of direction. Still, the roar of the falls sounds off in the distance.

He frowns, turning toward me. "What the hells is that?"

My arms skim the sides of the tunnel to try to slow us down. "Waterfall."

"Ah," he says blankly, pinching the bridge of his nose. He grinds the broomstick into the rocks. I scan the walls for another way to go, a wyrmhole, something, *anything*, but the only places I see are so narrow that even I couldn't manage to fit through them alone.

The roar of the falls grows ever louder, nearly deafening us as we approach the end of the tunnel. A curtain of water slips past the entrance, chilled droplets splashing over my face. This tunnel is lower than the one Bran and rest of us usually took to the falls. It's hidden behind the rushing water, but it's still high enough that we cannot see the bottom.

"That's that," I whisper. We scoot off the door and watch as it floats over the edge. I can't even find the energy to despair about it, my senses growing numb to it all. The water here is shallow enough to wade through at this point, anyway.

I lean forward to gauge the distance to the tunnel above, rewarded with a splash of foam for my troubles. The rocks here are wet and slippery; climbing them would be difficult even in the best of situations.

Ghost cracks a lightstick and drops it below. It spirals into the darkness, its golden flare swallowed up as it plummets. He whistles. "No wonder there haven't been any survivors."

"We don't have a rope to try to climb down. Assuming there's even a way out."

"It's an offshoot of the Everdark River. I imagine it finds its way to the sea at some point. Doesn't mean I want to try it." He shrugs. "If this were one of those awful penny romances Lucian's always reading, we'd undoubtedly have a good shag and then plummet hand in hand to our deaths below in a fit of fatalistic lovers' foolishness."

"Lucian reads penny romances?" I snort.

"All the time," he replies cheerfully. "They're ridiculous, but as guilty pleasures go, I suppose they're harmless." He sinks to his knees, curving against the edge of the tunnel wall to stare out into the darkness. "Not exactly how I thought things would turn out, I have to admit."

"You and me both." I take the spot opposite him, my bones weary and my chest hurting from the whirring of my heart. I shuffle through the satchel I'd snagged from the wyrmhole and pull out another crust of bread, handing half of it to him. "Not a whole lot left in here," I muse, digging to the bottom.

A wry smile twists my lips when I find the cigarillo Penny had stuffed in the one tiny pocket. She'd known me well. Not that I have any way to light it. With a sigh, I dangle one leg over the edge, wincing at the icy chill as the foam splashes over my toes.

Would I be able to do it? Jump in and end it all in some swirling abyss below rather than starve to death in this hole over the next few weeks? I glance over at Ghost, his disheveled head bent over the last of his meal.

Dimly, I wonder what's happening topside. Is Lucian all right? Are the Rotters wreaking havoc? Did Bran manage to escape? Did any of it really matter?

Grasping at a desperate need to fill the silence, I blurt out the first thing that comes to mind. "Did Josephine ever get those wings to work?"

Ghost rubs his chin. "In a manner of speaking. Tin Tin was the only one light enough to pilot the damn thing to the top of the gates before an airship nearly shot him down. It was a test run, really, and he barely managed to escape, but it was proof that it could be done. Plus, it gave Josephine the idea of mounting an attack on the airships directly. That went much better, mind."

"She *what*?" I blink at him.

"Start small. Isn't that what they say? Turns out Josephine makes a hell of an admiral." He cracks a little grin. "Those airships aren't nearly as well protected from the top—ten or so Moon Children dropping out of the sky in the dead of night is a bit hard to prepare for."

"And the Twisted Tumblers have all those weapons..." My voice trails away, remembering Tin Tin's makeshift crossbow, created from leftover Meridian technology.

"Yes," he agrees. "Once we saw how things were going to go when you were in the Pits, Josephine doubled her work output, making sure the Chancellor's rebellion was as well armed as possible. At any rate, we took over one of the Inquestor Scout ships, and once we figured out how to fly it, we used it to start raiding their Interceptors. They're big but slow, so between the wings and the Scouts, we managed to hit them hard and fast." Pride ripples over his face. "We've got a little flotilla of stolen ships moored out in the fog in the Warrens. The Inquestors pay a bit more attention to us now, I'll say that much."

"I dare say." I hardly know what to think, marveling at Josephine's daring. A small twinge of envy flutters through me—at the idea of the rest of them being able to fly, to make a real impact. And here I am, buried beneath the ground for nearly a year with little more to show for it than a broken heart.

I gaze upward at the flowing water, scanning over the rocks again, as though I might somehow will an escape hole to appear. And then I see it. Something is gleaming beneath the waterfall, over to the right and down, all but hidden within a recess.

Something metal.

I frown at it. Bran never mentioned such a thing, but if it had been hidden behind the waterfall all this time, how would we have seen it? As far as I knew, none of us ever came out this far below the main part of the river.

I peer over the edge to get a better look at the curved edge. "A pipe," I breathe, exhalation leaping through me. A gods-be-damned pipe.

"Mags? I was only half joking about jumping." Alarm fills Ghost's voice.

A soft laugh escapes me. "But it's a good idea. More or less. Except we don't need to drop all the way to the bottom." I point at the shadows. "Just into that pipe."

"The what?" He leans out past me, craning his head. "I don't see anything..."

"Well, you can't see in the dark, aye?" I say dryly. "It looks like a pipe there, maybe a sewage runoff or some offshoot of the BrightStone stink pipes."

The thought of crawling through shit makes my stomach curdle, but the possibility of escape is worth it. "I can't tell how wide it is from here. One of us needs to climb down to see if it goes anywhere." I shift my shoulders and flex my fingers.

"I'll do it." Ghost holds my arm in a tight grip.

"No offense, but I've had more practice doing this in the dark."

"Please, Mags. Let me do it. I'll use a lightstick."

It's written all over his face. Guilt. Helplessness.

He *had* been the best roof dancer I'd ever seen. Even down here, he is holding his own so far.

But you'd trust Bran or Penny or the others, right?

Or maybe you're afraid of losing him... And mayhap he feels the same way...

"All right, then," I say finally. He snorts, a flash of his old self peeking through as he cracks another lightstick.

Placing it between his teeth, he inches out of the tunnel, his feet digging into the slick rock. I'm tempted to follow, but he doesn't need the distraction, so I grind my jaw instead, tracking each movement he makes, searching for the tiniest slip.

He slides only once, grunting as he rights himself, one hand now gripping the edge of the pipe. Craning his head, he spits the lightstick into the pipe. "It's empty," he calls. "And dry. Whatever it is, it hasn't been used in a long time."

"Can we fit?"

"It will be tight, but I think we can manage."

"We'd better," I mutter. "I'm coming over."

"Okay. Watch that third rock down. It's crumbling."

I half expect him to start crawling into the pipe, but he clings and waits for me. On closer inspection, I notice the pipe is green with age, a faint copper sheen peeking through cracks in the patina.

"Who goes in first?" I don't know if it's better or worse to be the one waiting on the outside, and I fidget at the thought.

"Me. If I get stuck, you can help pull me out. And the lightstick will give us a better idea of how far this goes." He tucks his hair behind his ears, shaking himself a little, working himself up to it.

"Suit yourself." My tone is casual, but I can't help but shiver as I watch as he creeps in first, holding out the lightstick to give himself a better view.

I keep my head down when I follow him in, trying not to think about the way my shoulders rub against the sides. Parts of the pipe are corroded, flaking off into my hands. It stains my fingers until it seems as if we are moving through a bloody intestine, but I quickly clamp down on that thought. Wyrmholes and tunnels aside, I don't need to borrow *that* particular mental image. Ever.

The temperature rises, sweat dripping from my forehead and making me sticky. I'm not sure if it's the air growing warmer or that there are two bodies in such close quarters, but it does nothing to inspire confidence.

Ghost slows, and I nearly butt into his backside. "Hold up," he says. "There's a bend in the pipe."

"Which way?"

He sighs. "Straight up. I can't tell how far it goes."

I laugh. Of course, it goes up. "If it leads to the surface of BrightStone, that's going to be a hell of a scramble. Not that I'm complaining, mind. I'd climb the Mother Clock naked if it meant getting out of here."

He climbs into the bend and stands up, his hands running over the sides. "I'll look forward to it."

I smirk, trying to peer past his shoulders. The lightstick is flickering now, threatening to go out, making it easier for me to see. But even I can't tell how tall the pipe is. "So now what?"

"Whatever's up there, nothing has flowed through this thing in some time, but here"—he points to part of the pipe—"it's corrugated. Should be doable if we go slow." He raises a brow in challenge. "Feel like a climb?"

"Not really, no." But I wriggle past him. "I'll take point this time. I don't fancy being crushed if you fall."

He snorts and flattens himself against the side of the pipe so I can squeeze by him, one hand lowered to give me a leg up. "This seems familiar," he says when I brace my other foot on his shoulder to get a little higher.

I let out a grunt, remembering when he'd boosted me up a fire escape so we could break into the museum. "History has a tendency to repeat itself. Let's hope things turn out a little better this time, aye? At least there aren't any Inquestors here."

My fingers slide over the wall of the pipe. Corrugated or not, there's not much here to cling to. But I curl my toes into the pipe indentations, and I shove off him, my arm reaching up to find another grip. "Shit on a shingle." My fingers struggle to find purchase. "We'll be lucky if we don't break our necks."

"At least that would be quick." He pauses, waiting for me to get a few lengths ahead of him before following.

"Speaking of history, where's my dragon?" My words grind out in tentative gasps as I fall into a working rhythm. Push, cling, pause. Push, cling, pause.

"Gone. Lucian had it for a while, after the two of us fled to Josephine's territory. But despite our best efforts, it had a tendency to disappear for periods." He sighs. "Maybe it was searching for you. Eventually, it just never came back."

"Well, it never made it down this way." A twinge of sadness brushes over me. I've had far more important things to worry about than steam-powered mystery dragons, but there'd been something special about it.

My foot slips, and I grind my hands into the pipe to keep from falling. "Hells, it's slick."

"Don't take too long, Mags." He shifts below me, and if his legs are trembling anything like mine, I know we need to keep moving. I suck in a deep breath of air, wiping my sweaty brow on my shirt-sleeve, and try again, this time balancing on a slightly different part of the pipe.

Crack!

Pain lances through my forehead. "Oy!"

"What is it? Are you hurt?"

"There's somewhat here," I say, elation surging through me. "Gods above, Ghost. It's a ladder." I let out a whoop as my foot finds the first rung, its tarnished metal still sturdy enough to bear my weight. My arms ache with relief.

Before long, we come to a dead end. Or at least the beginnings of one.

"Why have we stopped?" Ghost stretches his neck with a groan.

"The pipe ends here. But there's a wheel of sorts above. Maybe we can twist it open." Being this seemingly close to escape renews me, and I give the ladder a cursory tug, grunting when it doesn't budge. "Can you get any higher?" I ask. "It's going to take two of us. I think the steel edge has rusted shut."

I shift as much as I can to let him up, leaving us pressed tightly together with barely any room to move at all. "You know, some people paid extra for this sort of thing at Molly Bell's," he murmurs.

"Which part? Being crammed in a tube like sardines, aye? Some people have too much money and none of the sense," I retort, hissing when he bumps into my chest, causing my heart panel to jostle uncomfortably.

"Truer words were never spoken." He loops one knee over a rung for balance before reaching up take the other side of the wheel. Panting, his arms strain as he tries to turn it. I add my own strength to the effort, my voice an angry buzz until we have to admit defeat.

He punches it suddenly, the clang reverberating through the pipe. "Dammit!"

"Here." My hammer still hangs from my makeshift belt loop, and I pull it out. "Let's see if we can't loosen some of the rust with this. Or use it for leverage—something."

I give the wheel a sharp rap, wincing when a sprinkle of rust flakes into my eyes and nose, burning.

"Let me try." Ghost takes the hammer from me and hits the wheel himself, along the edge of the seam. More rust rains down on us, but I brush it away when he shoves the hammer at me and grips the wheel again.

I tuck the hammer into my belt again and take the other side of the wheel. This time we're rewarded with a wailing moan, the breath of spirits trapped within whatever we're about to open. "Come on, Mags. Again. Nearly there." Ghost's voice rings with encouragement.

I bite down on my lip, tasting blood as I strain against the wheel. It creaks, the porthole of an entrance popping open on dying hinges. Light floods the pipe in a wash of gold, and I turn away from it, even as Ghost thrusts his way through, then reaches down to pull me up.

My arms and legs go limp and I sag, my entire body trembling. When the fire in my feet sets in, I barely notice except to wiggle my toes feebly. Somewhere along the way, I've also cut my soles, but I don't remember doing it.

I squint from the sharpness of the illumination. Ghost's shadow slips in front of me, allowing me to see better. He's squatted down to my level, his head blocking the light. Superficial cuts mar his cheek where he must have scraped it on the side of the pipe. His pale hair is scruffy and damp, slick against his head.

"You look like you've been dragged to the Hells and back," I say.

"That makes a pair of us, then." Ghost pushes the hair away from my eyes. "Let's see if we can do something about this light."

He stands, and I'm forced to shut my eyes again, my ears pricking as he shuffles about. There's a creaking noise and then the blessed relief of darkness. There's still a shaft of light pointing into the far corner of the room, but it's no longer aimed at me, and that's enough to make it bearable. I blink rapidly, getting my bearings.

"It's a laboratory," I breathe, my feet forgotten.

But what a wondrous laboratory it is. Lucian would have killed to see it. Dust coats nearly everything in a fine powder, but that doesn't stop the shine of the brass beneath it. Above us, something glitters, golden light reflecting off a massive round mirror. It's a simple thing, purely functional, without the ornate bearings I've seen in so many of the shops in the square.

Ghost stands beneath it, his fingers brushing the top of the mirror to shift it slightly. Immediately the light in the room dims even more, and he cranes his head, looking at a series of small pipes that seem to disappear into the ceiling.

"They must be lined with mirrors to reflect the sun's rays." He turns toward me, full of hope. "We must be close to the surface if it can be directed down here. It's wickedly clever, even if somewhat limited."

"As long it's not a rainy day." I pull myself up to stand and look around. Every cranny of useful space is filled—workbenches, books, dirty glass vials. A map of Meridion hangs on the largest wall. I peer at it, wiping away the dust with a careful hand. I've never seen one so intricate, inked and shaded, with a hint of gold leaf to make it gleam. Every part of the layout of the floating city is etched in minute detail, giving me a bird's-eye view—tall spires and curved staircases, standing pools and exquisite gardens with narrow pathways twisting in elegant fashion throughout. I can see myself there, surrounded by glass and lights and the surely musical tone of utter perfection.

I trace the outline of it. "What's this?" The diagram of the lower bowels of the city is a series of coils and pipes, the inner works of its turbines far greater than my ken. Except for the center, where a dragon of glittering brass, bronze, and glass lies chained, spouting great bouts of flame and steam. My throat closes. It's so like the dragon I found, though if this picture is to scale, the dragon nested within is monstrous in size.

Something is written beneath it in faded script. I squint at the letters, struggling to make them out. "I...R...O...N...H...E...E... No, A...R...T. IronHeart." I roll the word on my tongue. Its meaning tastes heavy, beats in my chest as though my own heart were made of such weighty stuff.

Ghost has come to stand beside me. He's studying the map of Meridion and points at one of the smaller estate homes nestled within some sort of park. "I used to live here. That's where my bedroom was." An aura of melancholy falls over him, and I limp away to sit on the floor.

He squats, turning my injured feet up with a careful hand. "Damn. I didn't realize... We should get those cleaned up."

"If you can find anything. Whatever this place is, it's been abandoned for a long time."

An odd look passes over his face, something tight and full of sorrow. He rummages in one of the cabinets, finally pulling out a couple of rags and a tube of salve. He sniffs it. "Lavender. It's so familiar..."

I raise a brow at the comment. "So what do you think this place is?"

"I'm not sure, but we can explore later." He blinks owlishly. "I don't know about you, but I could use a nap. After we get you fixed up," he amends, yawning.

A sink next to one of the workbenches still functions, a fact for which I'm dreadfully grateful, however it's managed. It sputters rusted, dirty water at first, but the longer Ghost lets it run, the clearer it gets until it's finally about as close to normal as anything I'd seen up in BrightStone.

He wets the rags with the freshly running water and gently blots at my feet to rinse off the worst of the blood and dirt before applying the salve. It smells like the stuff Georges had used on my lash wounds, though fainter. It stings, too, but there must be a numbing agent in it because a few minutes later, there's barely any pain at all. I wriggle my toes, pleased they still work correctly.

"We'll have to bind them if you're going to walk," Ghost notes. "But let them dry out some first."

I glance up at the mirror light, grateful we aren't at risk of running out of air at least. Old shunting pipes weave their way into the wall. The ceiling vaults high and narrow, with one column that disappears into the darkness above. It's too wide to climb as we did the pipe, but perhaps we can use some of the things we find in here to aid us.

Wherever *here* is.

Ghost must've followed my gaze because he says, "That seems promising, doesn't it?"

I smile ruefully. "It does... Listen, when we do get topside, I'm going to need your help. I can't bear the light anymore. I can hardly tolerate the little bit put out by that mirror right now; I don't know if I'll ever manage the sun again."

He gives my hand a squeeze. "I'll be your eyes up there. Like you are down here for me."

We're silent for a time, and I start slipping into sleep when he shifts, fumbling with something at his neck and pressing whatever it is in my hand. I turn it over. It's Sparrow's necklace.

I bite my lip, the image of the green beads scattering on the cobblestones at my feet filling my vision. "But the Inquestors broke it..."

"I was there," Ghost says, bitterness coating his words. "I watched as they whipped you, and I could do nothing. Collecting the beads was a poor victory, but it was the only thing I had left of you." His hand clenches into a fist. "Lucian did everything he could to try to get you out of the High Inquestor's keeping. But he had to be so careful. Plenty of witnesses saw him dancing with you the night you rescued me from Balthazaar's estate."

"He had a cane when I last saw him." I idly rub one of the beads between my fingers. "Did he injure himself?"

Ghost laughs wryly. "He fell partway off the roof and sprained his knee. I'll spare you the details of how we escaped, but it wasn't very pretty. We were like a pair of spavined horses. Here," he says, taking the necklace from me and fastening it around my neck.

I shiver when it settles against my skin. After so long without it, it feels like a jeweled noose, pulling me into memories I've allowed to fade away. But that's silly—I'm chained to my past, necklace or no. I don't require an old piece of jewelry to realize I'll never be free of it. Sparrow meant far too much to me for that. I pat it anyway, exhaling raggedly as I wipe away a rush of tears. "Thank you."

"It's a poor gift. You're deserving of far more than this, Mags. So very much more." His fingers trail over the necklace and settle on my shoulder. He pulls me against him and leans us back so we're lying on the floor.

"You'd be the first to think so, then." I've been used my entire life. That anyone might consider me worth something simply for being me is a foreign concept.

Ghost presses his lips to my forehead and he curls his body around mine. "We'll figure it out, Mags. I promise."

Tears continue to well up until I finally admit to myself that it's not the light that's the problem. In the end, I sigh, letting myself go limp in his arms. And for the first time in very long time, I sleep.

From a whisper to a scream
Secrets shadowed while I dream.
Digging deep while I turn about
No matter how I shut them out.

— CHAPTER FIFTEEN —

My limbs won't move. I'm encased in ice upon a pedestal in Balthazaar's receiving room. Long tables are piled high with fine cheese and fruits and bloodied slices of meat, cups filled to the brim with wine. Fingers point at me, laughter and amusement and cruel curiosity upon the face of everyone who watches.

"Blackbird, magpie, raven, crow. Where do you fly to? Where do you go?" Penny's corpse emerges from the crowd, her voice a mocking singsong. "With broken wings to search and seek, voiceless song and shattered beak."

I'm sorry. I'm sorry. My mouth cannot seem to form the words as I vibrate within this prison of…of what?

Plip. Plip. Plop.

Something drips onto my forehead, hot rivulets slipping over my face. My vision scans up to see Ghost hanging from the rafters. His throat is slit, and the last of his life drips down on me, filling my eyes with tears of blood.

"You let me die, Mags," he whispers. "Just like Sparrow."

I jerk awake, whimpering when I accidentally open my eyes to a flare of light, my lopsided heart pounding. Ghost is singing softly, his back turned toward me, some sad little line from an old nursery rhyme, over and over and over. "One for my master, one for my dame, and one for the wee lad who lives down the lane..."

His voice and its pleasant timbre echoes in the laboratory. I stretch, wincing as my feet brush the floor, pinpricks of pain lancing into my shins. A quick inspection shows the result of yesterday's exertions. As tough as my feet are now, even they aren't impervious. My soles are sliced up, the cuts scabbing but still dreadfully sore. I attempt to get to my feet but quickly decided against it, contenting myself with pulling my legs beneath me so I can sit up.

"Mad Brianna sang that to me, too," I grunt, finding the salve Ghost used before and applying it until the pain ebbs. "Though she twisted it like she did everything else. The version I learned had the lad hanging himself with the lamb's wool."

He hesitates. "Since her...death, the day you were sent to the Pits, the townsfolk have raised her up to be a prophetic martyr. There's a shrine dedicated to her on the docks."

"Brianna? She was nutters. Everyone knew that." I say it lightly, though a soft pang strikes me hard as I realize the woman who raised me is now dead. Not that I'd really expected otherwise. I'd seen the High Inquestor strike her down, but part of me had been pretending the poor woman had somehow survived.

"BrightStone is a city without hope. Those last words of hers, coupled with what happened to you... 'Meridion will fall if you bury the moon. IronHeart's flight is Meridion's doom.'" He sighs. "If we do make it topside, you're likely to be taken as a... I don't know. A savior?"

"There's a laugh. I haven't saved shit." I wiggle my toes. "All they want is someone they can pin their disappointments on if things don't go the way they want. And I've had quite enough of that."

Ghost gets to his feet and rummages around one of the work-benches, coming up with an old striker. He grabs a nearby lantern, and after a couple of tries, he lights it, whooping when the wick catches. "Let's see what else there is in this place, shall we?"

I nod in agreement but remain seated. Exploration is all well and good, but I'm not inclined to do much walking until I bandage my feet. I shield my tearing eyes with my hand as he holds the lantern to illuminate the other corners of the room. Scattered on the floor are signs of domesticity: random pieces of crockery, an empty can of beans, blanket scraps, and a rotted mattress on the floor in the far corner.

Oh…

A skeleton covered by a threadbare blanket lies in gentle repose upon the mattress, its finger bones curled almost into fists. A tattered bit of tendon still remains upon the hands, but the rest of it has fallen apart, whatever flesh that holds a person together long since gone. A few traces of white hair linger on the pillow. A Moon Child, perhaps. Or someone simply lucky enough to die of old age. There's no way to tell which.

I slide across the floor on my hands and knees for a closer look. A thick notebook sits on the floor, its parchment pages looking fragile and dusty. I can't make out the words upon the cover, but I do recognize the symbol beside them.

Three black dots, connected by a faint design of a cog.

I lick my lips. "Madeline d'Arc." The words echo in the quiet of the room.

Ghost's breath stills until he's no more than a statue, trapped like some otherworldly spirit. Then a small whimper escapes him as he approaches Madeline's remains, kneeling beside the decaying mattress with its sagging springs and stained fabric.

"It must be odd, aye?" I'm desperate to break up this strange tension. "Seeing the founder of all our troubles here like this?"

"It's not that," he says raggedly. Regret and sorrow and something far more secret flits over his face when he turns toward me. "She was my mother."

I gape at him. "What?"

"Lucian and I… We're the children of Madeline d'Arc," he says, not meeting my eyes.

A flush of hurt rolls through me. "Why didn't you tell me?"

He barks out a laugh. "Would you have believed me? Or Lucian? That the sons of Madeline d'Arc, the famed architect of Meridion, the traitor who left the flying city in chains, were reduced to living in squalor in a brothel in BrightStone?"

"Maybe not at first," I admit. "But after everything that's happened…after you swore to me there weren't any other secrets, that you would tell me the truth even if Molly Bell and Lucian would not…"

"I know. I know. But this…this was personal." He tries to smile, and it fails utterly. "And I thought if you knew, you wouldn't help us."

My nostrils flare wide, and I touch the panel on my chest. "I suppose that explains why Lucian was so interested in this. It bears her mark. No wonder he was so desperate to know where it came from." It's on the tip of my tongue to ask if that's why they kept me around at all, if Lucian would have still patched me up the night I'd been left for dead, if the panel hadn't been there. Would he have sent me on my way that much faster?

Stricken, Ghost takes my hand. "It's not like that, Mags. It never was. It was a mystery, yes, but even aside from that—"

I wave him off. "I always wondered how you planned on taking me to Meridion as you promised when all this started. My 'reward,' I suppose, though I'm not sure I'd take you up on it now." A soft sigh escapes me at the irony. I'd spent my entire life wishing to find a way to the floating city. It had been a fairy tale turned into a nightmare. "At least I know you've got the connections, aye? Did Molly Bell know?"

"Maybe. Probably?" He shrugs. "If she did it wasn't from us telling her. You know how she is with secrets. Nothing happens in BrightStone that she doesn't know about sooner or later."

"Flesh, information, or jingle," I mutter in agreement. "She trades in all of it."

He nods, but the tremble in his hands tells me how shaken he really is. "Would you mind leaving me alone for a few minutes? It's going to take me a little time to wrap my head around all of...this."

"Aye." Were our roles reserved, I would want some privacy after such a discovery, too. I let his hand slip from mine as he turns away, but not before I catch a glimpse of tears streaking across his cheek.

I sit on the floor, flipping through one of Madeline's notebooks and frowning at the maze of schematics of Meridion's underbelly. It was the only thing within reach and I'd long since given up on Ghost breaking the silence of his own volition. He's been sitting by his mother's bedside for at least an hour, lost in his own thoughts.

And why wouldn't he be? I have no reason not to believe him. In fact, so much makes perfect sense now. Why he knew so much. Why he was so well spoken.

But to think Madeline d'Arc had a Moon Child for a son?

I study the curve of his back and the angle of his shoulders. His clothes are tattered and nearly as filthy as mine are, but there's a pride in his posture that I've never quite understood until now. Perhaps it's one thing to be a Meridian, but to have the Architect's lineage resting on your shoulders?

But given Buceph's explanation of the immortality serum and the Rot, how is Ghost's presence even possible? Moon Children are born of BrightStone women, and Madeline d'Arc was never one of those. Lucian said his people had come across the Emerald Sea, but beyond that, their origins were a mystery.

I have no doubts this lab is part of what the Meridians were sent to the Pits to find so long ago. I don't pretend to understand most of the woman's esoteric diagrams and sketches, but I recognize blueprints when I see them. Immortality serum or not, if there's a way to restart their floating city, it's going to be somewhere in this dusty room, lost in the copper models and brass coils. But it's all beyond me, no matter how I puzzle over it.

I flex my toes again, restless. Ghost turns and helps me to stand. Pain prickles through my legs, and I hiss, easing onto my heels.

Ghost tightens his grip to steady me. "I didn't expect to see her here. I mean, I knew she was most likely dead by now. I'd only hoped to find out where she'd had gone, if she'd found a way to stop the plague." His nostrils flare. "To think she's been here this whole time, that she died like this…alone?"

"I'm sorry." I can't think of anything else to say.

"Don't be. She's been gone a long, long time. In some ways, it's good to know. I will never be able to live up to her legacy," he says, "but I can make sure it lives on. Lucian was only twenty when she left me with him, but he was brilliant, even at that age. If we can find a way to get him here, he might be able to put the equipment to good use. If not…"

"Let's find a way out of here first."

"In a moment." He gestures at me. "Sit down. I'll bind your wounds."

I find a stool and sit, my legs dangling over the edge. He rips up the remainder of the rags he found on the workbench and wraps them over the still-oozing cuts, knotting the makeshift bandage by my ankles. I circle my feet, pleased to see there is plenty of give to walk easily.

"Nothing like a new pair of shoes, aye?" I say.

He snorts. "When we get out of here, I'll buy you a new pair of boots. A new *everything*. After all, can't have you wandering the streets of Meridion dressed like a vagabond, can we?" His voice is teasing, but there's such an abject misery in his eyes that I'm forced to look down.

"It's what I am, Ghost. Put a dress on a pig and you've still got a walking bacon factory."

"Trystan," he says suddenly, seeming desperate to change the subject. "That's my real name. I just thought you should know." Before I can figure out a response to this, he pulls a notebook from the pile, snatching it in a white-knuckled grip. "She talks about me in here. When I was little."

The confession has stripped away his outer shell, exposing him. If I ask him about it, I know he'll break, and I've no right to do that.

He tucks the journal into his waistband. "I need to read it. But I can't, not yet."

My fingers drift over the tangled mess of his hair. There's no comfort I can offer him. Nothing that wouldn't be a lie anyway. And I think we've both had enough of those. So I simply lean against him. "Maybe you'll find somewhat written in there about my heart. What it was meant for, even."

He sighs. "So much here and so little time to figure it all out—all these secrets and inventions. And if it falls into the wrong hands…"

"Well, we probably ought to worry about getting out of here first," I remind him. "Hands later."

"I don't believe she would have sealed herself down here without an exit. Not counting the drainage pipe we climbed up," he amends. "And that's what it is. She probably dumped anything caustic or dangerous down there if she couldn't vent it properly." A soft chuckle escapes him. "She was always meticulous about proper ventilation."

"You remember a lot, for being so young. What were you, five? Six? I can't remember what Lucian told me."

"About that," he agrees. "And it's in bits and pieces, mostly. I was always underfoot back then. She set me up with my own corner in her workroom. I'd twist the bolts on and off one of her projects all day long. And then one morning, she was gone. Left us a note and, poof, she disappeared. Lucian and I were kept under close watch by the Meridian Council for a long time after that, especially once people discovered that Meridion could no longer fly."

"A note, eh? Well, now I know where you got it from." I nudge him, teasing.

He gives me a sour look. "The Meridian Council accused Lucian of murdering her, but obviously that wasn't true. According to Lucian, what they really wanted was access to her estate. She had a lot of technology ferreted away in her various labs and even in our home." He frowns, shaking his head. "With us out of the way, they could declare her property for the city. They never pinned anything on him, but our family name was so tarnished, we had no choice but to leave. So we came to BrightStone. On the surface it was to search for her, but really..."

"The Rot," I finish for him. "Lucian told me his theories. And that he was accused of murder, but I didn't realize it had been d'Arc he supposedly killed." I rub my temples against a sudden headache. "All these secrets and the lies. There's no sense to be made of any of it. And no one to trust."

"Yes, well, I don't think we had much choice. Exile was better than execution, and by the time Lucian thought he might be able to convince them of his innocence, Meridion wasn't communicating with BrightStone anymore. We were stuck here."

"So now what? We might be able to scrounge up some more supplies here, but food is at a premium, if you haven't noticed. We need to get topside...and fast." My stomach rumbles loudly at the thought, making us both snort.

Ghost nods absently. "As much as I'd like to read through all of these notebooks, you're right. I... It's my mother's legacy. It belongs to me and Lucian. And it's our ticket to restoring our family name."

My mouth twists into a wry smile. I can't really pretend to understand, with me having no family name at all. "I'm sure it will be helpful in that regard."

"As long as the Inquestors don't get wind of it." His face grows grim. "I don't have to tell you how things might go if they find my mother's writings."

"Maybe you should. I mean, how bad would it be if they got their city going and left? With them gone, we might be able to make BrightStone a normal place to live in. No more plague. We could actually leave the city, find a new place to live—with grass and wind, even." I freeze, pointing to one of the worktables. Piles of metallic pieces are laid out in apparent haphazard fashion, but it looks familiar, too.

Scales. Crested wings.

My eyes widen. "Oy. Come here."

He peers over my shoulder, his breath against my ear. "Dragons? But..."

I reach out to pick one up. No ember beats in its glass chest. "It's like the one I had. But why? I thought they were coming from Meridion. The dead architect Sparrow and I found had one."

Ghost turns a piece of tail over in his hand. "I don't understand. Why would she be building them?"

"Maybe she couldn't get out," I say quietly. "Maybe she was communicating with someone up in Meridion. Or something." I study the dragons again. Their edges are rough, lacking the refinement of my dragon. It reminds me of the half-finished wings Josephine had been making.

It's almost as if she was testing their shape...

I spot a torn piece of parchment next to them, heavily charcoaled with various designs and measurements.

"Prototypes," Ghost says, picking up a delicate wing membrane. "That's what these are."

I turn the parchment around. "There's somewhat here about them."

I strain to read the writing: *To guard the fail-safe if I cannot undo the damage. She has indicated her displeasure at my leaving...*

The rest of it is smeared beyond comprehension, but a prickle runs down my spine at her words. A fail-safe for what?

"There must be a clue in your mother's notes. They aren't just messengers. And who do you think is 'she'?"

"I don't know. But maybe Lucian does." He gestures at the pile of notebooks, snagging a few, and sits beside the lantern. "I'm going to see if there's anything that might show us how to get out."

I pace slowly, still having trouble adjusting to the light. In the darker corners my vision is better, and it's here I retreat, my hands skimming the walls. When I come to a pillar on the far side, I pause and lean against the metal so its chill flushes over my skin. My gaze falls upon d'Arc's body, her skeletal figure forlorn with the rotting blanket askew on her bones. What had she been thinking in those last days?

Thrum.

Something hums beneath my fingers. "What's that?"

Thrum. Thrum.

Ghost turns from where he studies another sheaf of papers. "What's what?"

"That noise. Don't you hear it?"

Thrum.

My clockwork heart whirs, speeding up in a grinding rhythm I've never felt before. "That humming thing..."

A panel slides away on the pillar, revealing a keypad etched with a decorative cog—Madeline d'Arc's symbol, matching the one on my heart. The keypad is made up of six square buttons, each one glowing with a symbol I don't recognize.

Thrum. Thrum.

The beats echo out twice more and then cease. Ghost comes to stand beside me. "It's a Meridian door lock. They're usually coded to a certain pattern, depending on the button symbols. Don't need to worry about keys as long as you can remember your pattern." He taps the keypad, tsking when nothing happens.

My heart jolts, and I step away from him. Instantly, my heartbeat slows.

What the hells...?

As I approach the pillar again, my heart begins to vibrate once more. But it's different this time, off by a few beats from the first time I was near it.

"My heart," I say hoarsely. "It's reacting to...to it."

"It shouldn't be." He frowns. "Often it's a family code, passed between generations, but it's not responding to any of the ones I remember. If Lucian were here—"

"But he's not," I snap. "Stop wishing for what we don't have." A wave of guilt washes through me. "At this point, we've only got each other, aye?"

"Understood. No wishing," he says dryly. "But this makes no sense. What would your heart have to do with Meridian key codes? Or..." He pales. "That's it."

"What? What's it?"

"The key." He looks up at me, his expression a mix of terror and wonder. "It's you."

"*Me?* I have a clockwork heart, Ghost. It's what actually keeps me living. How the in the hells does that make me a key?"

His brow furrows, and he retreats to the pile of notebooks. He leafs through the pages with careful precision, and when he glances up at me a few minutes later, his face is ashen. "What happened to your mother?" he asks.

I shrug. "I don't know. I was only about two when Mad Brianna found me abandoned on the docks. There was a dead woman nearby, but I never learned who she was." I suppose I should feel saddened by this, but you can't miss what you never had. "Why? What does that have to do with anything?"

"This is a medical log," he says faintly. "There's a note in here about a heart surgery my mother performed on a two-year-old girl." He swallows. "The fail-safe. Listen."

He meets my eyes briefly and then starts to read aloud. *"Two weeks ago, a woman brought an ailing child to Surgeon's Row, who was presenting with signs of severe cardiomyopathy. Unable to find anyone with the skills to save the child, the woman sought solace at the Salt Temple, indicating she wanted to leave the child there to die peaceably. The salt priests allowed me to tend to the girl in secret, releasing her into the woman's care some time later, under the instruction never to tell anyone what had transpired and to guard the girl well.*

"The woman drove a shrewd bargain, nonetheless, and I was forced to promise her a great amount of money to be delivered in several years, as long as the child remained unharmed."

I sink to trembling knees, blood pulsing in my ears. "I don't understand. That was me? And Mad Brianna? Or was it my mother?" I blink at Ghost, but he clenches his jaw before beginning again.

"The mechanics of the clockwork heart are much the same as a proper heart, but without a sufficient medical environment and medications, the girl would surely perish shortly after the replacement due to organ rejection. Her blood type indicated she was of hybrid origin with the standard Meridian genetic predisposition, though she would not reap the advantages of that until she reaches menarche. On the hunch that the serum my cohorts and I attempted to develop might enable the girl's body to accept the device, I injected her with what small amount I had left. I did, after all, already test it with a modified structure upon another test subject, namely my youngest son..."

"Wait, what?" My mind is spinning so fast that I nearly miss the last part. "The immortality serum... I was injected with it? And you? You..."

He grips the notebook tighter in his hands. "You heard me. I was a...a test subject. For you, apparently, as far as the serum went." A shiver visibly runs through him, but the damage has already been done. My heart aches for him; such innocence is hard lost. As for me, I don't know if I should laugh or cry at this revelation, and a sudden wash of despair rolls over me because the lies will never be over.

"I'm sure she wasn't trying to hurt you." The words are empty, even to me. I'm not much good at consolation, and for all I know, Madeline d'Arc had been as skilled a manipulator as any of the Meridians I'd met down here.

Ghost's face flattens as though he's retreated into himself, and then he shakes his head, retrieving the notebook once more.

"That I have hidden away the fail-safe within the heart of this child seems ludicrous, but I have no other choice at this time. Should I not find success in my endeavors within the next several years, the messengers shall become the guardians until such time as she may be of use. I have programmed a skeleton key within the device, as well, to ensure access to that which remains hidden..."

"What in the *hells* does that mean?" I slump against the pillar, and a bark of laugher escapes me. "Mad Brianna's last words to me... 'I know what you are, lass. I know what you carry.' I'd assumed she meant the dragon in my bag, but she meant *this*." I tap the panel on my chest. "All this time she was trying to tell us with those befuddled wits of hers. And I was too stupid to understand her nursery rhymes about IronHeart."

"I'm sure I don't know. But if that scrap of paper with the dragon prototypes has the right of it, I think the little dragons were searching for *you*." I snort as he approaches me and pulls me to my feet. "Don't you see? That clockwork dragon of yours...that's why it was so attracted to you, why it was constantly trying to follow you everywhere."

"But to what end? I mean, not that it's not utterly fascinating in a really fucked-up way, but what is the fail-safe? Setting what free?" I slap the floor, frustration biting my belly. "The gods can take Meridian logic and shove it down a privy."

"I don't know, Mags." He sags. "I guess it means that whatever my mother took from Meridion to make it stop flying is...well, it's in you. Your heart."

"IronHeart in truth, then," I say bitterly, numb and sick to my stomach. "Nothing more than a walking prophecy come true. And when the Meridians find out, they'll tear me apart to get at it. After all, what's the life of a Moon Child compared to the freedom of an entire city?"

"Then we won't tell them," he says simply, as if there's nothing more to discuss.

"You know it's not that easy." I look away. "Don't make promises you'll have to break."

"But..." He takes a deep breath. "All right. Let's focus on getting out of here, then." He stands and heads to the panel on the pillar. He taps the buttons again. "Listen, I want to try something. Would you come here?"

I limp over to him. "What's this about?"

He gestures to me and taps on the keypad again. "Don't worry if your heartbeat changes a little. Can you just tell me the pattern?"

Immediately, my heart revs up like before, and I grit my teeth. "There isn't one. It gets faster and then short, and then it feels like it's going to fucking vibrate out of my skin," I snap, pressing against my panel and backing away from the pillar as a sharpness slices through my chest. I gasp. "Something's wrong."

I wobble on unsteady legs, Ghost helping to lower me to the floor. "What is it?"

My mouth moves, but I'm not making any sound, pain whisking my voice away. Ghost tears open my shirt, gingerly pressing against the bindings I had tied around my chest to keep the loose panel in place.

"Oh hells, Mags. It's shaking like crazy..." Whatever else he says is lost in the roaring of the blood in my ears. He's removing the wrap and flipping frantically through his mother's notebook at the same time. I catch an image of a diagram on the pages.

My heart...

His head lowers. "Breathe, Mags. In and out. In... Out... Okay, good, just like that."

My body shudders, the vibrating song of the heart echoing in my bones and through my teeth. "What's...going on?"

"I'm going to have to open the panel completely to see." He lays his hand on my forehead. "It's probably going to hurt, Mags. I'm sorry."

I nod, swallowing hard. My jaw is locked in place, as are my limbs, and it's all I can do to keep from screaming.

Click.

Click.

Clunk.

The silence is horrifying. For the first time, there is no whirring sound pulsing in my chest, pumping the blood. Ghost's breathing is labored, nervous, and there's an awful pressure pushing down on my lungs. I look up and immediately wish I hadn't. He's holding something metallic and says something to me, his face blurring.

Pop.

I shriek, and then everything goes black.

"Mags... Wake up. Please, oh please, wake up..."

Dampness is the first thing I feel, a wet cloth pressed against my forehead. I roll to my side, sucking in a deep, burning breath. Every nerve in my lungs is sparking. Fire sluggishly pumps through my veins, and I let out a sobbing moan.

Ghost exhales in relief as I blink blearily at him, even as he wraps his arms around my shoulders. "You're alive."

"Am I?" My voice shakes. "I'm not entirely sure I wouldn't rather be dead. Did you fix me?"

"I think so. For now. There was water in there from the flooding." He sucks on his lower lip. "But the skin around where your panel is… I think it's starting to get infected. I made a couple of adjustments, but I don't know how long they'll hold. This sort of thing is beyond me."

I cough. "Need a bonewitch."

"Lucian will know what to do when we get topside," he says, but his confidence feels forced through the dark circles and the weariness upon his face.

"It will be all right," I murmur softly, reaching up to stroke his head. "Let's see if the code works now."

"Aye." He doesn't say whatever else he's thinking, but he gathers me to my feet so I can limp over to the pillar. My shirt hangs in tatters from my thin frame, the heart panel peeking out of its low collar.

This time, the *click-whir* of my heart speeds up, but instead of the crazy grinding of before, there's an obvious pattern to it. I gape in amazement. "It's doing something."

Ghost places his fingers upon the heart-shaped panel on my chest, his head cocked as he listens. "Two short, one long…three staccato. And then it repeats." He finds the keypad with his other hand and taps out the pattern.

"My mother was either insane or a genius," he mutters when the panel lights up. "Whatever would have possessed her to lock herself down here with the key in the body of a little girl? Anything could have happened to it, to *you*."

"But if it only opens the door out of here, so what?"

"I'll bet you Lucian's best hat, it does more. She was too smart for that. If it's truly a skeleton key, then it probably fits every lock she ever made."

"Guess we won't know unless we test it," I say, imagining the fallout when the Meridians realize a Moon Child is the answer they've been searching for.

"Yes." The softly glowing panel now shows two sets of buttons. Ghost presses the top one, and the recessed edge of the pillar slides back to the right. Not a door exactly, more like a shell of metal rolling away into the wall, revealing a cylindrical room just large enough to fit us both standing. The floor is dusty, but dim lights in the ceiling illuminate the fading patina.

"This is it, Mags." Ghost's voice is tight as he looks at the remains of his mother's workshop, but he takes my hand to pull me into the pillar room beside him. He's stuffed several of the notebooks into a satchel he found, including the one about my heart.

The inside of the tube has a second panel with a few more buttons. He exhales sharply and presses the uppermost one.

I swallow hard. "It's like a moving coffin."

The door shuts closed, eliciting an involuntary hiss from me, but Ghost squeezes my hand. "It's an elevator. They use them on Meridion all the time to get to the tops of some of the spires." His mouth purses as the floor lurches beneath us. "Let's hope this one doesn't decide to stop working partway up."

"Quit borrowing trouble." I punch him in the arm a little harder than I intended, but he merely chuckles.

The elevator jolts to a stop, and for a moment, I'm afraid it actually *has* gotten stuck, but the door grinds open in the end and we find ourselves in a rather plain, empty room. The walls are a dull ash color, the floor slate and octagonal, just like the laboratory below, with a spiral staircase leading upward and a set of double doors directly across from us. The only windows are far above, the sunlight slipping through to wash over us in a playful splash of blood-colored shadow.

It's too bright, and I'm forced to cover my eyes with my hands, even as I let out a small sob of relief. We've somehow made it to BrightStone, alive and more or less in one piece. The reality of it shakes me to my core.

"Where...where are we?" It takes me a few tries to get the words out, but as the first *bong-bong-bang* rumbles its way down the stairwell, I laugh aloud. "The Mother Clock. We're in the gods-be-damned Mother Clock."

Ghost hugs me close for a moment, then sobers. "All this time and we never knew she was here... I'm so sorry we sent you down below, Mags. If we'd been smarter about it, maybe we'd have found our way in properly."

"No, you wouldn't have. We never would have figured it out without finding the lab first." I snicker, despite myself. "Though, really, I guess she couldn't have made it any more obvious, aye? I mean, it's called the *Mother* Clock. She was practically inviting you."

"Maybe she was," he admits ruefully, pressing a button on the panel beside the elevator. The doors close, blending seamlessly into the wall. "That looks hidden enough, but I don't want to risk anyone else coming in until we know what's going on outside."

"Agreed," I say and point up to the top of the clock. "Shall we?"

He laughs softly, and together we mount the spiral staircase, Ghost taking my hand to lead me. We reach the upper landing and are immediately confronted with a series of enormous cogs and whirring gears, the guts of the Mother Clock spinning and shifting with ragged surety. Even if time were to stop, she would remain ticking, ticking, ticking.

We step cautiously around the landing, careful of the moving gears as we head toward the window. We pass by a large control panel that I can only assume is meant for running the Mother

Clock. Yet I pause here and there, waiting to see if my heart clicks in answer, but aside from the vibration of the machinery itself, I feel nothing.

Until I do.

"Hold up. There's something here." This time there's not a door hidden away so much as a panel that slides back to reveal a series of numbers and symbols I don't recognize. A small scroll is tucked in a hollow tube, the barest hint of parchment peering out from its shadowed shell.

I pluck it from its hiding place and unroll it. My lips move as I try to sound out the words, but then I give up and hand it to Ghost. "I don't understand."

"That's because it's written in Meridian code. It wasn't intended for anyone but a Meridian."

"What's it say?"

"It's a series of signals. Most of them are simple things: danger, warning, all clear." He cocks a brow at me. "It's almost disappointing, really. I was half expecting an ancient prophecy in iambic pentameter, but I think this is a communications beacon. The bigger question is why?" He studies it and then shakes his head. "This one, though...I think this one is something else. It's coded differently. It's got the word for *aria*. Whatever that means."

"Maybe it's somewhat to do with her contact on Meridion. It's probably best not to start hitting buttons." I pause, remembering Mad Brianna had said something about this too. "'When the Mother Clock sings—'"

"'—the dragon takes wing'," he finishes. "Maybe *you're* the dragon. I don't know. Maybe she really *could* tell fortunes." He waves off the thought. "Never mind that, now. Let's try to open the window."

The window itself is too small to crawl through, but there's a latch so I crack it open, nearly weeping at the breeze that flutters in. Ghost holds me tight as I suck in deep pulls of air. The waning sunlight blurs my vision, but I squint out over the city anyway.

My city.

In the distance come screams and gunfire, the buzz and whine of weapons discharged, the scent of smoke and flares of light that burn hot against my retinas. The thrum of an airship engine wavers as it circles the city. "What's going on? I can't see." Panic lances through me to be topside and blind in the middle of what seems to be a war.

"The rebellion, I think. Come on." Ghost nudges me. "We have to find Lucian and the others."

"You'll move faster without me." I let out a sad little laugh.

A hint of anger seeps through his words. "You really think, after everything we've been through, that I would leave you alone, injured, and blind. And—"

I place my fingers against his mouth. "Everyone else would."

"I'm not everyone else." He tips his forehead toward me so it rests against mine, his fingers tracing the brand on the back of my neck. "Am I?"

I swallow hard. "No. You aren't."

This time, I meet him halfway when we kiss, a pair of vagabond Moon Children beneath the shelter of the Mother Clock, silent under a setting sun I never thought I'd see again.

Fire and ash are the sun's delight
And the moon's unending bane,
It scorches me as I take flight,
My feathers bursting into flame.

— CHAPTER SIXTEEN —

The door to exit the Mother Clock creaks open, a cool breeze shivering in from the outside. Goose bumps ripple over my skin, but that doesn't stop me from lurching outside, the need to be free overriding everything else.

"Easy there." Ghost holds me up as I slip on the cobblestones.

I take a deep breath, but smoke and ash burn my nostrils, a wall of heat making me forget the chill damp of the puddle I'm standing in. Another fire has broken out—this one much closer than the others. The flicker of flames from a nearby building sears itself into my retinas. It's so bright I nearly vomit, and in the end, I tear off a scrap of cloth from my shirt to wrap around my head and cover my eyes. It stinks something fierce, but it's better than nothing.

"Come on." Ghost shuts the door behind us and takes me by the hand.

My fingers brush the brickwork of the far wall. "All right, all right."

I go as slow as I dare, one hand skimming the sides of the buildings as he guides me. I still stub my toe three times and crack an ankle when my foot rolls on a piece of debris. If I had any guts at all, we would take to the rooftops, but that would be a death trap.

Suddenly I'm shouldered against the wall, and I stumble against Ghost.

"Hey, watch out where you're going!" a man shouts at me.

"Watch yourself," I snap. "I'm blind."

"Well, so am I!"

I cock my head. His voice is achingly familiar...

There's a pause, and I feel Ghost shift beside me. "It's Bran!"

"Bran? It's Magpie!" Relief floods through me. "How'd you get away?"

He snorts. "I should ask you the same. But not here. Between Buceph's Rotter army, the BrightStone rebellion, and the Inquestors damn near shooting everyone on sight, there's no real safety anywhere. Don't go near Surgeon's Row, either. It's overrun with Rotters."

I chance a peek out from beneath my wrap, wincing at the light. But it's enough to discover which side of the park we're on. Gunfire crackles in the distance, the buzz and whine of weapons being discharged. We can't afford to be caught up in that. Not yet.

"I've borrowed a room about two blocks over," Bran says. "In the old brewery pub. Third floor. Might be worth hiding out there until it gets dark enough that we can see without pain."

"Borrowed, aye?" Ghost's voice is tinged with amusement.

Bran grunts. "The whole place is nearly burned out. Not like anyone will notice. The others are waiting there, too."

My chest swells with the knowledge that our tiny clan has somehow managed to survive, and my mind fills with questions. I leave them unasked for now; any unwanted noise will make us targets. Ghost leads the way to the brewery, but random airship patrols and gunfire have us moving far slower than any of us like.

The abandoned wagon of a fruit seller becomes another hiding place, the scent of the rancid apples roiling my stomach and making it rumble. Soft cries of people in fear rush all around me, the rhythmic sounds punctuated by quick intakes of breath. It's a form of poetry, this panic.

Ghost nudges me when we get to the steps of the pub. "You two wait up there. I'm going to find my brother. I'll be back for you."

He gently squeezes my hand, and I nod. As much as I dislike the idea of him leaving us, I have to admit that he'll move much faster on his own. Besides, my feet are burning something awful.

At least it's dark inside the pub, and I'm able to remove my blindfold. The steps creak and wail their warnings beneath our weight, but our passage upward is uneventful, save for the taste of ash that still fills the air.

"Magpie?" I barely have time to glance up before someone barrels into me, Gloriana throwing her arms around my neck so that we tumble to the floor. "Oh," she sobs. "You're alive. You're alive."

"Aye," I say raggedly, hugging her. "For what it's worth. And— Oof!"

More of them pile onto me— Rosa, Dafyyd, Haru... I hold them all as tightly as I can and there's nothing but quiet sighs as we reaffirm our own existence, that we are here, in this place. A hot flush of tears brims down my cheeks.

Bran sinks into a broken stool, leaning against the wall. His face is equal parts sadness and bemusement as he watches us, and I know he's thinking about Penny. I shrink away from the thought, clearing my throat as I realize we're missing someone else. "Where's Tin Tin?"

Bran grunts. "That little shit took off as soon as he made it out of the Arse. Can't blame him though. He could see, after all. I hope he made it to Josephine, seeing as she's supposed to be helping to lead this little rebellion, aye? At least from what you told me." He smirks. "Not that any help came, but seeing the state of the city, I cannot blame her for that. So now what?"

I extricate myself from the pile of Moon Children and wipe my eyes. "We wait for Ghost. You have somewhat to eat?"

"There's a package of crackers in the corner. Think a rat's been at it."

I'm not picky, so I find them and scarf a few down. He shifts on the stool. He's favoring his right leg, his knee bent at an odd angle. A closer inspection reveals a large amount of swelling.

"You should get that treated." I poke his leg gently.

Gloriana flushes. "I tried, but I don't have any supplies, not even anything to clean it with." She nudges Bran. "No luck in Surgeon's Row, I take it?"

He shakes his head. "The bonewitches are completely overrun by the dead and the dying. Those who are left, anyway. Most have been taken into 'protective' custody by Balthazaar."

My upper lip curls. "Still determined to make a profit dancing on the bodies of the crippled. Why did he even let you go?"

"Who said he did? After you…fell? Jumped? Whatever the hells you did to get into the Arse, there was enough confusion that the rest of our clan could get away. Except for me, of course. Noble self-sacrifice and all that. I'm sure Penny would have been impressed." He looks away. "Balthazaar locked me up right quick—threw me in the cellar. Tanith and the other two Meridians had better rooms upstairs, but I was in them while she stuck needles in me. It really didn't matter." He rubs his leg. "Scientist or no, she's shit with a syringe."

"Her supposed cure, I take it?" I don't know why I'm even disappointed that the woman kept her promise to Balthazaar. In the back of my mind I'd been hoping that Joseph would convince her otherwise, but a crow's feathers are black through and through, no matter if it's day or night. Why would Tanith be any different simply because she worked for a different master?

"Aye. Though I'm not sure Balthazaar will ever get over Lydia's death, he's certainly willing to make some jingle on a potential medicine. And it's not good news for any of us, by the by," Bran says with bitter surety. "When they round us up for their miracle cure? Get used to a life in chains, is all I can say."

I don't even bother pretending to chuckle. Nothing is ever good news for us. I lick the crumbs off my fingers. "What are you talking about?"

"Oh, turns out it's Moon Child blood that fixes the Rot after all, at least by what Tanith indicated," Bran says airily, reaching into his pocket to pull out a cigarillo and lighting it with a snap of a lucifer. "Guess Buceph was nothing more than a big fat liar. Go figure."

He puffs out a stream of smoke as I wrap my brain around that particular tidbit. "What the hell do you mean, our blood cures the Rot? And you still haven't told me how you escaped."

"Ah, well, I don't think the Inquestors are really used to us fighting them. After I got my hands free, I waited until nightfall, killed three of them outright, and strangled Tanith. The other Meridians tried to stop me, but I slipped out during all the chaos and stole one of Balthazaar's horseless carriages." He laughs. "Drove it right over a bridge and into the Everdark River, in fact."

I gasp. "You *what*? You killed Tanith?"

"Believe me, you'll thank me for doing it." Bran flicks the remainder of the cigarillo at me. I snatch it and take a deep drag of my own. "Balthazaar is already too ambitious by half. You think I'm going to willingly roll over and become his slave?"

The Mother Clock chimes out the hour, and I realize the sun has finally gone down completely. Fires or no, we should have a better time of it now. I peer out the window. Where is Ghost? I shift, pressing my hand over my heart panel. It hasn't been rattling since he messed with it, but there's a heat coming from my skin that I don't much like.

Bran cracks his neck. "Your erstwhile rescuer seems to be taking his sweet time."

I shoot him a glare. "Maybe he's having trouble finding the rebellion. He said they've been taking possession of airships."

"Sounds handy. Wish I'd thought of it." He stands and limps to the stairwell, wincing away from a sudden flare of orange light. "Well, isn't that a pisser. The pub's on fire again."

I sniff. The acrid scent of smoke is definitely stronger now, and Bran is already climbing out the window. I move to join him, my heart sinking when I see the flames licking up the front of the building.

Bran squints and gestures at the rest of us to follow. "You know, I've never been much good at waiting. Let's go see if we can find them, aye?"

When seen from the perspective of my naturally enhanced night vision, the entirety of the city appears to glow, every shadow in the fog seeming to burn with an inner illumination. The moon winks from behind the clouds here and there, and even that is too bright. Despite my pain, I bask in it, the sky weighing upon me with its terrible openness. If I were to jump from here, I would be a bird taking flight on wings of bone and ash.

Sucking in a deep breath, I leap across the first gap to the next building over. My cloth-wrapped feet burn as they scrape the copper roof, my balance wobbly. But I correct and then correct again, my hands finding purchase in the crenulations of a chimney.

I cough. "Out of practice." But it's more than that. I've forgotten the ins and outs of the buildings and the layout of the city. It's there, in my memories, overlaid across my vision, but tiny changes make it difficult to maneuver. A pipe gone here, a crumbling wall there. It will take time for my muscles to relearn the movements I once knew and remember the city that was my home.

The whole group of us creeps along as best we can, descending a fire escape when we reach a height none of us can jump down from. I stretch my calves when we reach the bottom. "Before, I would have tried it."

A chuckle escapes Bran. "Speak for yourself. I was never very good at this. There was a reason the Spriggans never chased you or Sparrow very far. None of us would have been able to keep up with you anyway. And your scrawny necks weren't worth a broken back."

"Keep talking like that and I'll start thinking you're sweet on me," I retort.

We slip through the alleyways, careful not to make eye contact with the few people who furtively skulk by.

"Have you been to the Warrens yet?" Bran pauses and scans the houses near us. "Whatever they did to collapse the Pits leveled half the buildings."

I blink at him. "What about the Banshee clan? I mean, our home was there."

Haru tugs on my sleeve. "I saw Rory last night, but I didn't let him see me. The Banshees are holed up over by the Cheaps for now, down by the docks."

"Good." Not that I bear my former clan leader any love at all, but if he's at least trying to take care of the rest of the clan, that will have to be good enough. "Sounds like a right mess."

A clattering of voices freezes us all. Bran cups his ears. "Rotters."

I can't hear much beyond a sudden high-pitched shriek, but I'll take his word for it. My fingers tap the hammer at my side, and then I pull it out of my belt. "Come on."

To his credit, he doesn't ask questions, merely takes up a long metal pipe from the ground. Scuttling forward, we reach the edge of the alley to see a cluster of townsfolk balancing precariously on a stack of barrels. Ten Rotters surround them, their broken fingers clawing at the wood.

Bran and I don't hesitate. I whistle shrilly to catch the creatures' attention, and the two of us fall into our usual attack pattern. The other Moon Children snatch up their own makeshift weapons and join us, swinging them with the careless confidence born of practice. And being able to see now only makes it that much simpler.

I crack one through the skull and slam my hammer into the chest of another as Bran twirls his pipe, mowing down three more. The report of gunfire shatters the bricks behind us, the roar nearly deafening me

The people huddled atop the barrels duck, one of the children moaning.

Another Rotter shambles toward us, and I dispatch it quickly. I'm wiping the blood off the handle of my hammer when a group of Inquestors trots into view, pistols at the ready. "You're all under quarantine for infection, by order of the High Inquestor," one of them announces.

"Don't be daft," I sneer, panting. I'm stalling for time in the hopes that my clan can escape. Fighting the Rotters has taken far more out of me than I'd like to admit, and none of us are in particularly good shape.

"It's orders, miss." He waves his men forward, and they fan out around us, avoiding the dismembered bodies of the Rotters. "Get them ready to put on the airship."

Their would-be leader approaches us, the distant rumble of an Interceptor looming ever closer. "What in the hells is wrong with your eyes?" I'd forgotten that I practically glowed in the dark. Before I can even answer, he points the pistol at my head. "I don't care what the High Inquestor says about collecting Moon Children. I'm not—"

Pop!

Bran shoves me down as a whistle echoes off the buildings. The Inquestor topples over, a crossbow bolt embedded in his brainpan.

"Not doing much of anything," finishes a voice from above us.

I look up. *Josephine.* And a very smug Tin Tin, who lifts his now-empty crossbow off his arm. And Ghost.

He's at my side in an instant, anger staining his cheeks.

"Someone's pissed you got off your leash," Bran mutters to me, earning him a snarl from Ghost.

All around, pale heads emerge from the surrounding buildings—Moon Children armed with crossbows and patchwork weapons. Josephine herself climbs down the nearest wall. My mouth splits in a wide smile. Breaking down in a sobbing heap of relief isn't a particularly good option right now, though, so I hold it all in, giving her a tight nod, one clan leader to another. Her brow raises, but she returns the gesture with an air of bemusement.

The other Inquestors retreat to form a tight ball, bristling with aggressive tension. There's something tired about the way they move, defeated, as though they don't want to be here any more than the rest of us. How many of them simply want to go home?

Josephine points at the townsfolk. "Go on. Get out of here. If you have no homes to return to, there's shelter at whatever's left of the Brass Button Theatre." They don't wait to be told twice and scatter into the darkness. She gestures curtly, and a handful of Moon Children follow, flanking them from the rooftops.

"As for you lot…" She turns to the Inquestors and shrugs. "Well, you know the drill." Another gesture and a surge of bolts twang from behind us, the Inquestors dropping to the cobblestones in a pool of blood. I should feel horrified at the carnage, but I can't quite bring myself to care.

"Why didn't you wait for me?" Ghost snaps at me. "I told you I was coming back once I'd found everyone else."

Rosa shoves her way between us, trembling in sudden fury. "Don't you talk to her like that," she roars, startling everyone. "Mags is our clan leader. Not *you.*"

I gape at the other girl. "Well done," Bran murmurs, his cheek twitching.

"Ah, it's all right, Rosa," I say, desperately trying to ignore Josephine's blatant snickering even as I wince at Ghost's sudden confusion. "He didn't know the pub caught fire, aye?"

"Next time we'll wait for the building to go up in flames completely so you can pick up her ashes, instead." Bran shoves past us to stand in front of Josephine, and I pinch the bridge of my nose.

Something unreadable crosses her face when she sees him, taking in the glowing eyes and hair shining from beneath his cloak. "My, my," she drawls. "To think I've been graced with the presence of the former leader of the Spriggans."

Bran's expression becomes appraising, and then he laughs. "There are no clans anymore."

"Perhaps. Perhaps not." She tips her head at Ghost. "Let's show them what we've got, shall we?"

The Interceptor is deep in the Warrens, drifting gently in the fog. The other Moon Children have gone ahead, fading into the mist without a sound, including our little NightSinger clan. Tin Tin has taken them under his wing and led them off somewhere to find a hot meal. Josephine is already onboard, and she lowers a rope ladder, leaving the three of us to climb up.

For the sake of keeping hidden, there is no light on the outside of the airship, but once we pass through the main cabins, I'm forced to replace the cloth over my face against the sharpness of the lanterns.

"Here we are." Ghost hasn't let go of my hand this entire time, but he does now, rapping sharply on a door. Behind it, there's the sound of a great deal of lively conversation. It's nothing I can make out, and it all goes quiet when the door opens and Ghost ushers us inside.

The tension hurts, prickles me through my skin with a painful sort of terror. That I've been gone too long. Seen too much. Changed beyond recognition.

And then someone lets out a whoop, and I'm pulled into a pair of arms that I can only imagine belong to Lucian, which is confirmed a second later when he says my name and a host of other things I can barely understand. He clings to me so tightly I might shatter from the pressure.

Questions. Shouts. Joyous laughter at Ghost's return. At *my* return.

It's too much. After so long, my heightened senses are nearly overwhelmed by the cacophony and the embracing, and I find myself pulling away, my hands behind me to press against the coolness of the wall.

"Leave off," I say to whoever is still holding my arm, swallowing a sudden rush of panic.

"What's wrong with your eyes?" Lucian asks softly, tugging at my blindfold.

"You think living in the dark for so long *improved* our vision?" Bran snorts beside me. "Turn down the lights and you'll see why."

Someone shuffles around the room. The lanterns squeak when they're turned to their lowest setting, but immediately, I sense a much more comforting level of darkness, despite the soft illumination from under one of the other doors.

"By the hells," Lucian says. "Your hair, Mags. It's glowing."

I tug at the knot of the blindfold and squint when it falls.

Even without the lights on, this place has got nothing on a pitch-black cave, but at least it doesn't pain me. Memories rock me sideways. Lucian. Josephine. Even the BrightStone Chancellor is here, albeit in far more casual clothing than the fine gown she'd been wearing the last time I'd seen her. It feels a lifetime ago.

She lets out a gasp when I blink, straining to focus. "You've got moonbeams in your eyes."

"Something like that," I agree wryly. "Thanks to the power of some rather interesting fungus."

Lucian takes a step closer, his fingers snarling in the tangles of my hair. "Remarkable."

"It was handy down below, I'll grant you. Not so much right now."

Josephine gives me a shrewd look. "Oh, I think it might prove to be very useful."

"And I think I'm done with being *useful*," I snap at her.

"You must be hungry," Lucian says abruptly, interrupting what would surely become a nasty conversation. My stomach rumbles at his words, and I realize I can't even remember the last time I've eaten.

Josephine hands me a partial loaf of bread. It's a few days stale, but I barely slow down long enough to taste it. Lucian breaks off another piece and gives it to Bran, and for a few minutes, there's nothing more interesting than the sound of chewing.

Ghost digs up another loaf from a cabinet somewhere, as well as some cheese, and comes to sit beside me.

There's a flask of ale on one of the tables, and I cock my head at Lucian. I don't bother asking permission, snatching it up to wash down the bread. He remains pensive as he watches me eat, and I nearly cry at the familiar expression. I didn't realize how much I missed the man until now.

But there's no time for tears and I swallow them, coughing to hide the half sob that escapes my throat, and I gesture about the room in an effort to hide my emotion. "So what is all this?"

"Ah, yes. I suppose there should be introductions and explanations." Lucian turns to the Chancellor. "You already know Ghost. And this young woman is the one I told you about, Magpie. She's been down in the Pits attempting to gather information to help our cause."

Bran shakes his head. "A cause? This is a nightmare."

"Yes, well, you're in the rather impromptu headquarters of the BrightStone rebellion," the Chancellor says coolly. "For too long, we have been under Meridion's thumb, and it has become all too clear that we must finally take a hand in our own fate."

Something inside me flutters at her words, but I can't bring myself to believe them. Buceph had pretty speeches, too. Even if Lucian and Ghost trust her, they had also trusted Molly Bell and that hadn't turned out particularly well.

"Aye, fate," Bran retorts. "Is that what you called that shit show up by the gates? You damn near collapsed the mines on top of us!"

Josephine's eyes narrow, darting toward Ghost, who flinches beneath the weight of her stare. "Well, *someone* decided to take matters into his own hands. But even aside from that, I used my airships to force the gates open once Tin Tin had been sent down there. We were planning on coming to get you, but we weren't anticipating an entire Rotter army to come pouring out of it." Her brow furrows. "It was a bit beyond our expectations. And besides, the Inquestors blew up the mine entrance. We hightailed it once we saw what was going on."

"It all happened rather fast, aye?" I point out. "How could they get that much firepower there that quickly?"

Lucian sighs. "I think the Inquestors might have had a contingency plan in place already. It wouldn't have been too hard to ensure explosives were situated around the mine structures when they were building the Pits so many years ago."

"It was an unfortunate hiccup," the Chancellor says, "but we've done the best we can. The bulk of the Rotters have been destroyed at this point; now we're fighting directly with the Inquestors over parts of the city."

"I'm sorry we can't offer you better accommodations," Lucian says regretfully. "We'd rather hoped things might be different by this point."

"We've been sleeping in caves filled with flesh-eating Rotters."
I wrinkle my nose. "So I've got a radically different definition of
better now. I wouldn't say no to a hot bath, though."

An awkward tension fills the room, but I've no sympathy for
their discomfort. This is what I'd been sent to the Pits to do. I might
as well share my findings.

The words spill out of me, then. The darkness, the scent of salt
and death, the soft glowing of the mushroom. The secret society of
Meridian scientists and their lab of sideshow experiments. At one
point, Lucian pulls out a notebook and starts writing, but by the
time I get to the part where the Moon Children were deliberately
butchered and sent to their deaths, he has paled.

Josephine's eyes are flashing with a terrible fury, but Lucian taps
his charcoal pencil on the paper with a frantic nervousness. "I've
heard those names before—Buceph and Tanith. I've seen their
work in papers with…Madeline d'Arc."

For a moment, I think he's going to slip up about the family rela-
tionship, but he's been hiding it for far too long to let it out now. I
can see the questions whirring in his mind and the frustration as
he bites his tongue to keep from asking.

"Yes. They were colleagues," I say. "I saw pictures of them
together from their time up on Meridion. For whatever that's
worth…" I take a deep pull from the last of the flask, the alcohol
burning my belly.

"Touching," Bran says, "but it doesn't matter. I made sure
whatever secrets that Meridian bitch brought up from the Pits died
with her."

"And you don't think it's worth sharing with us?" Ghost shoots
back.

I touch Ghost's shoulder. "Bran killed Tanith during his escape
from Balthazaar."

"And good riddance, given what I learned." Bran sits up on his
stool. "It's our blood that cures the Rot."

Lucian frowns at him, but it's tempered with a wary interest. "But I've been trying for years with Moon Child blood—with no results."

"You can't just inject a...a victim with Moon Child blood," Bran explains with more calm than he's shown thus far. "It has to bond with a donor first, aye? So the Rotter's blood is injected into a chosen Moon Child, and once the blood has mingled for a time, then it can be returned to the infected patient." Bran snaps his fingers in irritation. "I don't know. I don't understand this shit. Tanith had lousy notes."

Lucian grows thoughtful, scratching something else into his notebook. "Like a vaccine."

Bran shrugs at the word. "If you say so. But the worst of it is that it only works for that one Rotter, and according to Tanith, it only worked if the Rotter got regular doses and began them early enough to make a difference."

Horror lands in a cold lump in my belly as I realize the implications of this statement. Beside me, Josephine tenses.

The Chancellor's brow furrows into deep lines. "But surely that could be the start of something, couldn't it? With the beginnings of such research, perhaps the method could be streamlined—synthesized, even."

"No," Josephine snaps. "What it means is that Moon Children will be rounded up and chained, to be sold to the highest bidder as living cures. Surviving in poverty beneath our birthright and treated like trash is one thing, but slavery?"

"I cannot deny we have treated your kind poorly," the Chancellor says quietly. "But I would have us do better going forward."

Bran sneers at her. "You can start by sucking my cock then, because that's about all the satisfaction worth getting from your sort."

The Chancellor draws herself up, her eyes flashing, but I kick Bran in the shin of his good leg. "You're not helping our cause here, aye?"

His eyes drop. "Sorry," he mutters. He's hurting; I can see it in every move he makes, his bravado a cloak wrapped around him like a shield to avoid breaking any further. A soft trill escapes me, one of those calming whistles Penny used on him from time to time, and he startles, a half smile tugging at his mouth.

I glance over at the Chancellor with an apologetic shrug. "We're all of us a bit ill-used. Manners don't get us very far in the Pits."

"Undoubtedly," Chancellor Davis says coolly. "But that attitude won't get us very far in forging new alliances."

"Enough," Ghost says, interrupting the flow of conversation with a sideways glance in my direction. "Maybe you should all listen to what else Mags and I discovered before you start making decisions." His mouth tightens and I can hear the anger sliding beneath the tension of his voice.

I exhale sharply as all attention turns my way. I'm tired of fighting and tired of arguing, but mostly I'm tired of this unending conflict. Moon Child clans. BrightStonians versus Moon Children. And then there are the Rotters playing nightmare games in the city, trained to consume mortal flesh by their creators. They are all intricately connected to the Meridians in some way, merely puppets to the masters above and dancing to the tune they play.

I hardly know where to start. Misery seeps into me, raw and bitter. In the end, I undo my shirt so it falls open on either side of my chest, exposing my clockwork heart.

"Mags," Ghost hisses at me.

I know he doesn't want me to tell them. I'll be made a target for sure. One way or another, though, it has to come out tonight. Maybe I'm ready to show the world. Or maybe I'm a coward who doesn't want to decide the fate of my people.

Lucian leans forward. "What happened to you?"

I can't help but run my fingers over it, shuddering at the lumpy way it juts out of my chest and the burning beneath my skin. "Madeline d'Arc put it here," I say finally. "It's the key to restarting Meridion."

Bran lets out a low whistle and cocks a sardonic brow at me. "Maybe we should kill you, too, then. Because if they capture you, we're all fucked."

Josephine crosses her arms. "Why didn't you tell us earlier? By the gods, can you imagine what this means?"

I flinch as though I've been slapped, grabbing my hammer almost on pure instinct. "Because I didn't have any idea what it was for! It never served a purpose until I ended up down...there. And then Ghost and I—"

"We found Madeline d'Arc's laboratory," Ghost cuts in. "It's hidden beneath the Mother Clock." He lets his words sink in around us, but his attention rests solely on his brother.

Lucian's face becomes desperate, dropping into a ragged whisper. "Are you sure?"

Ghost pulls out a notebook from his pouch and tosses it to him. "I brought this back. She's still there. Her remains, that is. I mean..." His voice trails away awkwardly.

There's a tremble in his voice as he says it, and I can't tell if he's about to break down over the betrayal lying within those pages or lash out in anger. Something fiercely protective flares to life in me, hard enough to make my chest ache.

I interrupt him before he can say anything else. "My heart. It unlocked the exit from her lab through the Mother Clock. It reacts to technology she created and beats out a key or something. But I think it might be broken. Buceph tried to pry it off me, and Ghost..."

"She was dying," he says softly. "I had to crack it open to keep it from killing her, but I don't think I did it right."

I look over at Bran. "It's how we escaped the Pits. If I'd had any idea, I would have said something. I swear it."

"I'm sure." The way he says it I'm not convinced he believes me, but I have no more explanations, no more words. He fixes his broad stare on the others. "So now what?"

"Look away," Lucian says, snagging a lantern and turning it up next to the panel on my chest. His sudden exhalation brushes over my skin. "It's going necrotic, Mags. Whatever else is decided tonight, you're going into surgery immediately."

I swallow. "Can't it wait? I mean, I've gone this long…"

"Not unless you like having your chest rot from the inside out, no."

"But if… What if the key stops working?" The words vibrate in the silence of the cabin. Not that I really want to say them, but I know everyone is thinking it—the advantage we'll lose, our hold over Meridion. How much is one Moon Child's life really worth when confronted with all that?

Lucian's voice grows hard as he dims the lantern again. "Then we will find another way."

The Chancellor nods and then taps her fingers upon the map. "In the meantime, we study what's inside that lab, and then we use it as a bargaining chip with the Meridians." She presses her lips together. "And say what you will about this potential Moon Child cure, but if we know what it is and how it works, it will keep Balthazaar in check, simply because he will not have a monopoly on it. All in all, it's a good start. If we can manage to work together."

I meet her eyes. "The other Moon Children have to be told—all of them. If you wish us to give your words any value, then we need a say in our own destiny. They need to be educated, trained for something other than scavenging, allowed into society. We…we have given you enough." I curl into my seat, thankful for Ghost's presence when he reaches over to take my hand. His earlier anger at me is gone, lost in the severity of our situation.

"Agreed," Josephine says. "And the Twisted Tumblers will be notified later tonight. As to the others scattered about?"

"Leave to that me." Bran smirks, but it's full of self-loathing. "I can be rather persuasive. After all, I certainly didn't have any trouble convincing Penny I'd make for a good shag, aye?"

"We were in the dark for months," I retort, stung by how casually he refers to our fallen clanmate. "A doorknob would have made for a good shag."

"Fair enough. But a doorknob doesn't cut your fingers off, either." The words hang there for a moment as things suddenly fall into place. Penny's half-dropped hints, Bran's apologetic mien around her...

I blink. "That was *you?*"

"Well, it's not like I knew we'd be thrown in together after I found her roaming around Spriggan territory, now is it?" He scowls, but it's clear he's directing it at himself. "We can talk about it later."

Josephine glares at him. "Good. Get that leg treated, and then we'll go over the logistics of rounding up the clans together. It's going to take a little more than *persuasion* if we want to be seen as more than a genetic inconvenience."

Lucian gestures to Bran. "I'll see to it after we get Mags fixed up."

Bran makes a mocking little bow and takes his leave shortly after that. I can only marvel at his stamina, but he's had a few extras days aboveground and a few extra meals, and maybe that makes all the difference.

The conversation turns to other things and back to the discussion Bran, Ghost, and I interrupted with our presence in the first place. Who was captured, who was killed. What streets the Rotters are on. Where the fires continue to rage.

Their words are a blur to me, exhaustion and relief making my bones heavy. Somewhere along the way, Josephine and the Chancellor have disappeared, though the sudden thrumming vibration beneath my feet can only mean we're about to shove off. Part of me dearly wants to go above deck to see what it's like to fly, but Ghost has dozed off, his head in my lap.

Lucian takes my hand in his. His long, elegant fingers are as I remember, though far less polished now. The once neatly trimmed nails are jagged and dirty; the skin on his knuckles has seen its fair share of hard labor.

"Where are we going?" I slur up at him, my vision hazy.

"The Brass Button Theatre. Surgery or no, I have the feeling we're going to need Josephine's forge before we're through. I've never attempted anything like this before." He presses a kiss to my temple. "I know I'll never be able to repay you for everything you've done for us, Mags—for me, for him. But damned if I'm not going to try."

My name is Raggy Maggy,
Made of iron is my heart,
Cold and clean and metal sheen
And hollow when it's ripped apart.

— CHAPTER SEVENTEEN —

Time slips away while I sleep. Hours. Days. Years. An eternity passes between one blink and the next, the seconds stretched out into a wyrmhole of time from which I cannot seem to wake.

In the tunnels, none of us slept heavily. Even as high up as we were, there was always this wretched sense that something was seeking us out, that if we let down our guard beyond a certain point we were certain to be destroyed.

But here in this place of my past, the future has twisted in on itself, and somehow I'm on the rooftops of the Cheaps with Sparrow, staring up at Meridion and dreaming of climbing to its top and looking out at the blue and brilliant sea. A realm of possibilities for a history we couldn't remember. A future we'd never have.

And I'm clean and dry. And warm.

So dreadfully warm.

I shift, panic rushing through me as I realize I don't know where I am.

"Shh. It's all right."

My muddled mind sorts through the voice, recognizing it as Ghost's as the memories of the last few days flash in my mind. I'm on a mattress with an actual pillow, Ghost curled around me and a blanket covering us both.

A shiver runs through me. This can only be a dream. Any second I'll wake up in the caves below, tucked between the *plip-plop* of dripping water and the shambling moans of the dead.

I have no idea what time it is, or even what day. My last memories are a blur, a hazy recollection of an injection of medication and my thrashing panic at being put to sleep. Then pain and more medicine, and a pulling sensation on my chest.

My chest.

I jerk up, throwing off the blankets, my hands slapping at the panel.

"Whoa, Mags." Ghost rolls off the mattress, his hair tousled.

"My heart..."

"Is as good as new," he says, his whole face lighting up. "Though the argument between Lucian and Josephine as to who should actually try to fix the mechanics behind it was fairly epic. My mother's notes on the subject came in rather handy."

Unconvinced, I try to peek beneath the bandages, peeling them carefully away. The panel is new, but d'Arc's symbol is carefully carved upon it like the old one. The skin around it is raw but healing, with no trace of any infection that I can see. And below the panel there's a salmon, tattooed in soft blue ink.

Ghost smirks. "Josephine wanted to brand her initials under that, but Lucian convinced her it would be a bad idea while you were still healing."

I shudder. "But do you think it still...works? The key part, I mean?"

"No idea. We should probably head over to the Mother Clock when you feel up to it and make sure. You hungry?"

I yawn. "I could probably eat every minute of the next few days and still want more."

He stretches and stands, pulling on his trousers. "I'll see what I can find. Rest here awhile."

"Like I have a choice?" Successful surgery or no, I'm tired. It's easier to slide back beneath the covers than to think of anything at all. The mattress is the most luxurious thing I've felt in ages, and I'm in no rush to get up. I drift into another fit of dozing, my bones soaking in all the warmth.

When I wake up for real some time later, Ghost is still gone, though the blankets have been tucked tightly around my shoulders. Not exactly the silk cocoon of a butterfly, but it will do. My stomach twists into knots of hunger, pulling me from the bed at last.

Poking around reveals an additional loaf of bread and a packet of greasy bacon on a nearby table. Both are gone within minutes as I gobble them down and lick my fingers clean. There's a fresh shirt and a pair of trousers there, too. They're far looser than any I've ever worn, but a rope belt takes care of the worst of it, and I holster the hammer snugly at my hip.

Nearly like old times, but without my dragon. Its absence is oddly noticeable now—maybe because I'm back in something akin to civilization.

I catch a glimpse of myself in a mirror on the wall and stop, staring at whatever I've become. My hair is ragged, body worn down to nothing more than a thin bit of skin stretched over bone and sinew. I'm covered in bruises, blotching reds and purples, from the swollen knuckles of my hands to the angry slash on my collarbone and the bite on my arm.

I touch my face, my cheeks pinched, lips cracked, and eyes sunken. I'm nothing more than a hollowed-out shell of a woman, a doll with a wind-up heart meant to be discarded on a rubbish heap like any other Meridian plaything. It's a wonder Ghost had recognized me at all.

"But I am alive," I say to my reflection with an air of rebellious satisfaction. I'd beaten the Pits, after all. "And that is more than enough for now."

With a soft sigh, I head for the door, covering my eyes with my hands as I exit just in case. Thankfully, the hallways are dim enough that my vision isn't too painful.

The scent of the burning metal and liquid fire of Josephine's forge are easy to recognize, and I follow it. Lucian comes storming past me, nearly knocking me into the wall. His expression softens when he recognizes me. "Sorry, Mags. Didn't see you there," he apologizes. "Not my day it would seem... It's good to see you up and about. How are you feeling?"

"Sore, but I'll manage." I wiggle my toes. "Even the cuts on my feet feel better."

"Good, good. I'll check those bandages a little later." He squeezes my shoulder gently. "You came through it so well. We were able to stop the infection in time, too. With fairly minimal damage from what I can tell."

"Aye," I say gratefully. "Where's Ghost?"

His face shutters. "Out cooling his heels. He and I had a bit of a disagreement. Maybe you can talk to him. He doesn't want to listen to me."

Irritation prickles over my skin. "He's not the child you think he is," I point out. "You might want to remember that. *He* came to find me. *He* helped me escape. Whatever your argument, perhaps he's got a reason for how he feels."

He shoves his glasses onto his forehead. It's as though he finally sees me, that despite the warm welcome from the other evening, I am not the same creature he thought I was.

He gives me a faint smile. "Mayhap you're right. Sometimes I forget... Well, it doesn't matter. Josephine is waiting in the forge. I think she would like to see you. I'll see if I can't find my erstwhile brother in the meantime."

"All right." I press past him toward the forge as he sighs and heads down the hall.

Inside, Josephine sits at a table studying a map of BrightStone. She immediately dims the lights when she sees me. "I didn't think you'd wake for at least a fortnight, given everything you've been through." Her mouth purses as she scans me. "You're a little less like a Rotter now. Smell better, too."

I snort. "Guess we're high-class."

"When it comes to dealing with the BrightStonians, apparently not stinking like a corpse is an advantage. Go figure."

I cross my arms against a sudden chill. "So what's the plan?"

"The Chancellor is doing whatever the Upper Tier sorts do. Win the people to our cause. Reduce casualties. Try to stop whatever's coming by wrapping it all in a big blanket of peace and treaties. It's all bullshit, but it's probably the only way the rest of BrightStone will rally." She shrugs. "At least the Rotters aren't as big of a threat in the daytime. Turns out the sun doesn't do much for their complexions; they have a tendency to fall apart." She strokes her chin with a pensive air. "By the way, I might have something that could help you with your light issue. Wait here."

She disappears into a closet. Metal clinks from where she's clearly shuffling drawers about, and she reappears with spectacles and a pair of boots. "I used to wear these sometimes, when I did more intricate work with a blowtorch. I've no call for that sort of thing now, but the lenses are smoked glass."

I peer at the copper banding and the silver filigree. The lenses are thick and set deep within their brass fittings, blocking out the light from the sides as well as the front. I slide them on, uncertain at the way they settle into place. But I blink. And then blink again, turning directly toward the forge doorway. "It's like I'm looking through shadows. And it doesn't hurt at all."

Josephine gives me a tight smile. "Good. I'd rather hoped they would work."

"How much do you want for them?" I ask. "Not that I have anything."

"Nothing. The information you've gathered is worth so much more than some tinted glass. And we've no way to really repay you. Besides, I gave Bran my other set this morning after Lucian sewed up his leg. Figured it was only fair. I'll see if I can't make a few more sets for the rest of your other...clan."

Her gratitude seems genuine enough, so I leave it be. "What time is it?"

"Late afternoon, actually. You might not even need the spectacles in a few hours, but at least you have them."

"Mayhap I'll catch up with Ghost and see what this fight with Lucian's about," I muse, sliding on the boots and tying them loosely. My feet are bandaged, but I'm glad for the extra protection.

"Might not be a bad idea. I don't know what was going on, but it didn't seem particularly pleasant." She chews on the inside of her cheek, waiting for me to fill her in on it, but I shrug at her.

"He missed you, you know," she says. "They both did. Lucian may have been more aloof about it, but he blames himself for what happened to you."

"Ghost said Lucian had given me up for dead," I say, tapping my fingers on the table.

"Well, to be honest, we all had. It's been nearly a year, after all, and none of us have ever seen any survivors. But Ghost never doubted you. He tried several times to convince Lucian to let him go find you, though I'm sure you know how that went." She cocks her head at me. "If you want to talk about a fight, you should have been around for that one. I damn near had to tie them up in separate corners."

I snort at this, but I'm not sure it makes me feel any better.

The main door from the hallway bursts open, and another Moon Child pelts in, gesturing wildly. "There's an automaton wandering the ruins upstairs. It's carrying a box."

Josephine snaps her fingers at the boy. "Go round up the others. I want them flanking the theatre. Full weapons."

He nods and disappears down the hall in a flurry of movement.

A grumpy sigh escapes her. "It's probably nothing, but let's go check it out. If you're up to it, that is," she drawls.

"I'm not a doll." I can't tell if she's serious or lightly mocking me, given the recent surgery, but now I'm curious.

"No, but getting a chance to see inside your heart was fascinating. What I wouldn't give to take it apart and really see how it was made." She smirks at me.

"That was a onetime shot," I say. "But I appreciate your assistance."

I adjust the spectacles on my nose for greater coverage and follow her down the hallway and up several flights of stairs until we find ourselves in the lower levels of the Brass Button Theatre. It's an empty, hollow place of dust and decay, and my feet make no noise on the rotting velvet rugs. The scent of old smoke and charred wood fills my nose, but it's not the smell that makes me pause.

At the entrance to the theatre stands Copper Betty, Molly Bell's mute automaton. It's been a long time since I've lived at the Conundrum, but I can't help but feel a little pang of regret when I see her. I'd always been fond of the robotic girl, even if her mistress had betrayed me. It's not like she could choose who to serve.

Copper Betty's head cocks when sees me, and the gesture is familiar and terrible all at once. The shiny polished gleam of her metal skin is long gone; she's become a dusky brown. Not rust so much as a lack of care. Her forearms are covered in scratches, and a partial dent shows from beneath the metallic coils of her hair.

"I know her," I murmur to Josephine. "She belongs to Molly Bell."

"She?" The other Moon Child quirks a brow at me. "It's an automaton. There's no gender involved."

I approach Copper Betty carefully, my fingers resting on my hammer. Familiar or not, she's one of Molly's creatures. I cannot trust the messenger any more than the message. Copper Betty holds out a wooden box to me, something insistent in her expressionless face. An envelope rests atop the box, fixed with a wax seal.

"Because this isn't suspicious in the slightest," Josephine mutters. "You should bash its chest in and be done with it."

She's right. I should. But my fingers clench around the hammer and I don't move. Eventually Copper Betty sets the box down, her feet clanking heavily against the creaking wood as she moves to stand beside the front doors of the theatre.

I approach the box with caution and snatch the envelope from the box with a trembling hand. I peer at the elegant script.

Raggy Maggy.

My lips press together. Molly knows I'm here. And if *she* knows, others do, too. Information is what she sells, after all.

The seal breaks easily beneath my fingers, the parchment unfurling like a flower with petals coated in poison. For all that it matters, the words within might be as dangerous as the real thing.

But the script is too fine for me to make out, and I'm reduced to sounding the words out a little at a time until Josephine takes it from me in irritation, her thick hands crumpling the corners as she reads aloud.

"*My dear Raggy Maggy,*

"*If you are reading this, then my suspicions are correct and Copper Betty has, indeed, found you alive and well.*

"*I will not apologize for my actions, nor do I have any words of comfort to offer you as we both know they would be dishonest. With that in mind, I do have a few small things to give you that were somehow left in my keeping. I thought you might want them returned.*

"*To that end, I am also leaving you Copper Betty. You will find her a good and loyal servant. Truthfully, I am loath to part with her, but she has indicated her time with me is over. Please take good care of her.*

"*Best wishes,*

"*Molly Bell.*"

I stare at Copper Betty. How did a mute automaton indicate anything?

"Something isn't right," I say. "This doesn't make any sense at all."

"Open the box," Josephine snaps.

But I'm already there, my hammer smashing open the side of it when the latch doesn't give.

Flame erupts from beneath my fingers, and I dance back, my heart whirring madly. The box explodes into splinters as my dragon bursts from within, its ember chest blooming red and orange. I laugh as it takes to the air, hissing small puffs of steam. It circles us and then lands abruptly on my shoulder. Its talons dig into my neck, and I wince. I'm half expecting my heart to change its rhythm to match that of the dragon, but then I realize the dragon has changed its heartbeat to match *mine.*

My hands find its head and stroke it, already drawn to the soothing *click-whir* of its own clockwork heart. "I missed you, you silly wee thing." Guardian or toy, it doesn't particularly matter to me anymore.

"What a cunt that Molly Bell is." Josephine kicks what's left of the box, ignoring my impromptu reunion. "The waters might be muddied, but the shark always finds a place to feed."

Click.

I stiffen at the sound, knowing full well the cocking of a pistol when I hear it. Josephine reacts to it first, snatching my shoulder and driving us both to the floor as a bullet zips past us and takes root in the rotting boards of the wall.

"Oy!" My shout reverberates through the nearly empty ruins. A flash of red catches my eye. Inquestors, flanking us from the perimeter of the theatre.

Another betrayal?

"Damn her." Josephine ducks behind a piece of rubble. She lets out a high whistle, but it's a signal I don't recognize. "That was a warning shot." She frowns and whistles again. "Where are they?"

One of the Inquestors stands tall, staring coldly down upon us. "There is no hope for escape," he intones. "Surrender to us now and we'll—" His words cut off as a rock cracks him upside the head, and he disappears from view.

"That's it." Josephine smirks as the Inquestors turn toward this new distraction.

I snicker as Bran drops from one of the nearby rooftops, at least twenty Moon Children brandishing weapons behind him. The hum of the Inquestors' electrical wands surges in an angry buzz.

Before any of us can take another step, the wounded Inquestor staggers to his feet. Blood pours from an ugly cut on his brow. "Belay that. We've taken one of your leaders into custody. He's been scheduled for execution in about twenty minutes unless you yield to us now. *All* of you."

Josephine snarls. "Prove it."

The Inquestor throws a pair of glasses at us, and my belly rolls. *Lucian.*

"We have to stop this." The words come from my throat mechanically. I don't want to believe it, though a grim certainty twists in my chest. To have come this far only to have it all crash down around me so soon after finding my freedom is almost too much to bear.

Josephine whirls on me. "We'll deal with this. Can you make it to Prospero's Park? That's where they've been doing the public executions. Find some way to stall whatever the Inquestors are planning."

"Aye." Butterflies beat heavy in my gut. I don't know what I can do in the shape I'm in, but I have to try. I glance over at Copper Betty, unsure of what to do with her. For now she'll have to stay here. I can't waste time thinking it through.

Josephine nods curtly to where Bran is standing, and chaos erupts as he and the others charge the Inquestors. Gunfire whizzes past me again, but I'm already sprinting for one of the windows. The dragon leaps from my shoulder to take to the air above me.

Josephine calls out something, but her voice is distant and I'm far too focused on finding the fastest way to Prospero's Park. I cross the street, ducking past cringing citizens, and crawl up the brickwork of the nearest building.

After feeling my way in the dark for so long, climbing the side of a building is shockingly easy. And with the spectacles in place, I no longer have to hide from the glare of the sun or streetlights. I reach the rooftops, scanning the city as I run. My awkward leaps and jumps are a thing of strained locomotion, my once nimble limbs hesitant and jerky. The dragon glides from building to building, chirping encouragement at each successful landing.

"Easy for you. Wings would make all the difference." Soon I'm crossing the trestle over the Everdark. In the daylight, the bridge seems to sway in the breeze like it's made of matchsticks, but I don't stop.

I crouch upon the roof of one of the houses lining the edge of Market Square. The ashen remains of the Conundrum poke out of the earth like bones, and bodies of Rotters are sprawled below in bloodstained puddles, limbs still twitching. The other buildings are boarded up, silent with weary fear. An air patrol circles around the square, and I flatten myself into the shadow to watch it fly by, but whatever it's searching for is long gone.

A cleanup crew, perhaps.

I slide down the ruins of a drainpipe to the street below and spring along as fast as I can, only slowing down when I reach the edge of Prospero's Park. My gaze darts about in search of Lucian or Ghost. But Inquestors line the streets, rounding up the injured to lead them in front of a gallows.

"They're nutters," I breathe. "Clear out of their gourds."

Something sharp lands on my shoulder, and I startle, only relaxing when I realize it's the dragon. Absently, I reach up to stroke its head as it curls its tail around my neck. Its metallic skin burns against mine, but I make no move to dislodge it. I cannot turn away as Lucian comes into view, as he's forced to mount a makeshift set of stairs pushed up against the gallows. He limps to the top step, a red stain blooming beneath his shirt.

My breath hitches, and I look around, frantic. The guards are lining up with their long guns, finding their positions at the end of the square, ready to fire on any who might rush the gallows. Crowds of people crush against me, cries of indignity and anger filling the air. The taste of violence coats my tongue, beating in my blood like a wave about to break over the city.

There is no sign of Ghost anywhere.

"No!" I'm screaming it, but somehow my voice is only a whisper, my mouth dry as parchment. "No."

My feet slap against the muddy cobblestones. Slippery blood. Old fish. Guts and shit and the cold fluids of the dead. I step through all of it. *Plot. Plat. Plot.*

Click. Click. Click.

My newly mended heart whirs and shakes, and the dragon lets out a cry I've never heard, a whine like that of rusty cogs and twisted hinges. It takes flight so sharply its wings scratch my cheek.

Startled, the Inquestors stop their preparations and the mob goes silent. I use the distraction to work my way through the crowd, easily darting to the foot of the gallows and around the guards. My dragon belches a gout of flame. Tears burn my eyes despite the spectacles, but I force myself to ignore it and keep running toward Lucian.

I whistle shrilly, knowing it's a long shot, but what else can I do save call the other Moon Children here? If any will come. But they need to hear what I have to say, to carry the message if I cannot. I need to show them the truth of what I am, what any of us are.

I mount the steps two at a time, sliding to a halt in front of the doctor.

"Ghost," Lucian says weakly. "He's escaped to the Mother Clock."

I open my mouth to speak, but an Inquestor shoves me roughly from behind, knocking me to my knees. "Quiet!"

"Enough!" bellows a voice I think I recognize. "Let me through!" A contingent of BrightStone guards parts the crowd, escorting Chancellor Davis toward us. "You will release these citizens at once. At *once*." The Chancellor mounts the gallows, a calm fury upon her face. "Citizens are not yours to execute upon your whim. Even in these troubled times, due process is required."

One of the Inquestors sneers and points at Lucian. "This one is an exile from Meridion, and therefore doesn't fall under BrightStone jurisdiction. And Moon Children are under ours."

Spotlights shine down upon us from an air patrol, even as a mechanical carriage displaying Balthazaar's livery pulls smoothly through the crowds, flanked by twin rows of Inquestors. The High Inquestor emerges from its shadowed interior with a crimson cloak drawn tight around his shoulders, Balthazaar at his side, and they mount the steps to where we are. Behind them are Rinna and Joseph, the two Meridians pale and wan as they see the spectacle in the square.

I must have made some sound, a whisper of a scream when I see him. *Do something. Say something. Help us.* But Joseph is fixated on Lucian, unable to tear himself away.

The High Inquestor bows when he sees the Chancellor. "I do believe we find ourselves at odds once more." He points at me, and I'm suddenly snatched from behind, guards holding my arms tightly. "And now we'll begin rounding up the rest of the Moon Children vermin and finish this."

The dragon lands on my shoulder with a thud, hissing a blast of hot steam at my captors, who quickly release me. I snatch my hammer, ready to lash out at anyone who might try it again.

The High Inquestor cocks a brow at me. "You have nowhere to go."

"Mags," Lucian pleads. "Don't go down like this. They'll kill you."

"Then let them. We are not commodities to be used!" I whirl around and around, my guard up, waiting for an attack to come. Around us, the silence is ugly. A whistle echoes down to us from the rooftops. And then another. And another.

Moon Children from all parts of the city slip from the shadows atop the surrounding roofs. The glint of weapons shines easy in the sharp relief of the late-evening sun, cutting through the fog in a rare display. And above them all, the thrumming vibration of three airships—an Interceptor and two Scouts—bearing down upon us. Moon Children perch upon the rails, hovering in time like birds about to take flight.

And then they do. Gold wings snap out from their backs, and they launch themselves into the air in groups of twos and threes. I cannot help but gape at the sight, Josephine's winged prototype refined and modified to metallic perfection into the swooping forms of Moon Children armed with crossbows sparking with electric menace.

The High Inquestor lunges at me, ripping off my spectacles. The dragon claws at my attacker's arm, only to be knocked away by a gloved fist. I roll to the ground, lashing out with a leg to knock him down and grunting in satisfaction when I hear the thud of his body beside me on the floor of the gallows.

Someone has stepped on my wrist, forcing me to drop my hammer, and I flail with my other arm, trying to find purchase in the wooden platform for leverage. The pitch of weapons being drawn and fired rings in my ears. Moon Children signal their attacks, even as the crackling Inquestor wands are drawn and BrightStonian guards rally to the gallows.

Slam!

Something barrels past me, lifting the weight off my wrist. I roll to my hands and knees, squinting against the light to make out Bran straddling over the prone form of the High Inquestor. He's got my hammer from where I dropped it.

"This is for Penny!" he roars, swinging the hammer down, down, down.

And then the world stops.

It's a tiny thing at first—just the tolling of the bells of the clock tower. But the miniscule pulsing in my ears rocks me to my very core with all the tenderness of a thunderclap. These aren't the normal hour bells. It's something deeper, churning and grinding with a timed pulse.

Like a song.

Or a code.

Or an *aria*...

The Mother Clock groans, a rusty shriek of cogs and gears forced into sluggish movement. The sound startles Bran, causing him to drive the hammer into the gallows with enough force to split the wood sideways.

The High Inquestor doesn't hesitate and rolls away from the Moon Child. He runs for the security of his Inquestor guards. I feel around for my spectacles, only to have someone thrust them into my hand.

I look up at Lucian. The doctor's face is a swollen mess on one side, but he's wriggled his way free of his captors. Joseph stands beside him sheathing a knife, and I realize the he was the one who cut the ropes from Lucian's wrists.

Joseph smiles sadly at me, his brows nearly lost behind the brim of his hat as he lifts his head. "The bells. Madeline d'Arc's signal. It was supposed to tell Meridion we'd found a solution."

I frown at him, scooping up my hammer from where Bran left it. "You understand it?"

"Of course," he says, his voice trembling. "I helped her build it."

Lucian gapes at the other man, struggling to find something to say to this, but Joseph simply walks away. Lucian sighs and takes me by the hand. Together we stumble away from the gallows as the crowd surges all around us. The dragon lands on my shoulder from wherever it had escaped to. Behind me, more Moon Children follow, until the streets are awash in a sea of pale white heads and naked feet, tattered cloaks and broken hearts.

Spriggans. Banshees. Twisted Tumblers. I lose count at how many of us are here, and it doesn't matter anyway. Bran shouts out orders, and the several Moon Children split out from the main group, flanking us through the alleyways. It appears random, but I've lived with him long enough to understand his tactics when I see them. I can't help but feel a twinge of pride. He's everything a good leader should be. Everything Rory wasn't.

The bells continue to ring, deafening me more the closer I get. All around us doors and windows open, curious and confused faces peering at us from rooftops and doorways. Some hide where they are, but many emerge from their houses and follow us, chanting Mad Brianna's prophecies.

When the Mother Clock sings, the dragon takes wing...

By the time we cross through the main square, there are thousands of us—Moon Children and BrightStonians alike.

Meridion hangs motionless far above. Not even a wind balloon stirs from its moorings. And through it all, Ghost's name beats a wild cadence upon my breast, terror and hope warring with each other. To come so close now to finding the answers we need, to restoring the Moon Children into society, it's almost too much to comprehend.

When we reach the Mother Clock, there's a moment of confusion. The bells have faded, but their sound continues to echo between the buildings. Lucian and I mount the steps, and my dragon alights upon the crested statue of a gargoyle, its serpentine neck curved artfully. Bran emerges from the crowd and gives me a tight nod. Shadows still darken his face, but a faint glimmer of hope shines through.

I grasp the door knocker, rapping it sharply upon the wood. I nearly fall over as it abruptly opens inward, leaving me to confront a hollow-eyed Ghost.

"I'm sorry," he says. "It was the only thing I could think of to try to stop...this." If I were to pluck a loose thread from his coat, it would be him that unravels. But relief flickers over his face when he sees me. Before he manages much more than a wisp of breath, Lucian sweeps past me to wrap his brother in a tight embrace.

"Thank the gods," Lucian murmurs. "Are you hurt?"

The pressure of arms around my waist startles me, but I let myself be drawn into their embrace, my throat tightening because I have a family now, despite it all. I lean against Ghost, and I don't fight it in the least when he captures my mouth, because in that instant, it doesn't matter at all if I make it to Meridion or not.

I'm home.

Ghost glances up then and flushes as he realizes the size of our audience.

A buzzing sound fills the air, and the white sails of a Meridian airship descend upon us.

It anchors off one of the steeples of the Mother Clock, ropes carefully tied in place. And then a gangplank is lowered—not with the clattering, clumsy *thunk* of one of our ships but with the quiet smoothness of well-oiled technology.

Ghost takes my arm, but my hand slips over my hammer all the same. An awful mix of excitement and fear settles inside me, and I wonder what new violence might unfold.

Armored Meridians stride down the plank in uniforms of silver and white, pistols at their sides. They flank an ebony woman with a bright-blue sash about her hips and a silver cowl over her inky-black hair.

Her skin *glitters*. There is no other word for it. A true Meridian, then. Not like the hapless Inquestors living so long away from their home. If this is how they looked when they first came to BrightStone, no wonder they had such an easy time inserting themselves into positions of authority. She's like a living star, flesh made of magic.

"Which of you has struck the bells? Where is Meridion's Architect? We have been waiting for her to return to us what is ours." Her voice cracks like a whip with the command of one who is very used to being obeyed. But she does not look upon us unkindly. It's an odd dichotomy, given the circumstances.

Ghost bows slightly. "I did, Your Eminence. Trystan d'Arc."

A hush rolls through the crowd at his name, and she pauses. "And so the exiled children return." Her nostrils flare when she sees Lucian, but she remains otherwise impassive.

Lucian bows. "Lady Fionula. My brother and I... We wish to come home, to reclaim our birthright and work together to strike a balance between the Meridians and the citizens of BrightStone. And to restore the legacy of the Moon Children." He places one hand on my shoulder and the other on Ghost's. "My mother knew there was enough space for all of us to live peaceably. Why else would she have turned her own flesh and blood into that which is hated most?"

She stiffens. "Do not address me so informally, sir. I am the liaison between Meridion and BrightStone, not your peer. And as to your request...the council will never allow it. Your mother was stripped of her titles when she became a traitor. You have nothing to reclaim. And no way to keep it, even if you did." There is nothing malicious about the way she says it. Her words are simply a bureaucratic statement of fact. She is merely declaring that water is wet and the sun is hot.

My temper flares. "Typical Meridian logic." I sneer, disregarding the strangled sound Lucian lets out. "How high and mighty will you be when we come to take that floating city off your hands?"

The Meridian wrinkles her brow. "And who are you, then, to dictate to me what is proper for the good of my people, little half-breed?"

I overlook the slur to pull down the collar of my shirt, exposing my clockwork heart and ignoring her sharp intake of breath and the quiet chatter of the people around us when they see it. "I am IronHeart—the key to restarting Meridion. And if you don't hear our terms and requests, I'll smash it right out of my chest and you'll be stuck here. Forever."

"I see." Her eyes narrow as she appears to weigh my threat.

"Do you?" Chancellor Davis shoves her way through the crowd to stand beside Lucian. Behind her, the High Inquestor and Balthazaar are prodded along by her guards, their arms bound behind them. "I'm not sure you understand the stakes here. Your people have much to answer for." Something electric buzzes at her side and I realize she's holding one of those modified Inquestor Tithe wands in her hand, pointing it low at the Meridian. The Chancellor raises her chin to the silent faces in the park. "Good citizens of BrightStone, there is nothing to be done here but to return to your homes. Rest assured we are working on a peaceful resolution to the Rot." She turns to the High Inquestor. "And those responsible will be punished."

The Meridian liaison's jaw tightens. "Very well. What would you have of us?"

"Our birthright," Josephine chimes in, mounting the steps to stand beside me. "Meridion belongs to us as much as BrightStone does. Take responsibility for the mess your people have made. That's all we've ever wanted."

"I can see there is no point in discussing this any further here." Lady Fionula points at her guards. "You three—take a contingent of our men with you and help these people in any way they deem necessary. I will send reinforcements, along with Captain Derbinshire, to oversee things here. Any remaining Inquestors will report to her." Her eyes fall upon the bound form of the High Inquestor, and her mouth twitches. "A day for reunions, it would seem. We will take him into custody, if you will allow it."

The Chancellor shakes her head. "Not yet. He has committed the most heinous of crimes, along with several of our own citizens, and they *all* must answer for it."

The High Inquestor sneers. "A farce. You can prove nothing."

"But I can." Joseph cuts through the crowd, the lines on his face as deep as canyons. "And so can Rinna." He points behind him to where the Meridian bodyguard stands, her upper lip curling with a nearly predatory satisfaction. "As one of the original serum developers, I think my word will go a very, very long way." He bows to Lady Fionula. "Your Eminence, I will provide what evidence I can, but after that, I would dearly like to come home."

"It has been a long time." Her tone softens, regretful. "Very well. The council must be informed of this. The sons of d'Arc will accompany me, should they wish to have their demands met. And IronHeart, if she will."

Chancellor Davis lowers the wand. "Typically I would insist on attending such a meeting, but much of BrightStone will need to be rebuilt and the remaining victims of the Rot found. I trust Lucian to look out for our interests, as we have discussed many times."

Josephine takes a long drag from a cigarillo and shoves me forward. "Go on. Bran and I will keep tabs on the situation here. For now. But I'll be expecting the grand tour within the month, aye?"

Bran's shadow falls over me as he climbs the steps to me. "I'll watch over our clan," he says. I squeeze his shoulder, pulling him into a tight embrace. It's a forward thing to do, but he doesn't fight me on it. There are far too many emotions for me to put into words, and I'm out of time.

"I'll be back for you. All of you. Oh...and what of Copper Betty?" I'd nearly forgotten about her. I scan the crowd, though I'm not surprised the automaton isn't there.

"Copper Betty?" Lucian asks blankly. "What are you talking about?"

"Molly Bell appears to have gifted her to me," I say, discomfited beneath his champagne gaze. "I don't know what to do with her."

"How very amusing," he mutters, though he sounds anything but amused.

Josephine snorts. "Fine, I will watch over your precious Copper Betty. For now. But I suggest you figure out what to do with it soon. I'm not a charity, mind."

"Will you be coming today or shall I rescind my invitation?" Lady Fionula's voice cuts through our conversation, her drawl an edged blade cutting me away from my companions as she turns to look at us from where she stands midway up the gangplank.

Lucian bows in the Meridian's direction. "Of course, Your Eminence. Please, if I may have one moment." He turns to me and Ghost. "We have to go. We'll settle this Copper Betty business later, but if we don't take this chance now, who knows if we'll ever get it again."

Ghost squeezes my hand. "Don't be afraid." He bends down to whisper in my ear. "You're the key to all of this, Mags. The Moon Children will need you as their voice."

Now that the very thing I've wanted for so long is finally here, my feet are rooted in place. Terror, anger, and an anxious nervousness flutter in my gut.

But there's no time to ask anything else. He pulls me along, Lucian bringing up the rear as we follow the Meridian liaison up the gangplank to the airship. My dragon croons a mechanical purr in my ear as he lands on my shoulder.

Lady Fionula looks at it in bemusement, and then sighs, gesturing at us to take a place in one of the teakwood booths next to a window. I follow Ghost's lead as he and Lucian do as she bids. The engines quickly roar to life, great propellers spinning with a massive rush of power. We lurch forward when the ropes are freed from their moorings. Ghost squeezes my hand again when I let out a little cry of surprise.

Across the table, Lucian stares at the city below, the expression upon his face changing rapidly before settling into something like a resigned melancholy, but I don't have the heart to ask him why. Besides, if what Ghost told me about their mother was true, I don't doubt they both have their own memories to reconcile.

Lucian tugs at a chain about his neck but otherwise remains perfectly still, dried blood staining his hands. I nudge him with a knee. "What a sight we make, aye? Two Moon Children, a vagabond doctor, and a dragon."

"It's not how I'd have guessed it would happen," he agrees. "While it's unlikely to help our situation much, we'll do the best we can."

The city shrinks as we rise up and up. The sea spans out like a brilliant sapphire in the distance, beyond what appear to be rolling hills and tiny mountains far outside the walls of BrightStone.

"Oh," I mumble, my voice thick with a terrible grief as Sparrow fills my mind. "You can see the sea from atop it."

"Yes," Ghost says gently. "We'll be docking on the lower levels, but I'll take you to the highest spire if you want."

I can only nod at this, numbly quiet until the ship slides into the relative darkness of the berths in the port beneath the city. The dragon squirms on my shoulder and huffs a burst of steam at the window. I lean forward to write Sparrow's name on the glass and suck in a deep breath.

I am on Meridion.

— ACKNOWLEDGMENTS —

Thanks to Danielle Poiesz, as always, for her dedication to making this the best book it could be—I'd be lost without her!

Hugs to my family—your love and support is always appreciated. Thank you for granting me the time to tell stories. I adore you all.

And of course, all my love to the usual suspects: Piper J. Drake, Debbie Bliemel, Jim Moore, Tonia Laird, Jaime Wyman Reddy, Sarah Cannon, and Aimo. I couldn't do any of this without your help, and I'm eternally grateful.

— ABOUT THE AUTHOR —

ALLISON PANG is the author of the urban fantasy *Abby Sinclair* series, as well as the writer for the webcomic *Fox & Willow*. She likes LEGOS, elves, LEGO elves...and bacon.

She spends her days in Northern Virginia working as a cube grunt and her nights waiting on her kids and her obnoxious northern-breed dog, punctuated by the occasional husbandly serenade. Sometimes she even manages to write. Mostly she just makes it up as she goes...